the BLOODSTONE chronicles

BY BILL MYERS

NOVELS

Eli
The Face of God
The Fire of Heaven Trilogy:
    Blood of Heaven
    Threshold
    Fire of Heaven

NOVELLA

When the Last Leaf Falls

CHILDREN'S AND YOUNG ADULT SERIES

McGee and Me
The Incredible Worlds of Wally McDoogle
Blood Hounds, Inc.
Secret Agent Dingledorf
Forbidden Doors

a journey of faith

the
Bloodstone
chronicles

formerly titled *journeys to fayrah*

Bill myers

ZONDERVAN™

GRAND RAPIDS, MICHIGAN 49530 USA

ZONDERVAN™

The Bloodstone Chronicles
Copyright © 1991, 1992, 2003 by Bill Myers
Formerly titled *Journeys to Fayrah*

This title is also available as a Zondervan audio product.
Visit www.zondervan.com/audiopages for more information.

Requests for information should be addressed to:

Zondervan, *Grand Rapids, Michigan 49530*

Library of Congress Cataloging-in-Publication Data
    Myers, Bill, 1953–
        The bloodstone chronicles : a journey of faith / by Bill Myers.
            p. cm.
        "Formerly entitled: Journeys to Fayrah series."
        ISBN 0-310-24684-9
        1. Christian fiction, American.   2. Fantasy fiction, American.   I. Title.
        PS3563.Y36B58   2003
        813'.54–dc21

                                                                    2003001707

Published in association with the literary agency of Alive Communications, Inc., 7680 Goddard Street, Suite 200, Colorado Springs, CO 80920.

Illustrations by Clint Hansen
Interior design by Todd Sprague

Printed in the United States of America

03 04 05 06 07 08 09 /❖ DC/ 10 9 8 7 6 5 4 3 2 1

for brenda,
who believed in this series more than any of us

contents

book three
the WHIRLWIND

book four
the taBLet

BOOK ONE

the
PORTAL

the ROCK

It wasn't Denise's fault. It was just some weird rock she'd found in her uncle's attic. And what better gift to give a weird kid than a weird rock. How'd she know it would start to glow in her coat pocket? How'd she know by exposing it to the light of the full moon it would send out a distress call to some sort of "alternate dimension"? What'd she know about glowing rocks? Come to think of it, what did she know about alternate dimensions?

Now it's true, a rock for Nathan's birthday probably wasn't the best of gifts. Then again, Denise and Nathan weren't the best of friends. To say that she hated him might be an exaggeration. To say that at least once a week she had this deep desire to punch him in the gut, well, that at least would be the truth.

The problem was that Nathan was spoiled—big time. But it wasn't all his doing. Ever since the last operation—ever since the doctors said his hip would never be normal, that he'd always limp and have those sharp, jagged pains whenever he walked—Nathan was treated differently. And, being a fairly bright kid, Nathan did what any fairly bright kid would do . . .

He milked it for all it was worth.

He milked it when he didn't want to go to school. He milked it when he didn't want to take out the trash. And he especially milked it to get whatever he wanted from his grandfather.

Yes, sir, Nathan knew all the tricks.

Denise rounded the corner and headed up the street toward Grandpa O'Brien's Secondhand Shop. That's where Nathan hung out when his folks were away on business. With any luck, his older brother, Joshua, might be there, too.

Good ol' Josh. A couple years older than Denise, he was always there for her. He was there to pull her off kids before she pulverized them in fist fights. He was there to help her with the math she could never quite master. He was even there when her father ran off. Denise was only four at the time and could barely remember what the man looked like. But she remembered Joshua. She remembered him playing with her and trying to make her laugh. And she'd never forget the time he held her when she couldn't stop crying. It made no difference how much the other kids teased him. He went right on holding her until she finally stopped.

Good ol' Joshua. Now if only his little brother could learn some of those traits.

As she moved up the sidewalk, Denise listened to the snow creaking and squeaking under her feet. She loved December nights—the way the stars were so close you could almost touch them, the way the store windows glowed with twinkling Christmas lights. She even loved the obnoxious ringing bell of the Salvation Army Santa Claus across the street.

Reaching the Secondhand Shop, she pushed open the door only to be knocked aside by two little kids racing out for all they were worth. Their reason was simple. Nathan and his grandfather were going at it again. . .

"Grandpa, that's the third toy you've given away this week!"

"To be sure, lad, and don't you think I'd be knowing that?" The stout old man had come from Ireland almost forty years ago but still insisted on keeping his accent—and his temper.

Even at that he was no match for Nathan's selfishness. The boy was a pro. Denise stood near the door watching the redheaded kid go after his grandfather with everything he had.

"Grandpa, how do you expect to make a profit?"

"Son, there's more to this life than making a—"

"You've seen the bank statements."

"Yes, lad, but—"

"You know what Mother's accountant said."

"Yes, but—"

"It's all there in black and white."

"I under—"

"If you don't start making a profit you'll lose the store."

"Yes . . . but . . . I . . ." The old man was running out of steam. Denise could see him trying to change gears, searching for a new target. Unfortunately the one he chose happened to be Nathan's heart—an impossibly small mark for anyone to hit.

"It's the Johnson children," Grandpa sighed. "You know how they've always wanted a puppy. And since we got them little wooden pop-up ones last week, and since times have been so hard for . . ."

The old man slowed to a stop. The boy wasn't even listening.

Denise watched as Nathan hopped up on the stool behind the antique cash register. He spotted her and grinned, making it clear that this was all a game to him. A game she'd seen him play more times than she could count. And, if she guessed correctly, he was about to enter phase two of the game—the woe-is-me-self-pity phase.

"Times are hard for all of us, Grandpa." He glanced over at the stuffed toy on the counter beside him. It was an English bulldog complete with sagging wrinkles and floppy jowls. By the way it was left half unwrapped, it was obvious that it hadn't exactly met up to his high standards for birthday gifts.

Slowly he turned to his grandfather. One aspect of the self-pity phase was to make sure you either had a catch in your voice or a tear in your eye. Nathan had both. He was good. Very good.

"Oh, Grandpa, I don't mean to complain"—he threw in a couple sniffs for good measure—"but the Johnsons aren't the only ones who want a real dog."

"I know, son, but—"

"And if you're always giving stuff away so you don't have enough money . . . well . . ." He let his voice trail off into silent sorrow.

The old man bit his lip. It was obvious he loved the boy with all of his heart. "I'm sorry, lad. Maybe in a few months I'll be able to afford a nice puppy."

Nathan looked up and gave a brave nod.

Denise could see Grandpa's heart melting.

"But for now, this ol' bulldog here, he ain't a bad substitute, is he?"

Nathan managed to smile and get his bottom lip to tremble at the same time. Yes, sir, he knew all the moves.

Denise wasn't sure what was next, but she'd definitely seen enough. She stepped from the door and started toward the counter. "Hi, guys!"

"Oh, hi, Denny," Grandpa exclaimed. "So how are you this fine winter evenin'?"

"Pretty good," she said. "So, where's Joshua? Still at basketball practice?"

"I believe so."

She turned to Nathan, who was giving her his famous death glare. She tried not to smile. Here he had gone to all this trouble getting Grandpa right where he wanted him and now she barged in completely ruining the mood. "Happy birthday, Nathan."

"Thanks," he grumbled.

"I brought you a gift." She dug into her coat pocket.

"You did?" Suddenly he didn't sound quite so depressed.

"Yeah. It isn't much, but I think you'll like it." She pulled out the crimson-colored stone and plopped it down on the worn wooden counter.

Nathan stared at it blankly. "A rock?"

"Yeah, but not just any rock. I found it in my uncle's attic. Look at the cool red sparkles in it."

"Great," Nathan groaned as he picked it up. Obviously he didn't share her excitement. "A stupid stuffed dog . . . and now a rock. Some birthday." He tossed the stone back onto the counter where it rolled into a patch of moonlight that streamed in through the window.

"Nathan," Grandpa chided, "where are your manners?"

"Well, it's the truth, isn't it? Mom and Dad are off on some vacation—"

"Business," Grandpa corrected. "They're on a business trip."

"Whatever. And all you do is look out for everybody but me."

"Now, that's not true."

"Isn't it?" Nathan spun around and nailed Grandpa with another woe-is-me look. "What do you call it when you give away so much stuff that you can't afford to buy your own grandson the only present he's ever really wanted in his whole, entire life!"

Nathan scored a direct hit. Denise saw the guilt wash over Grandpa—guilt over giving the toy to the Johnson kids, guilt over not buying Nathan a real puppy, guilt over the boy's parents always being away. You name it, Grandpa was feeling guilty about it.

"All right, all right!" he exploded. He turned and headed for the cash register.

"What are you doing?" Nathan asked innocently.

Grandpa punched the buttons on the old machine and the money drawer rolled out. "You want a puppy, I'll be gettin' you a puppy!"

Nathan slipped Denise another smile as Grandpa grabbed the bills from the drawer, then turned to face him. "I'm takin' whatever money we got here and buyin' you your puppy!"

"But Grandpa," Nathan protested.

"No," the old man said as he stormed toward the coatrack and threw on his cap and scarf. "You've been whinin' and complainin' all week and I'll be havin' no more of it."

"But not *all* the money."

"I've made up my mind, lad." Grandpa slipped into his wool coat, hiked it up onto his shoulders, and headed for the door.

"Grandpa, please, not all your hard-earned—"

"No, sir," he said, yanking open the door and causing the little bell above it to jingle. "I'm goin' to Smalley's Pet Shop to buy you a puppy, and that's final!"

Just before Grandpa shut the door Nathan was able to squeeze in one last protest. Well, it really wasn't much of a protest. "Make sure it's the black one with the white spots!"

The door slammed, once again jingling the bell, and the room fell silent.

Denise could only stare as Nathan broke into a grin. Finally, she was able to speak. "You—you had that all planned, didn't you?"

"Not the part about the rock," Nathan shrugged. "But that worked out pretty good, too, don't you think?"

Denise was stunned.

Nathan laughed. "Come on, lighten up. You'd do it too if you thought you could get away with it."

"No way." Denise could feel the tops of her ears starting to burn like they always did when she got angry.

"Gimme a break," Nathan said. "Of course you would—we all would. That's the only way to get ahead in this ol' world—figure out what you want and go for it."

Sounding like some sort of professor with all the answers, he plopped his feet up on the counter and continued his lecture. Denise watched, both awed and repulsed.

"The way I see it, there are only two types of people"—he leaned back and clasped his hands behind his head—"the haves and the have-nots."

Once again she had this overwhelming urge to punch him in the gut. But this time something other than self-control stopped her. It was the rock. It had started to glow! It was filling with red, sparkling light. And the more Nathan talked, the brighter it grew—as if his words somehow gave it energy.

"You think billionaires get that way by looking out for the other guy?" he asked. "No, sir. They get there by looking out for number one."

By now the glow was bright enough to light up the entire counter. Denise tried to shout, but she was too frightened to speak. She tried to back away, but she was too scared to move. So instead of shouting or backing away she just stood there pointing.

But it didn't matter to Nathan. He wasn't looking. He was too busy giving his speech. Eyes closed and leaning back, he went on and on . . . and just when you thought he had finished, he went on some more.

All this as the red stone behind him continued to grow brighter and brighter, lighting up more and more of the room . . .

the VISITORS

N*ow hold it, partner,*
that ain't how it's done.
if you're tryin' to be tops,
don't fight for number one."

The voice sent Nathan and his stool crashing to the floor. One minute he was leaning back, lecturing Denise on the advantages of being selfish; the next minute he was on the ground shaking like a leaf.

"Who . . . who said that?" he stuttered.

Denise would have joined him in his demand but she was still trying to find her voice. Come to think of it, she was still trying to move. By now the entire room was filled with the rock's glaring red light. And that voice—that weird poetry—it seemed to come from everywhere. Every wall, every shelf, everything in the room vibrated with its sound.

"Where . . . where are you?" Nathan demanded with obviously false courage. (But right now, false courage was better than no courage.) He barely finished the words before the voice answered:

"HOLD ON TO YER HORSES,
WE'LL BE GETTIN' THERE SOON.
JES' NEED THE RIGHT COORDINATES
TO ENTER YOUR ROOM."

Denise and Nathan exchanged looks of terror and astonishment.

The voice continued, this time talking to somebody else. "Got it this time, ol' buddy?"

An ultra-cool, gravelly voice answered, "Got it, do I."

"You sure?" the first voice asked. "Remember the last time when you—"

"Cool, is it," the second voice interrupted. "Got it, I do."

Next Denise heard four electronic sounds . . .

BEEP . . .

BOP . . .

BLEEP . . .

BURP . . .

. . . followed by a "YEOOOWW!" as the door to the pot-bellied stove flew open and three very strange creatures leaped out. As they sailed through the air, they grew in size until they were nearly as tall as Denise and Nathan.

The first was a furry-faced bearlike fellow with a checkered vest and walking stick. But right now he wasn't doing much walking. With the seat of his pants on fire he was doing a lot more jumping and yelling. Most of that yelling was directed at the second creature, who was tall and purple with a foxlike face, long fluffy tail, and a large Mohawk. He was dressed in a tuxedo.

"Ow, ooo, ooch, ow, ow! Put me out! Quick, put me out!"

The purple creature did his best to slap out the flames. "Man, got it. It, I got." But he wasn't having the greatest success.

Nathan and Denise watched speechless as the strange dance continued—the furry creature running around with his pants on fire, the cool purple dude trying to put him out.

"Won't you, ooo, ooow, ever get them coordinates right?"

"Cool man, is it!"

After a few more attempts, the purple dude finally managed to smother the flames.

The furry creature sighed and gave a heartfelt, "Thanks."

"Cool," was all the cool dude said. Then suddenly remembering his own clothes, he began checking them urgently. "Coat my? Okay, is it?"

The furry creature looked over the cool dude's coat, brushed off a few ashes, then glanced at him with a grin. "Cool."

Relief swept over the purple creature's face.

With the preliminaries taken care of, they finally turned to face Denise and Nathan. For a moment all four stood in silence. There was no movement in the room—except, of course, for the slightest trace of smoke still rising from the furry creature's rear.

Nathan, who had managed to get back on his feet, was once again trying to sound brave (and might have succeeded if his voice wasn't shaking so much). "Who—who are you guys? Where'd you come from?"

The furry creature pulled himself together, straightened his tie, and answered:

> "SO SORRY ABOUT THAT.
> FIRST, TO ANSWER YOUR 'WHO,'
> I'M ARISTOPHENIX T. XANTHROPE,
> AND THIS HERE IS LISTRO Q."

Denise glanced at Nathan. They may have got an answer, but it wasn't much help. She was about to step in and try a question of her own, when there was a sudden high-pitched squeal—like a tape recorder running at high speed.

They spun around and saw the third member of the party hovering behind them. At first glance he looked like a dragonfly. On second glance a ladybug. But neither dragonflies nor ladybugs have glowing blue tails. This one did. He had a glowing blue tail that flickered and blinked for as long as he talked. He also wore glasses.

When he finally stopped talking, the cool dude nodded. "Taken, good point." Then turning back to Denise and Nathan, he introduced the third and final creature. "Here this is Samson."

Samson let out another long line of high-pitched chatter, which Denise naturally took as a greeting. Not wanting to appear frightened or impolite (like all those stupid earthlings in all those stupid sci-fi movies), she tried to smile graciously and answer the little fellow. "Well, thank you, and it's certainly a pleasure to meet you." In an effort to show universal friendship and politeness, she held out her hand to shake.

Samson immediately swooped down and bit it.

"Ow!" she yelled, pulling back her hand.

"Samson!" Listro Q scolded.

Aristophenix cleared his throat and tried to explain:

> *you'LL have to excuse him,*
> *sammy's not being rude.*
> *in fayrah, opened hands*
> *mean you're offering food."*

"Fayrah?" Nathan asked. "What's that?"

"Home, for us," Listro Q answered.

"Yeah," Denise said, sucking her fingers, no longer quite so worried about universal friendship and politeness. "So why'd you come *here?*"

"Bloodstone threw you into moonlight." Listro Q motioned toward the rock Denise had given Nathan. It now sat on the counter just as plain and dull as any other rock.

"Bloodstone?" Nathan asked.

"Yes," Aristophenix said,

> *"a symbol to all,*
> *of imager's great compassion.*
> *of the price that he paid,*
> *to bring you back into ... uh ... fashion!"*

Denise gave a little shudder. It had been a long time since she'd heard poetry quite so awful.

"A universal call for help made you," Listro Q said. "By putting it in moonlight."

"Help?" Nathan said. "We don't need any help."

"You don't?" Aristophenix asked, sounding just a little disappointed.

"What do we need help for?" Nathan said.

"Selfishness, your speech?" Listro Q asked. "Number one looking out for, didn't just a minute ago hear we?"

"Huh?" Nathan asked.

Denise ventured a guess. "I think he's talking about your looking-out-for-number-one speech."

All three strangers nodded.

"Oh, you heard that?" Nathan asked, swelling just a little with pride.

"Believe that, do you?" Listro Q asked.

"Well, yeah, sure."

"Then more help need you than know you."

Nathan frowned in confusion.

Aristophenix explained:

> "IN OUR WORLD OF *fayRaH*,
> tHe oppoSite IS tRUe.
> we caRe LeSS foR tHe me's,
> aNd faR moRe foR tHe you's."

Nathan broke out laughing. "Yeah, right." He looked back at the group.

Nobody was smiling.

"Come on." He gave a nervous chuckle. "Who are you fooling? No one could survive in a world where you care more for the other guy than for yourself. That's impossible."

Suddenly, all three creatures began to laugh.

"What?" Nathan demanded. "What's so funny?"

"Never wrong, more have been you."

Once again, Samson began to chatter.

Listro Q and Aristophenix listened carefully, throwing in a few "mm-hmm's" and "goods" until the little guy finally finished.

"What did he say?" Nathan asked.

Listro Q explained. "A child is still Samson. Graduate to adulthood soon must he."

"Yeah?" Nathan said. "So what does that got to do with us?"

Aristophenix continued.

> *"to gRaduate in fayRaH,*
> *good deeds sammy must do.*
> *so come oveR to ouR kingdom,*
> *and let him show it to you."*

Nathan's face lit up. "You mean go with you? Like to another planet or something?"

Denise gave a little shiver and whispered, "Nathan."

"Actually," Aristophenix replied, "we call them *dimensions.*"

"No kidding?"

"Nathan," Denise whispered louder.

He turned to her. "What?"

She wasn't sure how to say it without hurting anyone's feelings, so she did what she did best. She just blurted it out. "We don't even know these . . . people."

"So?"

"So you just don't go along with a bunch of strangers . . . no matter what dimension they come from."

Nathan glared at her but Listro Q seemed to understand. "Correct, absolutely is she."

Aristophenix nodded, his furry face scrunched into a frown. "I understand what she's sayin', but—"

"Yes," Listro Q agreed, "however—"

"Exactly—," Aristophenix said.

"On the hand, other—"

"I see yer point, but—"

Samson joined in, long and loud.

Soon, Aristophenix was shouting to be heard.

So was Listro Q.

It had quickly turned into a free-for-all debate.

Denise and Nathan traded looks.

"Excuse me?" Nathan shouted.

No response, except for more arguing.

He tried again. "Excuse me! *Excuse me!*"

At last the three quieted down.

Somewhat embarrassed, Aristophenix pulled himself together, adjusted his tie, and answered:

> *"we understand your fears.*
> *you are right, this we know.*
> *but to prove nathan is wrong*
> *our kingdom we really should show."*

"That's right," Nathan agreed.

Denise started to protest. "But—"

"Come on, Denny. Don't be such a chicken!"

Again she felt her ears starting to burn. "I am not a chicken!"

"Sure you are."

"No, I'm not, but—"

In a sudden burst of maturity Nathan started clucking.

"Nathan," she warned.

He clucked louder.

"Knock it off!"

And louder still.

"Nathan!"

But he would not stop.

"Nathan, I'm warning you!"

Her warnings did no good. Finally, she'd had enough. You could call Denise a lot of things, but you couldn't call her a chicken. "All right, fine!" she shouted. "We'll go!"

Nathan grinned and the group nodded, pleased with her decision.

Then she added, "But just for a few minutes."

Everyone agreed. But, even as they thanked her and promised her everything would be all right, Denise felt herself growing just a bit colder. She couldn't put her finger on it, but somehow she suspected this little trip of theirs would be anything but "all right" . . .

Bobok, my precious and most trusted friend . . ." The Illusionist leaned forward on her throne, wrapping her leathery wings about her shimmering scales and war-scarred body. "Tell me on what occasion do you honor my humble kingdom with your wondrous presence?"

Bobok rolled back, just out of reach of her powerful hoofs. He knew she hated him almost as much as he hated her. In the past three thousand epochs they had fought hundreds of battles over the disputed border between their two kingdoms. But now he had put all of that aside. Now he had come here, to Seerlo, the waterless kingdom of wind and sand, to speak with her personally.

"I sense a stirring in Imager's tapestry," he purred as he rolled from side to side in the fire-hot sand. He had lost all of his legs and arms in the Great Rebellion. And over the epochs of time, as he propelled himself by rolling, he had worn off all the other parts of his body as well. He had become a perfectly round orb—no nose, no ears, not even a head—just a perfectly round, ice-blue orb, with two tiny eyes set deep within their sockets. He continued. "Two threads are tugging at the Weave; two threads from the Upside-Down Kingdom are about to enter Fayrah."

"What?" the Illusionist asked in astonishment. "Don't they know it is still your season in Fayrah? Don't they know that you still have two hours in which to tempt anyone you can to cross through the Portal and enter your domain?"

"Perhaps they have forgotten," Bobok offered.

"And Imager, he would allow this?" she demanded. "After the awful price he has paid for their freedom? You *did* say they were from the Upside-Down Kingdom."

Bobok smiled a sinister grin. "It is the supreme act of egotism, wouldn't you agree? Thinking his love would save them from our ways. But we must work together. If I succeed in wooing them through the Portal, I must cross your kingdom to reach mine."

"But of course, my kindest and dearest of friends. Whatever you wish. After all, it is your season. Of course there must be some minor charge—a tariff for such a crossing."

"Of course," Bobok softly agreed. "And what might that be?"

"Since we have been so close these many epochs, and since you are such a kind, handsome gentleman, the fee will be slight."

"I thought as much," Bobok cooed.

"Let me see," she thought aloud. "Your keen intellect perceived two threads, did it not?"

"Yes, male and female."

"And they've both been re-Breathed?"

"No, neither one has come to know Imager. Though the girl may be closer to re-Breath than the boy."

"Good . . . good—then you must let me try to lure the girl to stay with me."

"That is a hefty price, dear lady," Bobok protested, "to take half my catch."

In reply, the Illusionist gave the slightest wave of her hand. Instantly a thousand soldiers rose from underneath the sun-scorched sand. Part cockroach, part giant ant, they lay dormant to conserve their moisture until needed. Suddenly they scurried around Bobok, surrounding him on every side, buzzing their wings, clicking their pincer jaws, poised to attack.

But Bobok was not frightened. He had known this would be the Illusionist's response.

She smiled sweetly—no easy task with a beak for a mouth—and spoke. "Surely a sensitive man of your great heart and giving nature would not deprive me of the girl."

"Of course not, gracious lady," Bobok purred. "The girl is as good as yours." With that he turned and started rolling through the hot sand, past the soldiers, and toward the distant Portal . . . toward the Kingdom of Fayrah.

He could practically hear the Illusionist grinning over her powers of negotiation. But that was all right; he was grinning as well. It had gone exactly as he had planned. He had no interest in the girl—never had. All he wanted was the boy.

And he would do anything to get him.

the
JOURNEY
BEGINS

"**D**enny, Bloodstone," Listro Q ordered. "Make sure, take it you."

Denise nodded and headed for the counter where the Bloodstone rested. Though she had carried it all the way to the Secondhand Shop, she was a little reluctant picking it back up. But when she finally took it into her hands, it felt as cool and normal as always.

She glanced at Listro Q, who was pulling a small electronic box from his pocket. It looked like a remote control to a TV, but somehow she suspected it did more than pick up local cable.

"Sure you got the coordinates right this time, ol' buddy?" Aristophenix asked.

"Cool, is it," came the reply.

Aristophenix nodded and turned to Nathan. "Will ya grab a couple of them canteens there on the back shelf for us?"

"Canteens?" Nathan asked skeptically.

"If ya don't mind."

Nathan shrugged and limped down the aisle to pick up a couple of old army surplus canteens.

Meanwhile, Aristophenix gave the final instructions:

"to travel across dimensions,
there's some things you must know,
to help ease the trauma,
and allow you to flow."

"Most of the work, Cross-Dimensionalizer will do," Listro Q said, referring to the little box in his hand. "But weight either have you of hate, anger, even unforgiveness, far too heavy to carry through the Center. Mind free of these burdens must be you."

"That's right," Aristophenix added.

"think of things pleasant,
imager has made,
the breadth of his passion,
which never will fade."

Denise wasn't sure she completely understood, but she caught the general idea. Somehow the trip would be easier if she thought of happy things. No problem, she could handle that.

"Set everybody?" Listro Q asked.

Everyone nodded. Denise could feel her heart starting to pound in her chest. She took a deeper breath, forcing herself to relax. It didn't help.

Listro Q reached down to the control box, pressed four buttons . . .

beep . . .
> **bop . . .**
>> **bleep . . .**
>>> **burp . . .**

. . . and they were off.

Suddenly there was so much light that Denise couldn't see a thing. It was like looking into the sun. She closed her eyes, then squinted them open a crack until, slowly, gradually, she grew accustomed to the brightness. Only then did she notice that there were even brighter lights surrounding her. They were different shapes and every possible color imaginable, but they all had one thing in common. Like herself, they seemed to be traveling at incredible speed toward the middle of something.

We're falling, Denise thought. But there was no panic. Barely any fear. Instead, it was more of an observation. *We're all falling toward the center of something.*

Correct is that, Listro Q answered.

She turned and saw him directly beside her. Like the others he was also glowing. In fact, he was so bright that if it wasn't for his distinct shape, she might never have recognized him.

He continued to speak—but it really wasn't speaking because his mouth never moved. It was as if he was thinking the words and she somehow heard them. *All worlds and dimensions connected to the Center,* he explained. *Slow travel would it be around the outside from world to world. Faster travel is it through the Center.*

So we're going to the center of the universe? she asked.

Center of all universes. End and beginning of all things.

You mean like heaven or something?

Listro Q shrugged. *The Center—Imager's home is it. Imaged by him are all things—from him come all things.*

God? The Imager, is he like God?

Again Listro Q shrugged. *Intense pure—the Imager, is he. The Center, his home.*

Before Denise could ask any more questions she spotted Aristophenix approaching. Like Listro Q, he glowed with brilliant light. Beside him little Samson also glowed. And beside him was what looked like the stuffed bulldog that had been sitting on the counter— the one that had been Nathan's birthday gift. Apparently the Cross-Dimensionalizer had sucked it up into their journey as well.

But what really startled Denise was Nathan—at least she thought it was Nathan. Yet this Nathan was full grown. Not only was he full grown but he was incredibly handsome, and both of his legs were whole, his hip perfectly well. And his clothing? Instead of sweater and jeans he now wore some sort of bright metal all over him, like a suit of armor.

In one hand he held a shield. In the other, she noticed a couple canteens—the ones he'd picked up at the back of the store. But they were no longer canteens, not exactly. They'd changed their shape. Oh sure, they still had their black screw-on lids and the green camouflage cloth covers, but now they were shaped like . . . well, they almost looked like swords. And, on what would be the blades of those swords, there was the slightest spattering of . . . blood. But it wasn't human blood or even the blood of animals. Somehow Denise knew or felt that it was a different blood—like the blood of reptiles or maybe insects. *That's weird,* she thought, *insects don't have blood. Or do they?*

Aristophenix pointed toward the Center. They were approaching what looked like a thin layer of fog. And below that . . . below that was the outline of what could only be described as a city—but a city that glowed brilliantly!

> "start thinking them good thoughts.
> the center we're nearer.
> keep thanking images,
> so you'll pass freer and clearer."

Denise winced. The one thing that hadn't changed was Aristophenix's awful poetry. But she understood his warning and quickly searched her mind for something pleasant to be thankful for.

She had it. Toby, her cat. She thought of the first day her parents brought him home—an orange tabby kitten, all full of fluff and warmness. What wonderful feelings those were. She was only three or four at the time but she recalled how both parents knelt beside her, how they stroked Toby, how they smiled. Those were happy times—the best times.

The memory was so warm and tender that Denise barely noticed as they entered the Center—as the fog gently embraced and enfolded her. But, instead of cold and damp, this fog had the same warm cuddly feelings as the kitten.

And then it happened . . .

In her memory she looked up to see her parents smiling. There was Mom, looking like she always did. And there was Dad . . . But wait a minute. She couldn't see his face. There were his thick arms, his broad shoulders, even his wavy hair. But no face. Why couldn't she remember his face?

Then the anger started—a little at first, but it quickly grew. Anger over her parents' fights. Anger over his leaving. Anger over never seeing him again. Why? Why had he gone? What had she done? Why had he deserted her?

And, as the anger grew, the shaking began.

What's going on? she thought as she turned to her companions. But they were no longer beside her. They were several feet below, falling much faster and smoother.

For the first time since the journey began, Denise started to feel real fear. Cold, icy panic knotted her stomach. It quickly spread to the rest of her body. As it did, the shaking increased.

"*Listro Q!*" She shouted. "*Aristophenix?*"

But no one heard. No one noticed. Each was too immersed in their own thankfulness and joy.

Suddenly Denise felt alone. Alone and frightened. *Very* frightened.

As the fear grew, the shaking turned into violent lurchings and bouncings. She tried to scream but was thrown so savagely about that it was impossible to catch her breath. She clenched her teeth and closed her eyes—hoping through sheer concentration to ease the relentless shaking—to make whatever was happening stop. Again she tried to picture the kitten, but it did no good. There was too much fear now.

She noticed she was slowing. She was no longer falling as fast toward the Center. And the slower she fell the less shaking she experienced, until both the shaking and her falling came to a stop.

But only for a moment.

Instantly, she was flung away—like a slingshot in the opposite direction, *away* from the Center. Faster and faster she flew. The lights and colors were a blur as she streaked past them. She looked down and spotted the Center. It quickly shrank to a little ball, then a little dot, then finally disappeared altogether. Now there was only the light. But even that was beginning to fade.

For the briefest moment she was back in the Secondhand Shop— or thought she was. It came and went so quickly she wasn't sure. And then she entered a void—a hollow void that grew darker and darker.

Help me! she tried to scream. But she was going so fast the words were sucked from her mouth before she could shout them. The darkness increased, growing blacker and blacker, until there was no light at all. Nothing. Total darkness. There was no up, no down, only speed, terrifying, horrifying speed, hurtling her deeper and deeper into the blackness.

Then she saw them. She gasped. How could it be? How, in this total darkness, was there a blacker darkness? But not just one. Hundreds of them. Hundreds of black shadows racing through the darkness. Shadows feeding upon the darkness, devouring the existing darkness, sucking it into themselves and creating an oblivion so deep, so intense, that reality itself seemed to disappear.

Sensing her presence, they began turning in her direction. Then, to her horror, they started racing directly at her!

Denise threw out her hands to protect herself, though she couldn't even see those hands. She couldn't see anything. To be honest, she wasn't even sure if she was still alive. Of course she was alive. Why else would she feel so dizzy? Why else would she hear the pounding of her heart in her ears?

The shadows continued their approach from all sides. But that wasn't true, there were no sides. There was nothing.

The pounding in her ears grew deafening. Her head spun so fast that she could no longer think. *So this is what dying feels like,* was her last thought as she began losing consciousness. That and, *Are those Daddy's eyes?* For, suddenly, she was staring directly into her father's dark eyes. Well, they were his eyes, yet somehow they weren't. For these eyes looked like they understood every hurt, every sorrow, and every heartbreak she had ever had.

And then there was nothing.

aRRIVaL

At first the voices were a blur. Soft, velvet murmurings that floated above what sounded like a distant bubbling brook.

"Hold it, Partner. It looks like she's comin' around."

"How tell, can you?"

"HER eyes ARE A twitchin',
they're startin' to move.
it looks like HER CONDITION,
is 'bout to improve."

Denise struggled to open her eyes, but they were just too heavy.

"Minute now, any . . ."

"Come on, Darlin', you can do it—jes' concentrate."

The voices were much clearer, but she still couldn't understand the words. It sounded like they were talking a foreign language. But it was more than that. She wasn't certain, but they were definitely talking strange—very strange.

"SHE won't UNDERSTAND,
till you give HER some sips.
so take that there water skin,
AND put it to HER LIPS."

Denise felt her head being lifted and the cool rim of a container placed against her mouth. Instinctively, she opened up and took a swallow. It was wet and cool and perfect. Just what she needed.

"Careful, my good man. Not too much at first."

"And don't be forgettin' her ears."

Denise felt her head tilted to one side. She was more than a little startled as several drops of the cold liquid splashed into her ear. Then her head was tilted to the other side as more was splashed into the other ear.

"It's no fair making the rest of us wait till she gets better. Can't somebody just stay with her while we go check out the place?"

Suddenly Denise understood everything. Every word, every sentence—she even recognized that last voice. It belonged to the one and only Nathan More-Spoiled-Than-Any-Brat-She-Knew O'Brien.

"Patience, partner, patience," Aristophenix's voice said.

"Actually, Master Nathan, the greater number of amiable faces surrounding her at the time of consciousness will facilitate a swifter recovery, thereby allowing you to see the kingdom as quickly and as unimpaired as possible."

But whose voice was that? Denise had no idea. And since lying around and listening to voices was not exactly how she wanted to spend her time, she mustered up more strength. Focusing all of her concentration upon her eyelids, she was finally able to pry them open.

"Ah, there go we," Listro Q said, looking down at her. He was at her left with Samson hovering just over his shoulder. On the other side she saw Aristophenix kneeling and looking just as chubby and dapper as ever. And beside him with his head kind of upside down was Nathan. Much to her disappointment, it was the old Nathan—the spoiled, whining Nathan. What happened to the other one—with the shining armor and mighty swords? Had it been a dream?

"I do believe, Master Nathan, that the female will soon be as spry as ever."

It was the new voice again. Denise looked above her head and was astonished to see the stuffed bulldog peering down at her. She was even more amazed when he gave a stiff, stodgy cough and continued speaking!

"Note the color already returning to the cheeks, as well as—"

A stuffed animal speaking! What's going on? she thought.

"So is she going to be okay or what?" Nathan demanded. "I got things I want to see here."

Good old Nathan. Some things never change. With that strange and somewhat comforting thought, Denise struggled to sit up.

"Girl now, cool be," Listro Q cautioned.

By now everything had cleared and focused for her. Everything except Nathan. For some reason his face still remained upside down.

She tried to speak, but the words came out dry and choking.

"Water, more have some," Listro Q encouraged as he lifted the water skin to her mouth. She took a small sip, but soon found herself gulping in as much as she could. She had never tasted anything quite so good or satisfying.

"Now, easy, easy," Listro Q warned as he gently pulled the water skin away.

After taking a moment to catch her breath, Denise finally spoke. "What . . . what happened?"

"Enter you could not the Center," Listro Q answered. "Vibrate with thanks, all created things. Not, did you."

Confused, she turned to Aristophenix who explained,

> *"fROM ROCKS to tREES,*
> *to stARS to mAN,*
> *to vIBRAtE tHANKS,*
> *IS OUR pURPOSE AND pLAN.*
> *BY REfUSINg to JOIN,*
> *OR NOt KNOWINg HOW,*
> *NOWHERE IN HIS pRESENCE,*
> *DID ImAgER aLLOW."*

"Oh, so this was all his fault—that Imager guy."

"For your own protection was it," Listro Q explained.

"Yeah, sure," she scorned. "Some protection."

"Your vibration, your frequency out of phase. Kill you would it. By forbidding entrance, save you, did he."

"Right," she scoffed. Already memories flooded in faster than she cared to remember. Memories of the Center, and the awful shaking, memories of the terrifying darkness . . . and memories of those eyes . . . those sensitive, pain-filled eyes. Eyes that seemed to be her father's but were somehow deeper.

"Who caught me, then?" she demanded. "Who saved me?"

"Saved you?" Listro Q asked.

"Well, yeah, how did I get here?"

Aristophenix glanced at the others. He nervously cleared his throat and tried to explain.

> *"as best we can figure,*
> *you went the long way 'round.*
> *and doing it by yourself,*
> *makes it more than profound."*

"But my dad, didn't you see him?" Denise asked. "He's the one who caught me. Didn't you see him?"

"Denny," Nathan sighed impatiently, "your dad hasn't been around for years. You know that."

"Well, yeah," she faltered, "but it looked like him . . . except for the eyes. And what about you?" She turned to Nathan. "You just made it through there without any sweat?"

"Not at first."

Denise looked at him, waiting for more.

"I tried singing a bunch of songs—you know, happy stuff—but nothing seemed to work. I just kept getting knocked around harder and harder."

"Tell me about it," Denise said.

"Then I remembered one of Grandpa's hymns from Ireland—one he always sang to me at bedtime . . ." His voice trailed off as if he were lost in thought, as if he'd experienced something he could not quite explain.

"And?" Denise persisted.

He came to. Then he simply shrugged. "And here I am."

Denise's frustration grew. "What about all that armor you were wearing?"

He looked puzzled. "Armor?"

"Yeah, you were dressed in some sort of weird getup with swords and—"

"*I* was dressed weird?" Nathan said defensively.

"Well, not weird. Actually you looked kinda—"

"What about you in that wedding dress?"

"Wedding dress?" It was Denise's turn for surprise.

"And how did you get it to glow like that?" he asked. "You looked pretty cool." Then, catching himself, he added, "I mean, considering how stupid you normally look."

Denise was so puzzled she barely noticed the put-down. What wedding dress was he talking about? And why hadn't he noticed the armor he was wearing? Things were definitely strange. On the bizarre scale of one to ten, this was definitely pushing an eleven.

Suddenly Samson began to chatter.

"Right are you," Listro Q agreed. "To see much have we." Turning to Denise he asked, "Walk, you think can you?"

"Of course I can," she said.

With the help of the others Denise started to rise to her feet.

She wished she hadn't.

There was a loud *whooshing* sound and immediately she found herself standing upside down. Well, it really wasn't standing . . . her feet shot straight up toward the sky and her head rested firmly on the ground.

"What's going on?" she screamed.

"Don't panic," Nathan said.

"Yeah, right, like this happens all the time!" She threw a look at Nathan and was surprised to see that he was also upside down. But they were the only ones. Everybody else seemed to be standing perfectly normal.

"This is crazy!" she yelled.

Nathan answered. "They say it's because we're from the Upside-Down Kingdom."

"Upside-Down what?"

"Kingdom. They say our world is the only world in the universe that does things upside down."

"Upside down?" she repeated. Not only was she angry, but she was doubly upset that Nathan seemed to be taking it so calmly. "What do they mean, upside down?"

"In our world if you want stuff you take it," Nathan said. "Or if you want to be like the boss or leader, you make sure everyone else obeys you."

"So?"

"So here," he continued, "if you want something you give it away, or if you're trying to be the leader, then you help others."

"That's crazy!"

"No . . . just upside down."

"For them!" Denise sputtered. "They're the ones that are upside down—not us!"

"I guess," he shrugged. "Except for one little thing."

"What's that?"

"We're the ones standing on our heads."

Denise looked back at the group. "Great," she groaned, "so we spend the rest of our time here just standing on our heads."

"I say there . . . I do believe there is an expedient solution available." It was the bulldog again.

"And why aren't you upside down?" Denise demanded. She didn't mean to be so cranky, but all in all it hadn't been one of her better days. And at the moment it didn't seem to be getting any better. "If you're from our world, why aren't you flipped around like us?"

"Obviously, my dear human, because I don't have the potential of being Imager-Breathed."

"Oh great, more of this Imager stuff. He really knows how to show his guests a good time, doesn't he?"

"Get real," Nathan sighed. "We're not in the Center anymore. We passed through it to get to Fayrah."

"My dear Master Nathan"—the dog cleared his throat—"if you would be so kind as to allow me to continue?"

"Certainly, Mr. Hornsberry," Nathan said.

"Mr. Hornsberry, what a name," Denise muttered. "Doesn't that just figure."

Ignoring her, the dog continued. "In my humble estimation I believe your dilemma is an optical phenomenon." He turned to Listro Q and Aristophenix. "Am I correct, gentlemen?"

They both nodded.

"Then, by simply placing a few drops of your special water into their eyes—as you have already done with their ears, allowing them to hear right side up—will they not also be able to see right side up?"

"Mr. Hornsberry, you're a genius!" Nathan shouted.

The dog coughed slightly. "Yes, well, that goes without saying, doesn't it?"

"If that's all it takes, let's get on with it!" Denise demanded.

"Patience, female, patience," Mr. Hornsberry scolded. "Why you humans were ever given control is beyond me." He turned to Listro Q and asked, "My good man, would you be so kind as to do us the honors?"

"Cool," Listro Q said as he opened his water skin and knelt down to the faces of Nathan and Denise. "Your eyes, open keep you. Lots of water into them let you."

They nodded.

Listro Q poured the water into his hands. It was the first time Denise had seen it. Oh, she had tasted it, all right, with all its cool goodness. She'd even felt it as they poured it into her ears. But seeing it for the first time was quite a shock. Because it wasn't water at all! Well, maybe it was, who could tell in this place. But what it looked like was . . . letters and words. That's right, liquid letters and words. It was as if someone had taken the alphabet and somehow managed to turn it into liquid. There was an **S** pouring out, followed by a **W**, then an *L*. Next came an entire word, *тнe,* followed by **BEHOLD**, and *in*, and a half dozen more. Though they were all shapes and sizes, there was no missing the fact that they were actual letters and words pouring into Listro Q's hand.

All Denise could do was stare.

With his hand cupped full of the liquid, Listro Q said, "Go, here we!" and quickly splashed it into Nathan's face.

For a moment nothing happened. But as soon as he opened his eyes, as soon as some of the liquid fell into them, Nathan was standing right side up with the rest of them.

"All right, way to go!" the group cheered as they slapped Mr. Hornsberry on the back and congratulated Nathan.

"Excuse me . . . ," Denise called. *"Excuse me?"* Finally she managed to get their attention. "I don't mean to be rude or anything, but do you think maybe you could get around to doing me?"

"Certainly," Listro Q said as he kneeled back down to join her. He poured out another handful of the liquid letters and, without warning, quickly splashed them into her face. There was the loud *whooshing* sound again, and when she opened her eyes, she was also standing right side up.

There was more congratulating and backslapping, but Denise barely heard. She was too taken by the beauty . . .

Aristophenix saw her expression and softly spoke:

> *"weLcome to fayraH,*
> *tHe kinɡDom of Love,*
> *wHere tHe HarsHest assauLt*
> *is tHe cooinɡ of Doves."*

Denise didn't know about that, but she did know it was the most beautiful place she had ever seen . . .

First there were the colors. They were the same as back home, but somehow richer, more vivid. Yet none of them were too bright or glaring. Instead, each color gently blended into the next. Everything had its own distinct color and outline, yet each of those colors and outlines blended gently and naturally into its neighbor. It reminded her of a soft watercolor painting.

Then there were the trees. They were everywhere—each having their own shade of glimmering green leaves—leaves that she suspected would never fall; and if they did, somehow they would never need to be raked—at least by girls who had better things to do on Saturday afternoons.

Past the trees were rolling hills—jade green and as soft as velvet. And past the hills, well past the hills was something Denise had never seen before—mountains. But instead of the usual purple or violet hues, these mountains were a faint and very pleasant shade of . . . red. Not only that, but they seemed to be softly glowing and pulsating.

"Look!" she pointed.

"Ah, the Blood Mountains." Aristophenix nodded.

"Bloodstone from these mountains came yours," Listro Q said.

Remembering she still had the stone in her pocket, Denise pulled it out to take a look. Much to her surprise it was glowing again. Glowing and pulsating in exact rhythm to the mountains!

"Neat," Nathan said as he tried to reach for it—until Denise blocked him. It may have been *his* gift, but right now *she* was holding it.

"Celebration signal to all," Listro Q explained as he motioned to the mountains, "that arrived here have Upside Downers."

"What?" Denise asked.

"Because here visiting are you, glow in celebration do the mountains."

"You mean those mountains are glowing like that just 'cause we're here, visiting?"

Listro Q nodded silently.

"Why?"

Listro Q smiled. "Upside Downers very precious are to Imager." Then turning back to the mountains he continued, his voice lowering in reverence. "The Great Purchase . . . mountains these, reminder are they."

"Great Purchase?" Denise asked.

"Yes. Of Upside Downers."

A stillness crept over the group as everyone looked on in a gentle sense of awe. Well, almost everyone . . .

"Hey, everybody, take a look!"

Since Nathan couldn't hold the Bloodstone or be the center of attention, he had focused on something else. Denise turned to see him pointing at a stream a dozen yards behind them. But it wasn't a stream of water, it was a stream of those letters and words.

Aristophenix turned to him.

"THANK YOU, DEAR NATHAN,
I'D ALMOST FORGOT,
YOU MUST FILL YOUR CANTEENS,
SO TRUTH CAN BE SOUGHT."

"Alright!" Nathan cried as he grabbed the canteens and quickly limped toward the stream.

Of course Denise wanted to talk more about the Blood Mountains and the Bloodstone. But since Nathan had found another topic, and since Nathan loved to control the conversations, it was clear that she'd have to wait. She shook her head in mild frustration. Good ol' Nathan.

"Check it out!" he called.

The others had turned to join him. Denise started to follow, then felt a strange sensation. She slowed to a stop. Was somebody watching them? She turned and looked. Nobody was there. Just the shimmering grass, the jade green trees, and the—wait a minute, what was that? Behind those bushes? Something blue.

Denise shaded her eyes from the sun for a better look. It was about the size of a soccer ball and it glistened in the light like glass or—could it be . . . *ice?*

Yes, *blue ice.*

She lowered her hand and was about to investigate when Nathan shouted, "Denny!"

She turned to see him standing at the bank of the stream. "Come on!" he yelled. "You gotta see this!"

She hesitated, then turned back to the bushes. But it was gone. The little blue ball had disappeared.

"Come on!" Nathan shouted.

She looked in every direction, but it was nowhere to be seen. How strange. How very strange.

"Denny!"

She turned back to him.

"Will you come on!"

Finally, with a heavy sigh, Denise turned and headed off to join him.

the stream

Is this cool or what?" Nathan shouted as he dropped to the grassy bank and began untying his shoes.

"You're not going in there!" Denise cried in alarm.

"Sure, why not?" He'd already kicked off his shoes and was working on his socks. "We drank the stuff and it didn't kill us. And Listro Q splashed it all over our faces."

Denise turned back to Listro Q and Aristophenix. "Is it really safe?" she asked.

"Perfectly," Aristophenix smiled as he waddled closer to the stream.

"'Sides," Nathan called, peeling off his shirt, "I can't wait to tell Mrs. Barnick, my English teacher, that I took a dip in her precious alphabet. Maybe she'll finally give me an *A* this time."

Listro Q turned to Denise. "Welcome are you, to join him."

"I don't think so," she said, giving a dubious look at the stream. Call her old-fashioned, but somehow she felt words and letters were better suited for reading than for jumping in and swimming with.

But not Nathan. With a slapping splash he dove headfirst into the words and disappeared.

Denise watched and waited but he didn't resurface. She glanced at the others. No one seemed concerned. She tried to relax. *He'll be up any minute,* she assured herself. *After all, didn't Aristophenix just say it was safe? And if Aristophenix said it was safe, it was safe.*

Or was it? Seems her little cross-dimensional trip hadn't been so safe. Come to think of it, it had been downright dangerous.

Let's go, Nathan, she thought. *Don't be a jerk. Come back up.*

But Nathan didn't come back up.

The inside of Denise's palms grew damp. It's true, the two of them weren't exactly the best of friends, but Nathan *was* a human being (though there were times she had her doubts). Besides, what would she tell Joshua, his older brother, if something happened? "Hey, sorry 'bout losing your brother back in that other dimension, but, like, can we still be friends?"

Come on, Nathan, come back up!

She looked to the group. Maybe these creatures weren't so interested in their safety after all. Maybe this was all an elaborate trap, some way to lure poor unsuspecting earth kids into another world so they could be kidnapped and drowned. When you got right down to it, how long had she known them? Basically, weren't they just your common, average, run-of-the-mill strangers? Well, all right, maybe furry faces, purple skin, and glowing tails weren't exactly run-of-the-mill, but they were still strangers. And what did every kid know about taking rides with strangers?

What have we done?!

Her mind raced for a solution. *I could jump in there and save him. Yeah! Before they stopped me, I could kick off my shoes and leap in there to save his life! 'Course I can't swim, but—*

Suddenly, there was a stirring on the surface of the words.

Finally—he's coming up!

Wrong again. It was just a breeze rippling across the water's surface. Denise was definitely in a panic. And for good reason.

Then, just when she was about to jump back, point her finger, and blow the whistle on them—just when she was ready to challenge them to one of her world-famous fistfights, Nathan exploded from the surface laughing and gulping for air.

Denise was furious . . . and relieved.

"This is incredible!" he shouted. "Denny, there's no bottom to this thing!"

At first she was going to give him a good lecture. But what good would a lecture do? He'd just laugh and make her feel foolish—something she was becoming an expert at. By now she was sure everyone considered her the group idiot—first with her cross-dimensional detour, then her little stand-on-the-head routine. No, she'd been enough of a fool for one day, thank you very much.

So instead of giving Nathan the lecture he deserved, she tried to smile. She pretended to be Denise I'm-Having-a-Good-Time kid, instead of the Denise I-Know-We're-All-Going-to-Die fool.

She watched as the words **THEREFORE**, *surely*, and Beçat dripped from Nathan's hair. They fell to his shoulders and slid down his back before splashing into the stream where they swirled around his waist and disappeared.

Trying her best to sound calm and matter-of-fact, she turned to Aristophenix and asked, "So where does the stream come from?"

"The Center," Aristophenix answered.

> "It comes to fayraH
> and wanders around,
> for us to employ
> when truth must be found."

"But the words, the letters?" she asked.

"Imager's mouth, come from they," Listro Q answered. "Every word, every sentence, spoken by him."

"Hey, Denny, check it out!" Nathan squirted a handful of water at her. The word **PEACE** shot from his closed palms and landed on the bank just a few feet from her. She watched as it slowly seeped into the ground and disappeared.

Samson briefly chattered.

"Right," Listro Q agreed. "More to see much. Nathan! Come must you!"

"Ah, do we have to?"

"Come," he repeated. Then, stooping down, Listro Q grabbed the two canteens Nathan had left on the bank and handed them to Denise. "Filled must be these."

She took them and moved to the edge of the bank. *Typical,* she thought. *Nathan gets to play while I do all the work.* But the thought didn't last long. For when she knelt down and looked into the stream, she was in for another surprise. It wasn't the letters and words that startled her; it was her reflection. A reflection that wasn't her. Well, it was her and it wasn't. It did everything she did. It gasped when she gasped. It moved when she moved. But the reflection was of a much older Denise. And, she had to admit, a much more beautiful one.

There was something else above the reflection. It wore a breathtakingly gorgeous wedding gown. Intricately embroidered, it had long lacy sleeves and a sparkling veil made of tiny pearls—pearls so fine and shimmering that they could have been morning dew on a spider's web. Slowly, she raised her hand toward her face, to touch the veil. But of course there was no veil there. It existed only in the reflection.

Then she saw Listro Q's reflection over her shoulder, smiling. Unlike her, he looked exactly the same as in real life.

"I don't—I don't understand," she said, unable to take her eyes from the stream.

"Imager's words, show reality—things as they are, not as they appear."

"But . . . that's not me, that's not what I look like."

"You how Imager sees."

"But that . . ." She motioned to the reflection. "That's not real."

Listro Q chuckled softly and pointed at her reflection. "More real that"—he pointed to herself—"than ever will be this."

"Come on, Denny, are you going to fill those canteens or what?" Suddenly her reflection shattered into a million pieces as Nathan splashed through it to reach the shore. "Here, gimme one of those." He grabbed a canteen from her hand and quickly dipped it into the water.

"Quite so, Master Nathan," Mr. Hornsberry said in his typical snooty manner. "If one doesn't take charge, one may never accomplish anything."

"You got that right, Hornsey," Nathan said, pulling the filled canteen from the stream and grabbing the next one from Denise. "Especially when all some people want to do is sit around and gawk at themselves."

Denise would have fired off a stinging comeback, especially after the fright he'd given her with his little drowning imitation. But she didn't say a word. All she could do was stare at the reflection as it re-formed.

Only now it wasn't just her reflection, it was also Nathan's—the older Nathan—the one wearing the glowing suit of armor and carrying the shield and bloodstained swords. But it was more than just the armor that surprised her. It was those eyes. His eyes. Sure, his mouth was busy spouting the usual sarcasm and put-downs, but the eyes, they were different. In the reflection they appeared kind . . . even sensitive.

In his haste Nathan never saw the reflections. "Come on, let's get out of here," he said as he rose to his feet with the second canteen. "We've got lots to see."

Denise continued to stare.

"Denny, are you coming? Denny?"

Slowly she rose to her feet. She hesitated a moment and looked back at the stream a final time. Her reflection remained, as if waiting. But waiting for what?

"Heads up!"

She turned just in time to catch one of the canteens Nathan had thrown at her.

"Carry your own water," he scorned. "I'm not your slave." With that he turned and started limping up the path. The rest of the group joined him. Reluctantly, Denise followed.

Then, as if to remind everyone of their mission (and that he was in charge of it), Aristophenix raised his walking stick, and cheerfully spoke.

"TO SHOW YOU FAYRAH
IS OUR PURPOSE AND PLAN,
HOW DIFFERENT WE LIVE
FROM THE SPECIES OF MAN."

They'd only traveled for a few moments before Samson hovered over Nathan's head and chattered something.

"What's that?" Nathan asked.

It was Mr. Hornsberry's time to translate. "Master Nathan, I do believe he is referring to your shoes. In your admirable effort to hurry the female, you have forgotten your shoes."

Nathan looked down. "Oh, man," he complained. "It's this stupid path. The grass is so soft I forgot I wasn't wearing them. I gotta go back. You guys keep going, I'll catch up in a second."

"Back, go can we all," Listro Q offered.

"No way," Nathan said. "If Denny gets to looking at herself in the water again, there's no telling when we'll be able to leave."

The group chuckled.

Denise bit her lip.

"Over this knoll just, is the Capital," Listro Q said, pointing to the grassy hill in front of them. "Wait, can we."

"Go ahead," Nathan said as he started back. "I'll meet you there."

"Wait for me, Master Nathan," Mr. Hornsberry called as he scampered after the boy. "I shall accompany you!"

"Are you sure, ol' buddy?" Aristophenix called one final time.

"You go ahead," Nathan insisted. "We'll catch up."

Eventually, Nathan found his shoes, slipped them on, and plopped down on the side of the stream to tie them. And it was there, for the first time since he'd entered Fayrah, that he felt a chill. Strange, he'd never paid attention to the temperature before, probably because the climate was so perfect—not too hot, not too cold. But now he felt a definite shiver creeping across his shoulder blades. He threw a glance at Mr. Hornsberry, who sat beside him. By the way the dog flared his nostrils, he'd also sensed something in the air. Then, suddenly, there was a voice . . .

"Greetings, most favored."

Nathan gave a start. But he wasn't frightened. Maybe because the voice was so smooth and gentle that it almost sounded like his own thoughts. He turned and saw a little blue sphere near him. It was about the size of a soccer ball and was gently rolling back and forth. It had no arms, no legs, not even a nose or ears—just two deeply recessed eyes, and a mouth.

"Who—who are you?" Nathan asked.

"My name is not important. You are the only one of importance."

Mr. Hornsberry rose from his haunches and gave a low growl.

"Easy, Hornsey, it's okay," Nathan said. He reached out to pat him on the head and Mr. Hornsberry relaxed slightly. Pats on the head are good for a dog's relaxation—even haughty, intellectual ones. Turning back to the orb, Nathan asked warily, "Why am I so important? What did I do?"

"It's not what you did," the blue sphere purred, "it's who you are. You are one of Imager's chosen. A brilliant thread in his nearly perfect tapestry."

Nathan eyed the sphere carefully as it rolled closer. The chill grew deeper.

"But a thread not allowed to rise to its fullest potential . . ."

"What—what do you mean?" Despite the chill Nathan found himself strangely attracted to the creature.

"Have you never felt you were different—that somehow you were better than others?" The attraction increased with every word. "That you were somehow . . . *special?*"

"Well—well, yes," Nathan stuttered, "how did you know?"

"Because it is truth and I know truth." The creature turned to Mr. Hornsberry. "And you, my little friend—how clever you are to see your master's greatness."

Whatever concerns Mr. Hornsberry had, seemed to disappear. The stranger's words were as comforting as any pat on the head. "Well, yes." The dog nervously cleared his throat. "I am rather, as you say, *clever,* aren't I?" He gave his stubby tail a wag.

The creature grinned. He rolled closer to Nathan but kept a wary eye on the stream. Something about the water seemed to make him nervous. "When I speak of your greatness, oh Chosen Thread, don't you feel a stir of excitement? Does not your heart beat a little faster at the hearing of this truth?"

It was true. All of his life Nathan had felt that he was somehow different—special. He thought it when he saw the rock stars onstage or the movie stars on the screen. That should be him up there. He could do that. If he only had the right breaks he could be as great as any of them. Even better. He was sure of it. And now . . . could it be? Could all of those thoughts, those feelings, could they really be true?

"Listen to your instincts," the sphere cooed as it rolled even closer. "Trust them, trust what your heart whispers as truth."

"But . . . ," Nathan asked hoarsely, "I don't understand. How— how do I, you know, become . . . great?"

The creature chuckled. "You already are great—you simply have not experienced it."

"But . . ."

"Come, follow your humble servant to his kingdom."

"You mean a different kingdom than this one?"

The creature rolled back and forth in a gentle nod.

"Why?"

"To rule."

"What?"

"We have been waiting many epochs for your arrival. You are one of the great, a chosen thread."

Nathan's thoughts swam. Was such a thing possible?

"Surely this call to greatness does not surprise you. Listen to your heart, listen to its stirrings. Inside, you know you have been called to it."

"But—but what about Listro Q and Aristophenix . . . and Samson. They invited me to see *their* kingdom."

The sphere rolled so close that Nathan could now feel the coldness of its breath. It said only one word. "Why?"

Nathan was having a harder time concentrating. The stranger had filled his head with so many thoughts that he was thinking of everything and nothing all at the same time. "I don't . . . know . . . ," he stuttered. "Something about giving, about serving."

The blue sphere broke into laughter. "Don't you see, that is simply another trick to deprive you."

"Deprive me?"

"Yes, just as your hip has deprived you for so many years."

Instinctively Nathan reached down to touch his leg. The stranger had spoken another truth. He could do so much. He could be so great. If it just wasn't for his stupid hip.

"Do you think Imager wanted you to have that deformity?" The orb pressed in. "Not at all. It was thrust upon you to deprive you, to prevent you from finding your true self, from becoming all you were meant to be."

Nathan's heart pounded harder and faster.

The orb continued, "If you visit Fayrah and learn only to give and serve, you will never rise to your true stature of greatness. It is another merciless trick to deprive you of your destiny."

"My destiny?"

"Come with me, Chosen Thread. Mine is a different kingdom— a kingdom of owners. Only the weak are destined to give. You are destined to take. You are destined to possess. In my kingdom everything your eyes behold can become yours. No longer will you be deprived. No longer will your destiny be hindered. You will become exactly what you have been chosen to be since the beginning of time."

With that the orb turned and started rolling away from the stream. "Come . . . follow your trusted servant. Follow him. Your kingdom awaits."

"But where is it?" Nathan asked as he jumped up and limped to join him. Mr. Hornsberry trotted excitedly at his side. "What is the name of this special kingdom?"

"Keygarp," the sphere said as he continued forward.

"And your name, you never told me your name."

The sphere turned toward him and purred ever so gently. "My name . . . Bobok."

the
capital

Denise wasn't sure what to expect as they neared the top of the knoll. Except for Listro Q, Aristophenix, and Samson, she hadn't seen one other person from Fayrah. Granted, everything else in this world was beautiful—the trees, the hills, the glowing mountains, even that peculiar stream. But what about the people?

The question was short-lived. For as they reached the top of the hill, the valley came into view. And nestled in that valley was the capital of Fayrah.

It was breathtaking. Magnificent. And even more surprising was the fact that it wasn't surprising. Not to Denise. Not anymore. Somehow she'd expected breathtaking magnificence. And she was not disappointed. She saw it in the quaint cottages, the emerald green lawns, the perfectly manicured trees and shrubs . . . and most importantly, she saw it in the people—lots of happy, laughing, slap-you-on-the-back kind of people.

Well, maybe *people* wasn't exactly the right word . . .

Not only were there several of the Aristophenix and Listro Q varieties, but there were also dozens of even stranger and weirder types. Yet, even though the shapes and sizes were strange and weird, they weren't frightening. Like everything else in Fayrah, they were incredibly unique and yet perfectly blended.

Then there were the buzzing dragonflies or ladybugs or whatever they were—the ones that looked like Samson. Hundreds of these little critters zipped about chattering a mile a second. More than a few buzzed the group to check them out. It was then that Denise realized they weren't exactly like Samson. All the others had beautiful sparkling tails that glowed a pleasant red, like the Blood Mountains. But, for some reason, Samson's tail was the only one that glowed blue. Although it wasn't an ugly blue, it certainly wasn't red like all the others.

Poor thing, she thought. *Even in a place like this I bet it's no fun being the oddball.* And Denise knew exactly what that felt like—being the oddball . . .

—If she's so smart on those I.Q. tests, how come she's so dumb in school?

—What's a pretty girl like that trying to prove by beating up all those boys?

—Lots of kids don't have fathers. Why does she make such a big deal about it?

Denise had heard the questions whispered behind her back for years. And since no one ever had the answers, that made her, what else, but the *oddball.*

"Well, bless my soul, is this the Upside Downer?"

Denise turned to see a camel-type creature. It wore a large hoop-skirt and had two furry arms extending from its chest. At the moment it was reaching out those arms for a hug. Unsure what to do, Denise looked at Listro Q, who gave a nod. With more than a little hesitancy, she moved over to hug the creature.

"It's certainly a privilege to be makin' your acquaintance." The camel spoke in a charming Southern drawl while hugging Denise so enthusiastically that Denise could hardly breathe. "My name is Sally."

"How do you do . . . Sally. I'm Denise."

"What a charming name," the camel creature said, pulling back. "Will you all be staying long?"

"Not long," Aristophenix answered.

"we jes' want to show her,
some of the town.
how through givin' and carin,'
joy and peace can be found."

"Well, you all have the right guide for that," Sally said, referring to Aristophenix. Then lowering her voice she confided, "That is, if the poetry doesn't just drive you crazy."

Denise smiled back. She was already beginning to like this Sally camel-person.

"What was that?" Aristophenix asked.

"Not a thing, sugar," she grinned, "not a thing." Then, changing the subject, she asked, "Say, Listro Q, is that a new coat?"

Listro Q practically beamed with pleasure (which is a hard thing to do when you're trying to be cool). "Like it, do you?" he asked.

"Honey pie," she said, reaching out and stroking its fine texture with one of her hands, "it's simply divine."

Again, Denise had to smile. She couldn't say for certain, but it looked like Listro Q's chest actually grew an inch or two larger.

"Say," Sally asked, again changing the subject, "did you all know that today's my birthday?"

"Why, that's right," Aristophenix said. "Happy birthday."

The others offered similar congratulations.

"Thank you so much," she said, giving a little curtsy. "And since it is my birthday"—she turned to Aristophenix—"would you mind too terribly if I gave you this here pocket watch? It was my great granddaddy's." She pulled out an ornate gold watch from the pocket of her skirt and handed it to him.

"Woo-wee!" Aristophenix exclaimed as he took it into his hands. "Sure you don't mind, ol' girl? It's a beaut."

"It'd be my greatest pleasure."

And it was. Denise could tell by the look on Sally's face that she really enjoyed giving the gift away.

The others crowded around Aristophenix for a better look. After the appropriate *oohs* and *aahs*, Sally finally spoke. "Listen, there's plenty more people down thataway"—she pointed toward the village—

"who're just dying to meet your lovely friend here. And since I've got myself a lot more gifts to be passing out, if you all don't mind, I'll just be moving along."

Again she reached out to hug Denise. "It was nice meeting you, girl, and if you're ever in my neck of the woods, be sure to stop by, you hear?"

Denise smiled. "Thanks."

They finished the hug, more fiercely than the last, and Sally was off. "Bye-bye, now," she called as she drifted up the path as graceful as any four-legged camel with two arms can drift. The others called out their good-byes as Denise gingerly tested her side for any broken ribs.

Samson spoke again, and for the first time Denise thought she understood. Well, not all of it. Well, okay, so it was only a general impression, but a general impression was better than no impression. Maybe she was finally starting to get the hang of this place. Or maybe it was because her personality and Samson's seemed to be so similar.

In any case, Aristophenix was the one to respond. "Sorry 'bout that, partner, I'd almost forgot." Turning to Denise he explained,

> "to HeLp samson gRaдUate
> was tHe pURpose of tHis tRip.
> He must sHow you fayRaH,
> so fRom His дipLoma He дon't get, uH, gyppeд."

This time the entire group groaned. Usually they were able to endure his poetry, but once in a while he fired off a zinger that was just too painful to ignore. Still, Aristophenix paid little attention as he turned and led them down the knoll toward the village.

Denise threw a look over her shoulder and asked, "Shouldn't Nathan be here by now?"

"Worry, don't you," Listro Q assured her. "As long as stays he in Fayrah, perfectly safe is he."

Denise nodded. Although still a little reluctant, she turned to join the group as they headed down the hill toward the city.

How much farther is it? Do we have to walk so fast? Aren't we there yet?"

The boy's questions were wearing on Bobok. The only way he could continue was by reminding himself what a delectable catch the Upside Downer would be. But they'd have to hurry. Not only were Bobok's nerves wearing thin, but there was less than two hours of his season remaining in Fayrah. Less than two hours before the Portal sealed itself shut.

"Perhaps if you left that canteen behind," he offered, "it would be easier for you to travel." Ever since he had seen the canteen, Bobok feared it. But he wasn't afraid of the canteen; it was its contents.

"This stupid canteen's not the problem," Nathan complained, rubbing his hip. "It's how fast you're making us go."

"The Portal is just past the courthouse, most favored Thread. But we must circle behind the buildings to avoid the idle chatter of its citizens—lest they contaminate you with their weakness of thought."

"My leg is hurting," Nathan whined. "Besides, you never said it would take this long. Why can't I at least see some people? I still don't know why we have to go so fast."

Bobok continued forward, beginning to wonder if being the most evil and dreaded ruler in seventeen dimensions was really all it was cracked up to be.

Now they were inside the capital, and Denise was becoming quite the celebrity. It seemed everywhere she went she was surrounded by crowds of excited citizens. The glowing Blood Mountains had signaled everyone that she had entered their kingdom, and now they all wanted to wish her well. Apparently being a member of the Upside-Down Kingdom was quite an honor.

"Ain't this somethin'?" Aristophenix shouted over the crowd.

"I'll say," Denise answered as she reached up to shake claws with a giant twelve-armed crab. "Are they always this happy?"

"Sadness only have we," Listro Q called, "when out-give one another, try we."

Denise broke out laughing. Somehow she wasn't surprised. "Oh, and girl?" Aristophenix said.

"If ya' NEED SOMETHIN' ELSE
to ERASE ALL THEM FROWNS,
JES' LOOK OVER YONDER
WITH THEM BIG BABY BROWNS."

Denise turned. Despite everything she'd seen so far, there was no way she was prepared for this. In front of her stood a magnificent courthouse made of brilliant marble. Every stone was perfectly cut and gleaming white. In fact it was so white it almost hurt her eyes. Almost, but not quite.

High atop the building, past a hundred glimmering steps, twelve elegant pillars, and windows of what could only be pure crystal, stood the town clock. Its ruby hands glowed and shimmered in the bright morning sun as they pointed to half past ten.

Aristophenix spoke again,

"THIS HERE'S OUR COURTHOUSE,
WHERE OUR MONEY NEVER LAXES.
FACT, IT'S AT THIS VERY SPOT,
THAT THE GOVERNMENT PAYS US TAXES."

Next, Listro Q pointed to another building equally as beautiful and grand. "Library, here is it," he said. "All Fayrahnians keep we records do."

"Records?" Denise asked.

Listro Q nodded. "Every deed good of our, every kindness of action, written and recorded in the books."

Denise nodded. It sounded like the library was where they kept records of every Fayrahnian's good deed.

Suddenly Samson began to chatter. This time the tone of his voice said something was wrong.

Denise turned and looked down the street. She had never seen anything like it. It was as if the entire kingdom came to an end. But not all at once. Gradually, the sky drew lower and lower, while turning darker and darker. Slowly, the ground rose higher and higher, its grass and flowers turning sickly brown then black. And on the sides, the trees and bushes crowded closer and closer together, as they also withered and appeared to die. It was as if they were inside a giant pop bottle that narrowed into a tiny little neck. A tunnel. A tunnel where everything, every plant, every color, where all of life seemed to shrivel and die.

"There!" Listro Q pointed. "The Portal!"

Denise squinted. At the far end of the tunnel was a small round opening where wind and sand swirled fiercely—a small round portal that opened slightly and closed slightly, opened slightly and closed slightly . . . as if it were alive.

But it wasn't the Portal that caught Denise's breath. It was who was heading for the Portal. "Nathan!" she cried. "Mr. Hornsberry!" Then she saw a third creature who seemed to be leading them.

"Bobok!" Aristophenix cried.

She spun to Aristophenix for an explanation. For the first time since they'd met she saw fear in his eyes. "What's going on?" she demanded. "Where's Nathan going? Who's that with him?" Her voice grew high and shrill, the way it always did when she was scared. "Aristophenix! Aristophenix, answer me!"

The furry creature tried to sound relaxed and controlled. But he was as bad an actor as he was a poet.

> "THIS AIN'T A TIME TO WORRY,
> OR APPEAR TOO TERRIBLY GLUM.
> BUT THAT FELLA HURRYIN' NATHAN,
> WELL, HE AIN'T A FAYRAHNIAN CHUM."

"Bobok! You called him Bobok! Is he a bad guy?" Denise cried.

Aristophenix swallowed and tried to look the other way. But Denise wasn't backing down. She wouldn't quit until she had an answer. Finally he looked back at her.

> "NATHAN'S HEADING TO KEYGARP,
> THAT'S WHERE HE WILL BE.
> FROM BOBOK'S KINGDOM of WINTER,
> HE MAY NEVER GET FREE."

Denise's jaw dropped open and she stared helplessly. This is exactly what she had feared since the beginning. Something awful was going to happen. She had known it all along. She spun back to the Portal . . . just in time to see Nathan and Mr. Hornsberry crawl through the opening and disappear.

"Nathan!" she shouted. "Nathan, come back! Mr. Hornsberry!" But she was too late. They were gone.

Listro Q broke from the group and started toward the tunnel. "To go Keygarp!" He shouted. "Come, let's!"

But Aristophenix called out, bringing him to a stop.

> "HOLD ON ta yeR HORSES,
> I DON't tHINK tHat we SHOULD.
> If we gO ON INSIDe tHeRe,
> It miGHt Be foR gOOD!"

"What are you talking about?" Denise demanded. She could feel her ears burning with anger. "We've got to get Nathan. He's in danger—you said so yourself!"

> "tHe PORTaL seaLs at NOON,
> tHat ONLy gIves NINety mINutes,
> to get IN aND get OUt,
> OR Become peRmaNeNt teNaNts."

It was Samson's turn to argue with Aristophenix . . . and he did, long and loud, until Denise could take no more. "What's going on?" she demanded. "What's he saying?"

Listro Q's translation was quick and simple. "Help needs Nathan. Help must we."

Denise turned back to Aristophenix. It was obvious that he felt sick over what had happened and that he took full responsibility. It was also obvious that he knew something had to be done.

Once again Samson began to chatter.

And once again Listro Q agreed. "Choice no other have we."

Aristophenix stared at the Portal another long moment. Then, swallowing back his fears, he took a deep breath and started toward it.

Denise and the others followed. Of course Aristophenix tried his best to stay in the lead, because as everyone knows, leaders are supposed to lead. Unfortunately, his roly-poly body hadn't quite gotten the message. So with every step he waddled, he fell just a little farther behind.

> "sLow down on them tootsies,
> c'mon, Let me pass.
> I know there's a hurry,
> but I'm runnin' outta ..."

No one heard his final word. It was lost forever as they entered the howling tunnel of wind and sand.

the PORtaL

The first thing Nathan noticed as he stepped through the blowing Portal of wind and sand was the heat. But it wasn't the wet and sticky kind. This was hot and dry. The type that pounds your head and makes your eyes ache from its brightness.

The second thing Nathan noticed were the insects. Thousands of them. They were four or five inches long with pincer jaws. And each and every one of them had a single thing in common. They were racing straight for him!

"Bobok!" he cried. "What do we do? What do we do?"

"Close your mouth!" Bobok shouted.

"What?"

"Close your mouth! They smell the moisture from your breath and want it."

"But—"

"Close your mouth and breathe through your nose—*now!*"

Nathan would have argued but he barely had time to obey. He closed his mouth and just in time. The insects reached his legs— hundreds of them—and quickly scampered inside his pants around his ankles and calves. Instinctively he tried to kick and slap them aside, but there were just too many. As soon as he knocked off one a dozen more appeared in its place.

"Stop it!" Bobok shouted. "Let them have their way. It will only last a moment."

By now the creepy things were swarming around his knees in their desperate search for water. As they raced back and forth, his skin tickled and itched. But Nathan wasn't moving. Not anymore. He was too frightened. Forget being frightened. He was *petrified!*

"That tickling you feel is only their tongues," Bobok assured him. "They're licking the sweat off your skin—don't worry."

But Nathan *was* worrying, big time. He looked down and his eyes widened. He could no longer see his legs. He could see their shape okay, but his blue jeans were no longer blue. They were a mass of black and brown insects. Not only were they racing inside his pants but they were outside as well—thousands of hairy legs, fluttering wings, and hard-shelled bodies swarming as they slowly worked their way up his thighs.

Nathan tried his best not to scream. He clamped his jaw shut, he bit his tongue, he did everything he could do. But it was just too much. He had to open his mouth! He had to cry out! He had to—

"CHILDREN!"

All movement around his legs ceased.

"CHILDREN, COME DOWN FROM THAT HANDSOME UP-SIDE DOWNER THIS VERY INSTANT!" The voice screeched with power—like steel dragged across concrete.

In seconds Nathan's legs were completely free of the insects. Completely!

They pulled back into a teeming, swarming wall several feet high and several yards long. A teeming, swarming wall that had obeyed the voice, but remained close . . . just in case the voice changed its mind.

"You'll have to excuse their eagerness." The voice was much softer now, almost comforting. "It's been a long time since we've had the privilege of such a wonderfully handsome visitor with so much . . . moisture."

Nathan finally took his eyes from the quivering mound of bugs to see who was speaking. She sat on a throne and was gorgeous, heart-stopping—a woman more beautiful than any he had ever seen. She had soft blonde hair that fell to her delicate shoulders, a kind smiling mouth, and the most incredible violet blue eyes. Nathan liked her instantly.

"Who is she?" he whispered to Bobok.

"Don't be deceived by her looks," Bobok warned. "The Illusionist is as crafty with her disguises as she is with her words."

Pretending not to hear, the lady motioned to the wall of bugs. "You'll have to excuse the little ones. You Upside Downers consist of so much moisture that sometimes they forget themselves."

"She's trying to scare you," Bobok said. "Don't fall for it."

But Nathan wasn't frightened of her. How could he be? The lady was so lovely and kind.

The pile of droning bugs, however, was another matter. He glanced at Mr. Hornsberry to see how he was taking it. The dog didn't seem to mind them at all. And why should he? As a stuffed animal he was made up of cotton batting and cloth—not much moisture there. But the lady . . . for some reason he seemed very suspicious of the lady. And when she looked at him a faint growl escaped from his throat.

But instead of anger or concern, the lady broke into a gentle smile. "My, what a beautiful dog," she said. "Isn't he the most perfect thing?"

Immediately Mr. Hornsberry's tail thumped in the sand. So much for suspicions.

"Come here, boy," she called as she knelt down and patted her lap. "Come on."

He gave one of his throat-clearing coughs and nervously answered, "I don't wish to be too terribly rude at this juncture of our relationship, but it's probably best if I remain here with Master Nathan."

"Oh, and he talks," she said with a delighted grin. "Isn't he just the most clever thing." Turning to Nathan she added, "What a lucky young man you are to have such a friend."

Mr. Hornsberry's entire body gave a shudder of delight.

The lady rose from her throne and addressed Bobok. "My dearest and most trusted friend, you promised two specimens. I see only one and he's a boy—though an incredibly intelligent and handsome boy to be sure. But where, dear heart, is the girl you promised?"

"She will be coming soon," Bobok purred. "Trust me."

The lady smiled warmly before turning her focus back upon Nathan. "And why have you left her behind?"

Nathan swallowed hard and looked at the wall of thirsty insects. For the first time in his life he wasn't sure if talking was such a great idea. The lady saved him the effort.

"Of course." She smiled in understanding. "It is because a young man of your special genius and chosen talents would only be held back by someone of her mediocre skills."

Nathan's eyes widened in surprise.

"I am correct, aren't I?" she asked sweetly.

What could he say? When she was right, she was right. And isn't that exactly what Bobok had said—that he was special, a Chosen Thread? Nathan gave a modest shrug and finally spoke, "Yeah, I guess."

Immediately the buzzing from the wall of insects grew louder in agitation . . . or was it anticipation? Maybe it was both. In any case Nathan knew they definitely smelled the water from his breath and were hoping to race back for seconds on drinks.

However, the Illusionist gave a single wave of her hand and they immediately fell silent.

She continued, her voice filled with sympathy and understanding, "It must be very difficult for a good-looking young man such as yourself, with so many gifts and talents, to deal with such an *average* person as the girl."

Nathan looked at her carefully to see if she was mocking him. But there was no irony in her eyes . . . only the kindest, most sincere look.

He gave another shrug. "Sometimes."

The Illusionist nodded in compassion as she approached and gently rested her hand upon his shoulder. "Poor boy," she consoled. "I understand."

"Dear lady," Bobok quietly warned, "remember our agreement. The boy is coming with *me*."

"Of course, my esteemed friend. Though I must say I would give half my kingdom for someone with such looks and great intelligence to stay and keep *me* company."

Nathan looked up at her. He couldn't help smiling. She returned it and gave his shoulder the slightest squeeze. It wasn't much, just enough to say, *Even though we've only met, we really understand each other, don't we?*

"Dear lady . . ." Bobok's warning grew more stern.

"Oh, kindest Bobok, you needn't worry." Directing her gaze back to Nathan she continued, "All I am saying is that it must be terribly frustrating to be as great as he is and have to deal with commoners like that girl." She gave him another little squeeze.

"Oh, it's not so bad," Nathan said. "I mean, she can be pretty stupid sometimes, and, well, yeah, sometimes she's a real pain, but—"

Ahhhh . . ." Denise doubled over in agony. She had never felt anything like it. They had just entered the tunnel and had started for the Portal when a searing pain ripped through her mind.

"Wrong's what?" Listro Q was immediately at her side. He shouted over the wind, "Happened what?"

"My head!" she gasped.

But it wasn't her head. This was no headache she was experiencing. It was deeper . . . *much* deeper.

Then the pain suddenly left—disappearing as quickly as it appeared. Denise lifted her eyes, dumbfounded.

"Okay, are you?" Listro Q yelled. Even above the roaring wind and whistling sand it was possible to hear the concern in his voice.

"Yeah," she said, slowly rising. "What was that?"

Aristophenix joined them. "What's wrong?" he yelled over the wind.

"I don't know," Denise shouted. "But I'm okay now."

"You sure?"

She gave him a nod.

"Good!" Aristophenix shouted as he pointed ahead. "'Cause we've not much time!"

Denise followed his finger to the Portal. Through all the blasting wind and sand it was still possible to see it widen and contract, widen and contract—as if it were breathing. And each time it contracted, the opening shrunk just a little bit more. She understood Aristophenix perfectly. It soon would close.

The pain that had filled her head was completely gone. Now there was only the stinging sand. It bit her face and arms, and it made her eyes water so badly that she could barely keep them open.

But she had no right to complain. Samson was the one who really had it rough. The little guy fluttered his wings for all he was worth and still barely held his ground against the wind. He chattered loudly for everyone to hurry and continue moving. They did.

Then it hit Denise again—only worse. This time the pain was so intense that it knocked her to the ground. She grabbed her head. But it wasn't just her head. It was as if all of her mind, her body, her personality—everything about her had been hit. Hit hard. In fact, the pain was so violent that all she could do was lie there and gasp.

"Is it what?" Listro Q cried as he dropped to her side. "Is it what?"

But Denise couldn't answer. She was too busy trying to breathe.

"Nathan!" Aristophenix shouted. "It's Nathan!"

Once again the pain shut off. But this time it left Denise much weaker . . . and confused. "What . . ." She panted, trying to catch her breath, trying to make sense out of it. "What's going on?"

Suddenly Listro Q understood. "Speaking bad about you, is Nathan. His words hurting you."

"It's because he's an Upside Downer," Aristophenix explained.

> *"YOUR WORDS CAN CUT,*
> *AND FORCE OTHERS TO BLEED.*
> *'CAUSE THEY'RE SPOKEN FROM MOUTHS,*
> *WHICH HAVE BEEN IMAGER-BREATHED."*

"You mean"—Denise coughed as they helped her to her feet— "Nathan is doing all this to me with his mouth? This is all happening because of what he's saying?"

Listro Q and Aristophenix nodded.

"Great authority have Upside Downers. Powerful very, blessing or curse their words."

"Okay, fine," she called. "He wants a fight, I'll give him a fight." Taking a deep breath, she shouted at the top of her lungs, "Nathan Hutton O'Brien, you are the world's most—"

"No!" Suddenly both creatures covered her mouth with their hands, or paws, or whatever you'd call them.

Listro Q looked stern. "Spoken *never,*" he said, "harsh words in Fayrah, *never.*"

Samson chattered again. By now he was several feet behind them and losing ground rapidly.

Aristophenix nodded and yelled,

> *"OH, SAMMY BOY'S A-FADIN',*
> *Let's GET ON WITH THE SHOW.*
> *HE CAN'T Last MUCH LONGER,*
> *SO COME ON, Let's move IT, Let's GO!"*

Listro Q nodded and shouted, "Form a wall, quickly let's!"

"Good idea, partner."

With that, both creatures raced back to Samson. Turning to face the wind, they formed a type of shield with their bodies to protect their little friend. Samson ducked behind them and was able to avoid most of the wind as they struggled back toward Denise. Once they arrived, they linked arms with her and continued forward.

The Portal was only twenty feet ahead, but with the blasting wind and sand it could have been miles. And the opening was growing smaller, there was no doubt about it. It wasn't shrinking quickly but, like the hour hand of a clock, it continued to make progress—slowly but surely.

And still they pressed on . . . heads lowered and shoulders bent to protect their faces from the biting sand. Two steps forward, a slip and one step back. One step forward, a stumble, another step back. Yet, somehow, they made progress. Like the Portal itself, they may have been slow, but they were determined.

It happened a third time—a blow to Denise stronger than the other two combined.

She wasn't sure, but she thought she might have lost consciousness. One moment she felt the impossible pain. The next moment

Aristophenix and Listro Q were on the ground beside her shouting, "Denny, can you hear us? Denny!"

When she was finally able to speak, she groaned, "Thanks, Nate, that was a beaut."

"Stand, can you?" Listro Q shouted. "Denny! Stand can you?"

Denise wanted to break out laughing. And she would have if she'd had the strength. "You gotta be kidding," she moaned. "Stand? I can barely breathe . . ."

a HASTY exit

Well, that's enough talk about that silly old girl," the Illusionist continued in her soothing, silky voice. "But please, you've been so modest. Tell me more about yourself. What a wonderful life you must live, being a Chosen Thread, traveling in and out of dimensions as you do."

Once again Nathan looked into her understanding eyes. Somewhere deep inside he felt a stirring—that same rush of excitement that came every time he manipulated a situation to his advantage. It was a wonderful mixture of victory and self-importance. And the best thing was that he didn't even have to work to earn that feeling. Not here. It just came naturally. All he had to do was listen to her compliments and look into those eyes.

Bobok rolled back and forth as if growing nervous. "Dear lady, we would love to talk, but there is much to be done."

Ignoring him, the Illusionist looked directly at Nathan. "Oh, please stay," she begged. "Your visit has given me such courage and strength. Just to be in the presence of someone like yourself. Please, don't leave—not yet."

What could Nathan do? That little rush of excitement he'd felt growing inside was now a raging current. How could he say no to someone who admired him so much? How could he refuse to allow her to adore and worship him? Without taking his eyes from hers, he spoke to Bobok, "We can stay a couple more minutes, can't we?"

"I think not, Chosen Thread. There is much to give you in my kingdom, and it will take much time for you to acquire all of its possessions."

"But," the Illusionist protested, "if he stays here with me, he will be loved and admired for his greatness."

"Admiration is important, dear lady. But what of taking? Acquiring possessions is of great importance to a thread of this stature. Am I not mistaken, Chosen One?"

Nathan faltered a moment. It was true. The little blue guy had a point. Being admired was one thing. But having whatever he wanted whenever he wanted it, well now, that was quite another. Still, why couldn't he have both? Again he spoke to Bobok, "But if I'm so great and everything, then why can't I be, you know, adored *and* have all the things?"

"Precisely," the Illusionist agreed. "In my kingdom you would not only have our worship and adoration, which you so richly deserve, but you would share in all our possessions as well."

"*Share?*" Bobok's voice grew sharper. "Such a thread does not *share!*"

"A poor choice of words." The Illusionist quickly backtracked. "I did not mean *share,* I, too, meant *possess.* He would *possess* all that I have."

Bobok broke out laughing. "And what a lucky creature he would be. Imagine, possessing all of this sand, all of these insects. To think, Chosen Thread, someday this could all be yours."

For a moment the spell had broken. Nathan was able to turn from the Illusionist's eyes and look at the grinning Bobok. It was a grin Nathan couldn't help returning. After all, it was true. What did this woman have to offer but bugs and sand? Sure, he'd be loved and adored—treated like a king. But a king of what? A king of sand dunes and insects? "I'm afraid Bobok's got a point," he said as he turned back to the woman. "I mean, you really don't—"

But that was as far as he got. For as soon as their eyes met, he came to a stop. He wasn't sure if what he saw was inside her eyes, or if it was a reflection upon their surface . . . or if he was even looking into her eyes at all.

Whatever the case, the barren desert had suddenly exploded with life. Everywhere he looked there were marvelous castles of crystal, sprawling pathways of gold, and lovely parks and gardens filled with flowers. But what impressed Nathan the most were the people. Thousands of beautiful, perfect people—waving, smiling, and applauding. More importantly, they were all waving, smiling, and applauding for him!

"You were saying?" the Illusionist softly whispered. Now she was standing beside him. It was odd; one moment he was looking into her eyes and the next moment they were standing together gazing over the beautiful city and its thousands of citizens.

"Where—where did they all come from?" Nathan asked, breathless with emotion. "They're . . . beautiful."

"Their beauty is only a reflection of yours," she assured him. "Where they came from is of no importance. The fact that each loves and adores you—that is all that matters."

"Who loves you and adores you?" Mr. Hornsberry asked as he looked about nervously. "Master Nathan, I fail to see to whom she is making reference."

"Gracious lady," Bobok sternly warned. "We agreed. Your reflections are most unwelcome!"

"This is *his* illusion, not mine. This is what *he* wants to see."

Bobok turned back to Nathan, speaking louder to get his attention. "Chosen Thread? The canteen you have about your waist, the water."

But Nathan barely heard. He was too mesmerized by the thousands of adoring people calling out to him—beautiful people begging him to come closer so they could admire him, so they could reach out and touch him. How could he refuse? He started toward them. And to his amazement, he discovered that his hip no longer hurt. He didn't even have his limp!

"Master Nathan," Mr. Hornsberry shouted. "What are you doing—where are you going?"

"Those are my people . . . my fans."

"What people? What fans? Master Nathan, you're proceeding directly toward that multitude of insects!"

Nathan had no idea what Hornsberry was talking about. All he saw were the fans.

"Chosen Thread!" Bobok called.

"Leave him be," the lady warned. "If this is the reality he wishes, let him live it!"

Closer and closer Nathan approached the excited, teaming crowd—every one of them desperate for his attention, for his presence, for his slightest touch.

"Chosen Thread!" Bobok shouted. "Your canteen—your water!"

Nathan could barely hear him. The cheering fans were just too loud. He was only a few feet away now. Just a couple more steps and he would be in the center of their loving, adoring arms.

"Master Nathan!" Mr. Hornsberry cried. "Master Nathan!"

Bobok rolled toward him, shouting over the noise. "Chosen Thread! Chosen Thread, aren't you thirsty? Does not this hot, dry sand make your throat ache for water?" Now he was beside Nathan, then under his feet, nearly tripping him in an effort to get his attention. "Chosen Thread, how about a drink of water! It is so hot. I'm so thirsty—aren't you? How about some cool, refreshing water?"

Nathan glanced down at the creature and smiled. *Poor little guy,* he thought. *He's obviously feeling left out. Probably jealous. But why's he making such a big deal about taking a drink?*

"Just open your canteen! Just one sip!" Bobok shouted. "Just one little sip!"

Nathan shrugged. The little guy had obviously been helpful. If he wanted a drink so badly, there was no reason he couldn't have it. And he was right, it was awfully hot. It probably wouldn't hurt to take a few gulps himself. So, partially for Bobok, partially for himself, Nathan reached for his canteen and opened the lid.

That was all it took.

Immediately the adoring fans began screaming. But they weren't screaming in adoration . . . they were screaming in horror. They began pushing and shoving each other—not to get closer to Nathan, but to get *away!* They were shoving and shouting and screaming to get *away* from him!

"Bobok, what's going on?" Nathan cried. "Bobok!"

"Stop it!" the lady screamed from behind them. "Stop it at once!"

"Pour it on the ground!" Bobok yelled. "Pour the water on the ground!"

"But they're leaving!" Nathan cried. His lifelong dream was dissolving before his eyes. "Why are they leaving?"

By now the crowd was trampling over one another in their desperate attempt to flee.

"Stop it!" the lady screeched.

"Pour the water on the ground!"

Mr. Hornsberry began running in tight little circles of frustration, shouting, "Do what he says, do what he says!"

"Bobok, I don't understand!"

"Pour the water on the ground!"

"Do what he says! Do what he says!"

"But—"

"NOW!" Bobok shouted.

Mr. Hornsberry could stand no more. Suddenly the chubby fellow leaped into the air, opened his mouth, and chomped down on Nathan's wrist. Hard.

"OW!" Nathan cried as he grabbed his hand, dropping the canteen to the sand.

And then it started . . .

As the water of letters and words poured from the canteen onto the ground, they started to sizzle and pop. Like some sort of powerful acid, they began eating into the sand, turning it into a clear, dark liquid.

"Get back!" Bobok shouted as he rolled away from the rapidly growing puddle. "Get back! Get back!"

Nathan and Mr. Hornsberry didn't need a second invitation. They leaped backwards and watched as the liquid letters ate into the sand, making a bigger and bigger pool—a bubbling pool that began to swirl as it liquefied everything it touched.

But it was not just the pool that held Nathan's attention. It was the reflection in that pool. Now at last he was able to see the illusion for what it was. There were no castles, no golden paths, no flowery hills— just sand. And there was definitely no crowd of adoring fans. As

Nathan looked at their reflection he saw them for what they were—a mound of teaming insects, a mound that he had nearly walked into and that had nearly devoured him! But now the mound was collapsing as the insects tried in vain to scurry away from the widening pool.

"My children!" the lady cried. "My precious children!"

But it did no good. The growing, spiraling pool continued to eat away at her kingdom. Maybe *eat away* wasn't the right phrase. Maybe *dissolve* would be better. In any case, Nathan watched with horror and fascination as the pool continued to grow and suck in the sand . . . the insects . . . everything that it touched.

"*Run!*" Bobok shouted over the roar of melting elements.

"What's happening?"

"It's the water from the stream—it is destroying the Kingdom of Seerlo! Run!"

Nathan spun around and started to run, but he wasn't quick enough. The very sand under his feet was being sucked into the pool, faster and faster. He began losing more ground than he was taking.

"Jump!" Bobok yelled. "Jump and run! Jump and run!"

Nathan understood and started leaping. So did Hornsberry. And with each leap dozens of yards of sand rushed by under their feet. Up ahead he saw a dark blue forest. But instead of racing toward it, it was racing toward him! As more and more of the desert was sucked into the pool, the forest approached more and more quickly!

"You'll pay for this!" the lady screamed over the wind and roar of melting elements. "I swear, you'll pay!"

Nathan looked up and was amazed at what he saw. It was the lady's voice, all right, but it was no longer the lady—or at least as he'd seen her. This time the Illusionist appeared entirely different . . . a scaled and war-scarred body, with huge cloven hoofs. She had black leathery wings that were now unfurled and flapping—wings that lifted her high above the swirling whirlpool of what had once been her kingdom.

"Hurry, Chosen Thread!" Bobok shouted as he rolled ahead of them, spinning so fast he was merely a blue blur. "Hurry!"

keygarp

Although the Portal was only a few feet away, Denise wasn't sure she could make it. She'd already used most of her strength just to stand. After the beating she'd taken from Nathan she doubted she was strong enough to fight any more sand and wind. Still, there was something about Samson's, Listro Q's, and Aristophenix's encouragement . . . and their love—the way they stayed right at her side, helping her. Somehow it gave her strength, and enabled her to stagger the last remaining steps toward the opening.

The Portal continued to expand and shrink, expand and shrink, as it grew smaller and smaller. Once they arrived, Samson was the first to enter. Then Listro Q, then Aristophenix. Now it was Denise's turn. It was more than a little spooky, stepping through something that seemed half alive. But taking a deep breath and closing her eyes, she crawled through the opening and entered . . .

> "NOW HOLD ON TO YER HORSES,
> I DON'T MEAN TO HARP.
> BUT WHAT HAPPENED TO SEERLO?
> THIS HERE LOOKS LIKE KEYGARP."

The group stood inside some sort of frozen forest. But instead of leaves, each of the twisted and gnarled tree branches was covered in layers of frost and ice. That was Denise's first impression of the place—frost and ice. And the color blue. It seemed everything was blue. From the midnight blue of the tree trunks and boulders, to the lighter shades of blue for the snow, to the clear blue layers of crystalline frost that coated everything. There was no yellow, no orange, no red . . . only blue. It was both eerie and beautiful.

Denise gave a shudder and pulled up her collar against the cold. Listro Q and Aristophenix did the same with their clothes—though Listro Q made an extra effort to ensure his tuxedo was free of any sand or debris.

"You there—Upside Downer!" The voice was harsh and raspy, like the cawing of a crow.

Denise looked up. "What on earth?"

The others followed her gaze. Through the twisted branches of the forest they saw a creature with cloven hoofs and covered in scales. It circled high over their heads, its black wings stark against the cold blue sky.

"I have not forgotten!" it cried. "You have been promised to me. I have not forgotten!" And then, with two mighty thrusts of its wings, the creature sailed off.

Denise gave another shudder. Turning to the group, she croaked, "Who . . . who was that?"

No one had an answer. But, even now, Denise suspected it would not be the last time they met.

"Look!" Listro Q pointed in the distance. "Castle Bobok's!"

Denise turned to see a craggy set of towers that seemed to defy gravity as they leaned and loomed in all directions.

"Alrightee then," Aristophenix took a deep breath for courage.

> "to HeLP NatHaN, Let's move,
> siNce tHat's wHat we cHose.
> 'cause tHere aiN't mucH time Left
> 'fore tHe portaL is cLoseD."

He started toward the castle and the others joined him. Denise hesitated, took her own breath for courage and followed.

The doors slithered open with a harsh hiss. Like everything else in Bobok's castle, they were made of smooth, cold steel. And like everything else in Keygarp, they were covered with a thin coating of frost that sparkled in deep blue light.

Nathan had learned the hard way not to touch the walls or doors or anything else in the castle. Actually, the touching wasn't the problem. It was the letting go that got a bit painful. The steel was so cold that once you touched it, it was impossible to let go without leaving a layer of skin forever frozen to its surface.

They had barely left the forest and entered the castle before Mr. Hornsberry sidled up close to Nathan. "I do hope I'm not speaking with impropriety," the dog whispered between chattering teeth, "but I don't fancy this place, Master Nathan—I don't fancy it one bit."

Nathan had to admit he wasn't too fond of it either. In fact, as they moved from room to room, he wasn't sure if he was shivering because of the cold or because of fear. Maybe it was both.

The next room they entered was like all the others—a large, cavernous hall that seemed to have no purpose except to echo their footsteps. And, like every other room, the walkway was lined on both sides with little orbs that rolled onto their faces as Bobok, Nathan, and Mr. Hornsberry passed. Each frosty-blue ball wore a helmet and had a small sword strapped to its side. But, since they had no arms, Nathan figured the swords were more for show than anything else. And, like Bobok, each had a set of sunken little eyes.

Nathan couldn't help thinking how everyone in the castle looked exactly the same. They reminded him of one of those assembly lines where the same part is stamped over and over again. That's what they were—stamped, carbon copies. Carbon copies of Bobok. Only these creatures had no personality. They were just stamped carbon copies that moved in perfect synchronization with no life or feeling.

Oh, and there was one other thing Nathan noticed . . . a hum. He'd heard it when they'd first entered the castle. And now, with every footstep, it seemed to grow louder.

They approached a pair of doors that towered a dozen feet over their heads. Bobok rolled to a stop and turned to Nathan. "You'll like this," he purred, his voice as smooth as when they'd first met. "You'll like this a lot."

He turned back to the doors and they whisked open. A blast of cold air hit Nathan so hard that he had to close his eyes. And when he opened them . . . well, let's just say he wished he hadn't.

The three of them approached the edge of a platform a hundred feet high. Before them floated dozens of strange creatures—some as thin as pencils, some as round as beach balls, some with three eyes and one head, others with three heads and one eye. Amazing. If you could imagine the strangest imaginables imaginable, and then imagine them just a little bit stranger . . . well, at least you'd be getting close.

"What—what is this place?" Nathan stuttered.

"Welcome to my menagerie!" Bobok beamed.

Nathan continued to stare. The creatures rotated inside a giant cone that stretched a hundred feet above them and a hundred feet below . . . a cone of energy that crackled and sparked every time someone or something bumped against its side. Each of the creatures looked like they had been in a thousand fights. They were scarred and beaten and battered. Their strange, exotic clothing was torn into a million shreds.

But what frightened Nathan even more was how everyone seemed to be in some sort of trance. Although their eyes were open, it was as if they couldn't see. When they drifted into one another, they automatically began to fight and scratch. Sometimes it was over a shred of clothing, or a scrap of floating food or even the remains of a shattered toy. But it was always done in slow motion—as if the creatures were being controlled. As if they couldn't help themselves.

Finally there was the matter of the hum. Nathan no longer wondered about its source. It came from here. And it really wasn't a hum. It was a groan. Dozens of groans. Long, slow, mournful groans coming from the throats of these strange creatures caught within the energy field.

"Who . . . who are they?"

"Oh, just different beings I've collected from different kingdoms," Bobok purred. "But they all have one thing in common—at least they do now." He chuckled. "Each is possessed with greed—pure, unadulterated greed."

Nathan stepped back as two creatures passed so close he could have reached out and touched them. Like the others, they kept fighting, slowly and mechanically.

Mr. Hornsberry let out a long, low growl.

Bobok paid little attention and continued. "Once they're in that energy field they are under my power. They're doomed to scratch and claw, to take and steal for eternity. Great sport, wouldn't you agree?"

Nathan continued to stare.

"Particularly for those who never give but want only to possess."

Nathan tried to respond but he had no voice.

"However," Bobok purred as he turned toward Nathan, "in all my years I've never had an Upside Downer in there . . ."

Nathan swallowed hard. Slowly he turned to look at Bobok.

He wished he hadn't.

The blue orb was grinning his grin again. A grin that said his wishes were about to be fulfilled.

the
menacerie

At first Denise didn't notice the guards at the drawbridge. She just thought they were a couple larger-than-normal snowballs. Granted, they were bluer than the rest of the snow, and granted, they just happened to be wearing helmets and swords, but, hey, it had been a long day. She was entitled to make a few minor mistakes.

Unfortunately, these two guards were anything but minor.

"Who goes there?" Guard One shouted.

The group slowed to a stop and looked at Aristophenix. The pudgy bear cleared his throat and announced.

> "we're from the Land of fayrah,
> and though meeting you is a treat,
> we're Looking for a boy
> and an orb who needs feet."

Listro Q rolled his eyes at him.

"Hey, it's the best I can do under pressure," Aristophenix whispered.

The two guards paid little attention. Instead, Guard One approached a tree stump next to Listro Q and effortlessly rolled up its side. Now he stood on its top, about waist high. "Fayrahnians?" he asked. His voice sounded mechanical and brittle—like some old-fashioned record.

"Right are you," Listro Q answered, obviously trying to remain cool. Though it's hard to remain cool when you're sweating from fear.

"Nice coat," the guard said as he rolled closer and rubbed against Listro Q's tuxedo jacket.

"Uh, er, thanks."

"Give me," the guard demanded.

Listro Q hesitated. It was obviously one of his favorite possessions. No way would he give it up. At least that's what Denise thought. But then the most amazing thing happened. Without a word, Listro Q reached down and started unbuttoning it.

"What are you doing?" Denise asked. "You love that coat!"

"Shhh," Aristophenix whispered.

Everyone watched as Listro Q took off his coat, then slowly laid it on the stump beside the little blue ball.

But instead of showing gratitude or even giving a "thanks," the guard immediately demanded more. "Nice shirt. Me want shirt, too."

Listro Q frowned and tried to reason. "Cold, freezing is it," he said.

"Me want shirt!" the guard insisted. "Me want shirt! Me want shirt!"

With a reluctant sigh, Listro Q reached down and started unbuttoning his shirt.

"This is ridiculous," Denise muttered as she pushed up her sleeves and started for the little orb.

"Denny," Aristophenix warned.

"There're only two of them and four of us," she said.

"It's not the Fayrahnian way."

"I don't care whose way it is," she argued. "They're just a couple twerpy little ice balls, and if you're not men enough to stop them, then I'll—"

But that was as far as she got. Because when she turned back to the guard she discovered the little "ice ball" had grown five to six times in size. Now it was as tall as she was!

"Whoa!" she cried in surprise. "What happened?"

"Your hate," Listro Q said, as he finished unbuttoning his shirt and handed it to the guard, "fed him did it."

"My hate did this?" Denise asked, marveling.

The blue ball grinned.

"But . . ." Denise turned in frustration to Aristophenix. "You guys just can't stand around and give them whatever they want."

Samson chattered off a response. Aristophenix nodded and translated.

> *"give what they want,*
> *do what they say.*
> *that's our code of Love,*
> *that's the fayrahnian way."*

"But that's not fair!" Denise could feel the tops of her ears burn again, a sure sign of her anger. The same anger that made her the terror of every bully in the school yard. The same anger that would attack any foe, no matter what their size, even five-foot-five, round, blue ones!

But when she turned back to the guard, he was no longer five foot five. Now he was ten foot ten!

"Augh!" she screamed. She threw a look over at Listro Q, who only shrugged as if to say, *I told you so.*

Before she could do any more damage, Aristophenix reached into his vest pocket, pulled out the gold watch that Sally the camel creature had given him, and took a look at the time.

> *"my, oh my,*
> *well, what do you know.*
> *we'd stay for a chat,*
> *but it's time we must go."*

Now Guard Two rolled forward. "Nice watch."

But he had a little competition. For even though the first guard had Listro Q's shirt and coat, he was still greedy enough to try for the watch as well. "Yeah," Guard One said, "*very* nice."

"WHY, THIS LITTLE THING?
SHUCKS, IT'S ALL RUSTY AND OLD.
THOUGH I GUESS THAT'S NOT RUST,
SINCE IT'S MADE OF SOLID—"

But no one heard Aristophenix's last word as he "accidentally" dropped the watch to the ground. Before he could complete his poem, the two blue balls rolled for it.

Now it's true, Guard Two was many times smaller than Guard One, but as they fought and shouted and struggled for the watch, he began growing in size.

"Quick! Go let's!" Listro Q shouted as he scooped up his shirt and coat.

"But—," Denise protested.

"Hurry!"

She obeyed and followed as they raced across the drawbridge toward the castle. Suddenly there was a violent explosion behind them, followed by another. Denise spun around. The giant blue orbs were nowhere in sight. Instead, a light blue snow had started to fall.

"What happened?" she shouted.

"Snow!" Listro pointed.

"I see the snow, but where'd those guys go?"

"Here," Listro Q said, again pointing to the snow.

"You mean . . . this is them?" Denise couldn't help grinning in satisfaction. "This snow is them?"

"Correct are you."

"They blew themselves up?"

"Critical mass," Listro Q nodded. "Their hatred blew up them."

"All right!" Denise laughed. "Well, I guess you guys really do know what you're doing, don't you?"

No one answered. Instead, all three stood there giving the weakest smiles she'd ever seen. Suddenly she wasn't quite as confident. "You did know that was going to happen . . . right?"

Again, they smiled.

"Oh, brother," she sighed. For if there's one thing she'd learned, it was that Fayrahnians couldn't lie. They could smile all they wanted, but they could not lie. "You mean to tell me you just guessed this would happen? You just winged it?"

Once again the trio smiled.

"Oh, brother," she muttered again as she turned and headed into the castle. "Oh, brother . . ."

Aristophenix, Listro Q, and Samson looked at one another, shrugged, and followed her inside.

If you think I'm going in there," Nathan said, backing toward the door, "you're crazy!"

"You are a chosen thread," Bobok insisted as he rolled toward him. "To take and possess without giving, to look out only for yourself— that is your dream."

Nathan continued backing away. "Yeah, but . . ."

"This is what you've lived for, what you've always wanted."

It was Mr. Hornsberry's turn to speak. The hair on his back was sticking straight up, and although he remained polite, there was no missing his determination. "Excuse me, but if you persist in rolling any closer, I am afraid I shall have to take a bite out of your head."

Bobok threw him a glance and chuckled lightly. "This is my kingdom, oh cloth stuffed with cotton. You will do as *I* say." Bobok continued moving toward them.

"I have given you sufficient warning," Mr. Hornsberry said, sounding as bold as any English bulldog could sound—although he would have been a little more convincing if he hadn't been shaking or crowding so close to Nathan's legs.

Bobok continued toward them.

"Please . . . ," Nathan stuttered. "Maybe we can talk, you know, work something out."

Bobok continued.

"It is quite obvious, Master Nathan, that the creature wishes no further dialogue." Mr. Hornsberry turned to Bobok. "Am I correct in this matter?"

Bobok said nothing, but continued.

"Very well," Mr. Hornsberry said, "have it your way—though please remember, I did give you sufficient warning." With that the dog leaned back on his haunches and with a fierce growl sprang directly at Bobok.

But the ruler was prepared. He fired off a blast of icy cold breath that hit the animal dead center. And there, in midair, Mr. Hornsberry froze. He didn't even fall to the ground. He just hung there, suspended.

"Mr. Hornsberry!" Nathan cried, racing to him. He reached out and touched him. The dog felt as cold and stiff as a chunk of ice. Spinning around to Bobok, he demanded, "What have you done to him?"

"It makes no difference," Bobok purred. "In a matter of seconds you will no longer care."

Nathan threw a cautious glance back at the menagerie. Another pair of fighting creatures drifted by, lost forever in their mindless trance of scratching and clawing, grabbing and owning, taking and possessing. "I . . . I don't want to go in there!"

"All of your life, Chosen Thread, you have been planting the seed of greed. Now it is only fair that you enjoy its harvest."

"But . . . that's not what I wanted!"

"It is precisely what you wanted. To live in a world where all you do is take."

"Yes, but—well, not like that." He threw a terrified look at the menagerie. "I didn't mean this. I didn't . . . what I meant was—"

Bobok started to laugh. It was cold and frightening.

Nathan's fear turned to panic. He had to make a break for it—past Bobok and out the door. But Bobok sensed his thoughts and signaled the guards. Their speed was amazing—blue blurs that raced to the doorway—hundreds of them—until Nathan's escape was entirely blocked.

Turning back to the menagerie, Nathan shouted, "I won't go in there! You can't make me!"

Bobok said nothing. Instead he simply nodded to the guards. Like a synchronized machine the little balls rolled out across the platform and slowly closed in. Nathan had to back up—closer to the edge of the ramp, closer and closer to the menagerie.

"Please . . . ," he begged. "Don't do this . . . I beg you . . . *please.*"

Bobok only smiled.

Nathan glanced over his shoulder. There was only a few feet of platform left. Just a few feet before he'd fall into the cone of energy. He turned back to Bobok. *"Please . . ."*

The orbs continued forward.

He reached the edge of the platform. He began fighting to keep his balance.

The guards pressed ahead.

"Please . . ."

"Enjoy yourself," Bobok grinned. "I know I will."

And then it happened. Nathan's foot slipped. He tried his best to hang on, but it did no good. With a chilling scream he tumbled and fell.

The energy cone crackled and surged with power as if Nathan had somehow fed it, as if his spoiled selfishness had given it energy—an energy that it would feed upon for many epochs to come.

the
RESCUE

"**H**urry!" Denise shouted as she ran ahead of the group into a giant hall of the castle. "This place is huge, there must be a hundred rooms to check."

"Shut and seals the Portal"—Listro Q looked at his watch—"in thirty-eight minutes!"

"Thirty-eight minutes?" she cried. "Can we find him in time?"

"And free Nathan," Listro Q added, "and return to Portal, and escape through Portal all of us. Doubtful, is it."

"But . . . we've got to try!" Denise insisted.

Samson began to chatter.

"Yes, I hear it," Aristophenix answered.

"Hear what?" Denise demanded.

"Low hum," Listro Q said, cocking his head to hear better.

Denise strained to listen. She heard it, too.

Samson chattered some more.

"Are you sure, ol' boy?" Aristophenix asked.

Samson gave a terse answer.

"What?" Denise demanded. "What's he saying?"

Aristophenix turned and explained,

"from his studies he has knowledge,
that to me seems far-fetched,
'bout a room full of moaning,
where bobok's prisoners are kept."

"That could be their moaning!" Denise cried. "If Nathan's his prisoner, all we have to do is follow the hum!"

The theory seemed as reasonable as anything else in this place.
Again everyone grew silent, straining to hear what direction the
sound was coming from.

"Over there!" Denise said, pointing at a door to the left. She raced
toward it. "Come on!"

The door hissed open and she dashed in, followed by the others.

Now, tracking a hum wasn't as easy as Denise had thought. Especially in a castle with a maze of twisting hallways—hallways that
often came to a dead end for no apparent reason. More than once the
group zigged when they should have zagged, and headed down a few
stairways when they should have headed up. But after plenty of frustration and confusion, they somehow made it to the front of a huge,
towering door—a door that slowly crept open as they approached.

Denise quickly entered, then slowed to a stop. She had never seen
anything like it. Apparently, neither had the others. They were on the
ground floor, at the base of some sort of energy cone. It stretched up
and out, high above their heads. In here the discordant groans were
deafening. They came from zombielike creatures that circled and
floated by—each slowly fighting and scratching for the slightest scrap
of food, clothes, or toys.

It took some searching, but Denise finally spotted him. "Nathan!"

On the far side of the energy field, several feet from the floor, he
was floating. Like the others he seemed to be in some sort of trance.
His sweater was already gone and he was slowly and mechanically
fighting a strange triangular creature for what was left of his shirt.

"Nathan!" Aristophenix shouted. "Nathan, ol' buddy!"

The others joined in. "Nathan, can you hear us? Nathan! Nathan!"
But Nathan did not hear. Not a word.

"Well, hello there," a voice called from above. Denise tilted back her head to see an ice-blue orb on a platform several stories above them. "Welcome to my little party."

"Bobok," Aristophenix whispered with a shudder.

Denise looked at him, then at Samson and Listro Q. All three seemed equally as frightened. But there was little time to waste on fear. She turned back to Nathan. He was drifting toward them. If she jumped high enough she might be able to reach him and drag him down. She crouched, preparing to leap into the energy field.

"No!" Listro Q shouted, grabbing her arm. "Energy field, touch don't you!"

Denise turned to argue but was stopped cold by the look in his eyes. For whatever reason, Listro Q was deadly serious. All right, fine, she wouldn't jump in. But there was nothing to stop her from getting as close to Nathan as possible and waking him by shouting. She broke free from Listro Q and moved to within inches of the field. "Nathan!" she yelled. "Nathan, can you hear me?"

He continued drifting around, closer and closer, until they were nearly face-to-face.

"Nathan? *Nathan!*"

But Nathan gave no sign of recognition. Instead, he continued the slow mechanical fight over his shirt.

The voice above their heads broke into cold laughter. "Call all you want, my dear, he'll never hear you. He's mine now—doing what he's always wanted."

Denise looked up at the creature. "I don't know what you are," she shouted, "but I want him back, and I want him now!"

He gave another ominous laugh.

"Listen, you little ice ball!" she yelled. "If I ever get my hands on you, you're going to be—"

Suddenly the energy field flashed and sparkled brighter. Suddenly the groaning and moaning grew louder. And suddenly Listro Q's hand was upon Denise's shoulder.

"What did I do?" she protested. "I was just—"

"Hate of yours." Listro Q motioned toward the energy field. "The more have you hate, the more has it energy—like the outside guards."

"But . . . ," Denise sputtered in frustration. "We have to do something!" She turned to the furry bear. "Aristophenix! What do we do?"

Aristophenix stared at her, blinking.

"Come on, you're supposed to be the leader! What do we do now?"

But he had no answer. There were no longer any pithy poems, no blustery proverbs. The only answer he had was in his eyes. And in those eyes she saw the look of hopelessness.

"Aristophenix?" she cried.

"I'm . . . sorry," he said.

Not believing her ears, she turned to his partners. "Samson! Listro Q?"

Both stared hard at the ground.

"I don't believe this!" she yelled. "I don't—"

Suddenly Samson interrupted. He spoke only a few words before the other two joined in.

"Yes!" Listro Q shouted.

"Of course!" Aristophenix cried.

"What?" Denise demanded.

"Bloodstone, still have you?" Listro Q asked excitedly.

"What stone?"

> "тне sтоne ғвом тне моunтаins,
> шітн шнісн уou sicnаleр us ғівsт.
> іт's а віт оғ а lоnc sнот,
> виt іт мiснt ввеак тне сивse."

"You mean Nathan's birthday gift—from your Blood Mountains?"

"Have it, still you?" Listro Q repeated.

"I think . . ." She began digging into her pockets. "Yeah, here it is."

"Wonderful," Listro Q exclaimed as she handed it to him.

Samson chattered again.

"Hope so, let's," Listro Q answered as he carefully aimed the slightly longer portion of the stone in Nathan's direction.

"What's going on?" Denise demanded. She seemed to be asking that a lot lately, and didn't seem to be getting any answers.

Once Listro Q had the stone carefully positioned in his hands, he gave a nod and Aristophenix spoke to Samson.

"okay, ol' boy,
Let's give it a shot.
it's all aimed and ready,
Let's see what you got."

Samson swooped down to the stone in Listro Q's hands. Hovering just a few inches above it, he began to buzz his wings harder and faster. And the harder he buzzed, the brighter the blue light in his tail glowed. Denise had always noticed it flickering when he spoke, but now it glowed brighter than ever. In fact, it was so bright that the light began to bounce and reflect inside the Bloodstone until the rock itself started to glow.

"More, lots need," Listro Q urged.

Samson bore down harder. Louder and louder his wings buzzed. Brighter and brighter his tail glowed.

"Hurry," Aristophenix shouted. "We haven't much time."

Samson continued to work until finally, to Denise's amazement, a single beam of intense red light began extending from the stone.

"Attaboy, partner!" Aristophenix shouted. "Keep it up!"

High above, Bobok laughed maliciously. "Surely, you are not serious?"

No one bothered to answer.

Denise watched with fascination as Listro Q continued to carefully aim the pointed section of the Bloodstone toward Nathan. Slowly the red beam cut its way through the energy field toward the floating boy.

"That's it," Aristophenix cried, "keep her a-comin', keep her a-comin'!"

The beam inched its way forward.

"Futile," Bobok mocked them. "Your efforts are futile."

And still the beam continued forward until it was just a few feet from Nathan's face. Then it began to sputter.

"More," Listro Q shouted. "Need we more!"

"He's giving it all he's got," Aristophenix cried.

As the beam continued to sputter it also slowed until its progress came to a stop altogether. It could push no farther ahead. It was as if it had hit a wall—a wall with Nathan just a few feet on the other side.

Bobok's laugh grew louder. "Fools . . . I warned you. Utter fools."

The little bug bore down even harder—buzzing louder, trying to glow brighter. But it did no good.

"Reach him, can't we!" Listro Q shouted. "More, Samson!"

"It's no good!" Aristophenix called. "That's all he's got!"

Denise watched helplessly. She wasn't sure what the red beam could do, but she knew it was important for it to reach Nathan. Important, and by the look of Samson's exhaustion, impossible. Then suddenly, an idea struck her: If she could increase the power of evil by hating and being mean, then maybe, just maybe she could increase the power of good by loving and being kind. It was a long shot, she knew that, but it appeared to be the only shot they had.

"Attaboy," she called to Samson. "Hang in there, fella, you're doing great!"

For a second Samson hesitated, shocked to hear Denise compliment anybody about anything.

"Keep it up, little guy! Come on, you can do it!"

But as she spoke, his determination seemed to grow. He bore down harder and his tail actually grew brighter. Not a lot, mind you, but right now every bit helped.

"That's it," she cheered. "Samson, you're doing it!"

His buzz grew louder, his light grew brighter. And soon the rock was growing brighter. The beam resumed its progress, slowly moving toward Nathan.

"Attaboy," Denise encouraged. "Way to go, Samson!"

The beam continued, inching closer and closer to Nathan—until at last it struck him squarely on the face.

"What are you doing?" Bobok shouted from above.

Life came back into Nathan's eyes. He gave his head a shake and looked around, trying to get his bearings.

"Nathan!" Denise shouted. "Nathan, over here!"

He turned and spotted her. He started to move, to try and free himself from the energy field, but he couldn't. His mind had been cleared, but he didn't have the strength to move his body. "Denny!" he called, "Denny, help me!"

"Nathan . . . listen to me! Listen very carefully!" It was Aristophenix. "We haven't much time. You have to break this power."

Again Nathan struggled against the energy field, but it was just too strong. He couldn't break free.

"You have to stop fightin'," Aristophenix shouted. "You have to stop fightin' them creatures in there and start showin' them love!"

"You're crazy!" Nathan cried. "It's impossible! Not in here—I can't!"

"Yes, you can!" Aristophenix shouted back. "With the power of that light on you, you can do anything!"

"You don't understand! They'll tear me to pieces! I *gotta* fight!"

The light started to sputter.

"Much, too," Listro Q cried to Aristophenix. "Can't last, Samson!"

Aristophenix nodded and shouted to Nathan more urgently. "You gotta show some love . . . trust me! Stop fightin' and show them love!"

But even as they spoke, the triangular creature Nathan had been fighting took advantage of his distraction. With sharp jagged claws he ripped off another piece of Nathan's shirt, deeply cutting into his back.

"Augh!" Nathan screamed in agony. "See what happens?"

"Let him have it!" Aristophenix shouted.

"What?"

"Let him have your shirt! All of it!"

"I can't!" Nathan gasped. "You don't understand, I can't!"

Samson was growing weaker by the second. The beam from the Bloodstone started to flicker.

Spotting it, Denise resumed her encouragements. "You're doing good, Sammy . . . you're doing real good."

But the truth is, he wasn't doing good. Not anymore. The truth is, he was nearly exhausted.

Aristophenix continued calling to Nathan. "You can give it to him! Give that shirt to him! You gotta!"

"On come!" Listro Q shouted. "Hurry!"

"I . . . I . . . ." Nathan's voice grew weaker. Not only weaker but flatter—sounding more and more like the dull monotone voices of the outside guards.

"Too bad," Bobok laughed. "Your plans have failed. They will always fail in my kingdom."

And then, at last it happened. Samson collapsed. He fell to the floor, panting, barely able to catch his breath. The light from his tail had gone out. The red beam from the Bloodstone vanished.

"Nathan!" Denise screamed.

But it was too late. Nathan had fallen back into the power of the menagerie. He was back in its trance.

a
SECOND
CHANCE

Samson! You okay, buddy?" Aristophenix dropped to his knees to help the little bug.

Denise quickly joined them as Samson gasped and tried to gulp in as much air as possible. "Is he going to be all right?" she asked.

Aristophenix hesitated a moment before nodding. "He's young," he said, "but like you, he's stubborn."

Denise threw Aristophenix a look. But it wasn't an insult. In fact, it almost sounded like a compliment.

"Easy there, fella," Aristophenix urged as Samson struggled to get up. "You've been workin' too hard. Easy, little guy."

But Samson would have none of the sympathy. In a matter of seconds he was back on his feet—all six of them. After a couple false starts, he was able to flutter his wings fast enough to slowly rise off the floor. Once again he was airborne—although his buzzing sounded much weaker than before.

Denise watched with awe and wonder. She could feel herself getting caught up in his determination. Once again she was back on her own feet. And, once again, she was cheering him on. "Attaboy, Sammy! You can do it!"

The encouragement helped. With every positive word she spoke Samson grew stronger.

Nathan had drifted completely around the menagerie and was floating back toward them. This time the beam from the Bloodstone wouldn't have to travel so far; it wouldn't need as much energy from Samson.

Without a word the little bug took his position over the stone in Listro Q's hand. He started buzzing his wings and glowing his tail. There was no missing the stress and strain he was under. But he wasn't about to give up—not this time.

Neither was Denise. She stepped up closer to the hovering bug and quietly whispered into his ear—telling him how impressed she was, what a big heart he had, how much she appreciated and, yes, even admired him for what he was doing.

And that made all the difference in the world . . .

A new surge of brightness shown from Samson's tail. The Bloodstone started to glow. Finally the shaft of red light burst forth and in moments it struck Nathan squarely upon the face. Once again the boy regained consciousness. By now he and his fighting partner, the triangle creature, were just a few yards away.

Spotting Aristophenix, Nathan again pleaded, "Please, you gotta help me!"

"There's nothin' more we can do!" Aristophenix shouted. "Only *you* can choose to break his control—and there isn't much time!"

"But—"

"You've got the power!" Aristophenix insisted. "Just use it!"

"Come on, Nathan!" Denise called. "You can do it!"

For the briefest second Nathan appeared surprised at her encouragement. Come to think of it, so did Denise.

"Watch it!" Aristophenix shouted. He pointed to a pair of fighting prisoners who started drifting between Nathan and the beam.

Listro Q dropped to his knees, shooting the beam underneath the fighters so they would not interrupt its flow of power.

"Nathan," Denise cried. "You can do it! I know you can! Just stop fighting and give that thing your shirt!"

Again Nathan looked at her. She wasn't sure if it was the power from the beam or from her words—maybe it was both. But somehow, somewhere Nathan found the strength to slowly lower his arms and begin unbuttoning what was left of his shirt. Of course the triangle creature went in for the kill. And, of course, his sharp, jagged claws dug deep into Nathan's chest.

"Augh!" Nathan screamed. But this time he would not give up. This time he continued unbuttoning his shirt.

"You are fools," Bobok mocked from his platform. "Fools!"

The beam started to weaken. Though Nathan was closer, Samson didn't have the strength he had in the beginning. Still, between seeing Nathan's efforts and hearing Denise's words, the little bug pressed on.

At last, Nathan unbuttoned the final button. He started pulling his arms out of the shredded sleeves.

"Attaboy!" Denise shouted. "You can do it, Nathan, you can do it!"

"Fools!" Bobok shouted. "Fools!"

Samson's light began to sputter.

"Hurry, lad," Aristophenix shouted. "Hurry!"

The shirt was off. But that was only half the battle. Now Nathan had to fight the menagerie's power. Now he actually had to reach out and show love to the creature. He had to actually *give* him his shirt.

"Enough!" Bobok shouted. He started rolling back and forth across his platform. "Chosen Thread, this is what *you* wanted. Nowhere in any dimension will you enjoy so much taking!"

Beads of sweat sprang to Nathan's forehead as he fought and struggled. If he could just overcome the menagerie's control—if he could just utilize the red beam's power and reach out to offer the shirt to his enemy.

He started drifting away again.

Samson worked harder, but the blue light of his tail grew weaker. The beam from the Bloodstone became more and more faint. Soon it was almost invisible. Almost, but not quite.

"Give it up!" Bobok shouted. "Give it up!"

"Come on, Nathan!" Denise called. "You can do it—you can do it!"

And then, ever so slowly, Nathan started reaching out his arms—arms that held the prized shirt.

"Come on, Nathan, I know you can do it!"

"Stop that!" Bobok shouted. "Stop that at once!"

Slowly, inch by torturous inch, Nathan made progress until, at last, his arms were fully extended to his enemy.

With a vicious growl the triangle creature snatched the shirt from his hands, and suddenly . . . suddenly, the entire energy field crackled. Then, to everyone's astonishment, it began losing power.

"My menagerie!" Bobok cried. "Look what you've done! Look what you've done!"

Like a giant machine the menagerie slowly wound down until it came to a grinding halt. The groans of the prisoners faded as each regained consciousness and gently floated to the ground. Many shook their heads in confusion, trying to remember where they were or what had happened. And, as the realization sank in, they began to murmur among themselves—a murmur that grew into shouts of joy!

"Nathan!" Denise cried as she raced to him. The others ran onto the floor right behind her. Before she realized it, she had thrown her arms around him in a giant hug. "I knew you could do it!" she shouted. "I knew you could!"

Nathan couldn't return the hug. He could only stand there, dumbfounded at the love he was receiving from her. Still, there was no missing the glint of moisture in his eyes. And there was no missing the thick hoarseness in his voice when he finally spoke. It wasn't much of a sentence—only one word. But a word Nathan hadn't used in years.

"Thanks . . . ," he said. Unsuccessfully he tried to swallow back the lump in his throat. "Thank you . . ."

By now the other three had managed to work their way into the embrace. In fact the entire floor was full of creatures hugging, celebrating, and congratulating one another.

But it didn't last long.

Bobok's voice echoed through the room. "After them!"

Immediately hundreds of little blue orbs that had surrounded Bobok began leaping from his platform onto the floor of the menagerie. Many of them were hurt by the fall or crushed by fellow orbs landing on top of them. But those who survived had one goal—to recapture the prisoners before they escaped!

Panic swept the crowd. "What do we do?" they shouted. "We're lost! He'll capture us again!"

Then, just before everything turned to chaos, Aristophenix raised his cane high above his head and shouted,

"ONWARD TO THE PORTAL,

THERE'S NOT A SECOND TO WASTE.

IT SOON WILL BE SEALED,

Let's move, Let's go, make haste!"

With his cane still above his head, the roly-poly bear waddled forward and the crowd followed. They raced out of the menagerie and through the rooms of the castle until they reached the drawbridge and crossed it. Then it was into the bare, frozen forest of Keygarp. Yet, for some reason, none of Bobok's little blue guards followed.

"Where are they?" Denise shouted to Aristophenix.

Panting hard, the bear tried to answer. "Look at your feet!"

Denise looked down and saw that the hard ice and snow were turning to slush. "It's melting!" she yelled in surprise.

"The whole kingdom—inside and out," Aristophenix shouted. "The guards can't roll in slush—not like packed snow."

They continued through the forest. Trees dripped with water as the ice on them melted. Icicles gave way, clattering and shattering as they hit the ground. Then, at last, Listro Q spotted it.

"There!" he shouted, pointing in the distance. "There is it!"

Denise looked and saw the Portal. But even from their distance, she could see the breathing opening was much smaller . . . and growing smaller by the second!

"Hurry!" Aristophenix called to the group. "It's almost sealed!"

Panic filled the crowd as they pushed forward.

"Samson!" Denise cried. She looked every direction but couldn't find him. "Where's Samson?"

"Here," Listro Q said. He held out his pocket—a pocket that glowed and pulsed as Samson looked up and chattered away at her.

Denise grinned.

So did Listro Q.

When they finally arrived at the windy Portal, Aristophenix took a position beside the opening and began directing the crowd through it. Listro Q joined him. For many of the creatures it was going to be a tight squeeze, but with Aristophenix and Listro Q's help they were able to make it. "Be careful of those antenna . . . tuck in all of your legs, ma'am . . . watch your heads, sir . . ."

"Mr. Hornsberry!" Nathan shouted.

Denise turned to see the bulldog racing through the forest as fast as his stubby little legs could carry him. "Master Nathan, wait for me, wait for me!"

"You're unfrozen!" Nathan cried.

"An accurate observation," the dog said as he arrived, then leaped into Nathan's arms, practically knocking him over. "Everything in the kingdom is thawing."

But their joy was short-lived. A noise filled the forest. It was an ominous chant—half living, half machine.

"LUMM-KUMM, LUMM-KUMM, LUMM-KUMM."

The ground itself vibrated with the sound . . .

"LUMM-KUMM, LUMM-KUMM, LUMM-KUMM."

Denise watched as Bobok's army emerged from the woods—hundreds of them—rolling in perfect precision. Although they were slowed by the slush, their progress was steady and constant—like a slow-moving machine—a machine that would not be stopped . . .

"LUMM-KUMM, LUMM-KUMM, LUMM-KUMM."

Terror filled the crowd. Desperately they began to push and shove at one another, doing anything they could to be next through the Portal.

"Please, everybody!" Aristophenix shouted. "Wait your turn!"

But his request was met with only more screams and shoving as the army of blue orbs continued their approach.

"LUMM-KUMM, LUMM-KUMM, LUMM-KUMM."

"Them all through," Listro Q called, "get can't we!"

"We gotta try!" Aristophenix shouted over the noise.

"LUMM-KUMM, LUMM-KUMM, LUMM-KUMM."

Suddenly there was the sound of a whinnying horse. All heads snapped back toward the forest to see Bobok appear on a midnight-blue steed. He quickly trotted past his troops to take command.

The prisoners' terror grew to near riot. Everyone knew Bobok's power—his persuasive logic—his overwhelming evil. And now he and his cold blue orbs were less than fifty yards away—fifty yards and closing in!

"No good is it!" Listro Q shouted to Aristophenix.

Denise turned to the crowd. Listro Q was right. It was hopeless. There were still twenty or thirty creatures to help through the Portal. They couldn't possibly get them through in time. Either the Portal would seal or Bobok's army would move in—or both! What could they do? Where could they turn?

Samson began to chatter.

"That's what?" Listro Q asked, opening his pocket and allowing Samson to fly out.

Samson repeated himself.

Immediately Aristophenix shook his head. "No, no, that's too risky."

"What?" Nathan shouted.

Denise joined in. "What's he saying?"

But Aristophenix wasn't answering. He was still debating with Samson. "No, I haven't got a better idea, but—"

Again Samson chattered.

"Samson . . . ," Listro Q warned.

Whatever Samson was saying, he was not giving up. He kept right on arguing until Aristophenix and Listro Q started running out of excuses.

And still he chattered away.

At last, his two friends exchanged uneasy glances.

"Sure are you, Sammy?" Listro Q asked. "This something is of sure are you?"

Samson answered even more impatiently.

Listro Q turned back to Aristophenix. Apparently a decision had to be made. And apparently it could only be made by Aristophenix. The furry creature shifted his weight uneasily.

He looked at the panicky crowd as they screamed and pushed their way to the opening . . .

He looked at Bobok's army who were much, much closer . . .

And finally he looked at Samson.

Then, slowly, sadly, he began to nod. "Okay," he said. But by the catch in his voice Denise could tell it wasn't okay. It wasn't okay at all.

Immediately Listro Q reached into his pocket and pulled out the Bloodstone. He threw it several feet behind them, directly in front of Bobok's approaching army.

Samson followed the stone and once again began hovering over it.

Fear shot through Denise. "Samson!" she shouted. "Samson, what are you doing?" She turned and started for him but Listro Q caught her. "Let me go!" she yelled. "Let me go!"

Listro Q's grip was firm.

"Let me go! He's not that strong!"

"No!" Listro Q said.

"Let me—"

"Stop it!" Listro Q shouted. And it was the intensity of that shout that caused Denise to stop struggling. She looked up into his face as he spoke. "Only way, is it." And then more quietly, "Only way . . ."

Denise blinked, then swallowed. She turned to watch as Samson buzzed his wings furiously over the rock . . . as the army continued its approach. Once again he generated a blue light from his tail. And once again that light started to bounce back and forth inside the Bloodstone until a bright red glow suddenly burst out. But since Listro Q wasn't there to direct it, the light was no longer a beam. Now it formed a huge red circle—a circle whose color the army could not look at—a circle that forced them to stop their advance.

"Aughhh!" Bobok yelled as his horse began prancing and bucking. "Stop that light! Get that bug!"

The army tried to inch their way forward, but they could not approach the light. It was an impenetrable wall of color. A wall that protected Samson and the few remaining prisoners as they exited through the Portal.

"Quickly now!" Aristophenix encouraged the group. "Don't look back! Quickly!"

Samson continued hovering over the stone, but his buzz was much weaker. He simply hadn't had the time to recover from his last ordeal.

Cautiously, the army surrounded the wall of color, until they had formed a circle around Samson and the stone.

"Destroy him!" Bobok shouted. "Stop the color! Destroy the bug!"

Yet the army would not, they could not, penetrate the red glowing wall.

Unfortunately, it was a wall that began to shrink as Samson's strength began giving out.

"Come on, Samson!" Denise shouted. "You can do it, you can do it!" But even Denise's words didn't help.

Samson's light grew fainter and fainter. The wall of color shrank smaller and smaller. Relentlessly, Bobok's army closed in tighter and tighter.

"He can't make it!" Nathan cried.

"Quickly," Aristophenix shouted to the last of the prisoners as he ushered them through.

Samson had nearly reached exhaustion. The wall was only a few feet around him now . . . and so were the hundreds of blue orbs.

"Destroy him!" Bobok screamed.

"Nathan!" Aristophenix shouted. "Nathan, you're next!"

Nathan looked up as the last prisoner squeezed through the Portal. There was just the five of them left.

"Now, Nathan!" Aristophenix shouted. He had wedged his way into the opening trying to keep it from closing completely. But his efforts were in vain. Although he was slowing it, it was obvious he could not stop it. "Nathan!"

Looking back at Samson, Nathan was obviously torn.

"There's nothin' you can do for him—not now! Trust me!"

Nathan continued to hesitate.

"Now, or we're *all* doomed!"

Finally, reluctantly, Nathan ducked his head down, and still carrying Mr. Hornsberry in his arms, he quickly squeezed through the Portal.

"Denny!" Aristophenix called. "Denny, you're next!"

But Denise wasn't moving. All she could do was stare at Samson. The poor little critter was near exhaustion. He had less than a foot of light surrounding him. Less than a foot of color to protect him from Bobok and his army.

"Denny!" Aristophenix shouted. "Denny!"

But she would not budge, she refused to budge . . . until Listro Q suddenly picked her up.

"Put me down!" she cried. "Put me down!"

And then it happened. At last Samson's light flickered out.

"Samson!" Denise's heart broke as Bobok's thugs lunged toward her brave little friend. "Samson!"

To spare her the awful sight, Listro Q covered her eyes and pushed her through the opening.

She cried one last time. *"Samson!"* But it did no good. Her voice was lost in the howling wind.

Listro Q followed right behind her. Then Aristophenix—and just in time. For as the pudgy creature unwedged his body from the opening, it slammed shut with a foreboding *boom.*

The Portal was sealed.

CHAPTER THIRTEEN

HOME,
at Last ...

Denise and the rest of the group stepped out of the tunnel and into Fayrah. As before, it was a perfect day with perfect weather. But for some reason the colors seemed more vivid than before—glowing reds, bright greens, vibrant yellows. Maybe it was because they'd spent so long seeing nothing but the blue hues of Keygarp. In any case, the colors of Fayrah were so pure and beautiful that for a moment Denise's eyes almost ached with pleasure.

Then there were the citizens—thousands of them. They had all come out to greet the newly freed prisoners. It was a time of joy and celebration. Everywhere there was laughter, backslaps, and shouts of delight as long-lost friends and relatives found one another in the crowd.

Denise and Nathan seemed to be the only ones having a difficult time of it. Granted, they tried to smile as they were congratulated and they did their best to look happy. But neither of them was too successful. They had lost a friend—a good friend. And no amount of backslapping or laughter could take that loss away.

"He was . . . *good*," Denise quietly said to Nathan.

Nathan nodded. "Yeah."

Seeing their sadness, Aristophenix cleared his throat and tried his best to encourage them.

> "DON'T BE SO DOWNHEARTED.
> THERE'S NO NEED TO STEW.
> AFTER ALL, SAMMY BOY JUST DID
> WHAT ALL FAYRAHNIANS WANT TO DO."

Denise forced a smile. It was almost good hearing Aristophenix use his poetry again. Almost. It would have been better if Samson had been there to complain about it with the rest of them.

"He did what all Fayrahnians want to do?" Nathan repeated. "What do you mean?"

"Same love as Imager," Listro Q quietly explained. "Able to experience same love, was he."

"All he did was die. What good did his dying do?" Nathan challenged.

"So free are you," Listro Q answered. Then, motioning toward the thousands of happy Fayrahnians before them, he continued, "So, too, are others."

Denise wanted to argue, but as she looked around to the crowd of freed prisoners . . . and as she looked at Nathan . . . well, somehow, the argument fell flat. Somehow she suspected that Samson's love *did* do some good. And she suspected something else. She suspected Nathan's speeches about looking out for number one would never again be spoken with the same conviction as before. That didn't mean he wouldn't still be a selfish brat from time to time, but . . . well, something inside Nathan was changing. She could see it. And she didn't mind it. Not in the least.

Finally, glancing up at the courthouse clock, Aristophenix cleared his throat and spoke.

> "DON'T MEAN TO BE PARTY-POOPERS,
> OR make you feel more LOW.
> BUT YOUR GRANDPAPPY'LL BE A-WORRYIN',
> IF toward HOME we DON'T ROLL."

"Home," Denise quietly mused. It seemed like a million miles away. Joshua, Nathan's brother, was probably just finishing basketball practice. Grandpa O'Brien was probably back in the shop with the puppy he'd bought for Nathan. And her mother—well, her mother would still be at the diner taking orders and clearing tables.

"Got them coordinates, ol' buddy?" Aristophenix asked.

Listro Q gave his standard answer. "Cool."

Aristophenix nodded and turned to the crowd. "Folks!" he called. "Folks, may I have your attention?"

The crowd grew silent and Aristophenix continued.

> *"OUR fRIENDS HAVE TO LEAVE US,*
> *IT'S SAD, WE ALL KNOW.*
> *BUT YOU JUST CAN'T TRAVEL TO,*
> *WITHOUT TRAVELING fRO."*

The crowd groaned slightly.

"Push them buttons," Aristophenix whispered to Listro Q. "I'm losin' 'em."

"Cool," Listro Q answered as he gratefully reached for the little Cross-Dimensionalizer.

The crowd began waving and calling out best wishes to Denise, Nathan, and Mr. Hornsberry, which the three returned—until Listro Q set the coordinates and pressed the four buttons.

BEEP . . .

BOP . . .

BLEEP . . .

BURP . . .

Suddenly the group was bathed in intense light. More suddenly, still, they were falling. Again they were surrounded by other lights who were also falling—falling gracefully and smoothly. Each headed toward the bright concentration of light in the middle—the Center.

The thought of heading back there didn't make Denise leap for joy. She remembered all too well what had happened the last time she took this route.

She looked around nervously. As her eyes grew accustomed to the light, she spotted Mr. Hornsberry, Listro Q, and Nathan. But once again this Nathan was the older, more mature Nathan—the one with the shield and the suit of armor. Only this time he didn't have his swords—the ones fashioned out of the canteens and covered with bug blood. Hmm, sometime she'd have to ask him if he knew what that was about.

Right now, though, the Center was coming into clear view. Already she could see the thin layer of fog and beyond that the bright, glowing buildings.

Closer and closer they came as Denise tried to think of a pleasant thought. She wasn't about to go through what she'd been through the last time. No way. She had to fill her head with something good. *Anything* good.

But she was trying too hard. Nothing came to mind. Maybe a Christmas present here, a compliment there. But they were such short thoughts she knew they wouldn't last—not all the way through the Center. She started to panic. They were nearly there and no thoughts were coming. Desperately, she searched for something . . . anything.

Aristophenix! she called. *Aristophenix, help me!*

Suddenly a pair of hands tenderly covered her eyes. For a moment she struggled, trying to fight them off, to push them away. But they would not move.

And then she smelled it. Aftershave. But not just any aftershave. It was the same aftershave her dad used to wear. It had been years since she'd smelled it. In fact, until now, she had completely forgotten about it.

She had also forgotten how her mother had kept his clothes in the closet. How they had remained there for what seemed like years after he left. And how as a little girl she used to sneak into the closet, stand on her tiptoes, and bury her face into his favorite flannel shirt. She would just stand there pressing her face to it, breathing in the smell of his aftershave . . . and remembering.

That was happening now—the remembering. She could feel her whole body start to relax. Slowly she leaned into what she remembered to be her daddy's arms. And, strangely enough, they were there to support her. Deeper and deeper she relaxed, as she continued to breathe in, as she continued remembering his strength and tenderness.

The light outside the pair of hands grew incredibly bright. Then there was the singing. It was beautiful. Denise wanted to look, but knew she would be too terrified at what she saw. Besides, this was better. Resting in these arms was safe—secure. As long as she stayed there nothing could touch her.

Eventually the light and singing started to fade. And finally the hands were removed. Denise didn't bother to turn and see who they belonged to. She knew no one would be there—not now.

She looked for the Center and was surprised to see that it was above them and not below. They had passed completely through it and had come out the other side. Now she was heading away from it—but not wildly and out of control like the last time. This time everything was smooth and easy.

The light from the Center rapidly faded. Then, the faint outline of walls, ceiling, and a floor appeared around her. At last the sensation came to an end. The group was back inside the Second-hand Shop. Everything was exactly as it had been. There were no surprises.

Well, maybe one . . .

"Samson!" Nathan shouted as he spotted the half dragonfly, half ladybug. The little critter was buzzing over the Bloodstone on the counter.

"Samson! You're alive!" Denise started running toward him, but she'd only taken a couple steps before she caught herself. It wasn't Samson. Oh, sure, it looked like Samson; it flew and sounded like Samson. But this one's taillight was red. Samson's was blue.

"Congratulations, ol' boy," Aristophenix called out to the bug. "Glad you could join us!"

Denise turned to Aristophenix. "Hold it," she said. "That can't be Samson. He's dead."

"Right is that," Listro Q agreed. "Dead and alive."

Denise frowned and for the first time that she could remember, Aristophenix broke into a big grin!

Suddenly the insect dive-bombed her a couple times, then began buzzing around her head—all the time chattering in delight.

"But . . ." Denise hesitated. "If he's, you know, *dead* . . . how can he . . ."

Aristophenix chuckled.

> "I'M SO SORRY, DENNY,
> I THOUGHT THAT YOU KNEW.
> FAYRAHNIANS HAVE TO DIE,
> SO THEIR LIVES ARE RENEWED."

Denise was lost. "But his tail, Samson's was blue—this one's . . . this one's *red*."

> "IN GIVING LIFE we FIND IT,
> SAMMY BOY'S PASSED THE test.
> THE RED MEANS HE'S GROWN UP.
> A CITIZEN LIKE THE REST."

"Samson!" she cried. "It *is* you!" She did her best to throw her arms around him. But hugging a flying bug isn't the easiest thing to do, as Samson zipped in and out of her arms chattering a mile a second.

"What's all that noise out there?" It was Nathan's grandfather. He was in the back room. "Nathan, is that you?"

Aristophenix quickly whispered,

> "WE'D BETTER GET A-GOIN',
> DON'T HAVE MUCH TIME to WASTE.
> WE'D LOVE TO SURPRISE HIM WITH A HOWDY,
> BUT HEART ATTACKS ARE IN SUCH BAD taste."

"Nathan?" Grandpa called again. The lights to the shop snapped on.

Suddenly Denise had a new concern. "Will we ever see you again?" she whispered. She had just lost one good friend and found him; she didn't intend to lose any more.

"Certainly, yes," Listro Q assured her.

"Are you sure?" It was Nathan's turn to sound worried.

> "JUST PUT THAT STONE IN THE MOONLIGHT,
> YOU KNOW THE SCORE AFTER THAT.
> WHEREVER WE ARE OR ARE GOING,
> WE'LL SWING BY FOR A LITTLE CHAT."

"Good-bye," Denise whispered. She gave Listro Q a hug. Then she turned and hugged Aristophenix, burying her face deep into his fur.

"Good-bye," Nathan said, shaking both of their hands and doing his best imitation of a grown-up . . . until his handshakes also turned into hugs.

Samson gave a chatter.

"And you," Nathan said, his eyes filling with moisture as he looked up at the bug. "I'll *never* forget you."

Samson answered and Listro Q translated, his own voice thick with emotion, "Nor we, you."

"Nathan?" By now the old man was shuffling up the far aisle toward them. "Nathan, answer me!"

"Quickly!" Aristophenix whispered to Listro Q.

To which Listro Q, with trusty Cross-Dimensionalizer in hand, answered, what else, but, "Cool."

Turning to the children Aristophenix whispered one last thought:

> "OUR JOURNEY'S BEEN NIFTY,
> IT'S REALLY BEEN SWELL.
> BUT NOW WE GOT TO BE MOVIN',
> SO BYE-BYE, TA-TA, FARE THEE . . ."

BEEP . . .

    BOP . . .

        BLEEP . . .

            BURP . . .

In a flash of light the Fayrahnians were gone.

And just in time.

"Ah, so there you are," Grandpa said as he rounded the corner. "And would you mind tellin' me now, just where you've—"

But the poor man never finished his sentence. Immediately he was attacked by Denise and Nathan, who smothered him with all sorts of hugs. And if that wasn't enough, they both began talking at once, using new words like *Bloodstone, Fayrah, Aristophenix, Listro Q*—

"Hold it, hold it!" Grandpa shouted until they finally came to a stop. "I asked you a simple question. Now if you don't want to be givin' me a simple answer, then—"

"But we are giving you an answer," Nathan insisted. And once again they bombarded him with even stranger words like *Seerlo, Bobok, Keygarp*—

Again Grandpa's hands flew up. "If you don't want to be tellin' me the truth, then—"

"But, Grandpa, we are telling the truth!"

The old man gave them a scowl and repeated, "If you don't want to be tellin' me the truth, then I'll be hearin' nothin' until you do."

Denise and Nathan exchanged glances. By the look of things, the truth wasn't exactly something he was prepared to hear . . . at least for now. Maybe for now it was better to keep their little journey a secret—just between them . . . and all the rest of Fayrah!

Suddenly, a dog began yelping. Denise turned and spotted an adorable black and white puppy scampering down the aisle toward them.

"Ohhh . . . ," she cooed.

Nathan stooped down to pick him up and immediately received a nonstop face washing.

"Whose is he?" Nathan asked, trying to avoid the wet, slippery tongue that seemed to find every part of his face at the same time.

"Why, he's yours, lad. Don't you remember?"

"But . . . but I have a dog." Nathan motioned toward Mr. Hornsberry, who sat on the counter near the Bloodstone. Only now he wasn't giving speeches or sounding stodgy or being pompous. In fact, right now he wasn't even moving. Instead, he remained as stuffed and silent as when he'd first been unwrapped.

"But that's just a toy," Grandpa said. "This one here's real—it's the one you've been saying you wanted."

Nathan looked back down at the puppy and got another face full of wet tongue.

Denise watched. From years of experience, she knew exactly what Nathan was thinking. Why couldn't he have both dogs? In fact, why couldn't he have as many as he wanted? If he played his cards right, it wouldn't have to stop here, he could get all the puppies he ever dreamed of.

But then Denise saw something else. Nathan was looking over at the Bloodstone. And by the expression on his face, she realized he was thinking other thoughts . . . thoughts of Blood Mountains, of a kingdom of giving, and of a little dragonfly-ladybug with a brand-new taillight.

Suddenly he turned to his Grandfather. "Grandpa, what time is it?"

"A little bit after nine."

"Do you think the Johnson children will still be awake?"

"Why?" Grandpa asked suspiciously. He obviously knew gears were turning inside Nathan's head. He just couldn't figure out which direction.

"Do you remember when they were here earlier—how badly they wanted a puppy?"

"What's on your mind, lad?"

"I was wondering . . . ," Nathan continued. "Would it hurt your feelings if I, you know, gave the Johnsons *this* puppy?"

"Nathan!" Denise didn't mean to cry out but she couldn't help herself.

"Lad, have you gone daft? I spent nearly every dime on this here fella."

"I know, and he's super—it's just . . ."

Denise looked on. She could tell this type of thinking was brand new to Nathan, and she wasn't surprised that it took a while for him to put it into words.

"It's just . . . well . . . they wanted a puppy so badly and, you know, I really do have one, and . . ."

"You feeling all right, lad?" Grandpa slipped his hand to the boy's forehead. "No fever . . . no headache?"

Nathan shook his head. "No, I'm fine. Could we, Grandpa? Do you think that would be all right?"

The old man stood there a long moment—first looking at Nathan, then at Denise, then back at Nathan. Then, without a word, he turned and started for the coatrack.

"Where are you going?" Nathan asked.

"After all of these years," Grandpa said, as he threw on his scarf and coat, "do you think I'd be missing out on seeing you actually give something away?"

"All right!" Nathan shouted.

"Yeah!" Denise laughed, "I'd like to see this myself."

Nathan shot her one of his famous glares but it quickly turned into a twinkle as they headed for the door.

Denise grinned back. She was almost beginning to like Nathan . . . almost. At least she didn't feel like punching him in the stomach. The thought struck her as a little strange. But then again the entire evening had been strange.

The tiny bell above the door gave a jingle as the three of them stepped out onto the sidewalk. It had started to snow again. A gentle snow—the type that slowly covers the dirt and grime of the city and gently smooths out its harsh edges.

Grandpa locked the door and they turned to head up the street. But as they passed the shop's window, Denise thought she saw something inside. She couldn't be sure, but it looked like a tiny red flicker near the counter. A tiny red flicker that could only come from a strange and very unusual stone. A tiny red flicker that seemed to say their journeys weren't exactly over . . . not yet.

Not by a long ways . . .

the
experiment

aNOTHER Day, aNOTHER fuLL mOON

I have not forgotten!" the harsh voice cawed. "You belong to me. I have not forgotten!"

For the hundredth time Denise looked up through the gnarled and twisted branches of the frozen forest. And for the hundredth time she saw the black leather-winged creature circling high overhead. Half woman, half who-knows-what, the animal was enough to give anybody the creeps . . . even if that anybody knew they were only dreaming.

It had been exactly two months since Denise had traveled to Fayrah and had seen the creature. And for two months the ugly thing kept coming back and haunting her in her dreams.

"Surely you've not forgotten?" the voice demanded.

Denise swallowed hard. It took a moment to gather her courage before she finally found her voice. "What do you want from me?" she cried. "Leave me alone!"

Suddenly the entire forest broke into laughter. And more suddenly still Denise realized that she wasn't standing in a forest. Instead, she was sitting in her classroom.

"All I want from you, young lady, is to tell me the subject of this sentence." It was Mrs. Barnick, her English teacher. She stood three desks ahead of Denise with anything but a pleased look on her face.

"Ahhh . . ." Denise stalled, desperately trying to push the dream out of her mind while she searched for the sentence. *What sentence? Where was it? On the blackboard? In her book?* There were more giggles and whispers from those around her. She could feel the tops of her ears start to burn like they always did when she got mad or embarrassed.

"Denny," Mrs. Barnick spoke evenly as she pointed to the side board. "It is sentence number three, from yesterday's assignment: 'The clown's humor was quite bizarre.'"

Denise peered at the board.

"What is the subject of that sentence?" Mrs. Barnick persisted. "What is *bizarre?*"

"She is," a blond-haired kid cracked from two rows over.

Again the room broke into laughter.

The kid grinned proudly over his sharp wit—until his eyes met Denise's—until her look made clear what every other person in Lincoln Elementary already knew . . . you didn't give Denise Wolff a rough time without paying for it with either a bloody nose or a black eye . . . or both.

Now it's true, since her return from Fayrah Denise had made great progress in controlling her temper. But self-control doesn't come overnight—a fact that the blond-haired kid would become painfully aware of.

"In the future, Denny," Mrs. Barnick said, "I suggest you do your sleeping at home."

"Yes, ma'am," Denise mumbled just as the bell to end class rang.

She gathered her books and crowded toward the door with the rest of the kids, where she received the usual "way to go's" and "nice work" from the ones who liked risking their lives. But it really wasn't her fault. She wasn't the one who'd put English at the end of the day. Who in their right mind would schedule the world's most boring subject for sixth period? No, make that the second most boring subject. She'd almost forgotten about math.

"But she scores so high on the tests," the counselor had told her mother. "If she'd just apply herself she'd be an *A* student," her teachers had said.

"Yeah? Well, let them try being me for a day," Denise muttered as she shuffled down the hall toward her locker. "That would show 'em."

Instinctively she glanced around the hall for the blond-haired kid. But he was no fool. Already he was heading for the exit. Already he knew it was best to stay out of her way—at least for the next couple decades.

Denise arrived at her locker and threw open the door. She began loading up with the evening's torture of homework when the thought suddenly struck her. *Wait a minute! Tonight's the night! Tonight we use the Bloodstone to signal Aristophenix. Tonight I'll finally prove to Joshua that it wasn't just make-believe, or mass hysteria or, how did he put it?...* "*A couple kids' overactive imaginations.*"

With dramatic flair she dumped the books back into her locker, slammed it shut, and headed for the next building—the middle school's gymnasium. That's where the older kids would be setting up their science projects. And since it involved science, that, of course, is where Josh O'Brien would be.

"Hey, Denny!" It was Nathan, Josh's little brother. She slowed down to let him catch up. His limp was just as painful to watch as ever. They'd both hoped it would disappear after their trip to Fayrah, after Denise had seen him without it in the stream's reflection. No such luck. It was still there, just as obvious as ever. But there were other changes. As with Denise there were deeper changes . . .

For starters, Nathan was no longer the most selfish human on the face of the planet. Oh, he still had his moments. Like Denise, there were still plenty of areas that needed work. But instead of some modern-day Scrooge, he was coming off more like your average, run-of-the-mill corporate CEO. Not a great improvement, but a start.

"Listen," he said, "I might be late tonight."

"What?" Denise came to a stop. "Tonight's the full moon. If we don't signal them tonight—" She spotted a group of kids straining to eavesdrop and lowered her voice. "If we don't signal them tonight we'll have to wait a whole 'nother month before—"

"I know, I know." Nathan interrupted. "But we're having a geography test tomorrow."

"So?"

"So Jerry Boleslavski's having a lousy time memorizing his state capitals."

"So?"

"So I'd promised to help."

"Nathan . . ."

"How'd I know our teacher was going to spring the test on us tomorrow?"

Denise took a deep breath. She was not going to get angry. Worse things than this had happened, she was sure of it . . . although at the moment she couldn't exactly put her finger on one.

"Look," Nathan said. "We'll get done in time, no sweat. But if I'm not there, you and Josh go ahead without me."

"Nathan . . ."

"I'm serious, there'll be other full moons."

"Nathan . . ."

Without a word he turned his back on her and hobbled down the hall.

"Nathan . . . Nathaniel!"

There was no answer.

Denise let out a sigh. Why'd he have to choose tonight to get all compassionate and help a friend?

I just don't want you to be too disappointed when nothing happens," Joshua said.

"Oh, I won't be," Denise answered as they rounded the corner and headed up the street toward Grandpa O'Brien's Secondhand Shop. She couldn't help grinning as she fingered the Bloodstone inside her coat pocket. The full moon was already high over their heads. In just a few minutes she'd be exposing the stone to its light. Then she'd see what ol' Josh had to say about "disappointments."

For the past couple hours he'd had been dragging her all around to see the different science projects, explaining what they were about and how they worked. Joshua loved science and for him the hours flew. Denise hated science and for her the hours crawled. But it wasn't a complete waste—during that time she had mastered the fine art of faking interest. In fact, she'd become quite an expert at using phrases like, "No kidding," "I see," "That's neat," and the ever-popular, "Uh-huh."

Denise didn't mind. Faking interest was a small price to pay for Josh's friendship—a friendship that lasted almost as long as she could remember. It lasted through those awful months after her dad left home . . . it lasted through her slowly but surely becoming one of the school's oddballs . . . it even lasted through Josh having to drag her off of wise-cracking bullies whose faces she kept pulverizing.

Yes, sir, if anybody qualified as a friend, it was Joshua O'Brien. The only problem was he qualified as everybody's friend. He made sure of it. Smart, athletic, funny—he worked very hard at being popular. And if there was anything that drove Denise crazy it was probably that. Still, his focus on being popular was a minor annoyance that she'd learned to live with.

"Look, I'm not saying something didn't happen to you and Nathan," he continued, "something emotional or even some sort of natural phenomena. But all this talk about a kingdom and Imager and stuff—well, no offense, but it's just a little too far out there for me."

"And you don't believe in anything too far out."

"I believe in science—in cause and effect. But if you're expecting me to buy some sort of magic performed by some sort of "—he searched for the word—"wizard in the sky, sorry, but I'm going to have to pass."

Denise smiled weakly. To be honest she didn't know much about this "wizard in the sky" guy either. Oh sure, everyone in Fayrah had talked about Imager—how he loved them and took a special interest in their lives. But she'd never seen him. In fact, she hadn't even been allowed to enter his city. Even if he did exist, she suspected he'd never have anything to do with her—not Denise Wolff—not the Lincoln Elementary all-school oddball.

The two of them finally arrived at the Secondhand Shop. Joshua pushed open the door and the bell above gave a little jingle as they stepped inside.

"Hey, Gramps," Joshua called, "we're here."

A stout old man with thin, graying hair shuffled out from behind the row of secondhand toasters. "Good evenin' to you, Joshua," he said. "Oh, and you brought Denny with you, too—what a fine thing."

"Hi, Grandpa." Denise grinned. She always wound up grinning when she talked to the old man. Then, glancing around the shop, she asked, "Did Nathan show up yet?"

"I haven't seen hide nor hair of him."

"Great," Denise sighed. If he didn't show up soon, she and Joshua would have to go without him. Now that they were safe inside the shop, away from the moonlight, she pulled out the Bloodstone. She fiddled with it nervously, dropping it back and forth in her hands.

Unfortunately the bad news had just begun . . .

"Listen, lad," Grandpa said to Josh. "I won't be needin' you to close the store tonight after all."

"No?"

The old man shook his head. "They've released Mrs. Thomas from the hospital this afternoon, so I won't be goin' to visit her."

Denise spun to Joshua in concern. But he didn't notice. He just shrugged and said, "No problem."

But it was a problem. A *big* problem! How could she signal for the Fayrahnians to come with Grandpa right there in the store? The creatures had barely missed giving the old guy a heart attack the last time they popped in. What would stop it from happening this time around?

Terrific, Denise thought. *First, no Nathan, and now no Fayrahnians. What else could go wrong?*

Unfortunately, she was about to find out . . .

Even though she was inside the shop, and was careful to stay away from the windows, Denise had made one little mistake. When she had pulled the Bloodstone from her pocket and nervously fiddled with it, she hadn't noticed the reflection on the pots and pans in the display window. She hadn't noticed the glint of moonlight that hit the bottom of one of the pots and reflected in her direction. She hadn't noticed that single glint of moonlight that struck the Bloodstone.

That is, until the rock in her hands started to glow . . .

CHAPTER TWO

JUST LIKE
OLD TIMES ...
SORTA

First Denise tried to stuff the rock back into her coat pocket. But her coat pocket started to glow.

Next she sidled up to one of the drawers behind the counter. When no one was looking, she yanked it open, dumped the rock inside, and slammed it shut. A good idea, until the drawer started to glow.

Things were not looking good. She leaned against the drawer to cover the glow with her body while at the same time trying to get Joshua's attention. If she could just get him to take Grandpa out of the room for a minute. Forget a minute, she'd settle for five seconds. But, no. He was too busy with some stupid conversation about sports or school or something. *Figures,* she thought. *Let him stand around having a good time while I'm over here trying to save his grandfather from the world's biggest heart attack.*

She began to whistle. Not a bad plan—get Josh's attention and appear to be casual all at the same time. The only problem was Denise knew nothing about whistling. Never had. So instead of a casual little tune, the only sound that came from her mouth was wet, puckering wheezes.

Next, she tried drumming her fingers on the counter. Maybe that would get his attention.

Maybe not.

By now the entire top of the counter had started to glow. So she did what any intelligent person would do. She hopped up on the counter and tried to hide the light with her body. First she sat this way, then that. But the light just kept on spreading until she had to lie down, and completely stretch out across the counter top.

So there she was—sprawled out on the counter, noisily drumming her fingers, while puckering and wheezing a pathetic whistle. And then it happened. It was fainter than normal but there was no mistaking the clear . . .

BEEP . . .

BOP . . .

BLEEP . . .

BURP . . .

. . . of Listro Q's Cross-Dimensionalizer.

She'd been expecting it. What she didn't expect was the crashing and banging that followed—the crashing and banging that came from the alley out back.

"What on earth!" Grandpa exclaimed.

"Prowlers?" Joshua asked.

"We'll see about that," Grandpa said as he reached under the counter for his nightstick. It was only then that he spotted Denise. By now the glow had completely vanished, but she still lay on the counter. "And would you mind tellin' me what you're up to?" he asked her.

"Oh." She quickly sat up, "I was just, uh . . . tired. Yeah, I was tired and thought I'd, uh"—she faked a little yawn—"you know, get some rest."

Grandpa and Josh looked at each other. It was clear neither of them had bought the lie, but before they could question her further, there was more outside banging followed by strange voices—strange, arguing voices.

With nightstick in hand, Grandpa turned and headed for the back door. "Who's out there?" he shouted. "Who's out there, I say? What's going on?"

"Stop him!" Denise whispered to Josh.

"What?"

"Those are the Fayrahnians—I'm sure of it."

Joshua stared at her.

She heard Grandpa throw open the back door. "What are you—" Suddenly his yell froze in midsentence.

"We've got to stop him," Denise cried as she hopped off the counter and started for the back.

But Joshua didn't follow.

"Josh?"

The boy didn't budge. In fact he wasn't moving at all. He just kept staring straight ahead.

"Joshua?"

Still no response.

She crossed to him. "Joshua, what's wrong? Josh, can you hear me?"

But he didn't move. Not a muscle. Not an eyelid. It was as if he had suddenly been frozen. She took a step or two closer and waved her hand in front of his face.

Nothing.

> "IT AIN'T OUR WISH,
> THE WRONG WAY TO BE RUBBIN'.
> BUT WE AIN'T USED TO WELCOMES,
> WITH YELLIN'S AND CLUBBIN'S."

Denise immediately recognized the awful poetry. "Aristophenix!" she shouted as she spun around to see the furry, bearlike creature enter, complete with his walking stick, checkered vest, and straw hat. Behind him loped Listro Q, just as tall and purple and cool as always. Without another word she raced to them and gave them both a hug . . . but only for a second.

"Whew," she said, quickly pulling away. "What's that smell?"

Aristophenix rolled his eyes over to Listro Q.

The cool purple dude glanced at the floor, cleared his throat, and finally replied. His speech was as scrambled and backward as ever. "Trouble still a little, with Cross-Dimensionalizer, have I."

"So?" Denise asked.

Aristophenix answered.

> *so the WRONG COORDINATes,*
> *HE ENTERED aGAIN.*
> *so INSTEAD of THIS ROOM,*
> *THE GARBAGE BIN we LANDED IN."*

Denise burst out laughing. She wasn't sure which was worse—Listro Q's sense of direction or Aristophenix's awful rhymes. Maybe it was a tie. "But, Samson," she asked, looking around for her favorite of the group—the cute bug with the glowing red tail. "Where's Samson?"

> *"THE LITTLE GUY GOT MARRIED*
> *to a sweet THING WHO'S DEAR.*
> *AND IN fayRAH after weDDINGS,*
> *you DON'T work for a year."*

"That's great!" Denise exclaimed. "So Sammy got married, that's terrific." She tried her best to sound excited, but she didn't quite pull it off. She'd really gotten to love the little guy during their last journey together. The fact that their personalities were so similar had a lot to do with it. Now they were saying he was married? Well, that was great. A part of Denise was really happy for him. But there was another part of her—a part that felt just a little bit sad, just a little left out.

Speaking of "left out," she suddenly remembered Joshua and spun back to him. "Is he going to be all right?" she asked. "I mean just standing there frozen like that?"

> *"HE AND HIS GRANDPA,*
> *ARE DOIN' JUST fINE.*
> *we've acceLERATED OUR CLOCKS,*
> *past THE speeD of THEIR TIME."*

"What?" Denise didn't quite catch the drift.

"Grab there pot," Listro Q said, pointing to the teapot that sat on the shelf behind her.

She looked at him a moment, then reached for it.

"Drop now it."

Denise hesitated, not entirely understanding. He nodded for her to go ahead. With a shrug, she let the teapot drop. But it didn't drop. It just hung in midair.

"How're you doing that?" she asked in amazement. "How're you making it float?"

Aristophenix answered.

> *"it ain't floatin' at aLL,*
> *quite factuaLLy, it's faLLin'.*
> *we're just speedin' so fast,*
> *that by our time it's crawLin'."*

"No kidding," Denise said as she grabbed the teapot and let it go again. The results were the same. It just hung there.

"So Grandpa and Josh aren't frozen? We're just moving faster than they are?"

"Correct are you," Listro Q answered.

"But I wanted Josh to come with us," Denise said. "He doesn't believe in any of this stuff and I wanted him to come see for—"

Aristophenix politely interrupted.

> *"we understand the probLem,*
> *we've been to the weaver.*
> *when it comes to imager,*
> *josh ain't no believer."*

Denise nodded. That was it in a nutshell. She wasn't sure what they meant about the "Weaver," but they were right about Josh refusing to believe in Imager.

"Worry not to," Listro Q assured her. "Coming with us will be he." Then, with a smile, he added, "But that's all not."

Denise waited for more.

"A problem says the Weaver still have you."

"Me?" Denise asked.

"How loved by Imager are you. Still understand not do you."

Denise opened her mouth to argue but stopped. It wouldn't do any good. Whoever this Weaver guy was he had her figured out just as well as he had Joshua. It was true. When it came to Imager Denise knew there had to be somebody out there running the show. After all that she'd seen and heard on her last trip, she knew that much. But for Imager to actually *like* her, to take a personal interest in her, when he was so awesome and powerful—well, to her it sounded like a lot of wishful thinking—a nice idea, but definitely fantasy time.

Yet, according to Listro Q, this sounded like another reason they had come—to prove to her it *wasn't* fantasy.

> "so pack up yer bags,
> Let's get ready to shove.
> for josh it's the proof,
> for you it's the Love."

"What about Nathan?" Denise suddenly remembered. "He wanted to come, too."

"Later come can he. But now move must we."

Denise hesitated, then gave Listro Q a nod. After their last adventure together she knew he could be trusted.

Without further ado, he reached for the little remote control box, pressed four buttons . . .

beep . . .
> **bop . . .**
>> **bleep . . .**
>>> **burp . . .**

. . . and they were off.

Suddenly the room filled with blinding light. And then, just as suddenly, there was no room at all—just the light. As with the last trip, Denise felt herself falling. Once again she looked around and saw thousands of bright, multicolored lights—all falling toward a city of much brighter lights below—all falling toward the Center, Imager's home.

It took a moment for her eyes to adjust to the brightness. But soon she could make out the glowing forms of Aristophenix and Listro Q beside her. They were quietly speaking to Joshua—at least she thought it was Joshua. But this Joshua was bigger and more powerful—especially in his shoulders. He had to be, because in each of his thick, muscular arms he carried a huge clay pot, filled to the brim with water—but not the water of earth. It was the water from Fayrah's stream—the water made up of the liquid letters and words.

So, you're finally with us, Josh spoke as he grinned at Denise. But he really wasn't speaking—it was more like he was thinking.

What do you mean? she thought back.

Speeded up his time past yours did we, Listro Q explained. *To tell him everything, so frightened not be he.*

Denise nodded though she wasn't thrilled about the idea. It was one thing to zip around somebody else who was frozen. But to be the frozen one was different. Who knew what type of idiot expression she'd had stuck on her face or for how long it had been stuck there?

Don't worry, Josh thought back as if he'd read her mind. *You looked incredible . . . you still do!*

Denise shot him an angry look. It wasn't like Josh to be mean. But when she saw his eyes, she realized he wasn't teasing. Instead, he looked at her with a type of . . . well, the only word she could think of to describe it was . . . *admiration.*

Flustered and caught off guard, Denise glanced down and immediately saw the reason for Joshua's comment. Once again, she was wearing the gorgeous wedding gown—the gown she had seen in the stream—the one made of the intricate lace and tiny glowing pearls. But the pearls weren't all that glowed. She could feel color racing to her cheeks. It was an amazing fact, but she had actually been complimented for her looks. And, worse yet, she was actually blushing over it!

Not sure what to say or what to do, she avoided the topic altogether. Turning to the Fayrahnians she asked, *Did you guys tell him about the Center? Did you tell him what he has to do to cross through?*

But neither Listro Q nor Aristophenix answered. Their eyes were already closed and their heads were tilted back. Already they were beginning to quietly speak words of love and appreciation for Imager.

Yeah, they told me, Joshua volunteered. *I'm suppose to think of happy stuff—maybe sing a song.*

No, more than that! Denise thought. Suddenly memories of the last time she tried to enter the Center rushed in. Awful, terrifying memories. Memories of being flung into an empty darkness. *You've got to sing one of your grandpa's songs. That's what Nathan did. The only way he made it through was by singing one of your grandpa's old Irish hymns.*

A look of concern crossed Josh's face. *A hymn?*

Denise nodded and looked down. The Center was quickly approaching. Already she could make out the bright glowing buildings. Already she could see the thin layer of fog that formed the subtle but impenetrable barrier.

I don't know, Denny—I don't remember any hymn.

Denise felt a wave of panic. And with the panic came the first vibrations. They were faint, but rapidly increasing.

Sure you do, she insisted, trying to push back the fear. *He used to sing it to you guys at bedtime.*

A hymn? I don't think . . .

The vibrating grew worse, turning into a shaking which became more and more violent.

Come on, Joshua! she urged. There was no mistaking the fear she felt. *You've got to remember!*

The scowl deepened on Josh's face.

Denise cast another look below. They were practically at the Center. Already the shaking was turning into teeth-rattling knocks and bone-jarring bounces. Any moment they would enter the fog where the shaking would increase a thousand times, where it would turn into violent lurching and lunging. But that would only last a second. Then they would be yanked to a screeching stop—and, without warning, hurtled in the opposite direction, back past the Secondhand Store and out into a black void—an empty blackness that was full of nothing but fear and even darker blackness.

Come on Joshua! Denise's mind cried. *Think!* She would not experience the terror of that darkness again—she *could* not. *THINK! THINK!*

The bouncings and bangings became nightmarish—like a carnival ride out of control, growing worse by the second!

Then she heard it. It was slow and halting at first, but it quickly grew in volume and confidence . . .

"Be thou . . . my vision, O Lord . . . of my . . . heart."

Josh was starting to sing! Sometimes there were pauses or he would hum if he couldn't remember the words. But he pressed on . . .

"Naught be all else . . . mm-mm-mmmmm that thou art."

That's it, Josh! Denise cried. Keep it up! Keep it up!

"Thou my best thought . . . by day or by night.

Mmm-mm mmm mmmm-mm, thy presence my light."

The shaking grew less . . . and just in time! Immediately they dropped into the first wispy layers of the Center. Denise closed her eyes and forced herself to concentrate on the words. Eventually she tried to join in—half singing, half humming . . . as Josh continued . . .

"Be thou my wisdom, mmm-mm my true word,

Mm mm-mm mmm mmmmm and thou with me, Lord."

The shaking continued to decrease.

"Thou my great Father and I thy true Son.

Thou in me dwelleth and I with thee one."

Finally the shaking stopped altogether. They had passed through— Denise knew it. Even with eyes closed, she could tell everything was much brighter now—much brighter. She was tempted to open her eyes but she didn't. She knew the sight would fill her with fear—and with that fear the awful shaking would return.

At last she felt the pressure of something under her feet. They had landed! They had landed at the Center! Still, she was afraid to open her eyes—afraid of what she might see. Yet she knew she'd hate herself forever if she didn't take one look . . . at least one little peek.

arrivals

As Denise and the guys landed at the Center, a welcoming party was preparing for their arrival just five dimensions away. The vice-governor of Biiq sat at his banquet table, giving last-minute instructions to Bud, one of the greatest scientists in the realm. "Click clickCLICK CLICKclick CLICKCLICKclick click CLICKclick."

Nearly 150 epochs had passed since they quit using words in Biiq. Words were so inaccurate when it came to real communication. And in Biiq, a kingdom of math and science, accuracy was supreme. So, instead of words, everyone simply clicked their tongues. The pauses between clicks, the number of clicks, and the loudness of each click said it all. Of course it made their poetry a little difficult to appreciate . . . but they were scientists. What did they care about verse or rhyme?

Information had arrived earlier from the Weaver. Biiq would finally play host to the two precious threads from the Upside-Down Kingdom. One thread, a female, knew of Imager but did not understand his love. The other, a male, refused to believe in Imager at all because it supposedly went against the laws of logic and science.

That argument always made Bud chuckle. It was *because* of Imager's infinite logic and awesome science that the Kingdom of Biiq was created in the first place. Here, people could spend their entire life exploring Imager—understanding him through mathematical formulas, marveling over him through scientific investigation. Here, people could understand and experience Imager more deeply than anyplace in the universe! Of course, the boys over in the art kingdoms might not entirely agree, but who cared. Today *they* were the ones to help the Upside Downers. *Their* kingdom was the one privileged to draw them closer to Imager's heart.

For several epochs Bud had been in charge of building the special laboratory called the Machine. Throughout that time, rumors had spread far and wide regarding who the Machine was being built for and when it would be used. Well, today those rumors would finally be put to rest.

The Machine was designed for the two Upside Downers, particularly for the one who didn't understand Imager's love. And now the vice-governor was giving Bud last-minute instructions on welcoming the Upside Downers to his kingdom and introducing them to the wonderful new invention.

Bud received his orders with an enthusiastic, "CLICKclick click CLICK clickCLICK," then turned and immediately fell over the nearest chair. Now that wouldn't have been a problem—folks around the palace were used to Bud being a little, how did they say it—*heavy on his feet?* But when he jumped up and crashed into the waiter carrying the vice-governor's mashed potatoes and mustard gravy . . . then spun around, tripped, and landed face first into the vice-governor's cream of caramel soup, well, it was bordering on being a problem.

The vice-governor stared down at Bud and pursed his lips in self-control.

Bud stared up from the soup and tried to smile. Then, without a word, he rose, wrung out his mustache, gave a weak sort of salute, and raced out of the palace for all he was worth. It's not that he was embarrassed. Such catastrophes were normal for Bud—too normal. He may have been one of Biiq's greatest scientist, but he was also one of Biiq's greatest clods. He was in a hurry because the Upside Downers were about to arrive. They'd only make a brief stop at the Center. Since neither of them were re-Breathed, they couldn't stay there long—Imager's presence would destroy them. So Bud raced off to make final preparations. There was much to do and little time to do it.

Denise's first impression of the Center was the blinding white light. Her second was the singing. It was not your average, run-of-the-mill choir stuff. It was a swelling, breathtaking, send-shivers-up-your-spine type of singing. In fact, it was so beautiful and awe-inspiring that before she knew it, a lump had formed in her throat.

At first Denise thought the song came from the various light-creatures that were strolling past her. But once she grew accustomed to the city's brilliance, she saw that the light-creatures weren't the only ones doing the singing. It came from everywhere—the buildings, the streets, the trees, even the blades of grass (a neat trick since none of these things had mouths). Still, somehow, some way, everything seemed to be singing.

But that was just one way the song was different. Another was that Denise not only heard it, but she *felt* it . . . inside her. Somehow the notes did more than enter her ears. They seeped into her whole body, resonating in her muscles, her organs, her bones. It was as if all of her insides had joined in the song.

Aristophenix grinned at the puzzled look on her face and explained,

"all that's of imager,
vibrates with his voice.
from stars to dirt clods,
all sing and rejoice."

Denise nodded, pretending to understand. Then something even stranger happened. Tears began filling her eyes . . . and for once in her life she didn't try to stop them. Suddenly, all she wanted was to sit down on the glowing street and have a good cry. But not a cry of sadness . . . these were tears of joy. Imagine Denise Wolff wanting to sit down on the ground and cry for joy? Amazing.

She couldn't put her finger on it, but she suspected that the emotion had something to do with the song. Because as she felt herself joining in, she also felt something else. For the very first time in her life Denise began to feel like she "belonged." It was a wonderful feeling. After all these years of searching to fit in and be accepted, Denise finally felt that she was . . . well, the word that kept coming to her mind was . . . *home*. Denise finally felt that she was *home*.

She glanced over at Josh beside her. He was crying, too. Good, that meant she wasn't totally out of her mind. Or was she? Because now she noticed something even stranger. She could see through him! Not clearly, mind you. It was more like looking at a stained-glass window. Josh's form and color were still there, along with most of the details. But now she could actually see some of the light-creatures moving behind him!

She raised her arm to look at her own hand. It was the same thing! *Oh, brother,* she thought, *now what's going on?* She looked to Aristophenix for an answer, but it was Listro Q's turn to explain.

"Super reality is the Center. Everything else is shadow of it."

Again she looked at her hand. He was right. Because she wasn't glowing like the rest of the Center and because she seemed to be transparent, she looked like . . . well, she really did look like a shadow.

The thought didn't exactly thrill her. But it didn't upset her either. Not here. Not with all of this joy and goodness and wonder.

She glanced at the passing light-creatures. Whenever she looked straight at them, all she saw was a blazing glare of light. But when she looked away and caught them out of the corner of her eye, she could make out some of their details—details that showed these little creatures really weren't creatures at all.

Like the light that was approaching her now. How could it be living? When she glanced off to the side all she saw was a hammock—that's right, a swinging hammock. But not just any swinging hammock. No, sir. It was the very same hammock that hung in her uncle's apple orchard! She was certain of it. It was the very same hammock that she, her mom, and her dad used to romp and play in—the same one that held all those wonderful memories of their times together, back when they *were* together.

As it passed by her, Denise tried to see who was in it, but with little success. Every time she looked directly at the hammock, the whole thing blurred back into a glare of brightness.

Then there were the sounds . . . laughing, giggling, and shouting. She recognized the voices immediately. They were her parents' . . . and herself. In fact, for a moment Denise actually felt like she was back in that hammock, nestled between her parents' loving arms. The joy was impossible to describe. She looked at Aristophenix.

He smiled and answered,

> "reality of the center,
> your logical mind cannot grasp.
> so your brain sees in symbols,
> to help lighten the task."

It was tough to find her voice with all of the emotion racing through her, but at last Denise was able to speak. "You mean that's not my uncle's hammock?"

"A hammock?" Aristophenix chuckled lightly. "Ask Joshua."

"No way," Josh whispered in awe as he watched the same light-creature pass. "That's my whole Little League baseball team back in fifth grade—back when we won the All-City Championship."

"Right," she laughed. "Your whole Little League baseball team." But when she looked at him she saw he wasn't joking. In fact, his face glowed with as much joy as hers. He obviously saw the light-creature as one thing while she saw it as something entirely different. But, whatever they saw, it made them feel exactly the same . . . wonderful, warm, and incredibly happy.

She turned back toward the hammock or Little League team or whatever it was. Now it was farther down the road and beginning to look like all the other glowing lights. Any detail she had seen was swallowed up by the overall glare. But it wasn't just the glare of the light-creature. It was also the glare from the horizon. Because just over the ridge was a light so radiant, so brilliant, that it made all of the other lights dim by comparison.

But it was more than just light. There was something different about this light. It had a type of *splendor* about it. A type of . . . *glory*. A glory so intense that it made Denise catch her breath.

Her heart began pounding in her chest. She breathed faster. No one had to tell her. Now she knew what the singing was about. Just over that ridge was the source of all the Center's light, all the Center's beauty, and all the Center's glory. Just over that ridge she knew she would finally see . . . Imager.

Without a word she started up the path toward the top of the knoll.

Aristophenix spotted her and cried out, "Denny, no!"

But Denise barely heard. She picked up her pace—breaking into a run.

Listro Q took off after her. "No! Denny! Back come here!"

But she wasn't listening. All she could do was stare at the light blazing from behind the ridge. It burned her eyes, making the back of them ache, but she would not stop looking . . . or running.

Listro Q caught up to her and ran beside her. "Denny!" he shouted. "Stop must you!"

"Why," she puffed, refusing to take her eyes off the approaching ridge.

"As close to this, dare get you!"

"Why?" she repeated, still not looking at him, still running for all she was worth.

"Re-Breathed not are you! Destroy you will his presence!"

If Denise had any extra air in her lungs she would have broken out laughing. "No way!" she panted. "I feel his love now. I finally see what you and Aristophenix have been saying!"

"But . . ." Listro Q was sounding desperate. "Unapproachable is he! Too pure for you is he!"

They passed other light-creatures that were heading toward the ridge—first the hammock, and then one creature after another as Denise continued to press on. Her lungs started to burn, crying out for more air. But she was nearly there. Nearly at the top of the hill.

The music grew louder. Denise's joy increased until she could barely think. The song was everywhere—inside her, overpowering her, consuming her.

And the light. It was so bright that it was all she could see. It was all she wanted to see. If Listro Q was still shouting she wasn't listening. If her feet were still touching the path she wasn't feeling it. There was only light. Then her thoughts began to dissolve. One concept after another slipped away. She tried remembering her name and couldn't. Her thoughts, her memories, her very identity were . . . vanishing. But it didn't matter, because there was only the light.

Stumbling, she glanced down and saw that her body was also disappearing! Vanishing memories! Vanishing thoughts! Vanishing body! Everything about Denise was vanishing! With every step she took toward the light, less and less of her existed!

"Denny! Listen to me you!" Listro Q cried. But she barely heard, nor did she care. There was only the light.

Then it happened. The unthinkable. Denise ran straight through one of the light-creatures. She had grown so unreal that she was able to pass through solid objects! It was as if she had become vapor. And with every step she took, more and more of her faded.

In desperation, Listro Q leapt at her. He grabbed her waist and tried tackling her to the ground.

But he fell to the path alone. Her body had passed completely through his arms.

"Denny!" he cried.

But Denise no longer heard. She no longer cared.

She no longer existed.

the
weaver

"Nine hours," Josh complained as he paced the gleaming white marble floor. "How much longer?" He threw another glance toward glass and steel doors. They had remained tightly shut ever since their arrival—ever since an emergency team had raced through them with the last remaining vapors they had recovered of Denise.

For the past several hours Josh had been eyeing those doors, studying the stark black letters that read:

**RESTRICTED AREA
ENTRANCE PROHIBITED**

And, with the passing of each hour, Joshua grew more certain that, *restricted* or not, he was going to have to break through those doors to find his friend. It was just a matter of time . . . and of getting past the two huge elklike guards who blocked the double doors with their antlers.

Aristophenix stood at the far end of the room near one of the crystal windows. They were in Fayrah now. Listro Q had cross-dimensionalized them over as quickly as possible. And, since Josh was an Upside Downer, Aristophenix had already given him the water from the stream so he could see and hear right side up.

Now the pudgy, bearlike creature gazed out onto the lush courtyard where a hundred Fayrahnians quietly waited . . . and prayed. Denise had been their friend. In fact, many of them had been rescued as a result of her last visit.

Aristophenix raised his eyes from the crowd to look at the distant Blood Mountains. They glowed and pulsed the way they always did when citizens of the Upside-Down Kingdom were present. "I shouldn't of taken ya there," he sighed heavily. "Until you were both re-Breathed, I should never have taken ya there."

Suddenly the doors leading to the courtyard flew open. Two Fayrahnians raced in. One looked exactly like Aristophenix—except for the four ears and two noses. The other looked like a walking seahorse with legs. Between them they carried a long hollow tube with something glowing inside it.

"More threads from the Center!" the seahorse cried. Immediately the Elk Guards stepped aside as the sealed doors whisked open.

It was now or never.

In a flash, Josh made his move.

"Joshua!" Aristophenix called.

But it was too late. Josh broke past the guards and ran down the glaring white hallway for all he was worth.

"Stop him!" the seahorse shouted. "He must not see her tapestry!"

The two guards galloped down the hallway after him, the sound of their hooves echoing against the marble walls and floor.

Josh glanced over his shoulder. They were gaining on him. No way was he a match for their powerful legs.

But he continued to run. He wasn't worried about being hurt. He knew that wasn't the Fayrahnian way. He *was* worried about the Elks leaping over him and blocking his path with their giant antlers.

The opening to a huge room lay just ahead. Josh bore down, straining with every muscle. Suddenly the clatter of hooves stopped. He looked up to see that they had jumped and were sailing high over his head. In a moment they'd land in front of him and block his rescue. He had no choice. He did what any ex-All City Little League Champion would do. He threw out his feet, leaned back, and slid across the marble floor!

It worked perfectly. The Elks landed in front of him but had no time to drop their antlers and block him. He slid right between their legs and into the room.

He leaped to his feet but quickly came to a stop. He was in some sort of giant lecture hall. He stood on a balcony overlooking hundreds of different creatures. Hundreds of different Fayrahnians who, because of his disturbance, were all looking right back at him.

Well, all but one.

In the center of the hall was a single man wearing what looked like a blacksmith's apron. He was old and balding. What hair he did have was gray and flyaway. He was hunched over and concentrating on an old-fashioned loom used for weaving. But the threads were no ordinary threads. They glowed. And not with ordinary light. These threads glowed with the same brilliance and beauty as the light from the Center. And the pattern the old man was weaving? It shimmered and sparkled with such depth and beauty that it made Joshua's chest ache.

"Bring him here," the Weaver ordered. He never looked up but kept concentrating on the pattern before him.

"But, Weaver," the seahorse called. "He knows the girl, he must not see."

"It is too late, yes, it is," the Weaver answered. "Bring him here."

The Elk guards exchanged anxious looks. Apparently approaching the Weaver as he worked was not something they relished. Luckily for them Aristophenix waddled into the room, huffing and puffing a storm.

"THE ERROR *was* (PANT, PANT) *ALL MINE,*
to THIS (PANT) *I* CONfess.
I'LL take HIM (PANT, PANT) DOWN *to THE* WEAVER
AND (PANT) CLEAR UP ALL THIS *mess.*"

The guards didn't have to be asked twice. Gratefully, they stepped back.

Still gasping for breath, Aristophenix came forward and took hold of Josh's arm. Well, to most it looked like he took hold of it. Actually, it was Josh who was doing the holding as he supported the exhausted bear. Together they started down the stairs toward the Weaver.

A moment later Listro Q stepped in to join them. Aristophenix turned to him and spoke in a hushed whisper.

> "wHat aRe ya doin',
> don't be a sap.
> as tHe LeadeR it's me,
> wHo sHould be takin' tHe Rap."

Listro Q only smiled. "Cool," was all he said.

Joshua looked on, impressed. Listro Q *was* cool. Cool and loyal. But right now Josh was more concerned about Denise. She was down there somewhere. And he had to help her. But where could she have—

And then he spotted it. Far from the Weaver, at the other end of the room. On a table beneath intense, glaring lights. It was the faintest outline of a human body.

"Denny!" Josh gasped.

"Correct," Listro Q whispered as they continued down the steps.

"But . . . why isn't anybody with her?" Josh demanded. "They're all with the Weaver when they should be at that other table trying to save Denny!"

Listro Q tried to explain. "Physical body of hers only at that table is it." He pointed to the table where Denise's remains lay. "But her *character*," he said, pointing to the Weaver and his loom, "her character over there is."

"What are you talking about?" Josh argued. He motioned toward the glowing pattern on the Weaver's loom. "That's just some stupid design he's making."

Aristophenix patiently explained:

> "tHat desiGn is HeR Life.
> eacH fibeR and stRand
> is woven toGetHeR,
> as imaGeR planned."

Josh stared at him. He knew his mouth was hanging open but he didn't much care. "You mean, *that* . . ." He pointed at the design on the loom. "*That's* her life—that pattern is who she is?"

Aristophenix nodded.

> *"each thread is a moment*
> *in her life's master plan.*
> *to create a character,*
> *both glorious and grand."*

Josh continued to stare at the pattern that was forming. Aristophenix was right. It *was* "glorious." It *was* "grand." No wonder he was so moved when he first saw it. But there was something else . . .

The more Josh stared at the pattern, the more it began to make sense. Somehow the design really was Denise. Not her body, not what she looked like on the outside—but how she was on the inside . . . her character, her personality. Somehow the pattern that was appearing on the loom was what Denise was like as a person.

Then Josh saw something else. "Wait a minute!" he cried. "What's that?"

The Weaver had picked up a dark ugly thread and was adding it to the pattern. It was an awful, sinister color, so repulsive that it made Josh shudder. Such ugly darkness had no place with such beauty. In fact it looked like the Weaver was about to destroy his wonderful work by adding the awful-looking thread.

"What are you doing?" Josh shouted. By now they had reached the bottom of the steps. They were only a few yards from the loom. "Stop it, you're ruining it!"

Everyone tensed as Josh's voice echoed about the hall—everyone but the Weaver. For a moment the old man did not answer but remained hunched over the loom, carefully working in the dark, ominous thread. When he did speak, it was only one sentence. And he did not look up.

"This thread will give her strength and depth, yes, it will."

But Josh barely heard. He couldn't take his eyes off the thread. It was hideous. If this pattern, this tapestry, really was Denise's life, that thread would bring her incredible pain, unbearable heartache. Even now, as the Weaver continued to work it into the pattern, it seemed to fight against and destroy the beauty of all the other threads, ruining the entire design.

"Stop it! You're hurting her!"

But the Weaver kept right on working.

Joshua had to do something. He couldn't just stand around and let the old man destroy his friend's life. He pulled his arm from Aristophenix and started for the loom. He'd rip that awful thread out of the Weaver's hand if he had to!

But the other Fayrahnians quickly moved to block his path. He tried to push and shove his way through, but there were just too many of them. If he managed to force one aside three more appeared in its place.

Desperately he looked about. There had to be something he could do. *Wait a minute! What about Denny's body? The physical one on the brightly lit table across the room?* There wasn't much of her there—just a faint outline. And of course, it was only the outside of her without her personality. But some of Denise was better than none of her!

Listro Q was the first to see the look in his eyes. "Josh—no!"

But he was too late. Joshua broke across the hall toward the table. The few Fayrahnians that stood between Josh and the table tried to stop him, but he was too fast and too strong. Those he couldn't side-step, he shoved out of the way as he sprinted toward the table that held the faint, quivering form of Denise's body.

"You don't understand!" Aristophenix shouted. "You'll cripple her character! You'll ruin her!"

For the first time the Weaver glanced up. And for the first time Josh saw a look of concern cross his face. But it lasted only a second. He quickly returned to his task, working faster than ever.

Josh continued forward. Just another twenty feet and a few more Fayrahnians. And then what? He wasn't sure. Maybe he'd scoop up the faint outline of Denise's body and try to escape with it. Anything to get her away from the Weaver and his awful dark thread.

He glanced across the room and saw the Weaver working faster, his nimble fingers moving the dark thread in and out of the strands as quickly as possible. It had become a race. The Weaver desperate to complete his task—Josh desperate to save Denise before he did.

A Fayrahnian reached out and nearly had Josh until he faked a left and expertly spun around to the right.

Now it was a clear shot to Denise.

That is, until the seahorse leaped off the balcony and landed between them. The animal had obviously seen too many movie superheroes and figured this was his big break to become one. Unfortunately, as he landed on the hard floor, the only thing that broke was his ankle. He grabbed it, writhing in agony.

Josh sidestepped the poor fellow and continued his race toward the table.

"Five strands!" someone shouted. "The Weaver has only five strands!"

Josh understood. The Weaver had five strands to go—five strands to finish weaving before the dark thread became a permanent part of Denise's tapestry. He looked up and saw the man's fingers fly.

In and out. In and out.

Josh turned back to Denise. He was practically there. Just two steps to go.

In and out.

He reached the table, raised his arms toward her. She was nearly in his grasp—

"JOSHUA, NO!" Listro Q shouted. "COMPLETE FIRST MUST SHE BE!"

But he paid no attention.

In and out.

And then, just as Josh's hands touched her semitransparent form . . .

In and out.

The crowd broke into cheers. The Weaver had finished! The dark thread was woven into place! The quivering, transparent image of Denise suddenly took shape in Josh's arms—she now had substance—she now had weight.

"Denny!" he cried.

"Joshua," she gasped.

Across the room, the Weaver leaned back in his chair. Removing his spectacles, he grabbed a handkerchief from his coat. It had been close, but he had succeeded. Now he blotted his face with his handkerchief and shook his head.

"Upside Downers," he wearily sighed. "Will they ever learn . . ."

a GUIDED tOUR

"Let me get this straight." Josh scowled. "You mean to tell me that you've woven the pattern of every person that's ever lived?"

"That's right, yes, it is . . . and that ever will," the Weaver added.

The scowl deepened as they walked through a series of large, cavernous hallways. On each wall hung hundreds of shimmering tapestries. Each was intricately beautiful, magnificently breathtaking. And each was fashioned from the same glowing threads as Denise's pattern. The whole place was like a giant art museum. But not like the ones that are full of dull, boring masterpieces—the ones they drag you through on school field trips. No way. These were full of life . . . glowing, shimmering, quivering-with-beauty life.

It had been several hours since Denise was revived. Now she walked between Josh and the Weaver as the old man did his best to fill them in on all that had happened.

"How could you keep up?" Denise asked. "I mean, weaving so many people? Where do you find the time?"

"Eternity is a bit longer than you can imagine," the Weaver chuckled. "We had a head start on you."

Josh was still having difficulty. "I'm sorry," he apologized. "This is just a little too weird. I don't think I can buy all of it."

The Weaver gave another gentle chuckle. "I knew that would be a problem, yes, I did. When Imager first asked me to weave that thread into you, I knew you'd have a hard time."

"What thread?"

"The logic thread of yours—the one always wanting proof."

Josh and Denise exchanged looks. Whoever this old-timer was, he certainly had Josh figured out.

"But that's okay." The old man smiled as they shuffled out of one hall and into another. "That's part of the plan, yes, it is. That's why your tapestry is in these most honored halls."

"You're kidding?" Josh's voice cracked. He tried again, clearing his throat, attempting to sound more adult. "That is to say, my tapestry, it's here?"

"Of course," the Weaver laughed.

"Well, can I, you know—is it possible to see it?"

"Yeah," Denise joined in.

"Sorry, that's out of the question. Yes, it is."

"Why?"

"An Upside Downer is never pleased with his pattern. No, he isn't. Until his thread, until his design is added to Imager's final tapestry, he always tries to change it."

"I wouldn't do that, I promise." Josh grimaced at the urgency in his voice.

"You wouldn't, you say?"

Again he attempted to sound more adult. "No, of course not. You can trust me."

"Just as I could trust you not to change Denise's tapestry?"

"You saw my tapestry?" Denise asked in astonishment.

Josh ignored her and answered the Weaver. "Well, that was, you know, different."

"You saw my tapestry?" Denise repeated.

"How, different?" the old man asked.

"You were putting in that ugly dark thread."

"What thread?" Denise demanded, growing more and more frustrated that no one was answering her.

"The thread will give her character, yes, it will. It will give her—"

"What thread are you guys talking about?" Denise's shout echoed inside the giant room. She hadn't meant to be so loud. All she wanted was some attention. Well, she definitely had it. For a moment both of them stared at her as if she'd lost her mind. She smiled weakly and repeated the question a bit more quietly. "Uh, what thread are we, you know, talking about here?"

"There is a reappearing thread in this season of your life, yes, there is," the Weaver explained. "It is dark and it is sinister."

"It's really awful," Josh agreed.

Denise looked first at the Weaver, then at Josh, then back at the Weaver. "Why? I mean, if it's so dark and bad, why do I have to have it?"

It was the Weaver's turn to clear his throat. Apparently he hadn't meant to get into all the details. But Josh had pulled him in and there was no way to get out but with the truth. "The thread will give you character and depth," he explained. "It will make you one of Imager's most valued creations. Yes, it will."

"But . . . what is it?" Denise asked. "What type of darkness is it?"

The Weaver gave her a careful look. Instead of answering, he slowly came to a stop in front of another glowing and shimmering masterpiece. "Tell me," he asked, "what do you two think of this tapestry?"

"It's terrific," Denise answered. "Just like all the others, but—"

"Take a closer look," he insisted. "Both of you. Step closer and look at the threads."

The two exchanged glances and obeyed.

"Are they all the same?" the Weaver asked. "The threads, I mean. Are they all the same colors and brightness?"

"Of course not," Josh answered. "Otherwise the tapestry would be boring; there'd be nothing to it."

The old man smiled at the answer. "I wove you well, Joshua O'Brien." Then, looking back at the tapestry, he continued. "And the darkest thread, do you see it?"

"Yes, it's right there near the center." Denise pointed. "It runs all the way to the bottom."

"Good. Now . . . step back and see how that one thread adds to the overall beauty of the piece."

Once again the two obeyed. And, as they stood staring at the pattern, Denise could see how that one dark thread, woven in and out, created a type of strength, a contrast for the rest of the threads. It seemed to give the entire tapestry its depth, its texture, its great beauty.

"If I would have disobeyed Imager—if I would have refused to add that thread, tell me, what would have happened?"

"The pattern wouldn't work," Denise answered.

Josh agreed. "The tapestry would be nothing without it."

"Right again, yes, you are."

"Who is this person?" Josh asked. "I can't explain it, but the pattern looks—it looks kinda familiar. Do we know him?"

Denise turned to the Weaver. Now that Josh mentioned it, there was something familiar about it.

The Weaver broke into a smile. There was no missing the love he had for his craftsmanship. At last he spoke. "This is your brother . . . Nathan O'Brien."

Denise gasped. It was true. She could see it now. Somehow the pattern of that tapestry perfectly showed Nathan's personality. Not just the spoiled selfish Nathan of a few months ago, but also the new, giving Nathan that had started to emerge. It was amazing—the design really did capture Nathan's character. Completely.

"And that dark thread?" Josh asked.

"The dark thread is Nathan's hip—the deformity that has caused him to limp with such pain over the years."

Denise stared at the tapestry, even more amazed.

The Weaver continued. "Look how all the brighter threads radiate from that darker one. Look how they're highlighted and magnified—how their beauty is intensified. Without that darker thread the tapestry would have little substance. It would have none of the depth, none of the extraordinary strength that we see."

Denise nodded. It was true. Nathan's greatest handicap, in the hands of the Weaver, had become his greatest strength. Incredible.

The Weaver finished with one last thought. "Imager has great plans for all of you. But sometimes the heart is not big enough to hold such plans—sometimes it must be enlarged through hardship."

The silence lasted several moments. Finally Josh turned back to the Weaver. "But . . . what about Denny's question? You never answered it. What about *her* thread?"

The Weaver looked curiously at Josh. "I'd forgotten your persistence. Perhaps I wove you too well."

Josh continued to wait for his answer.

With a deep sigh the Weaver began. "Denny first met that thread in Keygarp. She saw it circling high above her in the frozen forest."

Denise could feel the hair on her arms begin to rise.

"Since then she has also seen it in her dreams." Turning to her he added, "In fact, the last time you saw it was this afternoon—when you were daydreaming in your sixth period English class."

"The witch?" Denise gasped. "That thing flying around with those awful black wings?"

"She's no witch, Denise. She is the *Illusionist*—a queen. That is, until Nathan destroyed her kingdom. In any case, she and the evil Bobok have made a pact. You have been promised to her."

"*Promised* to her?"

The Weaver nodded gravely.

"What are you talking about!" Denise could feel the tops of her ears growing hot with anger. "Nobody can *promise* me. What do I look like—a baseball card? People can't trade me around without my permission."

"That's right," Josh agreed. "Doesn't she have some say in the matter?"

"Of course she does. Every decision you make is of your own free will. These threads are only the *final* outcome—the ones Imager knows you will eventually choose."

"And he knows I'm going to let myself be given to some ugly, bat-winged queen?"

"No. He knows that your struggle against her will be fierce."

"Will I win?"

The Weaver hesitated. Finally he shook his head. "I cannot answer that, no, I can't. The decision will be yours."

"But you know what I'll decide, you just said so."

"Please . . ." The Weaver motioned toward the doorway at the end of the hall. "They are waiting."

"Who?"

"Your friends, Listro Q and Aristophenix."

"But you haven't answered my quest—"

"I have said too much already."

"But—"

He raised his hand for silence. It was a gentle movement but one that made it clear the topic was closed. Starting toward the doorway, he changed the subject altogether. "Your purpose for this journey, has it been fulfilled?"

"What purpose?" Denise asked.

"For Joshua."

"Oh, you mean proving Imager to him?"

The Weaver nodded.

She looked at Josh. Her friend stared hard at the marble floor. She could tell he wanted to be polite, but she could also tell he wanted to be honest.

Finally he spoke. "Everything about this place seems real, I'll give you that. But it's so *different* from the reality we normally experience. How do I know I'm not just having some sort of dream or something?"

Denise let out a sigh of frustration and looked at the Weaver.

But the old man was nodding in quiet understanding. Then he turned to Denise. "And you?" he asked. "You still do not believe Imager's compassion?"

The question caught Denise off guard, until she remembered that was the other reason they'd come. She knew her answer was no better than Josh's so she said nothing, hoping the question would somehow go away.

But the Weaver continued to wait.

Finally she spoke. "How can I believe in his love when"—she swallowed—"when all he does if you try to get close to him is hurt and destroy you?"

The old man nodded, his eyes growing moist. "Then come," he said softly, "we must not be late." With that he turned and resumed shuffling toward the door.

Denise and Josh glanced at each other and followed. It appeared that their adventure wasn't quite over . . .

the machine

"Clickclick CLICKclickCLICK." Bud continued testing the microphone. He blew into it and stepped a little closer. "click CLICKCLICK." Suddenly the speakers squealed with feedback. The guests surrounding the outdoor stage cringed in pain until the noise stopped and they resumed their smiles and chitchat. After all, that was Bud up there on stage. Such things were expected.

Bud had been told that the Upside Downers had just left Fayrah and were heading for Biiq. They'd had a couple minor detours, but now they were on their way. Any second he would have the honor of welcoming them. Denise's Machine had been tested and retested for the thousandth time. It worked perfectly. Now it waited in the gigantic building behind him for her arrival. And, across the river, on the other side of Biiq, Olga, the kingdom's computer, was humming with life, waiting for Josh.

Everything was set. Now all he had to do was greet them and escort them safely to their destinations. A simple task even for Bud. Well, at least that's what he hoped.

"Pssst . . . Psssssssst."

Bud turned and glanced backstage. There he saw the most beautiful creature he had ever laid eyes on. Scientifically, she was perfect. Every part of her was a perfect mathematical ratio to the other—from the length of her arms to the diameter of her knee caps to the width of her toenails. The lady wasn't necessarily pretty, but to a mathematician she was more breathtaking than any unified theory equation.

"Most important and excellent of all scientists?" Even her voice vibrated in perfect mathematical frequencies. "Please, if you would be so kind as to tell me where I might find the Machine—the one you've prepared for the female Upside Downer? I have a gift for her."

"Cl–cl–cl–click cl–click CLICK cl–click," Bud stuttered as he left the microphone and approached her. The woman's perfection was definitely fogging his mind.

She frowned slightly, not understanding the clicks.

Realizing she wasn't from Biiq, he nervously fumbled for the translator attached to his belt. He turned it on and repeated himself. It translated his clicks perfectly. Well, almost perfectly. There seemed to be a slight short in the circuits which made it occasionally repeat a word or two. Then there was the problem of Bud's stuttering . . .

"I'm s–s–sorry s–s–sorry, but that's a s–s–secret s–s–secret," he said. "We have word that the Illusionist has s–s–stolen into our kingdom and is is is trying t–t–to destroy her her."

"The *who?*"

"S-some s–s–sort of ugly queen queen who c-c-can transform her looks looks into any any creature she wants."

"But what of my gift?" the lady asked, managing to smile, flirt, and pout all at the same time.

Bud was mesmerized. Her perfection had captured his heart.

"Surely the most important scientist in the kingdom could figure out something . . . hmm?" She batted her perfectly proportioned eyelids, each with the perfect number of eyelashes.

"D–d–don't worry worry," Bud volunteered, suddenly sounding very gallant. "I'll s–s–ee to it that she g–gets it it personally."

"Oh, thank you, sir." The lady smiled sweetly as she reached out to touch his arm. "You're as kind a man as you are important."

That cinched it. Bud was in love. No doubt about it. He gave a polite little bow as he took the gift into his hands. Then excusing himself (after all he was an important scientist who had important science-type things to do), he headed back on stage to the microphone. It was then he spotted it—a tiny hole in the bottom corner of the wrapped gift. He turned back to the lady but she was already gone.

That's odd, he thought. *Where could she be?* He glanced about but she was nowhere to be found. *Oh well,* he figured, waving off a pesky fly that had suddenly started buzzing the gift, *she's sure to be in the audience admiring my importance. I'll see her then. Maybe give her a little smile to make her day.* With a confident grin, Bud turned toward the microphone. Again, he noticed the fly. It had landed on the gift and was crawling for the tiny hole. He was about to shoo it away when suddenly . . .

BeeP . . .

BOP . . .

BLeeP. . .

BURP . . .

Listro Q, Aristophenix, and the two Upside Downers made their grand and long-awaited entrance into Biiq. It would have been a bit more grand if Listro Q had not missed his coordinates. Instead of landing on the stage, they landed in a nearby oak tree. Even that wouldn't have been so bad if they had landed right side up. But there they were, all four of them hanging upside down in the giant oak, trying their best to look like proper and distinguished visitors.

"Nice work," Aristophenix muttered between clenched teeth while pretending to smile for the crowd.

"Cool," Listro Q answered as he pretended to look cool for the crowd.

The girl, on the other hand, wasn't interested in pretending anything for the crowd. "Listro Q!" she shouted. *"Listro Q!"*

But, before Listro Q had a chance to answer, Bud began his written speech. "sgniteerG sgniteerg, tsom devoleb edispU srenwoD srenwoD."

He glanced up from the speech and smiled. But no one was smiling back. In fact, everyone looked pretty confused—as if they didn't understand a word he was saying. What was wrong? What was going on?

He glanced down at the translator attached to his belt. Of course! It was shorting out again. Only worse. Now it wasn't just repeating itself, it was also translating backwards! "diputS diputs, doog rof gnihton, on dnarb eman rotalsnarT," he grumbled before giving it a good thwack with his hand. That did the trick. The backwards problem immediately cleared up. Bud grinned, pleased that all those years in electronics school had finally paid off.

He started again. "Greetings greetings, most beloved Upside Downers Downers. It is with great pleasure pleasure that we welcome you to to the Kingdom of Biiq Biiq—the kingdom of Math Math and Science."

The audience clapped and clicked enthusiastically . . . in perfect mathematical unison, of course.

And so it continued as Bud introduced the governor, the vice-governor, the mayor, the superintendent of transportation, the assistant superintendent of commerce, and on and on—each and every one of them excited to meet the two Upside Downers, and each and every one of them boring the children to death. Bud could see the weariness fill their faces, and he tried his best to hurry through the ceremony. Finally, just a mere four hours, twenty-three minutes, and eight seconds later, the last speech was made and the last hand shaken. The official welcoming was over.

Now, at last, he could take them to his beloved Machine.

This thing is huge!" Denise exclaimed as they arrived at the giant six-story building. There were no doors, no windows, just walls of smooth, shiny metal. "How do we get in?" she asked.

Bud smiled and produced a skeleton key. He placed it into a nearly invisible lock and gave it a turn. A large door suddenly appeared in the wall, humming to life as it automatically swung open.

"Nice," Denise exclaimed. She threw a look over at Josh. His mouth was dropping open. Not because of the door. But because of what was inside . . .

Before them stretched the biggest laboratory Denise had ever seen. Besides the obligatory bubbling beakers and smoking test tubes, there were thousands of electronic thingamajigs and doohickeys that glowed and flashed everywhere she looked. Some towered several stories over their heads; others stretched hundreds of yards into the distance. But no matter how tall they rose or how far they stretched, and no matter how many different colored lights flashed on how many different panels, they all surrounded and focused upon one thing . . .

It lay ahead of them in the center of the building. As they approached, it reminded Denise of a large round table. But it didn't seem to have any legs or support of any kind. Instead, it simply floated about waist high. Yet the closer they got, the more she saw it was definitely no table. It was more like a round, floating platform. It consisted of two layers. The bottom layer looked like compacted sand and was about a foot deep. The second layer was a little thinner. It was clear liquid, but a liquid that glowed—almost as brightly as the Center. All around the platform's side, some sort of energy field buzzed and hummed. And high above it hovered a giant, circular TV screen with a single microphone hanging down.

"What . . . is it?" Denise asked in a hushed tone as they arrived.

"The experiment experiment," Bud said. He was grinning from ear to ear, obviously filled with pride.

"For what?"

"For you you."

Denise turned to him in surprise. "What?"

"The only way to clearly clearly understand Imager's compassion is to clearly understand his heart heart."

"Yeah, so?"

"So, with this experiment, you will will become a creator. You will gain gain a creator's heart."

Denise looked at him as if he'd lost his mind.

Aristophenix smiled and tried to explain.

*"what better way
imager's love to understand,
than to create your own life form,
to hold in your hand."*

Denise still didn't get it. "What are you guys talking about?"

"Denny?" It was Josh. "I think I understand. These guys have set it all up so you can create a life-form." He turned to Bud, "Is that right?"

"Correct correct," Bud agreed.

"And by doing this, they hope you'll experience the same feelings that this Imager supposedly has toward *his* creation."

"Correct correct again."

"You're not serious?" Denise asked.

"Oh, yes yes, very serious."

"But . . . but I don't know beans about science. I can't just go and create *life*."

"Don't feel bad," Bud chuckled. "Nobody else has had much much luck in that department, either."

"Then how—"

"Imager. His Breath has already been programmed into the Machine."

"What machine?"

"Why, this whole whole laboratory. We've spent the last three and a half epochs building it for you."

Denise stared, amazed. "For me? You built all this for me?"

Bud nodded. "At Imager's request."

"But . . . how do I . . . I mean, where . . ."

"Don't worry," Bud laughed. "Your only concern is this this platform in front of you . . . and this screen and microphone above you."

"But, I still don't . . ."

"All you have to do is speak speak into the microphone. No matter what you say, great or small small, the Machine will translate your words into action. The Machine will create everything you say within that liquid light. And you will will see what you create on the screen above you."

"This is crazy!" Denise protested.

"No," Listro Q quietly corrected. "Imager's love is this."

She turned to him. "You knew about this?"

Listro Q nodded with a gentle smile. "From our meeting, the very first."

"If you need need any help," Bud said as he turned and prepared to leave, "just tell tell the Machine, and we'll immediately return."

"Wait a minute!" Denise cried in a panic. "You're not leaving me!"

"Yes yes. It's important that you do this this on your own. No one must interfere with what you do do . . . and more importantly no one must interfere with what what you feel."

"But I'm sticking around, right?" Josh asked.

"Sorry," Bud answered.

"But *I'm* the one interested in science. *I'm* the one you were going to give a rational explanation for—"

"This isn't about the mind mind, Joshua. This is about the heart."

"Yeah, but—"

"Your studies of logic are with with Olga."

"Who?"

"Our computer—the best in the kingdom."

Josh frowned. It was clear he didn't think a question-and-answer session with some computer rated with creating your very own life-form.

Noticing his obvious disappointment Listro Q spoke. "Worry don't. For your best will be Olga."

Bud turned back to Denise. "Call us us whenever you want to quit quit or have finished finished. Anytime, day day or night."

"Day or night! It's going to last that long?"

Bud smiled. "That's up up to you."

Denise looked at the platform with its liquid light floating on top of the sand, then up to the Machine surrounding her on all sides. This was insane! And yet, if it really was designed for her, and if it really was safe, and if she really could quit anytime she wanted . . .

On the other hand, all she had was their word . . .

On the other hand, Josh would kill for this opportunity, so why was she dragging her feet?

On the other hand . . . no, there were too many hands already. It was time for a decision. She turned to Aristophenix, who gave the slightest nod, assuring her everything was okay.

"DON'T BE a-WORRYIN,'
THERE'S NOTHIN' to feaR.
to tHE HEaRt of HIS feeLINGS,
tHIS WILL HELP YOU DRaw NEaR."

Next, she turned to Josh. Good ol' Josh. He'd tell her if it was safe or not.

"Well, kiddo." He flashed her that world-famous grin of his. She could tell he was still envious, but that he was trying to be grown-up about it. "I'm guessing this makes you about the luckiest person I've ever met."

She tried to smile back. This was obviously a new definition of *lucky*. She wanted to tell him how terrified she was of the whole idea—especially the part of being left alone. But the excitement in his eyes made her feel like some little kid afraid of the dark.

"No one's ever had a chance like this," he said. "And I doubt no one ever will again."

Denise knew his words were meant to encourage her, that she should be grateful for such an honor. And maybe she should. After all, Josh was right, no one had ever had a chance like this. And it was true, no one probably ever would again. So how could she refuse? And if she did, how could she ever look at herself in the mirror again? Or look at Josh?

She finally had her answer—not because it was what she wanted, but because it was what she *should* want. She turned back to Bud and in her best, I-can-handle-anything tone said, "So when do I start?"

"Right away!" Bud grinned.

Denise swallowed.

"Atta girl," Aristophenix said, slapping her on the back. "It's gonna be great!"

"Oh, here here, I'd almost forgotten." Bud reached out and handed Denise the gift he had been carrying under his arm. "It came from a most extraordinary lady lady who wanted to make sure sure you got it."

Denise took the present but paid little attention. At the moment she had a few other things on her mind.

After more "good lucks" and a few hugs, the group finally turned and started for the door. Denise followed them. It wasn't until they were about to step outside that she was again struck with panic. "Joshua!" she cried.

He stopped and turned to her.

She swallowed hard and shook her head. She would be strong. Even if it killed her she wouldn't admit being afraid—especially to Josh.

He flashed her another grin. "Have fun, kiddo," he said. "What I wouldn't give to be in your shoes."

Denise smiled back, desperately wishing he was.

He turned and joined the others at the door. Everyone waved and gave a few more encouragements.

Denise nodded and waved back.

Bud turned and immediately ran into the side of the door. "Oooh, ouch, ouch!" he cried, grabbing his foot and doing a little jig. "I hate it it when that happens!"

Denise smiled in spite of herself.

After a couple more hops and a few more "ouches," Bud pressed a button inside the building. The door hummed as it started to close. He stepped outside with the others and gave a final wave. A moment later the door shut with a foreboding *boom* that echoed back and forth inside the Machine.

Slowly Denise turned to face the experiment. She had never admitted to being afraid of anything before—and she wasn't about to start now. So, after taking a deep breath, she started toward the platform of liquid light, all alone in the giant building.

Well, *almost* all alone . . .

the experiment BEGINS ...

Denise stood beside the platform of liquid light, more than a little puzzled. Creating your own life-forms was a lot harder than she imagined. Actually creating them wasn't so hard—all she had to do was think something up, say it, and the Machine did the rest. But thinking it up, that was the brain-bruising part.

At first she tried the obvious choices. In front of her was a world of liquid, so she raised her head toward the microphone and called out . . .

"Machine, give me fish."

There was a surge of energy, some flashes and crackles, and she got . . . fish. Billions of them. And from what she could see on the screen above her, there were thousands of different varieties. Which was nice . . . for a while.

But, let's face it, they were just fish. It's not like she could have some great, personal relationship with them.

Next she tried animals. You name it, she created it: lions, hippos, giraffes, aardvarks (though she had no great urge to create the smaller, creepy-crawly varieties).

Again, this was nice, but like any great zoo, you can only stand around gawking at the critters so long before you want a little inter-action. And since she couldn't get down in the liquid and play with them, they really didn't hold her interest that long.

Then, at last, she had it . . . People! Like herself. Of course! If she could create people like herself, then she'd have somebody to talk with, to relate to, to be friends with.

"Machine," she said. "Create a me."

The Machine hummed a little louder, the outside energy field sparked a little brighter, until Denise saw an exact duplicate of her-self up on the screen. Only, well, not to complain but . . .

It was *too* exact.

Every time Denise moved, it moved. Every time Denise had a thought, it had the same thought.

"This is no fun," Denise muttered.

"This is no fun," the copy of Denise agreed.

"What can we do different?" Denise asked.

"What *can* we do different?" her copy repeated.

"Don't you have any ideas?" Denise asked.

"Don't you?" the copy replied.

In many ways it was worse than the fish or animals. How could she be friends with her own reflection? It was like having a computer or a robot who, although it appeared human, thought and felt exactly like she thought and felt. If she said, "I love you," the reply from her other self would be "I love you." If she said, "You're cool," she knew she'd get the same response. It was more like talking into a mirror or a tape recorder than having a real friend.

There had to be another solution . . .

And then she had it. "Of course, why didn't I think of it before?"

"Of course, why didn't *I*?" came the reply.

Ignoring herself, Denise raised her head to the microphone and ordered, "Machine . . . make a me, that's me but not me!"

Once again the Machine hummed and sparked and flashed. Denise leaned over the platform, waiting breathlessly. She looked up at the screen in anticipation.

And then, at last, her greatest and best creation of all formed inside the liquid light . . .

Nearly twelve hours had passed before the Illusionist woke up, stretched her six hairy legs, and quietly crept out of the hole at the corner of the gift box. True, the nap might have been a bit longer than necessary, but even the most hideous creature in twenty-three dimensions needed her beauty rest. Besides, she figured destroying Denise would be easy. Since they were alone together inside the Machine it would be a piece of cake . . . which, now that she was in the form of a fly, sounded pretty appealing—especially the frosting part.

It wasn't that the Illusionist hated Denise. It was that Imager loved her. And since the Illusionist hated Imager, and since the best way to hurt someone you hate is to destroy someone they love . . . well, the Illusionist really didn't have any choice in the matter. She *had* to destroy Denise.

But instead of going immediately for the kill, the Illusionist decided to remain disguised as a fly just a little bit longer. That way she could buzz the Machine a few times to check it out and see what the big deal was. Even in her part of the universe, the Illusionist had heard plenty about this newfangled invention that was being built, and how Imager hoped to instruct an Upside Downer with it.

Soon, she was airborne. And looking down upon Denise and the glowing platform, the Illusionist grew sick to her stomach. She was not prepared to see such innocence and goodness, such sweetness and kindness. It was absolutely disgusting, thoroughly nauseating.

But that was okay because it would soon come to an end. Very, very soon it would all be over . . .

After Denise created her latest and best creation, she decided to make two of them. After all, the only thing better than playing with one person was to play with two. She suspected she would create more than that in the future, but right now two was enough—two little life-forms in liquid light, splashing, playing, and joking with each other and with her.

She called them *Gus* and *Gertrude*. She wasn't sure why; the names just seemed to fit.

Physically, they looked exactly like Denise—well, except for the extra set of arms. Denise always thought that human-types were a little shortchanged in that department, and she wanted her creations to have every advantage. "This way you can brush your teeth and comb your hair at the same time," she explained.

Of course they couldn't see Denise. She was too big. In fact, she was so big that they just figured she was everywhere. In a sense, they were right. But even though they couldn't see her, they could hear her. That was one of the orders Denise had given to the Machine. And it was one of her best. Now the three of them could talk and joke and laugh for as long as they wanted.

Gus was the funniest—all huffy and puffy and pretending to have all the answers when most of the time he didn't have a clue. How could he? He was only a few hours old! But that didn't stop him from trying.

Gertie (she made it clear from the start that she hated the name Gertrude) was also a crack-up. The little gal could get so excited over the simplest things. "Look, everybody! I have a toe! I have a toe! And I can wiggle it!" And when she wasn't getting excited about having toes or fingers or a belly button, she was constantly bombarding Denise with a thousand *whys, what ifs,* and *how comes?*

They were incredibly cute, reminding Denise of a couple puppies, the way they romped and climbed and played over each other. Better yet, they reminded her of baby-sitting the Jefferson twins (when they were on their *best* behavior and when they *didn't* need their diapers changed).

But it was more than just their cuteness and playfulness. There was something else. Denise couldn't put her finger on it, but she'd never felt anything quite like it before. As she continued to watch them, her chest began to ache. But it wasn't a bad ache, it was an ache of pleasure—in fact sometimes there was so much pleasure that it was hard for her to breathe. And the more she hovered over her creations, watching and encouraging them in their new adventure called *life,* the more wonderful the ache grew. Whatever this feeling was, it was safe to say that Denise was definitely becoming attached to these little folks.

And they were becoming attached to her. In fact, Gertie put it best when Denise had to leave for a bathroom break. She was gone only a few minutes, but when she returned Gertie had her arms folded (all four of them) and began to scold Denise for being gone so long. "It was awful," she complained in her cute little high-pitched voice. "It was like a part of me was missing. Don't you ever ever *ever* do that again!"

"Okay, okay," Denise chuckled. "I promise I won't ever ever *ever* do that again." But even as she joked with her, Denise knew Gertie was right. She *was* a part of them. And they were a part of *her*. And why not? After all, didn't they come from Denise's own personality and imagination? Gus with his know-it-all, I'll-tackle-the-world mentality, and cute little Gertie with all of her questions and that big, sensitive heart of hers. Both were definitely a part of Denise . . . and she was definitely a part of them.

Then it happened.

"Hey, guys," Gus shouted. "Watch this!"

He was showing off by swimming little figure eights in the liquid light. Denise looked down at the ripples on the platform. As he swam faster, the figure eights grew bigger and the waves grew taller. It was pretty impressive, even to Denise.

Gertie had floated to the surface to get a better view, and as Gus kept making bigger waves, she kept bobbing up and down, higher and lower. "*Whoa, whoo, wee* . . . Okay, Gus," she cried between bobs, "cut it *ow, wow, woooo* . . . I'm not kidding now, *stop, eeeee, ooh.*"

Soon Denise and Gertie were laughing so hard that tears streamed down their cheeks. But not Gus. He was really getting into it. And as his figure eights grew larger and larger, he began swimming closer and closer to the platform's edge.

"Okay, Gus," Denise finally called out through her laughter. "That's enough now."

But Gus didn't hear.

Denise called a little louder, "Okay, Gus."

By now he was much closer to the edge . . . too close. And he still wasn't paying attention.

"Gus . . . Gus!"

No answer.

Denise fought back the rising panic inside her. Any second he could swim out too far; any second he could accidentally swim over the edge and fall to his death.

"Gus!" she shouted.

Gertie joined in. "Gus!" she cried. "Gus!"

But there was still no response.

Denise's panic turned to cold fear as Gus started the next figure eight—his biggest one yet—the one taking him straight toward the edge. What could she do? How could she stop him?

"GUS . . . GUS, LISTEN TO ME . . . GUS!"

But Gus didn't hear.

Suddenly a thought came to Denise. As a last-ditch effort she quickly turned to the microphone and shouted, "Machine, create a wall!"

The Machine hummed and immediately a wall sprang up around the edge of the platform. And just in time! It had barely formed before Gus hit it . . . head on. It was close, but Denise had managed to save Gus just before he'd have fallen over the edge to his death.

Yet, instead of showing his appreciation, Gus glared up at the sky, rubbing his head. "Hey!" he shouted. "What do you think you're doing?"

"You were swimming off the edge," Denise explained. "I had to stop you with this wall."

"What do you mean *edge,* what's an *edge?*"

"It's, uh . . . an ending . . ."

"An ending?"

"Yeah, it's a . . ." But try as she might Denise couldn't find a word he'd understand. "It's something that would kill you," she explained.

"Kill?"

"You would stop living and thinking. You'd stop . . . existing."

"Go on!" Gus shouted.

"No, I'm serious."

Gus was still angry and still rubbing his head. "So why didn't you tell me? This wall thing of yours packs a pretty big wallop."

"She tried to tell you," Gertie called. "She shouted at you over and over again."

"I didn't hear a thing. Just the roar."

"The roar?" Denise asked.

"Yeah, a roar that kept getting louder and louder."

Denise threw a glance at the edge of the platform. "Oh that . . . that's the energy field all around the platform. I think it holds it together. I guess it just drowned me out."

"What do you mean, *energy field?*" Gus asked.

"And what's a *platform?*" Gertie wondered. "And what do you mean, *drowned?* And what—"

"Never mind," Denise laughed, relieved that they were back to asking questions, "never mind. Let's just say it's a good idea not to get so close to the edge."

"You're not kidding," Gus agreed. "That wall of yours is no treat, and this *kill* stuff doesn't sound so hot either. Thanks for the warning."

"No problem." Denise smiled.

But she wouldn't have been smiling if she had known what the Illusionist was thinking. By circling high overhead the creature had seen everything. Everything from the sickening friendship and love between Denise and the creatures . . . to Gus's near-destruction by swimming too close to the edge.

And, as she watched, a plan started to form. It was one thing to simply destroy Denise. But it was quite another to make her writhe and suffer in agony first. The Illusionist broke into a grin. *Writhing* and *suffering . . .* two of her favorite words.

Without a moment's hesitation, the Illusionist folded her wings back and dove straight for the platform. Then just before she splashed into the liquid light, she transformed herself into the shape of Gus and Gertie—complete with the four arms.

Across the river, on the other side of Biiq, Josh stood in front of another type of machine . . . Olga. She was no taller than a boy and no thicker than, say, your average, run-of-the-mill breakfast waffle (complete, of course, with all those little square holes). Like a giant fence, Olga snaked in and around the entire kingdom. She circled houses and buildings, she passed under overpasses and over underpasses, she cut through farmer's fields, and she crossed over streams—around and around and back and forth she wound as far as the eye could see.

"What is it?" Josh asked.

"She's one of the most powerful computers in our dimension." Bud grinned. "We use her to explore and better understand Imager."

Josh took a deep breath. He wanted to be liked by the folks, but all this talk about Imager was starting to get to him. "Look," he said politely. "I appreciate what you're trying to do. But there's just no way you can scientifically prove there's some sort of . . . *Supreme Being* out there—someone who knows all and sees all."

Bud started to speak, but Josh wasn't finished. "I'm not saying there isn't *something*. I mean I definitely experienced things at the Center. But like I told the Weaver, to try and prove it scientifically . . . I'm sorry, it's just not possible."

Bud traded smiles with Aristophenix and Listro Q. Then he reached over and pressed a single button on the computer. Immediately a thin sheet of water shot from Olga and floated before them. It was about three feet long and a foot wide.

Josh was impressed.

"It's only a projected image," Bud said. "See?" He ran his hands through it. "Just like a holograph."

Josh reached out and touched the water. It was true. There was nothing there. It was just a picture of water floating in midair.

"Tell me me," Bud asked. "What do you know about geometry?"

"A little. We haven't had it at school yet or anything, but I've done some reading."

"Good good. In the Upside-Down Kingdom, how many many dimensions do you live in in?"

"Three," Josh answered. "In our world we have three dimensions. Everything has length, that's one dimension—and width, that's two dimensions—and height, that's the third. Everything from a penny to a skyscraper has three dimensions."

"Very good. But what if there were more than three dimensions?"

"Some scientists think time is a fourth dimension."

Bud couldn't help smiling. "Interesting theory. But could five, six, or seven dimensions also exist? Is that that possible?"

"Mathematically, sure. But we could never see them—they'd be past our understanding."

"Precisely."

"Hold it, wait a minute. Are you saying this Imager guy lives in a dimension higher than ours?"

"The highest."

"But . . . if that's true, well, you could *never* prove him."

"Yes and no," Bud answered. "The only way way to understand higher dimensions is to use the dimensions we already have."

Josh looked at him, waiting for more.

"Let's pretend this sheet of water floating in front of us us has only two dimensions. It has length"—he ran his finger across the longer side of the projection—"and it has width." He motioned to the shorter side. "But it it has no height, no tallness. In other words, let's say there's a sideways and a back-and-forth, but no up-and-down."

Josh nodded.

"Now let's let's pretend there are people living in in this two-dimensional world—a world completely flat. They would understand back-and-forth and sideways, but they would have no understanding of up-and-down, correct?"

Again Josh nodded.

"How how would we in the the next higher dimension, in the third dimension, appear to them?"

"If they looked up they'd see us like giants staring down at them," Josh said.

"No . . . they wouldn't know how to look look up. Remember, they have no up-and-down . . . all they they have in their two-dimensional world is back-and-forth and sideways."

"Well, then, I guess . . . they'd never be able to see us at all."

"Precisely. Does that mean mean we wouldn't be here?"

"No, we'd be here. And we could see everything about them, all the time . . . from one end of this projection to the other . . . we could see their whole life."

"And if we wanted them to see see us, what would we do?"

"I guess we'd have to get down to their level." Josh began to chuckle. "It would sure be a shock to them, though." He reached toward the floating projection. "I mean, it would be like, *poof*"—he stuck his fingertip into the image—"we'd suddenly appear, then *poof*"—he pulled out his finger—"we'd suddenly disappear."

"But would we really disappear?"

"No . . . like I said, we'd be there all the time. But to them, we'd be like these . . . these . . ." Josh came to a stop. The thought boggled his mind. He looked up at Bud, his eyes growing wide with understanding.

"To them what would we be like like, Josh?" Bud gently asked.

After a moment Josh slowly spoke the words. "To them we'd be like . . . we'd be all-knowing, all-seeing." Josh swallowed hard. Then after another pause, he concluded. "To them we'd be like . . . God."

CHOICES

Dozing off was the last thing Denise had in mind, particularly after Gertie's lecture about leaving them. But after a day of school, traveling across dimensions, visiting the Center, nearly seeing Imager, ceasing to exist, being rewoven, the endless welcome ceremony, and all the hours of fun with Gus and Gertie, well, she didn't have much choice. She was just going to lie down for a second to rest her eyes. Unfortunately, that second turned into nearly an hour.

And an Illusionist can do a lot of damage in nearly an hour.

The first thing Denise noticed when she woke up and looked at the platform was that the wall she created had a hole in it. How odd.

The second thing she noticed was that on the other side of the wall, just a hair's breadth from the edge, were Gus's waves!

"Gus?" she cried as she raced to the platform. "Get away from the edge! Gus, what are you doing?"

But Gus couldn't hear her. He was too close to the edge. The roar was too loud.

Desperation gripped Denise. Any second Gus could lose his balance. Any second he could fall onto the floor and be destroyed! What could she do, what could be done?

Then she remembered . . . the Machine!

She spun to the microphone and yelled, "Machine! Pick up Gus and put him back into the center of—"

"Not so fast, dear heart."

The voice sent a chill through Denise. She recognized it at once. She had heard it a dozen times in her dreams. She had heard it high over the trees of Keygarp. But now . . . now it came from somewhere on the platform!

"What are you doing here?" Denise shouted. She tried to push back the fear, as she searched for a telltale ripple in the liquid light. "Where are you?"

"I'm right here."

"Where?" Denise demanded.

"Why, with Gertie, of course."

Denise stifled a gasp. *The Illusionist—with Gertie?* "Machine!" she cried. "Show me Gertie!"

Immediately Gertie's image flickered onto the screen overhead. Beside her was another creature who looked almost identical to her. The chill Denise had felt earlier grew to a cold numbness. This other creation was *not* hers.

"Hi, Denny," Gertie's voice called cheerfully.

"Hi, Gertie," Denise answered. Her eyes desperately searched the platform for their location. There! She spotted them! Two tiny ripples near the center. She continued talking, trying to keep her voice calm and steady. Whatever was happening, she didn't want to scare her sensitive little friend. "What's going on, Gertie? What's Gus doing?"

"Oh, he's just exercising his free will."

"His what?"

"The lady here explained it all to us," Gertie chirped. "If Gus wants to play at the edge, he has every right to."

"That's right," the Illusionist agreed. Her voice was smooth and seductive. "Otherwise you'd be living in a prison, wouldn't you?"

"Uh-huh," Gertie said, "and Denny wouldn't want that."

"No, of course she wouldn't," the Illusionist said. "Because Denny loves you, doesn't she?"

Gertie agreed, "With her whole heart."

Suddenly there was a piercing scream. "*Ahhhh . . .*"

Denise spun back to the edge of the platform. The little ripples that had surrounded Gus were gone. Instead, there was just a pinpoint glimmer of reflection falling from the platform.

It was Gus!

Without thinking, Denise dove toward the glimmer—arm outstretched, hand open. It was close, but just before she hit the floor, she felt the faintest tickle inside her palm. Gus had landed safely in her open hand.

"Wooo-eeee!" he shouted as Denise rolled onto her back and struggled to her feet. "That was somethin'! Hey, Gertie, if you can hear me, you ought to come over and try this!"

"What are you doing?" Denise shouted angrily at him. "You could have killed yourself. Gus . . . *Gus!*"

"It will do no good, dear heart," the Illusionist chuckled. "He can't hear you. You know that—not near the edge."

"Fine, then I'll put him back here in the middle where he—"

"But he doesn't want to be in the middle. He wants to be at the edge."

"I know that, but—"

"She's got a point, Denny." It was Gertie again—just as sweet and thoughtful as ever. "You wouldn't want to make him live someplace he doesn't want to. You want him to have free will, right?"

There was that phrase again. Already Denise was beginning to hate it. For a moment she was tempted to shout, "*I don't care about any stupid free will! I'm the boss and what I say goes!*" But she didn't. Somehow she knew that being a demanding bully wasn't exactly what their friendship was about. So she tried reason . . .

"Look, I know that's what he wants—to play on the edge. But I also know it'll kill him. So I have to save him. I have to tell him."

"But you already did," the Illusionist reminded her. "And he chose not to listen."

"But he listened to you just fine, didn't he?" There was no missing the anger growing in Denise's voice.

"I have my ways," the Illusionist chuckled.

"Yeah, well, I have mine, too." With a determined voice Denise turned to the microphone. "Machine, I want you to take this, this stranger here, and I want you to—"

"Hold on, child."

Denise stopped.

"So what are you going to do—destroy me?"

"The thought had crossed my mind."

"That's rich," the Illusionist laughed. "So is that what you do? Destroy anyone who disagrees with you?"

"No, of course she wouldn't." Gertie's little voice was also growing angry at the Illusionist. "Denny isn't that way. Are you, Denny?"

"Well, no . . ." Denise faltered. "Of course not."

"See?" Gertie challenged. "Denny loves us."

"Love," the Illusionist sneered. "You call this love? Making people live where they don't want to live . . . destroying those who don't agree with her? That is not love."

Once again the tops of Denise's ears started to burn. She'd had enough talk. Now it was time for action. "Machine," she shouted, "I want you to take this—this thing and—"

"I guarantee you!" the Illusionist shouted over her.

In spite of herself, Denise came to a stop.

"If you destroy me, I guarantee that Gus and Gertie will never love you on their own. They'll only pretend to love you. They'll be afraid that if they don't, you'll destroy them just as you did me!"

Denise's head began to swim. She knew there was some truth to the Illusionist's words. She also knew that she wanted to completely wipe the creature off the face of the platform. And if those weren't enough emotions raging inside her, there was also her worry about Gus.

"Why . . ." She turned back to the Illusionist, the feelings tightening her throat. "Why are you doing this to us? Things were so good before. Everything was so perfect."

"Since when is a dictatorship perfect?" the Illusionist demanded.

"But I'm no dictator, I'm . . . I'm—"

"Hey, are you going to put me down or what!" Gus demanded.

Denise looked back into her palm.

"Put me on the edge, put me on the edge!" he shouted. "I want to jump off again, I want to jump off!"

Denise stared into her hand, angry at the tears welling up in her eyes. "Gus," she stammered, "don't you see. It will kill you."

But he didn't hear. "Put me down! I want to jump off again! I want to jump off!"

"Gus . . . please . . ." By now the tears were forming faster than Denise could blink them away. "Please, listen to me. Gus . . ."

"Cry all you want," the Illusionist taunted, "but he won't hear you. It was his choice to go to the edge. Now he will *never* hear you!"

The words cut deeply into Denise. One of her closest and best friends was trying to kill himself. No, he was more than a best friend. He was a part of her. A part of her was trying to kill himself . . . and there seemed little she could do to stop him.

"Gus . . . ," she croaked hoarsely, "please . . ."

But there was no answer except, "Put me down, put me down! I want to jump off again! I want to jump off!"

"Isn't there . . ." She looked back at the platform where the Illusionist was, hoping for some way out, *any* way out. "Isn't there *something* I can do?"

"Not a thing," the Illusionist smiled.

Denise looked back at her palm.

"Put me down! I want to jump off! I want to jump off!"

She stood a long moment, listening, thinking . . .

The Illusionist was right: Denise could demand that Gus stay in the middle, but then she'd be a dictator. She could build an impossibly thick wall around him, but then she'd be a prison guard. She could wipe out the Illusionist, but then she'd be a murderer.

The realization pressed heavily upon Denise's chest, making it difficult to breathe. The knot in her throat continued to tighten. But there was nothing she could do. She saw that now.

"Gus . . . please?"

"Put me down! Put me down!"

Denise remained listening to his demands, her mind racing, probing every possibility. But there was no way out.

"Gus . . . ," she pleaded one final time.

But his answer was the same.

Then, her heart aching, Denise lowered her hand back toward the edge of the platform. "Good-bye," she whispered softly. "Good-bye, my friend."

"Put me down! Put me down!"

"Good-bye . . ."

He leaped from her palm and she saw the ripples as he landed back in the liquid light.

"Don't worry, Denny."

She looked back to the monitor and saw Gertie. Her little friend was also crying.

"You still have me," Gertie sniffed. "And I'll never leave you. I promise I'll never, never leave you."

Denise tried to smile. Good ol' Gertie. Always the sensitive, big-hearted Gertie. But wait! Suddenly a thought came to mind. Of course, why hadn't she thought of it before? It was a long shot. But maybe . . .

"*Eeee-yaaaa . . .*" Once again Gus had raced to the edge of the platform and was leaping off.

Immediately Denise slid her hand underneath the edge and caught him.

"What are you doing?" the Illusionist yelled. "You're depriving him of his free will!"

But Denise paid no attention. "Gertie!" she called. "Gertie, will you do me a favor?"

"Of course, Denny, whatever you want."

"Will you give a message to Gus?"

"Now wait a minute," the Illusionist protested. "That's not fair."

"Of course it's fair!" Denise grinned, wiping away the tears with her free hand. "He may not be able to hear me, but there's nothing saying I can't write him a note."

"Put me down!" Gus shouted from inside her palm. "Put me down!"

"Unfair!" the Illusionist shouted. Her voice grew shriller. "Unfair!"

But Denise no longer listened. "Machine," she commanded. "Write a message. Put it on something that will last and see to it that Gertie gets it."

The Machine hummed a brief moment in preparation and awaited further orders.

"This is unfair!" the Illusionist continued to shout. "Stop it at once!"

"Put me down! Put me down!" Gus kept demanding.

But Denise wasn't stopping for anyone. She'd found the solution. Speaking to the Machine, she ordered, "Have the message read: *Do not jump off the edge—it will kill you!*"

The Machine gave a faint crackle. Suddenly there was another ripple in the liquid light. Denise looked up to the monitor to see a large steel sign appear close to Gertie.

It was more than the Illusionist could bear. As quickly as the sign appeared, she disappeared. One minute she was there, the next minute she was gone. Denise had no idea where she went and hoped never to see her again.

But, even now, she had her doubts . . .

the
SIGN

"Oh, look," Gertie sighed. She slowly drifted toward the gigantic steel sign resting on the floor of her liquid light ocean. "It's so . . . so . . . beautiful."

Now the truth is, it really wasn't all that beautiful—just an ordinary sign with a message engraved on it. But the fact that it came from her creator, that it came from her Denny, well, that brought tears of gratitude to young Gertie's eyes. "Thank you *soo* much," she kept repeating over and over again. "Thank you so very much."

Denise was deeply touched. It seemed the tiniest of things brought joy to Gertie. And somehow that made Denise love her all the more.

"You're so beautiful," Gertie exclaimed, as she tenderly reached out to touch the sign. "And your letters . . . they're carved so perfectly."

For a moment Denise was confused. Who was Gertie talking to? Then realizing Gertie wasn't addressing her but the sign, Denise politely cleared her throat. "Ah, Gertie . . . Gertie, it's me, Denny. I'm still up here."

"Oh, sorry." Gertie gave an embarrassed giggle as she glanced up to the sky. "I knew that."

Denise smiled. "Now, listen, I need you to take that message to—"

"Put me down, put me down!" It was Gus. He was still in her palm. She lowered her hand and let him jump back onto the edge of the platform. She quickly turned to Gertie, who had already resumed her conversation.

"Wonderful sign . . . perfect sign."

"Gertie?"

"Your letters say such truth, such—"

"Gertie . . ."

But Gertie was so busy admiring the sign that she barely heard. *"Gertie!"*

That did the trick. "Oh . . . uh, hi, Denny." But even as she answered, she sounded a little confused, a little distracted. "What were we talking about?"

"Will you ask Gus to read this sign?"

"Of course I will—I'd love to."

"Thank you," Denise said. "I'll just order the Machine to move it over to him and then you can show him—"

"Oh, no, I can carry it," Gertie volunteered cheerfully.

Denise couldn't help smiling. Once again she was moved by her friend's love and desire to help. But she didn't need her help. "That's okay," Denise answered, "there's no need for you to—"

"No, no, I'd love to carry it for you."

"Thanks, Gertie, but I don't think—"

"You're *so* beautiful." Gertie's voice grew dreamy again. "Your letters are so perfect, so full of truth . . . I'll carry you everywhere you want to go."

"Gertie, it's just a sign. You're talking to a—"

"I'll carry you anywhere—forever and ever."

"Gertie . . . *Gertie!*"

But Gertie didn't answer. Before Denise could stop her, she took the huge sign into her four hands and, with great effort, heaved it onto her back. It was so heavy that she sank into the sandy ocean floor. It was so big and bulky that it stretched out far over her head. But she forced herself to start walking. The awful weight caused her to groan with every step, but Gertie seemed happy to bear that weight. Honored to bear it. She would do anything for her Denny. Anything.

"Gertie!" Denise felt a twinge of panic. "Gertie, listen to me!"

But Gertie no longer heard. The steel plate that stretched over her head blocked all sound from above.

"Gertie, listen to me!"

Gertie continued to stagger forward, groaning under the weight, deaf to Denise's voice . . . as if she had more important things to do.

"Please, Gertie . . ." Denise could feel the emotion rising to her throat again. Could it be? First she'd lost Gus and now . . . "Gertie! Gertie, listen to me!"

But her voice continued to bounce off the steel plate, never reaching Gertie's ears. Suddenly Denise felt very alone. "You're cutting me off," she called. "Gertie, please . . . don't do this!"

There was no answer.

Gus gave another scream as he jumped from the platform. Again Denise leaped forward to catch him. But again, at his insistence, she put him back on the edge—none too gently this time.

"Hey! Watch it!" he shouted before starting his run toward the edge again.

Denise was lost. Something had to be done. Gertie could never carry that sign—not for long. She wasn't created to carry it. She'd wear herself out. In desperation, Denise turned back to the Machine and gave another order. "Machine . . . Another sign!"

The Machine hummed in preparation.

"Have it read: *Listen to me!*"

The Machine gave a faint crackle and immediately the sign appeared in front of Gertie.

But to Denise's horror, Gertie's gruntings and groanings grew twice as loud.

Denise looked back to the screen. Instead of obeying the second sign, Gertie had placed it onto her back with the first one!

"No!" Denise shouted.

But she was too late. Now Gertie's burden was doubly hard to carry. Now it was doubly hard for her to hear Denise's warnings.

"Gertie," she cried, "please don't do this to yourself! Please listen to me . . ."

Feeling light-headed from all the emotion, Denise grabbed the edge of the platform for support and looked down to watch Gertie's ripples of light moving slower and slower. The poor thing was obviously wearing herself out. Denise looked back to the screen. The weight was causing her friend to sink further into the sandy bottom. With every step she took, she sank deeper and deeper. Soon, she was waist deep in the sand and still sinking. In a matter of minutes the ocean floor would swallow her. The sand would cover her neck, her mouth, her nose; and then, in her stubborn desire to serve Denise, Gertie would suffocate and kill herself.

"Ahhhh!" Gus screamed as he jumped off the edge.

Denise dove forward and caught him, then returned to Gertie. But Gertie was gone! There were no sounds, no ripples, no image on the screen!

"Gertie!"

Desperate, Denise shoved her free hand deep into the liquid light where she had last seen Gertie. It was an impulsive move that could have crushed her little friend, but she had to do something.

At the same time Gus continued his demands, "Put me down, put me down!"

Then Denise heard her. She was coughing up sand and screaming hysterically, but there was no mistaking Gertie's voice. "Let me go, let me go!"

For a moment the tiniest relief filled Denise. But only for a moment.

"Put me down! Put me down!"

"Let me go! Let me go!"

"Stop this . . . ," Denise shouted into both of her hands. "You two are killing yourselves! Don't you see? Stop it!"

But neither was listening.

"Put me down! Let me go!" Their voices were blending into one. "Put me down! Let me go! Put me down! Let me go!"

Then another voice joined in. Denise wasn't sure where it came from, but there was no mistaking who it was. "You must let them go, dear heart, or they will be your prisoners. Without free will you will become their dictator."

"But they'll kill themselves!" Denise shouted.

"Put me down! Let me go! Put me down . . ."

Moisture again filled Denise's eyes. She was cut off from both friends now. Friends that were destroying themselves. Her two best friends were destroying themselves, and there was nothing she could do to stop them!

Her throat ached. The pressure inside her chest was so great that she had to fight for breath. "Please, Gus," she begged, "Gertie, please . . . you two have to listen to me!" Her head grew lighter as she struggled for breath. Hot tears spilled from her eyes and ran down her face.

"You need me!" she screamed in anger. "Listen to me! You need me!"

But there was no answer. Only their continual demands—

"Put me down! Let me go! Put me down! Let me go!"

Denise's vision began to blur. The hours without sleep, the intense emotions, and the ongoing fight to save the ones she so deeply loved was more than she could bear.

"Please . . . ," she groaned, "please . . ."

But it did no good. By now both Gus and Gertie were in a mindless rage. Gus was the first to add the new phrase. "I hate you!" he shouted. "I hate you! I hate you! Put me down! I hate you!"

Soon Gertie had joined in. "I hate you! Let me go! Let me go! I hate you!"

The words hit Denise hard, slamming into her gut . . . and breaking her heart.

"I hate you! I hate you! I hate you!"

Her head began to reel. She had only fainted once in her life. She hated the feeling then, and she hated it now. She had to fight it off, she knew it. But she also knew something else. She knew the Illusionist was right. She knew there was nothing more she could do for them.

Slowly . . . sadly . . . Denise unclenched one hand. Her mind screamed with anguish as Gus jumped off into the liquid light and swam back to the edge of the platform—for the very last time.

Then, no longer able to see through her tears or to stop the room as it started to spin, Denise opened her other hand. Suddenly she closed it and pulled back, yelling, "No! I can't!"

"Let me go! Let me go!" Gertie screamed.

"Nooo!"

"I hate you! I hate you! Let me go! Let me go!"

"You have no choice, dear heart," the gentle voice cooed. "You know that. No choice . . ."

Denise was weeping now. The Illusionist was right, there was nothing she could do. Once again she opened her hand and slowly brought it toward the platform. Once again the pain pierced her heart as Gertie dove into the liquid light and swam toward her precious signs.

Denise tried to speak, to say something. But as she clung helplessly to the platform, no words would come.

The tears turned to sobs—gulping, gut-wrenching sobs. She had never cried so hard, never felt such anguish. She wasn't just losing friends, she was losing her heart.

It was cold inside the Machine now . . . very cold.

She could no longer stand to watch. The pressure was too great. Hanging onto the edge of the platform, Denise slowly eased herself down to the floor. The sobs continued, only now they were silent sobs—sobs of hopelessness.

She released her grip on the platform and drew herself into a tiny little ball on the cold concrete floor.

The pain was unbearable.

aNOTHeR Last cHaNce

Across the river with Bud and the guys, Josh was still learning about Imager. He didn't believe everything they said, but gradually, scientific theory by scientific theory, and mathematical formula by mathematical formula, he was beginning to realize there must be *somebody* out there.

"But what about the future?" he asked. "Everybody—you guys, the Weaver, folks at Fayrah, they all say this Imager knows our future, that he knows what I'm going to do before *I* do."

Aristophenix, Listro Q, and Bud all nodded in agreement.

"But that's impossible!"

"Impossible more, that doesn't he," Listro Q offered.

"How?"

Bud grinned. "It's simple. If you would just just imagine—"

"No imaginings," Josh said firmly. "Your theory about higher dimensions is interesting but that's all it is—theory. I still need proof."

Aristophenix and Listro Q exchanged nervous glances.

But Bud simply smiled and pushed several buttons on Olga. Immediately a long paper slipped out of a slot.

"What's that?"

"Your future future."

"Yeah, right," Josh scoffed.

But Bud was perfectly serious. "Every one of your personality traits is given given a number. See . . ." He held the paper out but an immediate frown crossed his face. "This is strange strange. All the information seems to be be printed upside down."

Josh looked over Bud's shoulder a moment and then, without a word, gently took the paper from him and turned it right side up.

"Oh, thank you, much better." Bud grinned sheepishly. "Now where where were we?"

"Something about my personality traits having a number?"

"Precisely. See, your athletic abilities are number 706, your interest in science is 245, your desire to please people is—"

"Wait a minute, how do you know all that about me?"

"We know everything about you you."

"Everything?"

"Everything," Bud grinned. "Remember, we look down down from a higher dimension."

"Oh, yeah, right." Josh swallowed a little uncomfortably. Suddenly he wasn't so thrilled that everything he did was always watched.

"Anyway," Bud continued, "everything about you is given a number and everything that could happen to you is given given another number. Then, using the laws of probability, we run run these numbers through the computer and it mathematically tells us what you'll do do in every situation."

"What if I want to change my mind?"

"You can change your mind mind as often as you want. But we know what your final decision will be be."

"No kidding?"

"And we can predict how that decision will affect other people people in their mathematical future."

"And if you put all of our mathematical futures together . . ."

"We know the entire future future of your world."

"Incredible."

"No," Bud answered. "Just Imager's mathematics."

"Can I see it?" Josh asked, reaching for the paper.

"No, uh, I don't think so so."

"Why not? It's *my* future."

"According to these figures figures, you would try and alter these numbers."

"No way," Josh protested.

"Yes, you would."

"Absolutely not."

"Just as you didn't try to alter the Weaver's tapestry?"

"Well, that was different."

"How how?"

"Well, because . . . I mean . . ." Josh was running out of arguments. As much as he hated to admit it, Bud had a point. "Well, okay, I guess maybe I might try—just a little."

The group chuckled quietly. Even Josh had to smile. Then an idea came to mind. "What about Denny?" he asked. "Could I see her future?"

Bud glanced at Aristophenix and Listro Q. They hesitated a moment, then nodded.

Bud reached over and pressed another set of Olga buttons. Immediately another long sheet of paper shot out. He picked it up and began showing the figures to Josh. "See, this number here is your friend's stubbornness, this one is her doubt doubt over Imager's love—the reason she came here in the first place."

Josh nodded.

"This one is her love for the creatures she's just just created over at the Machine. And this this . . ." Bud's voice trailed off.

"What?" Josh asked.

"No no, this can't be right." Immediately Bud re-pushed the buttons on the computer and immediately another piece of paper shot out.

"What's wrong?" Josh asked as Bud quickly scanned the paper.

Bud's face grew pale.

"Bud?" Aristophenix asked. There was no missing the concern in his voice. "Bud?"

Finally the scientist spoke. "According to these calculations, Denny is experiencing a love for her creation similar to Imager's."

"Well, that's great!" Josh exclaimed. "I mean, that's what she wanted to understand, right?"

Still staring at the figures Bud could only shake his head. "But too too similar," he quietly murmured.

"Too similar, how?" Listro Q asked. "Similar love, how to Imager?"

Slowly Bud looked up. "Completely," he said. "A love so similar that it would destroy itself to save its creation."

A chill swept over the group.

Then, without a word, Aristophenix quickly turned and started waddling down the path toward the bridge.

"Where are you going?" Josh shouted.

The pudgy creature called over his shoulder:

> "OUR TOOSHES SHOULD BE a-MOVIN',
> 'CAUSE I'M AFRAID IF THEY DON'T,
> DENNY'S CHANCES OF LIVIN',
> ARE LESS THAN REMOTE!"

D enise wasn't sure when the idea first came. But there, curled up on the cold floor, she realized she hadn't tried everything. There was still one last thing she could do to try and save her friends.

She struggled to her knees, then rose unsteadily to her feet. A wave of dizziness swept over her, but she wouldn't give in to it. Those were her friends on that platform and nothing would stop her from saving them.

She glanced quickly over to the edge. Gus's ripples were still there. Good. That meant he hadn't jumped off yet. Apparently he enjoyed teetering on the edge as much as he did the actual falling.

She glanced up to the screen for Gertie's location. To her amazement her little friend had already reached the wall. Gertie's fierce determination surprised her. Then again, Gertie was part of her, and if there was one thing Denise had, it was determination. But Gertie was so much weaker now. As with Gus, it was only a short matter of time before she also destroyed herself.

It was an awful risk. Denise didn't even know if the Machine could pull it off—let alone if she'd survive. Then there was the matter of coming back. But it was the only hope Gus and Gertie had. If they wouldn't let her help from above, then maybe, just maybe she could help from beside.

"Machine!" she shouted.

The Machine hummed in readiness.

"Put me in their world! Make me like Gus and Gertie!"

The Machine crackled and sparked longer than normal. This was obviously no common request. At last a beam shot out and struck her, shrinking her to the size of a pinhead. Then, instantly, it transported her into Gus and Gertie's world.

The whole process took less than a minute and it definitely caught her off guard. Shrinking to the size of a pinhead is not your everyday experience. Then there was the matter of swimming and breathing in the liquid light. And finally, let's not forget the four arms. It took lots of concentration not to tangle them up and even more not to accidentally clobber herself with them. But finally she got the hang of it. And just in time.

"Who are you?"

The voice was faint and weak but Denise immediately recognized it. "Gertie?" she cried, desperately searching. "Gertie, where are you?"

"I'm right here," Gertie groaned. "Down here."

Denise looked down to the sandy ocean floor and let out a gasp. By now Gertie had sunk up to her neck. Yet she still hung onto the heavy signs—holding them high over her head. Nothing would make her let go.

"Quick, let me have those," Denise shouted as she swam toward Gertie and grabbed hold of the signs.

"What are you doing?" Gertie shouted. "These are Denny's signs. Let go of them, let go of them!"

"Gertie, give them to me!"

"Let go!"

There was a brief struggle but being stuck in the sand greatly hampered Gertie's efforts. Still, her four hands gripped the signs so tightly that it was all Denise could do to pry them loose from her. Then, despite Gertie's screams of protest, Denise lifted the heavy signs and threw them to the side.

"*Noooo!*" Gertie screamed. She started to fight and claw her way out of the sand. Denise reached down to help, but Gertie would have none of it. At last she dug herself out. But instead of throwing her arms around her creator, as Denise had hoped and dreamed, Gertie raced to the signs, dropped to her knees, and threw her arms around *them*.

"These are Denny's," she cried. "She told *me* to carry them!"

"Gertie, I *am* Denny! Gertie?"

But Gertie wasn't listening. Instead, she spoke to the signs. "Perfect signs, beautiful signs." She gently stroked their surfaces. "Did that mean, awful creature scratch you, hmm?"

Denise approached her cautiously. "Gertie . . . Gertie, it's me, Denny."

But there was no response as Gertie continued talking to the signs.

"Gertie, please, it's—"

Suddenly Gertie turned on her. "Stay back!" she screamed, pulling the signs closer to protect them.

Denise came to a stop, puzzled and perplexed. "Gertie?"

"I don't know who you are or what you want, but you keep your hands off my signs!"

"Gertie, it's me . . . it's Denny."

"Liar! Denny would never hurt these signs—Denny would never take them away. These are good signs, perfect signs." She began rocking back and forth on her knees, holding the signs like a lost child clinging to a doll.

"Of course they're good," Denise said as she cautiously resumed her approach. "That's why I made them. But look what's written on them, look what they—"

"Stay back!" Gertie warned.

Denise slowed, but she wouldn't stop. "They say you have to quit hurting yourself and to pay attention to me."

"Stay back, I said!"

"But you're so busy carrying them and loving *them*, that you don't even hear *me*."

"These are perfect signs, good signs," Gertie repeated.

"I know they're good signs, but you're not obeying them." By now she'd reached Gertie's side.

"Denny told me to carry them!"

"No, I didn't." Gently, carefully, Denise knelt beside her friend. "That was your idea. I just wanted you to obey them. You don't have to carry them."

"But I . . . I love Denny . . . ," she faltered. "I love Denny and, and she wants me to . . ."

"No," Denise gently answered. "All I want is your safety . . . and your friendship."

"But I . . . I have to help."

Again Denise shook her head. "By trying to help, you were cutting me off."

Tears filled Gertie's eyes. "No, that's not true. I love Denny, I didn't mean to—"

"I know . . . ," Denise said, feeling the moisture well up in her own eyes. She tenderly wrapped her arms around Gertie. ". . . I know."

Barely aware of it, Gertie returned the hug. The two of them knelt there for several moments—each giving and returning the other's embrace. Slowly the anger and hurt began to fade. Slowly the love and affection returned.

Finally Denise reached for the signs. "Here," she gently offered. "Let me help you with those. Let me take—"

"No!" Gertie screamed, pulling them back. "These are Denny's signs! Perfect signs! Good signs!"

"But if you'd just—"

With fierce determination, Gertie hoisted the signs over her head and threw them onto her back.

"Gertie, no—"

The poor thing let out an awful groan as the weight crushed her body. But she would not stop. These signs were her life. They had been given to her, and nothing would separate them from her.

"Gertie, please . . ."

There was no answer. Gertie turned and staggered toward the hole in the wall. Every step forced a moan of agony, and every step pushed her deeper and deeper into the sand.

"Gertie, please listen to me!"

But Gertie would not listen to Denise. She was too busy serving her.

fight
of Love

Josh was the first to arrive outside the Machine's giant door. He was followed by Bud, Listro Q, and in the distance poor Aristophenix, who, as usual, was bringing up the rear and gasping for breath.

"Come on!" Josh called over his shoulder. "Hurry!"

At last Aristophenix arrived, wheezing out an apology.

"I'm so sorry that I'm tardy,
but we've run so very far.
and we poets are artists,
not olympic track stars."

Josh found himself cringing. No matter how many times he'd heard Aristophenix's awful poetry, he still hadn't got used to it. He reached for the door and with a mighty heave tried to pull it open.

It didn't budge, not an inch.

"Wrong, what's?" Listro Q asked.

"It must be locked," Josh said as he tried to pull again with exactly the same results. He turned to Bud. So did the others.

Suddenly Bud remembered. "Oh, the key key, of course." He reached into his coat pocket as he crossed to the keyhole. "Can't get inside without the key key."

But there was nothing in that pocket. So he tried the next . . . "Yes, sir, it always helps to have the key key."

Still nothing.

He tried his pants pockets. "The key key," he muttered.

Then, finally turning to the group, he asked, "By the way, have any of you seen it?"

They stared at him blankly.

"No, I guess not," he mumbled as he retried each pocket.

"Where last use it did you?" Listro Q asked.

"Why, right here at this door door," Bud insisted. "I unlocked this door door and put the key key someplace where I'd be sure to remember."

"Where was that?" Josh asked, already fearing the worst.

Bud looked at him and shrugged. "I don't remember."

The group groaned.

"Wait a minute!" he shouted. "Of course! I put it someplace safe safe where no one could find it."

"*Where?*" everyone shouted in unison.

"Why, right on the console beside Denny."

The group stared at him in disbelief. Once again he shrugged.

Then, without a word, all four turned and began banging on the door. "Denny! Denny, can you hear us? Denny! Denny, open up!"

But Denise did not answer. Apparently, she couldn't hear.

But the group did. And what they heard brought a look of surprise to all of their faces. It was an electronic sound, one they all recognized . . .

BEEP . . .

BOP . . .

BLEEP . . .

BURP . . .

Gertie, please!" Denise shouted. "You've got to listen to me!"

By now Gertie was dragging herself through the hole in the wall. The bone-crushing weight of the signs took their toll with every step, but she had to get away. Apparently Denise had started to make sense, and that was something Gertie could not allow.

But Denise wouldn't be shaken. She stayed right at her side. "Gertie, please, let *me* carry those . . . please."

Finally they passed through the hole and—

"Hey, Gertie, who's your friend?" Denise looked ahead to see Gus. He was standing right on the edge of their world—teetering back and forth like a tightrope walker in the circus. And beyond him? Beyond him was an awful black void of nothingness—a void that roared and screamed as it smashed into the liquid light—a void as dark and terrifying as the one Denise had experienced on her first trip to Fayrah.

"Gus!" Denise cried, "Get away from there!"

But Gus barely heard. The roar was too loud. Instead, he gave a grin, leaped high into the air, and made a perfect 360-degree spin— well, almost. His right foot slipped and he started to lose his balance.

"Nooo!" Denise screamed as she started for him.

But at the last second Gus caught himself and turned to her, laughing. "Listen, I don't know who you are, but you're gonna have to loosen up a little. Besides, fallin' over the edge is the best part. Come on over here and give it a try."

Denise shook her head and shouted over the roar, "Gus, you've got to listen to me! You're going to—"

But Gus wasn't listening. If she wasn't interested in his little hobby, he'd find somebody who was. "Hey, Gertie!" he called. "You oughta try this."

Gertie just stood, panting—slowly sinking under her heavy burden. "No, thanks," she groaned. "I've got these signs to carry."

"Signs? What for?"

"They're from Denny—to make us happy. She wants us to carry them!"

"No, that's not true!" Denise shouted.

"Happy?" Gus scoffed.

"Yeah!" Gertie shouted. "Carrying them makes you happy!"

"Right," he laughed. "Looks like you're havin' a terrific time!"

"They're not so bad, once you get used to them." She adjusted the weight and grimaced slightly. "Want to try one?"

"Forget it!" he yelled back. "If you're looking for good times, this is the ticket!"

Gertie gave a doubtful look past him and into the roaring void.

"Don't worry about that," he shouted. "It ain't as scary as it looks."

"I don't know," Gertie answered nervously.

"What's the matter?" he teased. "Chicken?"

"Maybe."

"Come on," he laughed, doing a quick little 180-degree hop. "You won't know till you try. What do you say?"

"Don't listen to him!" Denise shouted. "He doesn't know what he's doing!" There was no hiding her desperation. If Gertie joined Gus on the edge, she could lose them both. "I'm not there anymore!" she shouted. "I can't catch him! I can't catch you!"

"Come on, Gertie!" he called, giving a little hop and a spin on one foot. "Give it a try, it's a real hoot!"

Almost against her will, Gertie was starting to listen.

"—and you can bring those signs," he continued. "I mean, if you really think you have to."

"I can?"

"Gertie . . . no!" Denise cried. "Gus, please!"

"Sure," Gus answered as he leaped into the air, landing on all four hands. He did a little jig before hopping back to his feet. "Come on! You gotta try it!"

Gertie readjusted her load. "You're really sure it's safe?"

"Hey, I'm still here, ain't I?"

"Gertie, no!"

Gertie threw Denise a quick glance, then looked back at Gus.

Denise knew exactly what she was thinking. It had been so long since the two of them had played together. Gus had always been fun and he'd never done anything to hurt her. Why would he start now? Besides, she'd worked plenty hard serving Denise by carrying the signs, so she was entitled to a little fun.

"All right!" Gertie finally shouted. "But just for a bit!" She staggered toward him.

"*No!*" Denise screamed. She raced forward and leaped the few feet separating them. She grabbed Gertie and tackled her hard to the ground. The signs fell to the sand as the two rolled back and forth, all four feet kicking, all eight arms flying.

"Let go! Where are my signs!" Gertie screamed. "Let go of me!"

"Listen to me, Gertie, listen to me!"

As they rolled and tumbled in the sand, Gus looked on laughing.

"Gertie, please—"

"I want my signs!"

"Gertie—"

At last Gertie managed to grab the closest sign. As she pulled it to herself, Denise tried to break her grip. "Gertie . . ."

"My sign . . ."

"Gertie, let me have it . . ."

Finally, rolling onto her back, Gertie tucked her legs into her chest and kicked out. Her feet landed squarely in Denise's stomach, throwing her backward with an *ooaaaf!*

But Denise was determined. Catching her breath and crawling onto her hands and knees, she gasped, "Gertie . . . please!"

Gertie was already reaching for the other sign.

Denise staggered to her feet and lunged again.

But this time Gertie had a weapon. Raising the sign high over her shoulder, she leaned back like a batter waiting to hit a ball.

Denise saw what was about to happen and tried to stop. But the momentum in the liquid light kept her moving forward until suddenly, *swooosh*, Gertie took a swing. The steel sliced through the liquid. Its sharp corner caught Denise hard, ripping through her clothing, cutting into her side.

At first all Denise noticed was the look of shock on Gertie's face. She glanced down and saw blood clouding the liquid around them. Next she saw the gash in her side—deep and ugly. Finally she felt the pain. Sharp, searing, relentless. She slowly raised her eyes from the bleeding wound and looked back at Gertie.

No one said a word. Everything was silent as the liquid light grew more and more cloudy.

Denise tried to breathe, but each breath sent the burning, jagged pain deeper into her body. Slowly the edges around her vision started to grow white and blur. Her legs turned weak and rubbery, but only for a second. Then, they gave out altogether and she crumpled to the ground.

"Ha!" Gus laughed. "Serves her right!"

Gertie continued to stare, horrified at what she had done—unsure what she should do . . . as the liquid light grew darker and darker . . .

CHAPTER TWELVE

REUNION

Aristophenix! Listro Q!"

The group spun around to see Josh's little brother, Nathan. He had just popped in with his stuffed English bulldog, Mr. Hornsberry. Oh, and they had one other companion—Samson, the half dragonfly, half ladybug who had become such good friends with Denise on their last journey together.

"Nathan!" Josh cried. "What are you doing here?"

"Samson says Denny's in some sort of trouble."

"But how'd you get here?"

Nathan held up another Cross-Dimensionalizer exactly like Listro Q's. "It's Samson's. He let me try it out. How'd I do?"

"Good, pretty," Listro Q answered half-grudgingly. Then under his breath he added, "Maybe lessons give me should he."

Samson interrupted with a high squeal question.

Aristophenix answered,

> "DENNY'S IN THERE,
> DYING FOR LOVE.
> BUT WE'RE ALL OUT HERE,
> 'CAUSE THE DOOR WE CAN'T BUDGE."

Again Samson chattered.

Bud answered, "The fault is mine. I left the key key inside."

For a moment the group was unsure what to do. That is until Mr. Hornsberry cleared his throat and spoke up. "Although no one is seeking my advice, would it not be advantageous for us to utilize all of our man and dog power?"

"So how?" Listro Q asked.

"My good man," Mr. Hornsberry answered in his usual why-am-I-surrounded-by-morons tone of voice. "All one need do is remove the door from its hinges."

As much as everybody hated to admit it, Mr. Hornsberry had a point. Now there was just the detail of how to do it. It was so tall and huge. Unfortunately everyone had their own opinion and no one was afraid to voice it. Suddenly the air was full of a hundred "if you ask me's . . . ," "we should try's . . . ," and the ever popular, "I'm telling you my way is better."

On and on they argued as if each was an expert door remover. Of course none of them were, so nothing happened—except more arguing—until, finally, ever so slowly, the door began to swing open by itself.

"What on earth," someone gasped.

"How do you suppose?" another asked.

Then they saw the reason: While everybody was voicing their opinion, Samson simply flew in through the keyhole, unlatched the door from the inside, and with considerable effort pushed it open.

"All right, Sammy!" everyone cheered as they poured into the laboratory. But the celebration was short-lived.

"Denny!" Josh shouted. "Denny, where are you?"

The others joined in, calling her name. "Denny? Denny!"

But there was no answer. She was nowhere to be found.

Josh turned to Bud. "What's going on?" he asked.

"I don't know know," Bud said as they approached the deserted platform of sand and light. "Denny!" he called. "Denny!"

Still no answer. "You must know something!" Josh demanded.

Bud gave no reply. Instead, he turned to the platform and ordered, "Machine!"

The Machine hummed louder.

"Where is Denny?"

With a faint crackle the monitor above the platform flickered. Everyone gasped as the image of Denise appeared—not because of her four arms or because she was lying unconscious in the liquid light. They gasped because of the bleeding wound in her side.

"Denny!" Josh called. *"Denise!"*

"She can't hear you you," Bud said.

"Listen to me!" Josh turned his anger on Bud. "You got her into this mess, now you get her out!"

"I . . . can't!" Bud stammered. "This was her decision, this was her—"

Josh grabbed the little man by his lab coat and pulled him directly into his face. "I don't care whose decision it was!" he shouted. "Do what you have to do to save her!"

"But . . . but—"

"Now!"

"The only way to save her is to to reduce someone to her size size and rescue her."

"Do it!" Josh shouted.

"But you don't understand how dangerous it is. It could—"

"Then do it to me!"

"But—"

"Do it to me, *now!*" Joshua glared at him, making it clear that he didn't have a choice.

Finally Bud nodded. "Machine Machine," he called.

The Machine crackled in response.

"Take Joshua here and—"

UNTIL ALL IS ACCOMPLISHED
DO NOT INTERFERE.

The voice stunned Josh. But it wasn't a voice. It was a thought that vibrated inside his head. He spun around to the rest of the group. By their expressions it was obvious it had vibrated in all of their heads.

"What . . . who was that?" he whispered.

At first, no one answered. Then, with a nervous swallow, Bud spoke, "Imager."

Everyone remained silent. Even Mr. Hornsberry. It was the strongest, most commanding voice Josh had ever heard. And yet, at the same time, it was the gentlest and most soothing.

Then he heard another. "Please . . ."

It was Denise!

His eyes shot up to the monitor. She had regained consciousness and was dragging her bleeding body toward two other creatures with multiple arms. One stood on the very edge of the platform; the other was being crushed by two large rectangular plates of steel on its back.

"Gertie," Denise gasped. "Gus . . ."

But the creatures did not answer.

Instead, the bigger one turned to the smaller one. "Hit her!" he shouted. "Hit her again!"

The smaller one hesitated.

Denise continued to approach. "Gertie . . ."

"Hit her!" the bigger one cried. "You have to stop her! She won't quit unless you stop her!"

Again the smaller one hesitated.

"Hit her! Hit her! Hit her!"

Reluctantly, the smaller one raised the steel plates high overhead and brought them down hard onto Denise's back.

Everyone in the lab cried out as the blow smashed her to the ground.

And yet, Denise wouldn't stop. She slowly rose to her hands and knees and continued toward them. "Please . . . ," she groaned.

Once again the smaller creature raised the plates and once again she slammed them hard into Denise's back.

Josh could take no more. That was his friend up there on the screen and, Imager or not, he wasn't going to stand and watch her beaten to death. He shouted at the thought or the voice or whatever it was inside his head. "What type of logic is this?"

There was no response, only silence—and a few nervous coughs among the group.

"Answer me!"

More silence.

"You claim to be so logical . . . so loving, then answer me! Answer me!"

Finally the voice spoke. But it wasn't angry. It was tender and understanding. Yet it was also firm—very firm.

UNTIL ALL IS ACCOMPLISHED
DO NOT INTERFERE.

"But she's dying!" Josh shouted. "She's killing herself! Where's the logic in that? Answer me! *Answer me!*"

The response rang loud and clear . . . and very, very gentle:

UNTIL ALL IS ACCOMPLISHED
DO NOT INTERFERE.

"Until *what* is accomplished? How will we know? What can we do?"

There was no answer.

Josh repeated, *"How will we know?"*

But the voice did not answer. Apparently it had said all that it intended to say. Now there was only silence.

Josh sighed loudly and turned to the others. Everyone looked equally baffled and confused. Everyone but Samson.

The little fellow flew closer to the platform and seemed to be waiting. Denise had often told Josh how close she and the little bug had become. How, of all the creatures in Fayrah, their personalities seemed the most similar. And, although the little guy said nothing, Josh could tell he was thinking.

But for now there was nothing they could do. Imager had spoken . . . three times he had spoken. Now they could only watch and obey . . .

As Gertie continued clutching the signs, their weight continued to force her deeper and deeper into the sand. But that was nothing compared to Denise's pain. Again and again Gertie had to strike her, and again and again Denise rose and continued toward them. Nothing would stop her. Not the gaping wound in her side that continued darkening the liquid, and not the brutal beating of the signs. Granted, each time Denise rose, she rose a little slower, but she rose, nonetheless. She had to in order to save her friends.

Soon she had backed them up to the edge of the platform, just inches from the roaring black emptiness. "Please . . . ," she gasped hoarsely. "Please . . ."

"What do you want?" Gertie screamed. "What do you want from us!"

"I want you to live . . ."

"You're crazy!" Gus shouted. "We *are* living!"

Denise shook her head and with great effort reached for the signs. "Please . . ."

"You're holding back!" Gus shouted at Gertie over the roaring void. "Stop holding back and hit her with everything you got! Make it hurt so much that she'll never bother us again!"

Denise looked up. She could see Gertie didn't like this, not one bit. The poor little thing was already crying over the pain she'd inflicted. Still, the look in her eyes said that she believed something had to be done.

"Go ahead," Gus demanded. "Everything you got!"

Gertie took a trembling breath.

"Don't hold back!"

Another breath.

"If you don't, she'll never give us rest. Go ahead! *Go ahead!*"

Finally, Gertie lifted the signs high over her head. She leaned back, closed her eyes, and—

"*No!*" Another voice shouted. Denise recognized it instantly.

"Who are you?" Gus shouted.

"She's our friend," Gertie answered. "The one who taught us about free will."

"Don't listen to her," Denise croaked, reaching up and clinging to Gertie's sleeve. "She's the Illusionist . . . she'll kill—"

"Destroy her!" the Illusionist shrieked.

"What?" Gus asked, obviously surprised at the outburst.

The Illusionist cleared her throat and regained control. "It's only a suggestion—after all, I don't want to interfere with your free will. But if you ask me, hitting her is not enough. You must completely destroy her by throwing her off the edge."

"But she'll come back," Gus explained. "I always have."

The Illusionist grinned. "Trust me, she won't come back—not this time."

"But . . . why?" Gertie asked, obviously confused. "Why do we have to destroy her?"

"It's for her own good," the Illusionist cooed. "It's the kindest thing to do, dear heart. Otherwise she'll just keep coming at you and you'll just have to keep hurting her."

Moved with pity, Gertie looked down at Denise.

The Illusionist continued. "You've inflicted such pain upon her already. But no matter how much she bleeds, no matter how often you strike her, she does not give up."

Gertie nodded sadly.

"It deeply grieves me"—the Illusionist pretended to have a catch in her throat—"but the only way you can stop her, the only way you can put her out of her misery, is to completely destroy her."

Then, turning to Gus, the Illusionist used an entirely different approach. "The wretched thing has no pride," she hissed. "If you don't destroy her, she'll always create problems. Just look at the way her blood is darkening your perfect ocean, just listen to the way she's nagging and begging. She'll never give you rest."

Denise watched Gus, hoping he'd see the lie.

"Do it!" the Illusionist cried. Then, turning to Gertie, she resumed her more gentle approach. "You can keep those perfect signs forever and ever." Then, turning back to Gus, she added with a sneer, "And you can jump off that edge anytime you want. No one will stop you. No one will stop either of you!"

"No one?" they asked in unison.

"Certainly not me." The Illusionist grinned. "I wouldn't dream of stopping you!"

The two glanced at each other, then down at Denise.

She no longer had the strength to speak. She could only shake her head, her eyes pleading with them.

The Illusionist stifled a yawn. "When you stop to think about it, you really have no other choice."

Gus was the first to agree. He began nodding his head and turned to Gertie. "Grab her arms," he ordered.

"There's no other way?" Gertie asked, her little voice filled with sorrow.

"You heard her, didn't you?"

Gertie nodded. Slowly she stooped down to Denise. "I'm sorry," she gently whispered, "but this really is for your best."

Denise shook her head violently, but Gertie would not listen. Instead, holding her signs high above with one pair of hands, Gertie tenderly took Denise's face with her other pair. "Maybe . . . maybe if you'd stop trying to help us—maybe, if you'd just let us have our way instead of always—"

Denise shook her head. She opened her mouth to explain, but could not speak.

Slowly, sadly Gertie rose to her feet. "I'm sorry," she repeated, tears streaming down her cheeks. "I'm so sorry." Then, taking Denise's arms with her two free hands, she gently raised her off the ground.

Denise clenched her eyes shut. The pain was too great. But it was not the pain of her wounds, or even the thought of being destroyed. It was the pain of a breaking heart.

Gus picked up her feet. Now she was suspended between the two of them.

"On the count of three," Gus ordered.

Gertie nodded.

"One." They swung her out over the edge and back.

"Two." They swung her further out and back.

"Three . . ."

But at the last second, using what little strength she had, Denise lunged for the signs in Gertie's other hands. She latched onto them as she swung out the third and final time. And, as she did, the momentum ripped them from Gertie's grasp.

Before they could catch her, Denise slipped from their hands and started to fall.

"My signs!" Gertie cried as Denise and the signs tumbled into the roaring darkness. "My beautiful signs!"

to the
RESCUE

The group inside the Machine cried out as Denise fell.

Everyone but Samson.

While the others had been staring at the monitor over their heads, Samson had hovered near the platform carefully searching the liquid light. He had spotted Gus and Gertie's location by the slight ripples near the edge. And, as soon as Denise began to fall, he made his move.

"Samson!" Nathan shouted. "What are you—"

But there was no time to explain. Imager had said, "Until all is accomplished." Well, as far as Samson could tell *all* had been accomplished. Now the little guy couldn't waste a second.

He swooped toward the platform's edge. And just as Denise had done so many times with Gus, Samson managed to spot the tiny pinpoint glimmer of her reflection. He raced toward it for all he was worth.

Faster and faster she fell.

Swifter and swifter he flew. He saw the approaching floor, but it didn't matter. He moved into position. Quickly he swooped under her. For the briefest instant he felt her hit his back. But they were traveling too fast. Although she landed, her speed forced her to tumble across him until she shot off the other side . . . and continued to fall.

Samson spun around and dove after her again.

But the floor was much closer. Much, much closer.

Common sense told him to pull out of the dive before it was too late. If he didn't, they'd both smash into the floor. *It's better to lose one life than two.* That's what his mind said. But Samson's heart was bigger than his mind.

He folded back his wings and dove even faster.

The floor raced toward him.

Now he was even with Denise. In just another second he would be able to swoop underneath and let her land on his back again. Unfortunately, they didn't have another second.

In desperation, Samson unfolded his right wing and thrust it into the roaring wind toward Denise. The air screamed and tugged at the wing, nearly ripping it out of its socket. But Samson endured the pain and continued to stretch his wing until it was finally beneath her.

Then he felt it—Denise's tiny presence landing on him. In a flash, he reversed course, using only one wing, buzzing twice as hard, struggling to navigate, until he was finally able to pull up. It was close. So close that he actually felt the lab's floor brush his hind legs as he zoomed away. But he made it. As he rose, he lifted his right wing until Denise rolled down it and onto his back. Now, he could use both wings. And now, at last, she was safe.

For Denise it had been quite a landing. She'd had the breath knocked out of her, but she didn't complain. She was just grateful to have breath to be knocked out! She was so tiny that she had no idea what she'd landed upon. As far as she knew it was some sort of elevator that was quickly shooting upward. Still, who had ever heard of an elevator with a gauzy, semitransparent floor ... and a huge flickering taillight in the back?

But Denise had little time to wonder, for suddenly the platform came back into view. And there, standing on its edge, were Gus and Gertie—both staring out at her in amazement. On the wall behind them the Illusionist was jumping up and down screaming, "Unfair! Unfair! Unfair!"

For a moment the "elevator" slowed and drew nearer to the edge. Gus and Gertie came so close that Denise could have reached out and touched them ... if she'd had the strength.

"Unfair!" the Illusionist continued to scream. "Unfair! Unfair!" But no one paid attention.

"I'll be back," Denise called. She was so weak her voice was only a whisper—barely audible over the roaring void. Still, somehow they seemed to understand. Gertie was the first to nod. Then slowly, almost reluctantly, Gus joined in. And then . . . was it just her imagination, or had the slightest trace of a smile started to cross their faces?

The elevator began to rise up and away. Faster and faster it rose. Soon Gus and Gertie shrank to tiny dots, and then to nothing at all.

But in her mind, Denise still saw them. She suspected she would always see them. "I'll be back," she whispered again. "I promise, I'll be back . . ."

F or the next several days Denise did little but eat and sleep. Once the Machine had transformed her to normal size, the group had whisked her out of the lab and off to Samson's home in Fayrah—well, at least to a huge tent they had erected beside his home. (Humans are a bit large for insect homes—especially newlywed insects just starting out.) Here she would rest until she was strong enough to return to the Upside-Down Kingdom. According to the doctor, her mind and body had been through a great trauma, and they needed time to heal.

"But what about Mom? What about Josh's grandpa?" Denise protested. "They'll be worried sick."

"Worry, don't you," Listro Q assured her.

Aristophenix agreed. "Remember,

"*we'Re RUNNING IN time,*
muCH fasteR tHaN you ReckoN.
foR us, wHat's a week,
to tHem's but a seCoND."

"Right is he," Listro Q agreed. "Teapot remember in Grandpa's shop that dropped you?"

"The one that floated?"

Listro Q nodded. "Floating, still is it."

Denise looked at him in wonder. But before she could say anything, Violet, Samson's new bride, buzzed in and began chattering a mile a second.

"What's she saying?" Denise asked.

Aristophenix gave a hasty explanation.

> *"SHE'S SAYING YER HER GUEST,*
> *AND THAT THERE ISN'T A DOUBT,*
> *YOU'LL BE GETTING SOME REST,*
> *'CAUSE ... WELL ... SHE'S THROWING US OUT!"*

Denise couldn't hold back a giggle as she watched Violet buzz and dive-bomb the guests standing inside her tent.

"All right, we're going, we're going!" they shouted, raising their arms and stumbling toward the exit. "Come on, Vi, give us a break. Samson, will you call her off!"

But Samson didn't call her off. And Violet didn't stop until every one of them was out of the tent.

"That's quite a wife you have," Denise said, grinning over at Samson.

Samson chattered back a proud reply but was cut short as he, too, was shooed out of the tent.

Six more days passed before the doctor finally gave Denise permission to travel. And once word spread that they were going, Samson's yard was filled with hundreds of well-wishers and bon-voyagers. Some of them had never even met Denise, but they'd all heard of her deeds.

"Now you take care of this side," the doctor warned as he changed the dressing and bandages on her wound for the last time. "It'll be a while before it's completely healed."

Denise nodded.

"And I'm afraid you'll always have a scar," he added. "Quite a large one."

Denise looked down at the red, jagged line that ran from the middle of her ribs all the way to her hip. "That's okay," she said quietly. "It'll help me remember." Then, before she knew it, tears filled her eyes and began to fall ... just as they had so many times throughout the week.

"Thinking about Gus and Gertie again?" Josh asked quietly.

She gave a quick nod and tried to brush the tears away. "And Imager too," she mumbled. Looking up she spotted Aristophenix and Listro Q standing nearby. She continued softly, "He really does care for us, doesn't he?"

They nodded in silence.

"I mean, if he only feels a fraction of what I felt for Gus and Gertie . . ." Her voice trailed off.

"More," Listro Q gently added, "more many times . . . for us each does he."

Denise could only shake her head in amazement. "How can he stand it?" she whispered hoarsely. "The joy . . . the pain . . ." Barely aware, she reached up and touched the scar in her side, remembering. "How can he stand it?"

For a long moment, everyone stood in silence. Until, suddenly—

"Step back, please . . . coming through, yes, we are. Stand back!" The silence was shattered by the Weaver's entrance. Following behind him were two of his assistants, each carrying an easel and small tapestry. Behind them several of the folks who had been patiently waiting in the yard squeezed in. Before Denise knew it, her tent was packed so tightly that no amount of buzzing and dive-bombing by Violet could unpack it.

"Oh, there you are," the Weaver shouted to Denise above the noise. "Getting better are we?"

She nodded.

"Good!" he said. Then, turning back to his assistants he called, "Just set those up anywhere, boys."

"What are you doing here?" Denise asked.

"Rumor has it you're concerned about Gus and Gertie, yes, you are. Well, no need to be. I brought their tapestries along to show you before you go."

"Gus and Gertie have tapestries?" Denise asked in astonishment.

"Of course! You don't think I'd let something like that slip by, do you?"

"Well, no, I guess . . ."

The assistants had placed the veiled tapestries up on their easels. The Weaver gave a nod and, with a dramatic flair, they removed the covers.

The crowd gasped, then broke into applause.

The Weaver grinned and nodded politely. Then, turning to Denise, he asked, "So what do you think?"

Denise could only stare. They were more beautiful than she could have imagined. Each thread shimmered and danced with light—each design, down to the tiniest detail, perfectly captured their personalities. In fact, the patterns were so perfect that as she stared she could practically see and hear Gus and Gertie again. Unfortunately this only brought on another grimace of pain and more tears.

"Come now, they're not that ugly," the Weaver protested.

Denise shook her head. "No, they were beautiful . . . wonderful."

"What do you mean *were*? As you can see by their length both Gus and Gertie will be living for many more epochs."

"They're still alive?" Denise cried.

"Well, yes, of course," the Weaver said. "As are their children and their children's children and their—"

"They have children too!"

Again the Weaver tried to overlook her interruption. "Of course, thousands of them. And according to this thread here—"

"They have thousands of children!"

"If you keep interrupting," the Weaver said evenly, "we won't get through this before you leave."

Denise nodded and did her best to remain silent, though her mind reeled with excitement. She'd just naturally thought that Gus had talked Gertie into jumping off the edge with him. But the fact that they were still alive and that they actually had children, well, the possibility had Denise so excited that she could barely sit still.

"Now where was I?" the Weaver asked. "Oh, yes. This thread here"—he pointed to the first tapestry—"indicates Gus's continual fascination with the edge. But, instead of leaping off, he has taken Gertie's advice and has devoted his life to studying it."

"Studying it?" Denise asked.

"Yes, *scientific evaluation* I believe they call it."

"Gus has become a scientist?"

"Yes, well, I'm afraid Bud has taken over leadership while you were away, and has had some impact upon—"

"Oh, no," Josh groaned. "Bud is their leader?"

Denise giggled. "I hope he doesn't drop anything on them."

Others in the tent also chuckled. Apparently Bud's reputation for grace was known far and wide.

The Weaver resumed. "And just as Gus has continued his scientific studies, Gertie has been writing and teaching her children poetry."

Denise kept listening, hanging on to every word. The news was so good. So very, very good.

"And do you see this scarlet thread here?" the Weaver asked, turning to the group, while pointing to a deep red thread. "This is most intriguing. See how it runs through the center of both patterns, seeming to hold them together?"

Everyone in the tent nodded.

He turned directly to Denise. "That thread is you, my girl, yes, it is. *You* are what they speak of in science class. *You* are what they write about in their poetry."

Suddenly Denise broke into laughter . . . and more tears.

"Good gracious, *now* what is it?" the Weaver demanded.

"I'm sorry," Denise said sheepishly while drying her eyes. "It's just . . . well, the thing is . . ." She tried to explain but couldn't. Everything was just too good. Too perfect. And that meant laughter . . . and more tears.

But it wasn't only Denise. It seemed everyone in the tent had suddenly come down with a good case of smiles and sniffles . . . everyone but Mr. Hornsberry. Stuffed dogs know better than to cry—they mildew.

"I say there," the animal said, clearing his throat in his usual snooty manner. "What about that dreadful Illusionist creature? Where is she in their tapestries?"

"Right here," the Weaver said, pointing to a dark, ominous thread. "As you can see, she makes an appearance from time to time, but her effect upon the overall work is minimal at best, yes, it is."

The Weaver pointed back at the scarlet thread. "But Denise's thread not only keeps appearing in their tapestries, but in their children's, and in their children's children. They will remember her life throughout their existence ... passing her exploits down from one generation to the next. In fact, until the end of time, they will insist she is the one responsible for the subtle rose hue that colors their ocean. They will say this is to remind them of her love as well as her promise to return. A promise"—he turned to Denise—"that as their creator, you are bound to keep."

Denise nodded eagerly. There would be no problem keeping that promise. In fact, she wouldn't mind keeping it right now. But that was out of the question. For now, at least, she would have to return home.

"That's all I have to say," the Weaver concluded. "You better get a move on, yes, you better. If I remember your patterns correctly, you'll be leaving here"—he glanced at his watch—"in less than forty-eight seconds."

The tent exploded into action. Everyone began hugging, shouting thank-yous, saying goodbyes, and making the usual promises to stay in touch.

It was during this confusion that Josh pulled the Weaver aside. "Listen," he said. "I just want to thank you. I mean, I know I was a bit of a pain, not believing and everything."

"Most of you are," the Weaver chuckled. "But we're getting used to it."

Josh smiled and continued. "If you could also tell Bud thanks for me—I mean, I didn't get to say much when we rushed Denny out of there and everything. But he really did help me ... a lot."

"You'll get a chance to thank him yourself," the Weaver answered. "Yes, you will."

"What?" Josh asked. "When?"

The Weaver lowered his voice and glanced about the room to make sure he wasn't overheard. "I shouldn't say anything, but in several months he will be cross-dimensionalizing over to your world."

"That's great!" Nathan exclaimed.

The Weaver scowled slightly. "Perhaps. But the reason will be most urgent."

"But everything will be okay?" Josh asked. "I mean, everything will be all right?"

The Weaver took a deep breath. For a moment it looked like he would answer, then suddenly he changed his mind. "I've said too much already."

"Oh, come on!" Josh pleaded.

"Josh, go let's!" Listro Q called. He had grouped all those heading back to the Upside-Down Kingdom at the far end of the tent.

But Josh paid little attention. He was still searching the Weaver's face. "You've got to tell me *something.*"

"Just . . . be careful. It will be a most critical time, yes it will."

"But we'll be all right," Josh insisted. "Won't we?"

"Go let's. Come on, Josh . . ."

The group started pulling him away, leading him toward Listro Q. With a few more tugs and jostles, they finally placed him alongside Denise, Nathan, Mr. Hornsberry, Aristophenix, and Listro Q. Josh searched the crowd for the Weaver, but he had already disappeared.

"Alrightie!" Aristophenix shouted.

> *"Let's move, let's go,*
> *Let's have no more stops.*
> *It's straight from fayrah,*
> *to grandpa's secondhand shop."*

"Good-bye," everyone shouted. "See you later . . . bye-bye . . ."

Denise caught Violet's and Samson's eyes. It was too noisy to be heard, so she could only mouth the words. "Thank you," she said.

Both insects understood and flickered their red taillights in response.

Listro reached for his Cross-Dimensionalizer and prepared to punch in the coordinates.

"Need any help with that?" Nathan teased.

"Manage think can I," Listro Q grinned back. Then he pushed the four buttons.

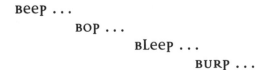

beep . . .

bop . . .

bleep . . .

burp . . .

Suddenly the group was crossing through the Center with all of its glory and splendor. And, although there was plenty more to see, they knew that it would have to wait for another time. They would return again. And when they did they knew they would not be disappointed. Unfortunately, at that moment, they should have also known something else. Listro Q's aim—

CRASH,

BANG,

CLATTER,

TINKLE-TINKLE-TINKLE . . .

—had not improved.

This time he only missed their landing coordinates by a few feet. But inside Grandpa O'Brien's cluttered shop a few feet was as good as a mile.

"Listro Q . . . ," Aristophenix cried.

"Cool, is it," came the reply.

And so, with the appropriate groans and complaints, everyone climbed out of the front window's display of pots and pans. For some it was quite a struggle. "It's stuck to my rear," Aristophenix cried. "Will someone please pull this thing off my rear?" But no one fussed too much. After all, practice makes perfect. And over the course of time Listro Q would have many more opportunities to get his coordinates right for traveling into that shop.

Many, many more . . .

the WHIRLWIND

CHAPTER ONE

WORRIES

D ON'T BE a-FRETTIN',
YOU'RE MAKIN' THIS fearsome.
IT'S PROBABLY GOOD NEWS,
AND HE WANTS US TO HEAR SOME."

Aristophenix's poetry was just as bad as ever. But Listro Q and Samson barely noticed their friend's awful rhymes. Instead, they were busy wondering why the Weaver had summoned them down to the Halls of Tapestry . . . and why he had called in the middle of the night.

"Doubt it, do I," Listro Q said, shaking his head. "At night this time of, Weaver calls us *not* for good news."

Samson, the half dragonfly, half ladybug, agreed in his usual high-pitched chatter.

Aristophenix took a deep breath and sighed. In his heart, the roly-poly creature also knew. Whatever information the Weaver had to share would not be good.

Their footsteps echoed as they entered another huge hall. In many ways each hall was like a giant museum. But instead of boring paintings or half-naked statues, these halls held tapestries. Tapestries that shimmered and sparkled with threads of light. Brilliant, breathtaking light. Light that came from the Center. Light that came from Imager.

Creatures from every dimension visited here to admire Imager's handiwork. Because each of these tapestries, each of these master-pieces, was actually an individual's life. Every joy, every heartache, every success, and every failure of a person's existence could be found in his or her own tapestry of glowing threads. Threads that were woven with infinite care to Imager's precise designs by none other than . . . the Weaver.

The three Fayrahnians rounded the corner and spotted the old man at the far end of the hall. He was peering into a magnifying glass, carefully studying one of three tapestries that hung before him.

"It's good of you to come, yes, it is," he called without looking up.

The trio said nothing as they approached. They were too busy staring at the tapestries before him, too busy trying to recognize them.

"Do you know them?" the Weaver asked, still not looking up.

Aristophenix took a guess.

> "tHey're our tHree Little buddies,
> from tHe upside-down kingdom.
> wHo are startin' to taste,
> and see imager's dominion."

The Weaver cringed. He'd obviously forgotten about Aristo-phenix's poetry. "Your friends will be tasting and seeing a lot more of Imager than you think, yes, they will," he said. Lowering his magni-fying glass, he pointed to a dazzling pattern of light in each of the three tapestries, a pattern so brilliant that it hurt the eyes to see. "According to these threads, all three children will have an opportu-nity to be re-Breathed."

Aristophenix, Listro Q, and Samson exchanged looks. This was wonderful news. To be re-Breathed by Imager was an Upside Downer's greatest honor.

But the Weaver wasn't finished. "Unfortunately, the evil Bobok and the Illusionist also know the special weave of these tapestries. And they'll do anything in their power to destroy the children before they step into the Whirlwind, before they're re-Breathed."

"Then help them must we," Listro Q said as he reached into a pocket for his trusty Cross-Dimensionalizer. "At once we'll there go and—"

"No." The Weaver cut him off. "To be re-Breathed is something the children must choose on their own, yes, it is. It must be of their own free will."

"But," Aristophenix protested, "if Bobok and the Illusionist are gonna—"

"Their plan is most evil. If you interfere before the correct time, you will not only destroy the children, you will destroy yourselves."

The statement surprised everyone. Finally Listro Q spoke, "But friends of ours, are they. Help should we."

"That is why I summoned you here," the Weaver explained. "You may watch their tapestries, you may even examine their threads. But until I give permission, you must not, you *will* not, interfere."

All three started to protest until the old man raised his hands. It was a simple gesture, but one that commanded instant respect. After all, he was the Weaver.

"I know this will be painful for you, yes, I do." His voice grew softer. "But they have much to learn. You must trust me on this . . . you must trust Imager. If you interfere before their time, you will destroy everything."

The three Fayrahnians looked at one another. What could they say? When he was right, he was right. And one thing about the Weaver . . . he was *always* right.

Back home, back in the Upside-Down Kingdom, Nathan and Denise arrived at Grandpa's Secondhand Shop. They pushed open the door, and the little bell gave a jingle as they stepped inside.

"And a good afternoon to the both of you." Grandpa smiled as they entered.

"Hey, Grandpa," Nathan said.

"Hi," Denise chirped.

"Listen, would you be doin' me a favor?" the old man asked. "Would you be lookin' after the shop a few minutes while I'm away?"

"Sure," Nathan said. "Where you headed?"

"I've got to be makin' a delivery over at the Burton's. You sure you won't be mindin'?"

"No problem."

The old man grinned and tousled the boy's red hair as he headed for the door. Nathan grinned back.

So did Denise. Nine months ago it would have been like pulling teeth to get Nathan to do anything for anybody. But that was nine months ago . . . before the Bloodstone, before their trips to Fayrah and its accompanying kingdoms. Now, things were changing—not all at once, but a little bit, day by day.

Grandpa had barely left before Joshua, Nathan's older brother, stormed into the shop. Josh was everybody's friend . . . super smart, super athletic, and most of all, super popular. He worked hard at these things (especially the popularity part), and that's what bugged Denise the most. Because, although they'd been friends since childhood, he was everything she was not. Instead of super smart, super athletic, or super popular, she was . . . well, she was just Denise Wolff, the all-school oddball.

"Stupid," Josh grumbled as he dumped his books onto the counter. He ripped the campaign button off his shirt and flung it across the store. "It's just not fair!"

Denise and Nathan traded looks. Anger and temper tantrums were *their* specialties, not Josh's. As the oldest of the three, he was always the wisest, the more "mature." So what was *he* doing acting like *them*?

"Why should I lose that stupid election?" he demanded of no one in particular. "Just because I'm honest? It's not fair!"

Denise knew she shouldn't try to reason with him, not when he was like this. Unfortunately, she never liked to let a good argument slip away. "Maybe if you'd have promised good times and no homework like that other guy, maybe *you'd* have won."

"But he was lying!" Josh said. "He can't deliver those promises!"

"He can't?" It was Denise's turn to feel depressed. She had just started middle school and there seemed to be a lot more homework.

Josh shook his head. "As student body president, do you think he can really replace algebra with video games?"

"I was just hoping he'd drop science," she mumbled.

Josh gave her a look. Science was his favorite subject, and she knew it.

Denise shrugged and hopped onto the stool behind the counter.

"Life's not fair," he repeated. "You guys know how hard I campaigned—how hard we all campaigned."

Denise did know. The past few weeks she'd done all she could do to help him win—she made posters, passed out campaign buttons, and threatened to beat up kids who wouldn't wear those campaign buttons. (Denise had a little problem with her temper.) But there was that other thing bothering her, and she figured now was as good a time as any to bring it up. "If you ask me," she sighed, "you're way too competitive and concerned with popularity, anyways."

Josh turned on her. "There's nothing wrong with trying to be the best."

"Sure, but you make it like a lifetime career."

"What am I supposed to do—not care what *anybody* thinks . . . like other losers I know?"

Denise turned to him, her mouth dropping open. Being mean wasn't like Josh at all.

Seeing her look, he immediately softened. "Hey, I wasn't talking about you."

She glanced away. That was another reason they were such good friends. Because even when he was a pain, like now, he was always kind to her. She gave another shrug. "Maybe I *am* a loser. And maybe life isn't fair." Then turning back to him she added, "But you . . . you're *way* too wrapped up in having to win."

Josh started to answer but couldn't. She had him and he knew it.

"I don't know about any of that," Nathan said as he limped back from the pop machine. "But you're right about one thing . . . Life isn't fair." He tossed them both a can of soda.

Denise caught hers and nodded. If anyone knew about life being unfair it was Nathan. Ever since she could remember he'd had that limp, that pain in his hip that no operation could cure. Sure, during their last visit to Fayrah the Weaver had promised that it would make him a better person, but that didn't exactly make things for him any easier . . . or fair.

She opened her can and immediately slurped up the foam that bubbled over the top.

"He's right, you know," Josh said, popping open his own can. "I mean, with everything we've learned about Imager, that's the one thing I still can't buy."

"What's that?" Denise asked, fighting back a belch. (She'd noticed her world-famous belches weren't quite as popular with Josh as they used to be).

He answered, "I mean, we all know about his love and stuff— what a good guy he is and everything, but . . . I don't know."

"Don't know what?" Denise persisted.

"It just seems that if Imager is so good, why doesn't he make life more fair?"

Denise looked on, waiting for more.

"If he's so just and everything, why does he let unfair things happen—instead of giving us what we really deserve?"

A brief silence settled over the group. It was true, Denise and the guys had learned lots about Imager from their past journeys. But it was also true that life really wasn't fair. Why? If Imager was in charge, why wasn't there more justice in the world? Why *didn't* people get what they deserved?

Denise coughed slightly and cleared her throat. "I suppose if we really want to find out . . . I mean, there is a way."

"You mean contacting Aristophenix," Nathan said.

"Think we're ready for another trip?" Josh asked.

Denise glanced out the window. "Not tonight. There won't be a full moon for a few more days."

Josh nodded. "Besides, the Bloodstone's at home in my room. I'm still running some tests on it."

"Maybe when you're done?" Denise suggested.

"Sounds good to me," Nathan said.

"Me, too," Josh agreed. "Should be in about a week . . ."

But it would be much sooner than that. For in the darkest threads of each of their tapestries, the faint sound of hoofbeats could be heard. Hoofbeats that grew louder by the second. Hoofbeats that would soon enter the Upside-Down Kingdom.

The truth of the matter is, the Illusionist had not enjoyed turning herself into a horse. She took even less pleasure in the evil Bobok riding atop her back. But what's the most sinister queen in twenty-three dimensions to do? Take a shortcut through the Center? Travel right through Imager's home? Of course not. She had her pride. Besides, there was the minor detail of being vaporized if she got too close to Imager's presence. Not a bad ending for the creature up there on her back, but an ending she'd prefer to avoid.

No, the best course was the one they had chosen. To take the long way around—to travel from dimension to dimension, slowly making their way toward their target—toward Imager's beloved Upside-Down Kingdom.

"Dear heart?" the Illusionist panted as she turned her head to speak to the ice-blue orb on her back. For three thousand epochs these two creatures had fought over the disputed border between their kingdoms—back when they had kingdoms—back before the Upside Downers had destroyed them. And for three thousand epochs the two had hated each other almost as much as they hated Imager.

Almost, but not quite.

"No talking, my lady," Bobok ordered. "Save your energy so we may travel faster. We haven't much time!"

The Illusionist bore down harder. Her legs and hoofs ached from the effort. It was obvious Bobok loved his position of power over her. But that was okay. The tables would soon turn. After all, she could transform herself into any being she wished, while Bobok would always remain Bobok. When they arrived at the Upside-Down Kingdom, he would have to wear the disguise she had prepared for him. And that would bring her pleasure. Immense pleasure.

Again she turned her head. "How much longer, dear heart?" she gasped. "You have the maps . . . how much longer before we arrive?"

"Soon," Bobok chortled, "very, very soon."

CHAPTER TWO

Deception

The Bunsen burner Josh borrowed from school had been roaring away for twenty minutes in his bedroom. And still, the Bloodstone did not melt. Stranger still, it wasn't even hot. The metal ring it rested on glowed bright red with heat, but the stone wasn't even warm. In fact, it still felt cool to the touch. Amazing. No matter how many experiments Josh ran on it, the Bloodstone never changed. It remained exactly the same.

The past few hours had been good for Josh. Because of his love for science, the experiments had completely taken his mind off losing the election. In fact, he felt more relaxed than he had in weeks—that is, until he heard the hoofbeats behind him. There's something about hoofbeats in your bedroom in the middle of the night that can set a person on edge.

Josh leaped from his chair and spun around. But before he completed his turn, the hoofbeats changed to . . . footsteps. And, instead of a horse, there stood before him a type of coach . . . but a very beautiful coach—complete with sweats, tied-back hair, and, of course, the ever popular stopwatch and whistle.

She held a leash in her hand that was attached to a living ice ball on a choke chain. The creature appeared to be some sort of pet, and not a very happy one.

It took more than a moment for Josh to find his voice. "Who . . . who are you?" he finally said. "Where did you come from?"

"Why, from Fayrah, of course." The coach grinned.

"But I, we didn't signal you." Josh threw a quick glance back at the stone. "The only way to signal you is by putting the Bloodstone in the light of a full moon. And it's not a full moon so how could—"

"Dear heart"—the coach smiled sweetly—"didn't they tell you?"

"Tell me what?"

"That you have graduated from such crude devices." She gave the Bloodstone an uneasy glance. For a *crude device* it seemed to make her a bit nervous.

Josh frowned. "What about Aristophenix?" he asked. "What about Listro Q and Samson?"

"They have served their purposes well and send their best."

"You've talked to them?"

"Of course. But Imager has now placed you in *my* care. That is, if you count me worthy of such an honor." She gave a slight bow and waited.

Still suspicious, Josh asked, "What is your name?"

"Oh, gracious, my name is of little importance when compared to your—"

"Just so I know," he interupted. "I mean, if I want to call you something, what would I call you?"

"Well . . ." She thought for a moment. "If you must call me something, I suppose 'Your Highness' is appropriate."

Her ice pet coughed slightly.

"You are a queen?" Josh asked in surprise.

"Of course. Only royalty is fit to train royalty."

"Royalty?" Josh exclaimed. "Who else around here is royalty?"

"Why, you are. I've been sent here to train *you.*"

Again her pet coughed. Apparently his master was holding his choke chain a bit too tight.

Josh looked down at the creature, his frown deepening. "And your little friend there. No offense, but he kinda looks like the thing Nathan described—the one who kidnapped him to Keygarp."

"Oh," the Illusionist chuckled. "You mean Fido here." She stooped down and patted the creature on the head. "Good Fido, good boy."

"Yeah," Josh replied, *"Fido."*

"Well, he is from Keygarp, I'll grant you that. But I've trained this little fellow since he was a pup." She reached into her sweatpants and produced a doggie biscuit. It took only a moment for the smell to reach Joshua. It was so awful it made his eyes water.

"And you wouldn't hurt a fly, would you, Fido?" she said as she reached down and held the biscuit to the creature's mouth. Fido did not look thrilled about taking it, until the coach firmly repeated herself, *"Would you, Fido,"* while yanking on the chain.

Half choking, Fido opened his mouth and she popped the biscuit inside.

"Now, chew, boy," she encouraged. "Chew the nummy treat for Momma, till it's all gone."

Reluctantly, unhappily, the animal began to chew. Joshua watched, guessing it tasted even worse than it smelled.

"Now," the coach looked up, turning her smile upon him. "Where were we?"

"You said something about me being . . . royalty."

"Yes." She nodded.

He shook his head. "You've made some sort of mistake. I'm just me."

Her smile grew. "Oh no, dear heart, you are indeed royalty. You are one of the elect, one of the chosen."

Josh felt a stirring inside his chest. The same sort of stirring he felt whenever he was praised or had won at something.

The coach moved closer, lowering her voice. "I guarantee you, my friend. After my training you will never lose another election again."

Josh looked at her in surprise. "How'd you know about the election?"

"Dear heart, I have studied every thread of your tapestry."

Josh nodded. The fact that she'd seen his tapestry gave him some assurance. Perhaps she really could be trusted.

She continued, taking another step closer, her words growing more and more persuasive. "I have been sent to train and prepare you."

His heart pounded just a little in excitement. "For what?"

"Under my guidance you will become more popular than you

have ever dreamed possible. In fact"—she lowered her voice to a mere whisper—"if you allow me, I will make you as popular as Imager himself."

"Yeah, right," Josh scorned.

"As you wish." The coach shrugged. "Perhaps I have overestimated your ambition."

Josh shifted uncomfortably. His mind raced, his heart beat faster. "How could anybody become as popular as Imager?"

"By becoming perfect."

Her second statement was more shocking than the first.

"You could do that?" Josh's voice cracked slightly. "You could actually make somebody perfect?"

"It's the only way," the coach explained. "If you're going to be as popular as Imager, you must become as perfect as Imager."

"But . . . how . . ."

"Oh, I wouldn't worry about that. It sounds like it's too much work for you." She turned to her pet. "Wouldn't you agree, Fido?"

The creature rolled back and forth as if nodding.

"I'm not afraid of work," Josh argued.

"Perhaps," the coach said, looking him over carefully. "But for you to become perfect, I am afraid it would take a great deal of effort . . . particularly for this body of yours and, of course, your personality."

"I said I'm not afraid of work."

The coach only smiled.

"How would you . . . I mean, what . . ." He caught himself and tried to sound less eager. "If somebody was interested in being perfect, what exactly would they have to do?"

"Why, dear heart, that's what the Kingdom of Perfection is all about."

"Kingdom of . . . Perfection?"

"Of course. It is divided into three levels. On the first level, you work toward physical perfection. On the second, you obtain perfect popularity."

"And the third?" Josh could no longer hide his eagerness.

"The third level is the Sea of Justice. A place where only the perfect may enter. There, at last, you would enjoy the rewards of all your hard work. There, you would finally receive all that you rightly deserve."

By now Joshua's head was reeling. Everything was moving too fast. He knew he should slow things down but couldn't. After all, the coach was promising popularity equal to Imager himself! He coughed nervously. "So, how would we start—I mean, if I were interested?"

"You would simply give me permission to transport you."

"To the Kingdom of Perfection?"

"That is correct."

"That's it?"

The coach nodded.

"But what about Nathan, what about Denny?"

"I'm afraid neither one of them is much interested in perfection. Wouldn't you agree?" She gave him a knowing smile.

Though he tried not to, he had to smile back.

Silence filled the room. It was clear she was waiting for his decision. He was cautious, of course. But, if he let this type of opportunity pass, how could he live with himself? Yes, it was a risk. He barely knew her. But look at what she was promising—popularity equal to Imager!

She continued waiting. So did her pet.

Finally, after taking a deep breath, Josh spoke. "Well . . ." He shrugged. "What are we waiting for?"

The coach smiled. "Not a thing, dear heart, not a thing."

Joshua turned back to the desk. "Just let me grab the Bloodstone here and—"

"No, don't!"

Josh turned to see the coach stumble over her pet, who was rolling behind her as if for protection.

"What?" he asked in surprise.

With some effort, her smile returned. "As I said, you have graduated beyond the stone."

"We don't need it?" Josh asked.

The coach shook her head. "It is now time to rely on your own powers. The stone was needed in the beginning. But now it would become a crutch that could slow your growth. You must put it out of sight. In fact, it would be best if you completely removed it."

"Remove it?" Josh asked.

"Yes. I will explain on our journey, but for now it would be best to place it outside your dwelling."

"Outside?" Josh asked.

"That is correct."

Joshua looked down at Fido, who rolled back and forth, nodding.

It was an odd request, there was no doubt about it. But she seemed pretty serious.

"Well," he said, "I guess I could put it out on the windowsill or something."

"That is an excellent idea, most excellent, indeed."

Still a little puzzled, Josh moved toward the window. "This seems kinda weird," he said, "but if you really think it's better . . ."

He arrived at the window, threw it open, and set the Bloodstone out on the ledge. "There," he said, shutting the window and turning back. "So why exactly is it—"

But he never finished his question. He was interrupted by the sound of approaching hoofbeats. Then an overwhelming numbness. Then nothing at all . . .

Denise bolted up in bed. At first she thought she was dreaming. Then she heard it again. A rattling. A clattering.

She fumbled for her bedstand light and turned it on. As usual it was about a hundred times too bright—at least for this time of morning. She squinted at the clock. It read 4:22 A.M.

The rattling grew louder. She searched the room. Nothing unusual. Just the everyday disaster of dirty socks, dirty clothes, scattered papers, coat piles, book piles, shoe piles, and a few baseball pennants tacked to the wall. Oh, and of course . . . the doll.

Some may have thought Denise was getting too old for dolls. But she didn't much care what they thought. The doll was the last present she ever received from her father. He gave it to her when she was four years old—the day he left. She would never part with it.

At last she spotted something . . . in the corner by the door— behind the broken bicycle pump and football helmet—right next to the spilled box of Josh's campaign buttons. It was the canteen. The one that still held water from their visits to Fayrah. The water made up of liquid letters and words from the stream. At the moment it was shaking and vibrating on the floor!

Denise threw off her covers and cautiously padded over to it. At first she was afraid to touch it. But that was silly. The water inside had always helped them before. It had helped them see and hear right side up. It had even saved Nathan from the Illusionist. So what was she afraid of?

Plenty. When was the last time anyone saw a canteen bouncing around on a floor?

But Denise wasn't about to let a little ice-cold fear get in the way. Not her. So, with a deep breath and a little shiver, she finally stooped down and picked up the canteen.

"Ouch!" she yelled, dropping it back to the floor. It was so hot it almost burned her. Almost, but not quite. She reached for the bottom of her sweatshirt, the one she slept in, and carefully wrapped it around the canteen. Carefully, she picked it up. It continued to vibrate in her hands. But it was more than vibrating. It felt as if it was . . . boiling—as if the water inside was actually boiling.

She started to unscrew the cap but burnt her fingers for good this time. She tried again, wrapping her sweatshirt around the cap and slowly opening it.

There was a loud hiss. And, before she knew it, a small cloud of steam escaped. But this was no ordinary steam. Like the water inside, this steam was made up of letters and words. The cloud continued to grow until it was two, maybe three feet across. As it grew, Denise stepped back. It wasn't that she was frightened, it's just . . . well, okay, she was a little frightened. Well, okay, she was a *lot* frightened. But not over the cloud. It was over what was happening to the cloud.

It hovered at eye level, just a few feet from her. As it cooled, it started to turn dark. And, as it turned dark, mist started falling from it—eventually turning to rain. That's right. Actual drops of rain fell from the cloud. It lasted nearly a minute, until the entire cloud had turned to rain and fallen to the floor. Now the water lay in a little pool next to the box of Josh's campaign buttons.

Denise stared in amazement. Nothing more happened. Nothing at all. Cautiously, she walked to the puddle on the floor. She stooped down to examine it. The letters and words had all disappeared. Now it looked like any other puddle of water. She carefully reached out, then touched it with a finger. It felt like any other puddle of water. She scowled. With all of the special effects, she expected to end up with something more than a puddle of water on her floor. But that was it. The canteen had quit boiling. The cloud had disappeared. Now there was just the puddle of water.

Annoyed, Denise rose to her feet. Then, just before she turned, she saw it. A reflection. One of Joshua's campaign buttons, the one pinned to the edge of the box. It was reflecting in the water.

But the water didn't reflect the photo of the smiling Joshua. It didn't even reflect the silly slogan, "Vote for Josh, by Gosh." Instead, it reflected a very sick-looking Josh. A Josh who seemed to be stretched out on some sort of bed or cot. His eyes were shut and he looked very, very pale. In fact, he almost looked—Denise sucked in her breath. He almost looked . . . dead.

She dropped to her knees for a better view but momentarily lost the reflection. When she moved and found it again, it had changed. Now it was just the reflection of the campaign button—stupid slogan and all. The sick Josh, the dying Josh, had completely disappeared.

Denise knelt there another moment. Then she sprang into action. She wasn't sure what she'd seen, but she knew it was a warning. An omen. She threw on her clothes and slipped into her shoes. Joshua was in some sort of trouble. He needed help. She grabbed her coat and raced out the door. A moment later she returned to scoop up the canteen, and then she was gone.

a cLose enCOUNteR

You're crazy," Nathan whispered as he opened the back kitchen door to let Denise inside. "It's 5:30 in the morning. Everyone's still in—"

"I just need to . . ." Denny gulped for air. Running halfway across town will do that to a person. "I just need to see Josh for a second."

"Suit yourself," Nathan mumbled as he rubbed his eyes and stepped aside to let her pass. "You always do."

Denise knew she could fire off a good comeback if she wanted. Firing off comebacks was her specialty. But right now there were more important things to do. She had tried waking Josh by tossing pebbles up at his window. Although she could see a strange flickering light inside, he did not answer. Nathan was her second choice.

They reached the steps and took them as quickly and silently as possible without waking the grown-ups.

When they arrived at the top they turned toward Joshua's bedroom. The door was shut but that same flickering light could be seen underneath.

"That's funny," Nathan whispered. "He never gets up this early."

"And what's with that light?" Denise asked.

Nathan shrugged like it was no big deal, but she could see he was

uneasy. As they approached the room she noticed something else—
a soft, whispering *whirrrr*. She slowed. "What's that sound?"

Nathan strained to listen, then frowned. They continued down the
hall . . . slower . . . more cautiously.

They were nearly there when Nathan started to snicker.

"What?" Denise asked.

He continued.

"What?"

"It's the burner thing he uses," Nathan said. "He's just doing an
experiment with it, that's all."

Denise took a deep breath and blew out the tension.

"Honestly," Nathan taunted. "Sometimes you're such a girl."

Normally, those were fighting words and normally Denise would
make him eat them. But considering his parents were sleeping just
down the hall, she refrained from inflicting any major bodily damage.

They arrived at the door. Nathan reached up to quietly knock.

There was no response.

He tried again.

Still, nothing.

Denise stepped closer and whispered through the crack. "Josh?
Josh, it's Denny. You okay?"

More in the nothing department.

Nathan turned the knob and pushed open the door. "Josh?"

But there was no sign of him anywhere. Just the eerie glow of the
Bunsen burner as it flickered light and shadows across the room.

Slowly Denise and Nathan entered.

"Josh?"

No answer—only the quiet roar of the burner.

"I don't like this," Nathan whispered. "Something's wrong."

"Now who's being chicken?" Denise scorned.

"I'm not kidding. Where would he go this time of morning? And
why didn't he shut off the burner?"

Denise looked around the room. It wasn't much. Just the usual bed,
the usual dresser, with the usual chair and usual clothes thrown on it.
Only the desk was unusual. It was covered with glass beakers, test
tubes, and all sorts of computer junk. Yes, sir, Josh loved his science.

"Maybe he went for a walk or something," Denise said.

Nathan didn't answer but moved toward the desk.

Denise gave another glance around, then spotted something—a half open closet door. Nothing unusual about that. But inside . . . inside she caught a glimpse of a moving shadow. Maybe it was from the flickering burner. Maybe it was just her nerves playing tricks on her.

Maybe.

Unfortunately, there was only one way to find out.

Carefully, cautiously, she started toward the closet. She heard nothing . . . unless you counted the pounding of her heart in her ears. And the closer she got, the louder that pounding grew.

Soon she stood directly in front of the closet. She hated this, but somebody had to do it. She reached out, grabbed the door, and threw it open to see . . .

Nothing. Nothing but clothes.

"Denny?" Nathan stood over Joshua's desk looking at an open notebook. "Listen to this—it's his journal." He began to read:

Friday, 10:05 P.M.

"That was last night," Denise said as she moved to join him.

He nodded and continued:

Have subjected the Bloodstone to twenty minutes of intense heat. Still no change. I am beginning to strongly suspect . . .

He came to a stop.

"Go ahead," Denise said. "'Strongly suspect' what?"

"That's all. It stops right there, right in the middle of the sentence."

Denise did her best to fight off a little shiver.

"That's weird," Nathan said.

For once in her life Denise didn't argue. She reached over and began rummaging through the different piles on the desk.

"What are you doing?"

"Looking for the Bloodstone," she said. "If he was busy running experiments on it, shouldn't it be around?"

"Denny, look!"

She glanced over to see Nathan staring down at the floor. Slowly, he knelt and picked up something. Then, even more slowly, he rose with it in his hand.

"What is it?" she asked. "Looks like a little shaving of ice or something."

Nathan nodded. "And it feels like ice. It's cold and slippery." He pushed the sliver around in his palm, squeezing it and pressing it. "But it doesn't melt." He squeezed it harder. "I can't get the stupid thing to melt."

Denise looked up at him. Fear crept across his face. "Nathan?"

He gave no answer.

"Nathan?"

When he finally spoke, his voice was trembling. "Denny, it's . . . *blue.*"

"So?"

"So what do we know that's icy and blue . . . and doesn't melt?"

She frowned, not understanding.

Nathan whispered, "*Who* do we know that's icy and blue and doesn't melt?"

It was Denise's turn to shudder. "Bobok!" she gasped. "You think Bobok was here?"

Nathan looked up. He tried to swallow but there was nothing in his mouth to swallow. He was frightened, and Denise knew why. Bobok was the evil ice ball who had lured him into Keygarp. Bobok was the one who had held him prisoner in the horrible menagerie. Bobok was the one who had nearly destroyed them at the Portal. And now, that very same Bobok had been in this very same room just a few hours earlier. Nathan had every reason to be terrified.

But Denise handled fear differently. When she got frightened, she got angry. And when she got angry, she paced. "Why?" she demanded as she started walking back and forth across the room. "Why would he come here? And what about Josh? You think he took Josh?"

Nathan gave no answer.

"And the Bloodstone—where's the Bloodstone?" She passed the window. Outside the clouds were starting to turn pink with the first signs of dawn. She moved closer for a better look. It was then she noticed the canteen attached to her belt. It was starting to bubble again.

"We got to do something!" Nathan cried.

Denise turned around, startled by the outburst.

"Josh's been stolen by Bobok! We've got to help him!"

"But how?" she asked. "Without the Bloodstone we can't signal Fayrah—we can't do anything."

"He's my brother!"

"I know, I know," she said, motioning him to lower his voice so he wouldn't wake the house. "But what can we do? Without the Bloodstone there's no way we can . . . Unless . . ." An idea began to form.

"Unless what?" Nathan demanded.

"Do you remember when we first got the Bloodstone?"

"Sure, for my birthday. You gave it to me for my—"

"No, before that. Remember I told you I found it up in my uncle's attic—in that old trunk of his?"

"Yeah, so?"

"So maybe there's more of it."

"More Bloodstone?" Doubt filled Nathan's voice.

"Yeah . . . or maybe, maybe something else. I mean, my uncle collected a lot of crazy stuff, right?"

"Denny," Nathan argued. "Going through your uncle's trunk isn't going to get Josh back!"

"All right then." She folded her arms. "What do you suggest?"

Nathan looked at her.

She looked at Nathan.

Finally, without a word, he spun around and started for the door.

"Where you going?"

"To get out of these pajamas so we can go to your uncle's."

Denise nodded. "I'll wait for you downstairs."

She moved to the desk, turned off the burner, and headed out into the hall. It was only then that she remembered the canteen and reached down to feel it again. But the boiling had stopped. How odd. When she was in the room, close to the window, it was boiling like crazy. But now as she headed down the hall toward the stairs it felt completely normal.

How very odd.

Faster, dearest of ladies," Bobok urged. "Faster."

Though her lungs cried for air, the Illusionist galloped harder. It was one thing to carry Bobok from kingdom to kingdom, but to drag the unconscious Upside Downer on the litter behind them—well, she was definitely feeling the strain.

Then there was their current direction. At the moment, they were traveling through Quurak-Bruuk—the Kingdom of Rock. And the *rock* wasn't just the land portion. It was *every* portion. Everything in Quurak-Bruuk was rock. The land, the sea, even the air. Of course, moving through such a kingdom can be a little tricky (breathing in it isn't so easy either). Fortunately, the molecules in this dimension were billions of times bigger, so the Illusionist could easily navigate between them, leaping from one molecule to another. Still, it was no picnic.

"Are you certain we are traveling in the correct direction?" the Illusionist panted. "I don't recall the Kingdom of Perfection being this way."

"My dearest friend," Bobok cooed, "you doubt my navigation skills?"

"Of course not," the Illusionist moaned. "I only hope this lengthy voyage has nothing to do with my little joke of feeding you the doggie biscuit."

"Gentle lady," Bobok chuckled, "I'm far above that sort of thing."

"Of course you are," the Illusionist agreed, knowing full well that he wasn't. "How is the boy?" she asked.

Bobok looked over his shoulder to the cot dragging behind them. In the bedroom, they had pressed the right combination of nerves on the boy's neck to put him to sleep. But he would not sleep forever. "Hurry, esteemed one," Bobok called. "We must arrive at Perfection before he wakes."

"I have little remaining strength," she groaned. "And my hoofs are splitting from the sharp edges of the rock."

"Then dwell on the beauty of our trap," Bobok chortled. "Dream of the pain we will inflict upon Imager. Dream of breaking his heart. Dream whatever you must, but hurry. *Hurry!*"

greetings from an old friend

Nathan was so concerned about his brother that he kept most of the wisecracks about Denise's uncle to himself. But it wasn't easy. The guy was a nutcase. Everyone in town knew it. He'd been some sort of filmmaker—always off in some strange country filming some strange tribe or some strange something.

Then, about three years ago, after telling incredibly weird tales that no one believed, he suddenly disappeared. That was it. Denise's aunt woke up one morning and he was gone. No one had heard from him since.

"Typical," everyone said. "Not surprising," they agreed. "A nutcase," they concluded.

Still, the man *had* found the Bloodstone . . .

Who knows, maybe there were other things in the trunk. Who knows, after their journeys to Fayrah, maybe some of his weird stories weren't so weird after all. At least that's what Nathan hoped as Denise's aunt welcomed them inside, as the two trudged upstairs into the dusty attic, as they found the old steamer trunk off in the corner, as they lifted its heavy lid.

The hinges creaked and groaned until at last they had it opened. And when they looked inside they found . . .

"*Nothing?*" Denise exclaimed. "How can that be?"

But she was right. There was nothing but a bunch of old, musty clothes and faded photographs. Well, almost nothing. Because when they dug through the pile of clothes and reached the bottom they did find something.

"Take a look at this," Nathan said as he pulled out a dusty old camera. At least that's what he thought it was. But it had no lens. In fact, it was even hard to tell which was the front or the back. After looking it over he shrugged and tossed it on the pile of clothes.

"How 'bout this?" Denise asked as she removed a thin, flat stone. It was gray, perfectly smooth, and about the size of a large writing pad.

"Let me see," Nathan said. Before she could stop him, he yanked it from her hands and turned it over. But there was nothing more to it. No writing, no markings, nothing. "Figures," he sighed as he tossed it beside the camera. "I was right, your uncle was a nutcase."

He glanced back into the trunk. There was nothing left but a rusty jackknife, some scratched sunglasses, and a dirty, beat-up audio-cassette tape.

"I knew there wouldn't be anything here," he scoffed as Denise pulled out the tape. It was caked in dirt and had no label. He continued, "I don't know why I let you talk me into these stupid things."

Denise didn't answer but licked her fingers and rubbed at the dirt. Slowly, something began to emerge. "Nathan," she said, "take a look at this."

He moved closer. Underneath the grime there was the faint scribbling of a pen. Denise kept rubbing, careful not to remove the ink, until they both saw the words:

"Greetings from Biiq."

They stared in silence. Nathan knew all about Biiq, the Kingdom of Math and Science. He knew this was the kingdom where Denise had created Gus and Gerty. And he knew it was the kingdom where Josh had studied Imager's logic on a computer.

He raised his eyes to Denise.

She raised her eyes to him.

Then, without a word, they both leaped to their feet and headed for the stairs. It was time to find a cassette player . . . and fast!

W here am I? " Josh groaned as he stirred on the cot. Finally he was able to pry open his eyes, but he was momentarily blinded by the glare of light. "What's going on?"

"We have arrived at the Kingdom of Perfection," a voice said.

Shading his eyes, he rose to his elbows, looking for the speaker. Then he spotted him. It was the blue ice ball!

"We are in the first realm," the creature was saying, "the Realm of Appearance."

"Your pet . . ." Josh searched until he spotted the coach standing nearby. "He talks!"

"Yes," the coach laughed. "It's amazing what you can teach them with a little patience."

The blue orb gave a tight smile then muttered, "It is one of my many talents." Turning back to Josh, he continued, "In this first realm, you may change your appearance until you are absolutely perfect."

Josh threw his feet over the side of the cot and stood. Well, *stood* might not be the right word. For there was no ground to stand upon. Neither were there any trees, or buildings, or mountains.

But there were people—layers of them piled as high as the eye could see. They weren't standing or lying on top of each other. Instead, they were divided into levels, each level floating about ten feet above the next. It was as if they were in a thousand-story office building but without walls or ceilings or floors—just layers of floating people. As Josh looked up he saw hundreds of these levels floating above him. And as he looked down, he saw hundreds more floating below.

The only other thing he noticed was the screaming. It was hideous.

The blue pet continued his explanation. "Each level is a step closer to physical perfection. The greater your perfection, the higher your level."

Although the floating was an interesting sensation, the screaming definitely concerned Josh. He'd never heard people in such agony. "What's with all that screaming?" he asked.

"Dear heart." The coach drifted closer, seeming to ignore his question. "What is your least favorite feature?"

"What do you mean?"

"What do you hate most about your appearance? What is your greatest physical imperfection?"

"I don't know . . ." Josh shrugged. "Probably my nose. It's always been a little too big."

"Then make it smaller," the blue orb suggested.

"What?"

"Push on your nose and make it smaller."

"Yeah, right," Josh smirked.

"Trust him, dear heart." The coach smiled. "Do as he says."

Josh looked at her. Then at her pet. They were serious. Of course it was a weird request, but let's face it, this place wasn't exactly *unweird*. Besides, what would it hurt? So, with another shrug, Josh gave his nose a little push.

"*AHHH!*" he screamed as incredible pain shot through his nose and face. But it was gone as quickly as it had come.

"What's wrong, dear heart?"

"I don't know," Josh said, rubbing his nose. "Wait a minute. I don't believe it. My nose! It's smaller! My nose is smaller!"

"Of course," the pet chortled. As he spoke, the three of them started floating up to the next level of people.

"What's going on—what's happening?" Josh cried.

"Do not worry," the coach soothed. "As we said, the greater your perfection, the higher your level. With enough hard work, you will reach a physical perfection greater than any of these others."

"This is incredible," Josh shouted as they finally arrived at the next level. "You mean I can change my looks any way I want?"

"Until you reach perfection," the pet purred.

"Cool!"

"Then it's off to the second realm of this kingdom," the coach said. "The Realm of Perfect Popularity."

"This is so neat!" Josh shouted. Then an idea came to mind. He reached down and grabbed hold of one of his legs.

"What are you doing?" the pet asked.

"I've always wanted to be taller," he said, giving his leg a tug. "Imagine what I could do on the basketball court if—*AHHHH!*" There was the pain again. Only this time it was in his leg. And it was worse. "What was that?" he cried. "Why does it hurt so much?"

The pet explained. "Each level of perfection is more painful than the next. That is the screaming you hear."

Joshua looked about. It was true. Everyone around him was shaping and re-forming their bodies. And each time they did, they let loose an agonizing scream.

"But . . . why?" Josh asked.

"Working toward perfection is a painful thing," the pet replied. "It requires much work. Only a few are strong enough to pursue it."

"And they are the ones you must beat to enter the next realm," the coach added.

Josh glanced about. "Is there only one winner?"

"In each group, yes. And this is *your* group," the coach said as she stretched out her arm to all the levels. Then, leaning closer, she added, "It is a strong group, but you're not afraid of a little competition, are you?"

Josh shook his head. "Of course not. But all of this pain . . . all of this screaming."

The coach's smile faded slightly before she quickly cleared her throat and changed subjects. "Dear heart, are you going to continue keeping one leg shorter than the other? Do you not wish to enter the next level?"

Josh frowned as he tilted back his head to see the hundreds of levels above him. "I don't know, guys, it's a long ways up there . . ."

The coach sighed. "Perhaps you are right. Perhaps it is too much effort for you to pursue a perfect body. Of course, that means you will never enter the second half of the kingdom, the Realm of Perfect Popularity, but—"

"Now wait a minute," Josh interrupted, "I didn't mean—"

"If he's *not* perfect in body and popularity," the pet argued, "then he'll never be able to enter the Sea of Justice, he'll never receive all that he deserves."

"I understand," the coach said. "But if he does not wish perfection no one can force him."

"Hold it, wait a minute!" Josh exclaimed. "I didn't say I didn't want it. I just said, well, what I mean is . . ."

The coach turned to him. "Yes?"

The blue pet floated closer, also waiting.

Josh coughed, then forced himself to continue. "No . . . great, good. It all sounds great to me. Let's get on with it."

The coach cocked her head at him skeptically.

"No, honest—I mean, who wouldn't want to have a perfect body and be super popular? After all, that's why we're here, right? Besides, that Sea of Justice is *definitely* something I want to visit."

"Are you certain, dear heart?" the coach asked.

"Yeah, sure."

"Because if you're not, we can—"

"No, I'm certain! I'm certain!"

"Well, then, Joshua O'Brien," the pet said, "shall we continue?"

Josh swallowed, then nodded.

They waited.

So did he—until he realized it was his move. Taking a deep breath, he bent down to his shorter leg, grabbed it with both hands, and started to pull.

"*Ahhhhh!*" he screamed. The pain was unbelievable, but as soon as he succeeded it stopped. As before, they slowly rose toward the next level. And as they floated, was it Josh's imagination or had he caught the coach and her pet exchanging grins? Maybe it was pride over his accomplishment. Maybe something else. It didn't matter. At the moment he had other things on his mind. There was so much more he needed to fix to become perfect . . .

"Hi, Denny, Nathan—these first few words, will sound upside down because you haven't put the water in your ears, yet yet."

Denise stood over the portable cassette player in her room and looked puzzled at Nathan. They'd raced all the way to her house, thrown on the cassette tape, and for what? To hear gibberish?

"What's he saying?" Nathan asked.

Denise frowned. "I can't make it out. I mean, it sounds like Bud, but—"

Again the tape spoke:

"Of course you can't make it out—you haven't put the water in yet."

Denise's scowl deepened. "It sounds familiar, but—wait a minute!" She quickly reached for the canteen on her belt and began unscrewing the lid.

"What are you doing?"

"Remember whenever we go to Fayrah"—she began pouring the liquid letters from the canteen into her hands—"how we have to put the stream's water in our ears to understand the people?"

"Right! Of course!" Nathan shouted.

Quickly, Denise splashed the liquid letters into her left and right ears. Then she poured them into Nathan's eager hands for him to do the same.

"Very good good, guys," the cassette player said. *"I knew you'd figure it out out."*

"Bud!" the kids cried in unison. "Bud . . . can you hear us? Bud!"

"Of course I can hear you you. I'm not deaf."

"But how . . ." Denise faltered. "How can you hear us? This isn't a cell phone, it's a cassette player!"

"And I'm talking to you on a cassette."

Denise and Nathan frowned at each other.

"Peculiar, huh huh?"

The children nodded.

Bud continued, *"Remember Olga, the computer?"*

Again the two looked at each other.

"Hello . . ."

"Of course," Denise finally spoke. "Olga, the super computer."

"Remember how, through probability, she knows knows everything you'll ever say or do do before you do do it?"

"Yeah . . ."

"Well, she's printed out exactly what you'll say say before you say it—complete with each of your pauses and facial expressions. So all I have to do do is answer them."

"You mean . . . ," Denise spoke slowly, piecing it together, "this is a tape you recorded ahead of time?"

"By your measurements, seventeen years ago, to be exact. In fact fact, I recorded this and gave it to your uncle before you were even born born."

"You knew my uncle!"

"Well, not yet yet, but we'll be meeting soon."

The kids stared at each other. Things were getting stranger by the second.

"You don't believe me me, do you?"

"Well, Bud," Nathan coughed slightly, "it's a little hard to—"

"Go ahead then, turn me off off."

"What?" Denise asked.

"Press 'stop.' Then press 'rewind' for a second."

They hesitated.

"Go ahead," the voice said.

Figuring they had nothing to lose, Denise reached over and pressed "stop." "Now what?" she asked.

But the tape machine did not answer.

"I guess, go ahead and press 'rewind,'" Nathan said.

Denise pressed "rewind" for a brief moment and then pressed the "play" button again.

"You don't believe me me, do you?" the tape repeated exactly what it had said before. There was a pause and then, "Go ahead then, turn me off off. Press 'stop.' Then press 'rewind' a second." Another pause. "Go ahead."

Denise and Nathan stood astonished. It really was a tape recording.

"Now do you believe me me?" the tape asked.

The two nodded in stunned silence.

"Good. Now listen listen very carefully. Nathan, it's just as you figured. Bobok and the Illusionist have taken Joshua."

"But where?" Denise asked. "Why?"

"Remember how Joshua wanted 'justice'? How he wanted wanted everything to be 'fair'?"

Again Denise and Nathan nodded.

"Well, Bobok and the Illusionist have talked him into the Kingdom of of Perfection."

"The what?" Nathan asked.

"The Kingdom of Perfection. It's a place where you work work on your body and your popularity until you finally think you have reached reached perfection."

"Sounds like Josh to me," Denise agreed.

"But it's a dangerous trap trap. No one can reach perfection by working at it. It is only a means to trick trick Josh into entering the dreaded Sea of Justice."

"What is that?" Denise asked.

There was a long pause on the tape.

"Bud?" Nathan said. "Bud, are you still there?"

At last Bud continued. "They want him to enter the sea so he'll be destroyed."

"What?" Denise cried.

"I'm sorry sorry, but that's their plan. In the Sea of Justice, Joshua will be destroyed by his own imperfections."

"Then we have to rescue him!" Nathan exclaimed.

"You will be destroyed as well. Only perfect creatures can enter the Sea of Justice."

"But we have to do something!" Nathan insisted.

"What about Aristophenix?" Denise asked. "Or Listro Q and Samson?"

"Theirs is a similar problem. They, too, are not not perfect."

"But that's my brother!" Nathan practically shouted at the cassette player. "We got to help him!"

"No, that's exactly what what Bobok and the Illusionist want. They're using Joshua as bait bait to lure both you and the Fayrahnians to destruction."

"So what are we supposed to do?" Denise demanded. "Just sit around on our hands?"

"I understand your frustration," Bud interrupted.

"So what are we going to—"

"Fortunately, Olga indicates there are a number of perfect people people in your kingdom—people people who have no imperfection. All you need do do is find them and convince them to rescue Joshua."

"Perfect people?" Nathan asked skeptically.

"How?" Denise asked. "How are we supposed to find them?"

There was a long pause.

"Bud?" she repeated.

Finally he answered, *"I honestly don't know."*

"What?"

"But you'll know know," he said. *"Olga assures me that when you find them, you'll know."*

"But ... where do we look?" Nathan demanded. "Where do we begin?"

Again there was no answer.

"Bud? . . . Bud, answer me!"

There was still no response except for a loud *click* as the "play" button popped up. The tape had come to an end.

Denise and Nathan traded looks of alarm.

"Turn it over!" Nathan ordered. "There's gotta be something on the other side!"

"Right," Denise said as she pressed the "eject" button and flipped the tape over.

"Hurry," Nathan said, as she fumbled with it. "Hurry."

At last she got the tape into the machine and pressed "play."

"Ah, I'm back, back," the voice finally said.

"Bud," Nathan tried to sound calm, but was doing a lousy job of it. "You said we'd know these perfect people when we see them."

"Yes yes."

"But how?"

"Go to the mall mall."

"What?"

"Please don't make me keep repeating repeating myself. We haven't much tape left. Go to the mall mall and we'll talk there."

"You want us to go to the shopping mall?" Denise asked incredulously.

"Yes, yes. Turn off this machine and wait until you're at the entrance to the mall mall before you turn it back on on."

"But—"

"Now." Bud's voice grew insistent. *"Turn off the machine and go now."*

"But—"

"NOW!"

the
maLL

T urn it on!" Nathan shouted. He limped toward the mall's parking lot doing his best to keep up with Denise, though he was falling behind with every step.

"Not yet," Denise called over her shoulder. "We're not at the entrance."

"We're close enough!"

But Denise refused until finally they arrived. She was first, followed by the gasping, wheezing Nathan. "Turn it on," he coughed. "Turn it on!"

She reached to the cassette recorder and pressed "play."

"Nice work work!" the tape blared. She fumbled for the volume control and turned it down. *"I'm glad you ignored Nathan and waited until you arrived."*

Denise and Nathan traded looks. It was still unnerving the way Bud knew everything they'd do before they did it.

"We haven't much time," the tape said. *"Let's get get going."*

Without a word, the two (or shall we say, three) turned to enter the mall. The doors hissed open and they stepped inside.

"So where do we go?" Nathan asked. "Where do we find these 'perfect' people?"

"You still have the water water from the stream?" Bud asked.

"Right here," Denise said as she held the canteen up to the cassette player. A couple businessmen in fancy suits gave her quizzical looks. She lowered the canteen a little sheepishly.

"Remember how you had to splash the water water in your ears to understand me?" Bud asked.

"Yeah."

"Well, now you're going to have to splash it it into your eyes."

"Why?" Nathan asked.

"The only way to see things as they really are are is by looking through the water—those liquid letters and words are the only way way you can see Truth."

Denise and Nathan hesitated.

"Hurry, we don't have much tape."

Denise reached for the canteen and quickly unscrewed the lid.

"Remember," Bud cautioned, "people in your kingdom do things upside down, so that's how they'll look look to you."

Denise nodded as she poured the liquid letters and words into her hand. For a moment she hesitated.

"Go ahead," the tape urged.

Taking a breath, she splashed the water into her eyes.

"Whoa!" she cried as she staggered backward, trying to keep her balance. Suddenly, everybody in the mall was upside down. Even Nathan.

But not for long. Nathan grabbed the canteen and splashed the water into his own eyes. A moment later he too was staggering.

Bud chuckled through the tape player. "Don't worry worry, you'll get used to it."

But they did not get used to it. Not by a long shot. Because there was something else the water was doing to their vision. Not only did the people around them look like they were standing on their heads, but they looked different in other ways . . .

For starters, Denise and Nathan could see through them. Not completely. They still could make out their bodies and their clothing. But now everyone was semitransparent. It was as if they were no longer made of flesh and bone. Instead, they appeared to be made out of some sort of vapor—a dark, misty fog.

"This is just like the Center!" Denise exclaimed as she raised her hand and looked through its mist to see Nathan. "Everyone's kinda clear—you can see through them!"

"*Correct correct,*" Bud answered.

But there were even greater differences . . .

Like the two businessmen standing nearby, the ones in the fancy suits and ties. Well, they *had* been in fancy suits and ties. Now they suddenly wore torn and smelly rags. And instead of standing, they were crawling around holding out tin cups to passersby and begging for money.

"What's going on?" Denise asked, motioning to the men. "What happened to them?"

"*The water lets you see see things as they really are,*" Bud answered. "*Those men may look rich rich on the outside, but inside they are some of the poorest people at the mall.*"

"What are you talking about?" Nathan scoffed. "They probably own the place."

"*They have nothing of Imager's life. They have nothing of real real value.*"

Before Nathan could argue, Denise pointed toward a tired and worn woman. She pushed a baby stroller with one hand while dragging a screaming three-year-old with the other. It wasn't too strange a sight—in fact, you could see it just about any day at any mall. Except for one detail . . . this particular woman was dressed as a royal queen! Complete with silk gown, velvet robe, and, of course, a golden scepter and sparkling jeweled crown!

"What's with her?" Denise asked.

"*She and those like her are the leaders of your world world.*"

"No way!" Nathan argued. "She's just a mom, just some housewife."

"*Precisely. They are the ones ones who prepare the next generation. They are the ones ones who shape and mold the future of your world.*"

The two stood staring.

"*This is is Imager's Truth,*" Bud explained. "*This is how Imager sees them, so this is is how they are. Now come, we must hurry.*"

But Denise and Nathan continued to stand, staring.

"Guys?" Bud's voice sounded more urgent. "*Guys, we better get going. I don't have much much tape left.*"

"Why didn't you send another one?" Denise asked. "Why didn't you send a whole case of tapes?"

"*I will, but your uncle will lose them. Please, we must must be on our way.*"

"Where?" Nathan asked.

"*I don't know know,*" Bud admitted. "*Anywhere, we just need to be moving.*"

The two started off. They half-walked, half-ran as they searched the mall, examining one misty Upside Downer after another. Each was clothed differently—this one like a baker, that one like a construction worker, another like a nurse. Several appeared as slaves with heavy chains wrapped around their ankles.

"I still don't know what I'm looking for," Nathan complained.

"*Imager's Breath,*" the tape responded.

"What?"

"*You are looking for those with Imager's Breath. They are the only only ones who can withstand the Sea of Justice.*"

"How do we recognize them?" Nathan demanded.

"*Everyone is transparent, correct correct? No one is solid.*"

"Sure, but—"

"*Even yourselves?*"

Again Denise and Nathan glanced at each other. Like everyone else, they were made out of the same dark mist.

"*Look for the persons who are are solid,*" Bud continued. "*They are the ones filled with Imager's Breath. They are are the only ones able to withstand the Sea of Justice.*"

Denise still didn't understand, but they continued the search anyway.

Eventually Bud called out, "*I've got one minute of tape tape left.*"

"One minute!" Denise cried.

"*Make that fifty-six seconds.*"

"But we haven't found anybody!" Nathan complained.

"We haven't even got close," Denise agreed.

"*You will. Olga's never been wrong wrong.*"

"You've got to give us more clues," Nathan said.

"If I had had them, I would would."

"Bud." Denise tried to reason. "This isn't working. It's not—"

"I've only got thirty-one seconds left left."

"You've got to tell us where to look!" Nathan demanded.

"As I've been saying saying, I'm not not sure."

"You just can't leave us here," Denise argued. "We've got to help Josh, you've got to show us where—"

"Olga says you'll succeed, so you'll succeed."

"Yes, but—"

"Four seconds . . . Sorry, guys guys."

"You just can't—"

"Good luck luck."

"Bud, you can't—"

Suddenly there was a loud click as the "play" button popped up. The cassette had ended.

"Bud!" Denise cried, coming to a stop. "Bud, answer me! Bud!"

But there was no answer. There was no more tape. Denise and Nathan were on their own.

Back in Fayrah, back in the Great Hall, Listro Q turned from Denise's and Nathan's tapestries. He could watch no more. It was too painful. He looked at the Weaver and tried to speak—to say something to convince the old man to let them go help the children. But the only words he could find were, "Uncool is it. Uncool."

The Weaver nodded. He seemed to understand, but would not budge from his position. Though the Fayrahnians had helped on earlier adventures, they must not interfere on this one.

Aristophenix gave another try.

> *"It doesn't make sense*
> *that we can't go and explain.*
> *'cause we'd be helpin' them miss*
> *all this confusion and pain."*

"And you would stop their growth, yes, you would," the Weaver gently replied. "Is that what you wish, to keep the children in the dark, to keep them ignorant of Imager's Breath?"

"Well, no," Aristophenix said, glancing at the floor, a little embarrassed. "I didn't, I didn't mean that."

The Weaver continued, "To be re-Breathed is an Upside Downer's greatest honor, yes, it is. Would you deprive your friends of that honor?"

Aristophenix did not answer. No one did . . . until Samson began to chatter loudly. He hovered right in front of Joshua's tapestry and sounded very concerned. Very, *very* concerned.

Aristophenix and Listro Q crowded in closer to him. They leaned forward and carefully examined some of the darkest, most sinister threads in the tapestry.

Samson was right, things did not look good for Josh. Not good at all . . .

physical perfection

AHHHH ..."

The pain screamed through every muscle, bone, and nerve of Joshua O'Brien's body.

"You're doing fine, dear heart," the coach encouraged. "Just a few more levels and you'll reach physical perfection."

But Josh was not fine. Not fine at all. It's true he had accomplished what most could not. He had nearly reached the highest level of the realm. In fact, as he looked around he saw only a few other contestants in his group who had made it this far. All the others had failed or dropped far behind. They could not withstand the painful tortures of changing themselves. But Josh could. Josh could withstand anything—especially if it meant perfection.

Unfortunately, Josh's ideas of perfection changed with each new level he entered.

For starters, there were his bulging muscles. At first, bulging muscles sounded great. Nothing like being the envy of all the guys in P.E. And let's not forget the benefit of a little extra female attention.

First he reshaped his arms by making them bigger than normal. But bigger arms called for bigger shoulders, so he made his shoulders bigger. But bigger shoulders called for a bigger chest, which called for a bigger waist, which called for bigger legs, which called for, well, you get the picture.

And just as soon as Josh had made his body big enough, he looked around and saw that his competitors had made their bodies even bigger. So he bore down harder to make his bigger yet. But, seeing what he was doing, they made theirs bigger still, which forced him to make his bigger, and on and on it went, each participant making themselves bigger and better for as long as they could endure the pain . . . since being bigger and better meant, well, being the biggest and the best.

Soon everyone had grown so large and monstrous that they stopped looking like humans. They'd become gigantic mountains of muscle—mountains of muscle that began losing their ability to move and keep their balance. The more muscles Josh created, the slower and clumsier he became. No longer could his giant legs easily transport his enormous weight. Something had to be done. He needed help. So Josh did the obvious. He created two more legs to help move the weight. And, as he continued to expand and enlarge himself, two more again.

The pain was unbearable, but to Josh, it was worth it. He was reaching perfection. He didn't understand the occasional chuckle he heard from the coach or her pet . . . like when he lost his balance and fell forward onto his six legs. Nor did he understand their whispered comment about him looking like some giant insect. But it didn't matter. He had to win this race. He had to become the best!

"What about your head?" the ice pet called. "You've become so wonderfully large you cannot see around yourself. Don't you need an extra head at the other end of your body?"

Of course, why hadn't he thought of that? The pain was unspeakable, but with his iron determination, Josh formed another head.

Next came the addition of a tail in the center of his body. Then fur for the tail. Then extra arms. And on and on it went. "How many more levels?" Josh gasped, the sweat pouring from both of his faces.

"Just two, Joshua O'Brien," the pet called, "just two more levels to reach perfection."

Josh nodded but felt himself growing dizzy. The edges around his vision became white and blurry. The pain was too great, too over-powering. He began losing consciousness.

But the coach urged him on. "You're nearly there, dear heart. You can reach physical perfection, we know you can!"

"What . . . what's next?" Josh groaned.

"Feathers!" the pet shouted in what sounded like glee. "Imager's most perfect and beautiful creatures all have gorgeous, multicolored feathers!"

"Are you sure?" Joshua moaned.

"Of course I'm sure. Look at the creature over there."

With great difficulty, Josh moved his heads and saw feathers start-ing to sprout from his nearest competitor. Having no other thought but to win, Josh groaned and followed suit. One by one, he forced the tiny hairs on his body to expand into brilliant, colorful feathers. This was no easy task. It required complete concentration. And as each hair blossomed into a bright, gaudy feather, Josh let out an ago-nizing scream of pain.

But he wouldn't stop. He couldn't stop. If this is what made him the most perfect looking of all creation, then this is what he'd be!

Finally, as the last feather grew and sprouted, Josh felt himself drifting up to the next level.

"Congratulations, dear heart!" the coach shouted. "You're in the lead! One more level!"

Josh lifted his heads. Above him was a ceiling of what looked like sand. "I can't . . . go through that."

"Yes, you can!" the pet shouted. "It is very thin."

"You're practically there!" the coach shouted. "One more level to go!"

Josh was in such pain that he could barely hear. "I don't—" He coughed. "I don't . . ." The words would not come; the pain was too great.

"You can do it!" the pet shouted. "Soon you'll be physically per-fect. You'll be through with this portion of the kingdom and enter the Realm of Perfect Popularity just above you!"

"I . . ."

"And then the Sea of Justice," the coach cried. "The sea is waiting for you!"

"What . . . do I have . . . to do?" Josh gasped.

"Just one more transformation," the coach shouted.

"What?"

"Your brain! Transform your brain to be like ours!"

"WHAT!"

"So you can hear our thoughts!" the pet cried.

"You're . . . crazy. I can't—"

There was a piercing scream just below them. All three looked down and saw the only remaining competitor sprout the last of his feathers and slowly rise toward them.

"Hurry, he's gaining!" the coach cried. "You must reach the next realm before he does!"

"I can't—"

"If you don't, he will win, you will lose!"

"All your work will be in vain!"

"But not . . . not my brain," Josh groaned. "I can't give you . . . my brain."

The other creature had finally drifted to his level. Now he and Josh were neck and neck.

"If you don't change your brain," the pet cried, "we cannot communicate—we cannot help you through the next realm!"

"But . . . it's . . . all I have left."

"AHHH . . . ," the other creature cried in pain and began to rise. He was about to pass Josh and enter the next realm.

"Here!" The coach shoved something hard and blue into one of Josh's hands. "It's a communicator. Wrap your ear around it."

"What?"

"If you will not give us your brain, then wrap an ear around this. It will allow you to hear us!"

"But—"

The creature continued rising. Any second and he'd break through into the next realm and win!

"Now!" the pet cried. "Do it now!"

"Hurry!" the Illusionist shouted.

Josh grabbed one of his ears and wrapped it around the tiny device. *"AHHHHH!"* he screamed and immediately shot upward. It was going to be close. He was beside the creature now. Just inches to go. He stretched out his necks as far as he could and . . . that did the trick! Josh struck the sand and broke through just a fraction of a second before the other creature.

"You did it!" the pet shouted.

"Congratulations, dear heart!" the Illusionist cried. "You're physically perfect. You've reached the next realm with all the other perfect creatures!"

Josh raised his heads and looked about. All around him were the winners from other races . . . each of their bodies as strange and different as his own.

Denise and Nathan raced through the mall continuing their search. Bud said they had to find perfect people, that only perfect people could save Joshua. But Bud wasn't there—the tape had run out, and now they were on their own.

"Look out!" Nathan shouted as they rounded a corner. He quickly yanked Denise back. Directly in front of them were dozens of runners. They were all dressed in track shoes and running shorts. Like everybody else, they were upside down and semitransparent. But these runners weren't running. Oh sure, their legs were pumping up and down, and they were breathing hard . . . but they never moved forward—not an inch.

"Who are you?" Nathan called to the nearest runner. "What are you doing?"

"I'm racing," the runner called back.

"Why?"

The runner jabbed his thumb at the rest of the group. "Because they are."

"Why are they racing?"

"Because I am!"

Nathan scowled. "Where are you racing to?" he asked.

"Wherever they are!" the runner shouted.

"And they're racing . . ." Nathan already suspected the answer.

"Wherever I am," the man shouted.

Well, that about wrapped it up in the logic department. This was weirder than the housewife queen or the beggar businessmen. Nathan had never heard such backward thinking. Then again maybe it wasn't backward, maybe it was just . . . upside down.

"What about you?" Denise called to another runner. "Why are you running?"

"Because they are!" came the answer.

"And they're running . . ." Denise paused, waiting for the obvious.

"Because I am."

"Come on," Nathan sighed, "let's get out of here." He turned toward the stereo and TV store.

But Denise had to try one last time. With a loud voice she shouted to the entire group. "Don't any of you know why you're running?"

The answer came back loud and clear, and in perfect unison: "BECAUSE THEY ARE!"

Denise shook her head, then turned to Nathan . . . and just in time. "Look out!" she cried.

Nathan looked up to see a slithering black tentacle shoot out of the display window of the stereo and TV store. It came from one of the big-screen TVs and passed through the window as easily as if it wasn't there. But where it came from wasn't as important as where it was going.

It was heading straight for him!

Nathan froze, unsure where to run. Denise saved him the effort. She dove into the air and tackled him hard to the ground—just as the tentacle swooshed above their heads, missing them by inches.

Quickly, they scrambled back to their feet and turned to the display window. What Nathan saw made him go cold. A dozen big-screen TVs were playing. And reaching out from each and every one was a long, slimy tentacle. A few of the tentacles, like the one that had tried to catch him, swished and flicked in the air searching for a careless victim, but most had already found somebody. Most had already wrapped around a passing child or adult and had dragged them forward until their faces were pressed flat against the window.

At first the people fought and struggled, but as the tentacles forced them to stare at the TV screens, they slowly stopped fighting . . . as if they'd lost the will to resist.

"Don't look at the screens!" Nathan warned Denise. "Whatever you do, don't look at the—"

But he was too late. Denise was already looking.

"What's that?" she asked, her voice sounding fainter and far away.

"Don't look at the—" But Nathan never finished his sentence. The tentacle that had nearly captured him was slithering toward her.

"Denny, get back!"

"Don't worry," she answered, her voice growing thinner, "there's nothing wrong with watching—"

"It's coming straight for—"

"—everybody's watch—"

Suddenly, the tentacle wrapped itself around her waist. It started dragging her toward the window. Nathan stayed at her side, punching and hitting the thing for all he was worth, but it did no good. "Denny!"

It pulled her up against the glass along with the other helpless victims.

"Denny!"

Nathan was frantic. Then an idea suddenly came to mind. He reached down and yanked the canteen from Denise's belt. He quickly unscrewed the cap. Then he began pouring the liquid letters and words onto the tentacle. Every place they touched hissed and smoked, burning deep into the creature. The tentacle thrashed and whipped in agony, its flesh sizzling and popping until it finally released Denise and made a hasty retreat.

"Denny, can you hear me?" Nathan shouted. "Denny!"

At first all she did was stare glassy-eyed at the TV in front of her. It wasn't until he forced her head around to look at him that life seemed to slowly return.

"Oh . . . hi, Nathan." She gave a confused smile. "What's up, what happened?"

"What *happened?*" he cried. Without waiting for an answer, he grabbed her arm and pulled her from the window. "Come on, we're getting out of here!"

"But the people," Denise protested, looking around the mall. "We've got to find the perfect people."

"There's nobody perfect around here," he snapped. "Everyone is upside down and all misty and just plain weird. No one here has Imager's Breath."

"So where do we look?" Denise asked.

Nathan didn't have a clue. Maybe Bud was wrong. Maybe they'd *never* find the perfect people. Maybe *no one* could save Joshua from Bobok and the Illusionist. Maybe he really would be destroyed in the Sea of—

"Wait a minute!" Denise's face suddenly lit up. "What about a church? If we're looking for perfect people, maybe we should try a church!"

"A church?" Nathan asked skeptically. He didn't know much about churches or churchgoers. Oh sure, a lot of kids in his class went to Sunday school and stuff, but from what he'd seen, they were *anything* but perfect.

"No, listen," Denise insisted. "Our neighbors across the street go to church—and they're pretty cool—and my cousins, they're all right."

"Okay." Nathan shrugged, figuring they'd give it a try. "So where's the closest church?"

"Over there." Denise pointed to a row of public telephones.

"What?"

"In the phone book! Let's look one up in the phone book!"

the
ReaLm of
PoPULaRity

What is this place? Josh wondered as he turned his two feathery heads from side to side. All around him were creatures of every imaginable shape and size. Some as big as buildings, others as small as bugs. Some with one body and a hundred heads, others with a hundred bodies and no head.

Anxious to investigate, Josh lumbered forward on his six legs. Well, actually he did a lot more falling than lumbering. When you're only used to two legs, having six can be a little confusing.

But at least there was ground to fall upon. Ah, blessed, beautiful, dependable ground. What a relief. No more floating around like in that last realm. There were also other features he appreciated like rocks, sand, trees, even a sun or two.

As far as Josh could tell, he was on some sort of beach. But it was the ocean that really caught his attention. Instead of water it seemed to be made of metal that was as shiny as silver.

"You there—the new kid!" a voice called.

Josh turned his heads to see what could only be described as a walking set of encyclopedias. That's right. The creature looked like twenty-six separate books all linked together. Somewhere in the middle, about the "M" volume, there was a small mouth and a pointed nose. And on both sides of that (about the "L" and "N" volumes), there were two narrow eyes.

"Hello," Josh said, trying his best to sound cheery. (Even here he was concerned about making the right impression.) He wanted to reach out and shake hands, but with four additional limbs to choose from he wasn't exactly sure which to offer.

"Welcome," the encyclopedia answered pleasantly.

Josh nodded. "Thanks. Listen, would you mind telling me where I am?"

The encyclopedia gave a gentle laugh. "My, you really are ignorant, aren't you?"

Suddenly, Josh felt a numbness rush through his mind—as if part of his brain had gone to sleep—as if his memory had been erased. He grabbed both of his heads and staggered backward. The creature's opinion of him had become true. He *had* become ignorant!

"No!" Josh cried. But it was too late. By the time he looked up, the creature had left. So had most of Josh's intelligence. In fact, Josh was so ignorant that it was all he could do to remember his own name.

"What's going on?" he shouted. "Somebody, please help me!"

"It is the second half of the kingdom," the coach's pet answered through the communicator in Josh's ear, "the Realm of Perfect Popularity."

It took all of Josh's concentration to remember the little blue ball. "What . . . what happened?" he stammered.

The pet's voice continued. "In the Realm of Popularity you become exactly what people think you are."

"That is correct," the coach's voice agreed. "Here, you literally become their opinion of you."

Josh stared blankly ahead, trying to understand.

"They think you're stupid," the pet's voice said, "so you become stupid. If they think you're smart, you become smart."

"But that's not fair," Josh protested, "becoming what people think of you."

"Of course it is," the coach replied. "You, dear heart, have lived your entire life for what people think of you. Here, at last, you will become exactly that. It is entirely fair because it is entirely what you've wanted."

"But . . ." Josh tried to argue; however, since he had no further thoughts on the subject, it seemed a little pointless. Come to think of it, he had no further thoughts on any subject. Not anymore. But he did have a question. "Can I ever, you know, get smart again?"

"Of course," the coach answered.

"How?"

"Just convince someone to think you're smart."

"That's it?"

"That's it."

"That's what this realm is about," the pet's voice said. "And that's the way you become perfect enough to enter the Sea of Justice. Convince everybody that you're perfect and, just like that, you'll be perfect."

"Hey you!"

Josh spun around just in time to see a giant rock rolling down the beach toward him. And we're not talking your average, run-of-the-mill giant rock. We're talking your top-of-the-line boulder . . . one big enough to crush a house!

"Oh, hi there," Josh called. He tried to sound calm as the rock continued rolling toward him. But even Josh's limited intelligence knew that this rock had no intention of slowing down for a friendly chat. Instead, it seemed to have only one purpose . . . to flatten him! And it was about to succeed!

"No . . . don't!" Josh cried. "Please! Please stop, don't hit me!"

The boulder gave a hearty chuckle and picked up speed, rolling even faster.

With Josh's lack of mental skills, it was tough to figure out what to do. But eventually he realized he had two choices: Run . . . or, well . . . run. It was a difficult decision. But after much concentration and one lucky guess, he made the right choice.

As he took off running the boulder roared with laughter. "My, oh my, if you ain't just about the scaredest, most cowardly thing I've ever seen."

Before Josh knew it, sheer terror filled his mind. Any courage he'd had quickly disappeared. His heart pounded. He began running around in panicky little circles screaming, "Help me! Help me! Help me!" until, at last, he spotted a huge piece of driftwood and scrambled under it for cover.

The boulder changed course and headed off in another direction, laughing all the way. He had decided Josh was a coward and that is what Josh had become. Now the poor guy was consumed by fear—mindless, irrational fear. And not fear of one thing or another, but fear of *everything*.

"Relax," the pet cooed through his communicator.

"What's happening?" Josh screamed as he continued to kick and fight his way further under the driftwood.

"As I said, in this realm you become exactly what people think of you."

"How do I change it?" Josh squealed in terror. "How do I change?"

"Convince them to think differently," the coach replied. "That's the only way to be perfect enough to enter the Sea of Justice. You must make everybody think you're perfect."

"But . . . they'll hurt me . . ."

"Joshua O'Brien," the pet's voice scolded, "you've devoted your entire life to impressing people. You'll do splendidly here. Splendidly."

By the time Denise and Nathan arrived at the church, the effect of the water was wearing off. Oh, they still caught glimpses of people as Imager saw them, but for the most part things were starting to look pretty normal again. And that was good. Denise in particular was getting a bit tired of looking at everybody upside down all of the time . . . not to mention seeing them as they really were instead of how they pretended to be.

What really cinched it for her was the traffic jam at Third and Franklin. Cars were backed up for blocks. Drivers honked and shouted and screamed. At least that's how it appeared to everybody else. But thanks to the water from the stream that was still in her eyes and ears, Denise saw things a little differently. True, everybody was still angry and upset, but instead of firing off their mouths at one another, they were firing off guns. That's right. Denise saw drivers using everything from pistols to bazookas, rifles to rocket launchers. For her the intersection had become a war zone . . . literally.

People were diving from their cars, shouting, cursing, blasting away with machine guns, blowing one another up with grenades. Needless to say, she and Nathan hightailed it out of there as fast as they could.

Now, they were seated in the office of some church. They'd already spoken with the Reverend for several minutes until he had to leave the room and take care of a disturbance in the lobby. He promised to be back in just a moment.

"Are you sure about this place?" Denise whispered as they waited for his return. "I mean, if this is a church, aren't there supposed to be crosses or Bibles or something?"

"How should I know?" Nathan said. "The phone book says it's a church, so it's a church."

Denise threw a suspicious look out the window to the fancy sports car in the Reverend's parking space, then to the expensive antique furniture filling his office, and finally to the plush carpeting at her feet. From what she'd heard of churches, this didn't exactly fit the bill. Or maybe it did. What did she know?

Suddenly the carved oak doors opened and the Reverend returned. "I do apologize for that," he said as he glided toward his desk. He was tall, handsome, and had a beautiful silk suit. Then there was his voice . . . smooth and understanding. "That was another one of those homeless people," he said, shaking his head in disgust. "You can imagine how bothersome they can be. But not to worry, we've called the police." Then, taking his seat, he smiled. "Now, where were we?"

"We were asking if you knew any perfect people," Nathan said.

The Reverend flashed a dazzling, every-tooth-in-place smile. "Ah yes . . . perfection." He toyed with the diamond ring on his left pinkie. "You must understand, Nathan, that here at Club God, we are *all* perfect."

"You are?" Nathan asked in surprise.

"Of course," the man laughed. "And you can be, too." He turned his perfect smile upon Denise. "And you, as well."

She couldn't help but smile back.

"How's that possible?" Nathan asked. "Everybody makes mistakes."

"It doesn't matter, my friend. Because once you join Club God, you automatically become perfect."

"I do?"

"That's right." The Reverend gave him a wink. "All you have to do is say the magic words and you're automatically forgiven. One hundred percent clean. For now and for anything you ever do in the future."

"You're kidding."

"No. And the best thing is, you don't have to do a thing. It's absolutely free."

"But shouldn't I, you know, feel bad for the stuff I've done, shouldn't I try to do better?"

"Nonsense," the Reverend chuckled. "Then it wouldn't be free, would it?"

Denise sat there staring at the man. Something about his mouth didn't seem right. The words he spoke didn't quite fit. It was like watching one of those old Japanese monster movies dubbed into English. He was out of sync. She threw a look at Nathan, but he was too caught up in the Reverend's words to notice.

"Just say the magic words, join the club, and you're free to do whatever you want whenever you want to do it."

Denise stifled a gasp. Before her eyes the man began to sprout hair all over his face. And we're not talking five-o'clock-shadow hair. We're talking thick, bristly hair. It was popping out everywhere.

At first she thought it was her imagination. Then she remembered the water. Maybe the effects hadn't entirely worn off. Maybe she was seeing the Reverend the way he really was.

"It doesn't get any cheaper than free, does it?" the man asked.

"No, I guess not," Nathan said.

Denise cautiously reached for the canteen and began to unscrew the lid. Maybe it was the water, maybe it wasn't. There was only one way to find out.

"As long as you show up at the club once a week and, of course pay your dues, you'll always be perfect."

Carefully she dipped her fingers into the canteen and raised them to her ear. She tilted her head to the right and managed to get a small drop of the liquid inside. And that was all it took. Suddenly, the man's words matched his mouth perfectly. And for good reason. Now she heard what he was *really* saying.

"I want power! Give me power!"

Denise's eyes widened as he continued.

"I'll make you feel good so you'll keep coming back so my empire can grow and grow and—"

"Well!" Denise said, suddenly jumping up. "Will you look at the time. I guess we better hit the road, huh, Nate?"

Nathan and the Reverend looked up at her in surprise. "What are you talking about?" Nathan asked.

"You know," she said, motioning toward the door.

"Know what?"

She gave him a look of exasperation, then tried another approach. "Uhh . . . homework! Yeah, that's it. Yes sir, got to crack the ol' books, got those big tests tomorrow, yes siree."

"Denny . . ."

"Yeah, Nathan?"

"Tomorrow's Sunday."

"Oh right, of course," she pretended to laugh as she walked over to his chair, put both hands on his shoulders, and tried to lift him. "But you know how I like to be prepared. Right, Nathan? *Right?*"

But Nathan was too stubborn (not to mention heavy) to move.

The Reverend turned his perfect smile upon Denise, and in his kindest, most sensitive voice screamed, *"Listen, brat, you're ruining my sales pitch! Keep your mouth shut!"* The outburst was a shock to Denise. But apparently she was the only one who heard it.

"Can't you see we're on to something here?" Nathan chided her. He turned back to the Reverend. "Now, what were you saying?"

Denise felt like an idiot. Of course that was nothing new. But the water from the stream had never been wrong before. No way was this place a church—at least, not a real one. And no way was this guy a real "Reverend."

"I was simply wondering," the man asked Nathan, *"how much money do your parents make a year?"*

Denise could feel the tops of her ears getting hot. She reached for the canteen. If Nathan wouldn't listen to her, then she'd make him hear for himself. As discreetly as possible, she poured a small handful of the liquid into her palm.

"Oh, Nathan?" she asked.

"What is it now?" he whined. "Can't you see I'm—"

She threw the handful of water at his ear. Well, that was her target. Unfortunately as he turned his head, the target moved. Instead of getting an earful of water, Nathan got a faceful. To be more precise, an eyeful.

"What are you trying to prove?" Nathan demanded as he angrily wiped his face with his sleeve. Then he looked back at the Reverend and screamed, *"AUGH!"* He jumped up and stumbled backward over his chair.

"What is it? What do you see?" Denise shouted.

"A wolf!" Nathan pointed at the Reverend. "He's a wolf!"

"What has the brat done now?" the Reverend snarled.

"See for yourself, Denny! He's a wolf, a wolf!"

Quickly, Denise splashed some of the water into her own eyes. Now she could hear *and* see. And Nathan was right. The Reverend was a wolf. A snarling, ravenous wolf. The hair she'd seen earlier suddenly made sense. But it wasn't hair, it was fur—fur that covered his entire body!

"I WILL BE THE BIGGEST!" the animal growled as he leapt to his desk and began pacing back and forth on all fours. *"MY KINGDOM WILL GROW! AND GROW! AND GROW!"*

"Well, thank you, uh, Reverend," Nathan stuttered as he backed up toward the door. "It was a pleasure meeting you." He groped for the doorknob. "We'd love to stay, but, like Denny said, we have a lot of things to do, so, uh . . ." He turned the knob and quickly threw open the door. "See ya!"

They dashed out of his office and were on the street in seconds. That's when Denise heard the eerie, unnerving cry. She'd never actually heard a wolf howl before, but that is exactly what she heard now. A lone wolf howling, crying over the meal that had just escaped its clutches.

CHAPTER EIGHT

PERFECTION at Last

It took all of the concentration Josh had left, not to mention courage, to finally start believing the coach. Maybe she was right, maybe he really could survive in this Realm of Perfect Popularity. After all, he had spent his whole life trying to be popular. He had devoted all of his energy to impressing people. Things really weren't that much different here.

First he had to regain his intelligence—to convince someone that he was smart so he could be smart again. That meant finding a creature even more ignorant than himself.

"Over there," the coach's voice called.

"Where?" Josh asked nervously.

"I hear a dog barking."

Not far away Josh saw a French poodle type of creature jumping up and down in the air. "But he'll bite me."

"Go ahead, he won't hurt you."

"But—"

"Do it! Convince him you're smarter!"

"But—"

"Do you want to stay like this forever?"

"No, but—"

"Then hurry," the coach urged. "Hurry!"

Reluctantly and more than a little frightened, Josh stepped forward. "Excuse me," he called to the animal. "Excuse me!"

"Yap, yap, yap, yap, yap, yap!" the poodle replied as she continued jumping mindlessly into the air.

"If it's not too much trouble, I mean if you don't mind, could I talk to you a second?"

"Yap, yap, yap, yap, yap, yap!"

"Right." Josh swallowed. He took a breath for courage and continued. "Look, I appear to be pretty smart, don't I?"

"Yap, yap, yap, yap, yap, yap!"

"I see," Josh replied, not seeing at all. "But at least I'm not jumping into the air and yapping my head off, right?"

"Yap, yap, yap, yap, yap, yap!"

"So . . ." He took another breath. "Since I'm not annoying everybody or making a total fool of myself as you are . . . well, wouldn't that at least make me smarter than you?"

"Yap, yap, yap, yap, yap, yap!"

Although the dog appeared to be thinking of nothing, something must have happened inside her little brain. Because suddenly Joshua felt intelligence returning. Not a lot, but a little.

Yet that was only the beginning. Now he had to find other folks with equal or less intelligence than the poodle and convince them. No problem. First, he approached a professional wrestler and asked the same questions. The results were the same. He grew smarter. Next there was the teen covered in tattoos who had more rivets in her body than a naval shipyard. Another success. And on and on he went.

Then he had to regain his courage by convincing someone more cowardly than himself that he was courageous. Fortunately, there was a chicken-like creature pecking away in the nearby sand. And since a chicken is the most timid animal in the universe (why do you think it's called *chicken?*) it took only a second to get her to run from him, flapping her wings and clucking for her life. As she did, she must have thought how brave he was because, suddenly, he had instant courage.

Next, he wanted to work on honesty. A brief chat with a used car salesman would take care of that. Unfortunately, there were no used car salesmen on the beach, so he had to settle for a politician. The results were even better.

Then came the sense of humor, then the winning personality, then the super friendliness, and so it continued—Josh moving down the beach convincing people that he was better than they were, and . . . becoming it.

His fame and popularity grew and grew until finally the big moment arrived. He had to convince someone he was the most popular creature in the realm. But with his fantastic new personality, that shouldn't be a problem. Still, not wanting to take any chances, he was careful to choose just the right creature. There, over by the rocks— a kid wearing a pocket protector whose glasses were taped together in the middle. The fact that he also wore a bowling shirt with the words *Chess Club President* embroidered on the back didn't hurt.

"Hey there," Josh called.

The kid turned to him, sniffing from about a thousand allergies. "You—you're Joshua O'Brien!" he said, sniffing some more.

Josh grinned.

"Why is someone as great as you (*sniff*) talking to a loser like me (*sniff, sniff*)?"

For the briefest second Josh felt compassion for the kid. "You're not a loser."

The kid's face lit up and the pocket protector disappeared. "I'm not?"

"Of course not."

Next to go were the taped glasses.

"What are you doing?" the coach cried through Josh's earpiece.

"I'm just trying to help the guy."

"You cannot win by helping! You must make him think you're the greatest creature alive!"

Josh frowned. "Yeah, but—"

"You must insult him. You must humiliate him into thinking you are the best!"

Josh hesitated. He'd always looked out for the underdog, he never put them down. "The kid's got some good qualities," Josh argued.

There was a ripping sound. He turned to see the kid's bowling shirt had been replaced by a muscle shirt. Not only that, but he'd stopped sniffing.

"He will overtake and destroy you!" the coach's pet shouted through the communicator. "Stop making him think he's somebody!"

"Hurry, dear heart, convince him you're better. Hurry or all your effort will be in vain."

Josh nodded. He wasn't crazy about this, but he understood. It was the only way to win. He turned back to the kid and said, "Nice shirt."

The kid stood straighter. "Thanks."

Josh hesitated, then added, "For a loser!"

Suddenly the boy hunched over smaller.

"Nobody wears muscle shirts anymore."

Suddenly the bowling shirt was back on. "They don't?" the boy asked.

"Of course not. And if you were cool and popular like me, you'd know that, wouldn't you?"

Now the glasses returned . . . until the boy looked down at the sand in embarrassment and they fell from his face. He dropped to his hands and knees, searching for them, but he couldn't see a thing.

Josh wanted to help, but he knew the rules. He had to win. "Hey, loser!" he called. "Look at me when I'm talking to you!"

Slowly the boy looked up, squinting toward Joshua.

"Who's the most popular person in the realm?"

The kid muttered something and returned to his search.

Joshua knew what should be done next, but he just didn't have the heart.

"Do it!" the coach shouted. "Do it!"

Reluctantly, Josh dug one foot into the sand.

"Do it! Do it! Do it!"

And then, sadly, he kicked the sand into the boy's face.

The kid started coughing and choking.

"Who's the most popular person in the realm?" Josh repeated. With even less enthusiasm, he dug another foot into the sand, threatening to kick more.

"You are," the kid gasped.

Josh felt terrible as the boy continued coughing and spitting. "You are the most popular! You are! You are!"

Suddenly the entire beach broke into applause. Josh looked up. Everyone was clapping and grinning at him. It had happened. He had convinced someone to think he was the most popular and, just like that, Joshua O'Brien had become the most popular creature in the Realm of Popularity.

"Congratulations, dear heart," the coach called through the earpiece. "You are nearly ready to enter the Sea of Justice."

"Nearly?" Josh asked. "What's left?"

"Simply convince someone there that you are perfect. Then you will be perfect and qualified to enter the Sea."

"No sweat." Josh grinned. He turned toward the fans who were still applauding. "Excuse me?" he shouted. "Excuse me?"

A hush fell over the group. The great Joshua O'Brien was about to speak.

"None of you can ever recall me making a mistake, can you?"

"Oh, no," the crowd insisted. "Absolutely not, you are too popular to make mistakes."

"Then, could that mean . . ." He looked to the ground, pretending to be modest. "Oh no, never mind."

"No, please," the crowd asked. "Please, tell us what your great mind is thinking."

"It's just . . ." He gave a shrug. "Well, since if I've never made a mistake and since I've got this perfect body and I'm the most popular person in the realm . . . doesn't that kind of, you know, make me . . . *perfect?*"

The crowd began to buzz. Apparently, the thought had never crossed their minds. But, now that he mentioned it . . .

"Yes!" they began to shout. "Yes, yes, you *are* perfect! You are the most perfect creature we have ever seen!"

And, suddenly, just like that, Joshua O'Brien became perfect.

"Excellent, dear heart!" the coach cried. "Excellent! Now hurry before someone challenges you. Hurry and enter the Sea of Justice."

"But where?" Josh asked, looking around. "I don't see any—"

"It's that ocean beside you," the pet's voice shouted.

"That?" Josh asked, pointing at the silvery water along the beach. "*That* is the Sea of Justice?"

"Precisely."

"But I can't swim in that. I can't—"

"Dear heart, it only appears to be liquid silver. Touch it with your foot. Enter it and you will see it is merely mirrors. Perfectly fashioned, beautiful mirrors."

"But—but I don't—"

"We'll be with you," the coach assured him. "In the reflections, we'll be with you."

Josh threw a look at the crowd. They were starting to fidget. Any moment one of them might think he was weak or afraid or worse yet, imperfect. And if anyone thought that, he knew what would happen.

Josh turned back to look at the silver water.

"Hurry, before you are challenged!" the pet called. "Hurry!"

Josh closed his eyes a moment. Then he took a deep breath and started toward the ocean.

It was exactly as the coach had promised. As soon as his foot touched the silvery liquid, he realized it wasn't liquid at all. Instead, the sea *was* made of mirrors. Nothing but beautiful mirrors. Mirrors reflecting in every direction. Mirrors that parted, allowing his feet to touch the dry sandy floor below.

The crowd cheered as Josh waded deeper into the Sea of Justice. Soon he was up to his knees, then his waist. Not a single mirror touched him. Each gently parted to the side as he waded in deeper and deeper.

"You should see this place," he said in awe to the coach.

"We are not even worthy to approach it," she replied.

"But we may enter its reflections," her pet added.

"I wish Denny and Nathan could see," Josh exclaimed.

"Oh, they will, dear heart, they will. Not only will they see it, but so will your friends from Fayrah."

"Aristophenix and Listro Q?" Josh asked, his excitement growing.

"And that bothersome bug," the pet added. "At last the trap has been set."

"Trap?" Josh frowned.

"Treat," the coach hastily corrected. "Fido meant *treat,* didn't you, boy. *Treat.*"

"Yes." The pet cleared his throat. "*Treat.* The *treat* of justice. The *treat* of receiving all that you rightly deserve."

"But how?" Josh asked.

"Look deeply into the mirrors, dear heart. Look deeply into the mirrors and you will understand perfectly . . ."

He lied to us," Nathan said as he slumped into the beanbag chair in Joshua's room. It had been a long day of searching with plenty of surprises, but no results. "The guy flat-out lied to us."

"I don't think Fayrahnians can do that," Denise said.

"Bud's not from Fayrah, he's from Biiq, remember."

"Same thing . . . and I don't think they can make mistakes, not with that Olga computer thing of theirs."

"Yeah, right," Nathan scoffed. Then motioning to the canteen on her belt, he added, "And a lot of good that water did us." He gave a sigh. "Who are we kidding? We'll never be able to find perfect people—we'll never be able to help my brother."

But Denise had stopped listening. She was looking down at the canteen. Nathan watched as she turned and headed for Joshua's dresser. There was a small dish that he used to dump his loose change and pocket junk into. She picked it up and dumped it out.

"What are you doing?" Nathan demanded.

She didn't answer. Instead, she removed the canteen from her belt, unscrewed the lid, and poured some of the water into the dish.

Nathan rose to join her. "Denny?"

Next she grabbed one of the dozen campaign buttons lying around. Carefully she positioned its photo over the dish of water. Then she lowered her head for a better view.

"What are you doing?" Nathan repeated.

"Look," she said in a breathless whisper. "Do you see it?"

"See what . . . where?"

"In the water? The reflection. It's different than what we see."

"Different? What are you talking about?"

"I saw it the first time we were in Fayrah. And this morning in my bedroom."

Nathan lowered his head until it was beside hers. At first he saw nothing. But as she adjusted the angle of the photo, he finally caught a reflection of it in the water. It was not a reflection of his grinning, good-looking brother. It was a reflection of Joshua, yes, but a Joshua with grotesque muscles, multicolored feathers and . . . Nathan sucked in his breath. This Joshua had six legs and two heads!

"Denny," he cried, "what's going on? Denny, we gotta help him!"

"But how?" Denise whispered. "How?"

Over in Fayrah, at the Great Hall, Aristophenix, Listro Q, Samson, and the Weaver stared at Joshua's tapestry. They studied with horror the thread indicating that he was wading into the Sea of Justice.

"Survive, cannot he!" Listro Q cried as he looked up from the tapestry to the Weaver. "Sea of Justice, it will kill him!"

Aristophenix agreed.

> "we have to assist him,
> there ain't not a doubt.
> no way can we stay here,
> without helpin' him out."

"Only perfect people can enter the Sea of Justice," the Weaver repeated. "If you enter the sea, it will destroy you." The old man tried to sound stern, but he knew what Josh was about to suffer. He knew something should be done.

And something *would* be done. He knew that as well. If the group could simply hold out and wait a few minutes longer, something would *definitely* be done . . .

the
sea of
justice

J osh waded deeper and deeper into the sea. And with every step he took, the mirrors continued to part before him. There were thousands of them. Millions. "This is incredible," he said. "Everywhere I look there are mirrors—miles and miles of mirrors."

Immediately, the blue orb's reflection appeared in a mirror beside him. "Gorgeous, aren't they?"

Josh gave a start, then nodded in agreement. "They're beautiful . . . But where's the rest of it?"

"The rest of what?" the coach asked as her reflection appeared in another mirror beside him.

"I mean, they're beautiful and everything, but there's more to this place than a bunch of mirrors, right? You said something about a *treat.*"

"I'm afraid you haven't looked deep enough," the coach replied.

"What do you mean?"

"Look into the mirrors . . . What do you see?"

"Nothing. Nothing but me."

"Precisely."

"But—"

"Have you ever seen such beauty, such perfection?" the coach asked.

Joshua looked more deeply. And the deeper he looked, the more he liked what he saw.

"Look at the curve of each of those muscles," the coach whispered. "Magnificent muscles . . . muscles you have worked so long and hard to obtain."

Josh continued to stare. She was right. His muscles *were* marvelous to look at. They *were* magnificent. And the longer he stared, the more he enjoyed their beauty . . . their *perfection*.

"That's the purpose of the sea," she whispered, "to enjoy the fruits of your labor. To receive your fullest reward." The coach's mirror moved a little closer. "And those feathers—have you ever seen anything so beautiful, so breathtaking?"

At first Josh wasn't so sure about the feathers. But the more he looked, the more he appreciated their intricate detail, their brilliant colors.

"And what of those wondrous heads of yours . . ."

As the coach continued to speak and as Josh continued to admire himself, a warmth of satisfaction flooded through his chest. This was *him*. This was the great Joshua O'Brien. The result of all his hard work was right here, reflected in these perfect mirrors. The warmth grew warmer; the satisfaction, more satisfying. At last, here in the Sea of Justice, Josh was finally able to enjoy the reward of his efforts. At last he was receiving . . . well, there was no other word for it but *justice*. Perfect, beautiful, *justice*.

"This is amazing," he whispered. "I've never felt so . . . so . . ."

"So proud?" the pet offered. "So full of accomplishment?"

Josh could only nod.

"But you've barely scratched the surface, dear heart. Look deeper," the coach encouraged. "Much, much deeper."

Josh obeyed. He couldn't help himself. He didn't want to help himself. And as he looked deeper, something within the mirrors began to shift. The reflection of his "perfect body" began to waver and change.

"That's it, dear heart," the coach softly spoke. "Look deep inside yourself. Find out who you *really* are."

In the mirror, Josh began to see a five-year-old boy. He was kneeling with a handful of kids beside a terrified puppy.

"That's me," Josh whispered in awe. "That's me when I was little."

"That is correct," the pet purred. "But look deeper still."

As Josh stared, the little boy grabbed a nearby milk carton and filled it with rocks. Next he tied the carton around the neck of the whimpering puppy. Then, as the other kids urged him on, he shouted at the animal and gave it a good kick.

The puppy scurried off like a frightened rabbit. The rattling milk carton only added to his terror and confusion. He yelped and ran helplessly in all directions as everyone laughed and congratulated young Josh for a job well done.

"I'd completely forgotten that . . . ," Joshua sadly mumbled as he stared into the mirror.

"Quite the little monster, aren't you?" the coach's voice gently accused.

The comment surprised Joshua. "That was a long time ago," he said. "I'm not that way anymore."

"You're not?" the coach asked.

Before Josh could answer, another reflection formed deep within the mirrors. It was Joshua when he was nine. He stood on the playground with a crowd of other kids. They were laughing and jeering at a smaller boy who was pulling himself out of a mud puddle—his face cut and bleeding.

The Josh in the reflection tried to look away, but he was too late. The little boy caught his eyes and staggered toward him, soaked and muddy.

"Make him stop," the boy pleaded. "Please, Josh! I never stole his pen, you know I wouldn't." He grabbed Joshua's shirt. "Please make him stop!"

"You sticking up for this weasel?"

Young Josh turned to see a huge bully striding toward him, obviously the cause of the boy's battered face. Josh swallowed hard as he looked at the bully, then down at the boy clinging to him for protection.

"Get out of there, O'Brien!" someone in the group shouted. Others joined in. "Move it! Get out of the way!" They wanted to see a good beating, and Josh seemed to be the only one preventing it.

The boy circled behind Josh, cowering, pleading to him for help. But Josh didn't look at him. Instead, he stared hard at the ground and said nothing.

The crowd jeered and shouted louder, "Get out of there! Get out of the way!"

"What will it be, O'Brien?" the bully demanded.

Josh had no answer.

The crowd grew more angry. He looked up at their faces. They meant business. *Real* business. He looked back at the bully.

The bully meant business, too.

Then, finally, without a word, Joshua O'Brien stepped to the side.

The bully lost no time in grabbing the little boy. Everyone cheered. Everyone but young Josh and, of course, the little boy. It's hard to cheer when you're getting the stuffing beaten out of you.

Squirming in discomfort, the older Josh tried looking away, but the scene filled every mirror in the sea. No matter where he turned, he saw the little boy being hit again and again and again . . . as the young Josh stood by refusing to help.

"There's nothing you won't do for popularity, is there?" the coach taunted.

Josh couldn't answer.

"Is there?"

He continued staring into the mirrors. His eyes filling with moisture; his throat growing thick and tight. "I didn't . . . I didn't know what to do."

The beatings continued. So did the crowd's cheers. And with each blow, the mirrors surrounding Joshua moved in a little closer.

"I don't . . ." Josh's voice was hoarse. "I don't want to look anymore. I came here for justice, not this."

"Oh, but this *is* justice," the blue orb purred.

"No, it isn't."

"This is what you're *really* like and this is what you *really* deserve."

"Those are exceptions," Josh insisted. "Mistakes."

"They are still truth . . . and truth demands justice."

"I didn't come here to see my mistakes." Josh croaked, still unable to take his eyes from the mirrors.

"You came to receive justice, and so you will."

"But . . ." Josh felt himself growing desperate. "This isn't . . . what I . . ."

The coach laughed. "This is exactly what you wanted. And it is only the beginning, dear heart! Only the beginning!"

The pet joined in the laughter as more reflections formed, as more memories flickered across the mirrors—memories of ugly mistakes, thoughtless actions, embarrassing failures. And, as their reflections appeared, as Josh stared, unable to look away, the mirrors moved in on him closer and closer . . .

Back in Fayrah, Aristophenix turned from Joshua's tapestry. "I don't understand what you're doin'!"

The Weaver simply looked at him.

"You keep tellin' us not to interfere—that Imager is using all this to get him re-Breathed!"

"That is correct." The Weaver nodded. "Yes, it is."

"But I don't see any sign of him gettin' re-Breathed. All I see is Josh gettin' tortured and Denny and Nathan gettin' more frustrated!"

Samson darted above Aristophenix's shoulder and chattered in loud, high-pitched agreement.

Listro Q also stepped forward. "Go in there and help him, now I say!" He reached into his coat and pulled out the Cross-Dimensionalizer.

It appeared the Weaver was about to have a mutiny on his hands. But instead of growing angry, his answer was gentle and firm. "If you enter the Sea of Justice, you will be destroyed."

"What about Josh? He's bein' destroyed right now!"

The Weaver continued evenly. "Your love for Joshua O'Brien is most commendable, yes, it is. But you must not interfere. You must trust that Imager's love is greater than yours. You must *not* enter the Sea of Justice."

"We have to do somethin'!"

The Weaver glanced at his watch. "In exactly two minutes and thirty-seven seconds you will Cross-Dimensionalize to Denny and Nathan."

"What!" Aristophenix exclaimed. "You're givin' us permission to visit the Upside-Down Kingdom?"

"Of course. Your visit has always been woven into these tapestries. If you would have looked more closely, you would have known this. It was simply a matter of time."

"Right all!" Listro Q shouted.

Samson darted above their heads with his own brand of high-pitched enthusiasm.

And Aristophenix found an opportunity to fire off a poem.

> "QUICK, GRAB that CROSS-DIMENSIONALIZER,
> AND ENTER THEM COORDINATES.
> WE'LL BE SEEIN' DENNY AND NATHAN,
> AND A-TELLIN' 'EM ... AND TELLIN' 'EM ..."

Aristophenix turned back to the Weaver. "Uh, what exactly *will* we be tellin' 'em?"

The Weaver smiled. "Tell them they are about to be re-Breathed."

"All right!" Aristophenix cried as he turned to the others. Then spinning back to the Weaver, he asked, "But ... how ..."

"You'll know," the Weaver chuckled. "Trust me, you'll know."

Without another word, and certainly before another poem, Listro Q reached for his Cross-Dimensionalizer, pressed in the coordinates.

BEEP ...

　　BOP ...

　　　　BLEEP...

　　　　　　BURP ...

And they were off!

Denise stared at the reflection of Josh in the liquid letters and words. As scene after scene of his ugly past played before him, as the mirrors moved in closer and closer making it impossible for him to look away, he slowly dropped to his knees. Denise couldn't believe it, but he was actually starting to cry, weeping over all the wrongs he'd done.

She could take no more. She turned from the dresser and began to pace. "I don't get it!" she said. "First Bud says we can't rescue Josh 'cause we'll be destroyed in that Ocean of Justice thing—"

"*Sea* of Justice," Nathan corrected.

"Whatever. Then he says we'll find perfect people who can go there. But, of course, there *are* no perfect people. But of course, *we* don't know that until *we* waste the whole day looking at people standing on their heads until we're nearly eaten by some wolf. And now we're back home watching Josh get tortured, totally clueless about what we can do."

Nathan nodded. "Yup, that about sums it up."

She shot him a look and headed to the window. "You'd think in this whole stupid town there'd be at least one perfect person." She pushed up the window and opened it. "What are we supposed to do!" she shouted at no one in particular.

The only answer was a startled crow that cawed as it took off from a telephone pole. Actually, there was one other answer. Just as she was about to turn from the window, Denise glanced down and noticed the Bloodstone resting on the outside sill.

"What on earth . . ." She reached down, picked it up, and brought it inside. "Look at this."

But Nathan was back at the dresser, staring at the dish of water.

"Nathan, take a look at—*ow!*" She dropped it to the floor.

Nathan spun around. "The Bloodstone!" he cried. "You found the Bloodstone!"

"Yeah," she said, sucking her fingers. "But the stupid thing burned me."

"Burned you?"

"Yeah, it was so hot that it—" Then she spotted it. The dish of water on the dresser was boiling! "Nathan, look! That's exactly what it did last night! That's exactly what happened to the water in the canteen last night!"

"I know," Nathan said as he turned back to the dresser. "It just started. As soon as . . ." He slowed, thinking. ". . . as soon as you opened the window and brought the Bloodstone into the room."

Denise frowned and looked at the Bloodstone on the floor. "Maybe it's trying to tell us something. Maybe—" And then she stopped. The Bloodstone had started to glow again. Not only that . . . but it was starting to melt!

Nathan took a step backward. "This is getting too weird," he said.

Denise hesitated, then carefully knelt down for a closer look. That's when she felt the heat.

"Don't get too close," Nathan warned.

She nodded but reached out her hand to feel its warmth. And with that warmth came the strangest sensation. It struck her outstretched fingers and moved up her arm and into her body. But it wasn't just warmth. It was . . . a peace. A peace that began filling her. She inched closer and reached out her other hand.

"What are you doing?" Nathan cried.

"I can't explain it." She felt a smile spreading across her face. "Nathan, do you remember the first time we were in Fayrah? Do you remember how they said the Bloodstone symbolized Imager's love?"

"Yeah, so."

Her smile broadened and she scooted even closer.

"Denny!"

"Do you remember the power it had to free you from the menagerie—to help us through the Portal?"

"Of course I do, but—"

"I think, I think this stone is more than just a symbol."

"What are you talking about?"

"I think this Bloodstone is . . ." She leaned closer to it and giggled.

"What?" Nathan demanded.

"I think this Bloodstone is like a *part* of Imager."

"You're crazy!"

"No," she said, shaking her head. "Come, feel the heat."

"No way," he replied. "I'm not getting near it."

"It's more than heat, it's . . ." By now her smile had broken into a full-fledged grin. "Nathan, there's a feeling to this heat. The same feeling I had when I was at the Center. Nathan . . . it's not heat . . . it's love."

For a long moment she remained, warming her hands . . . and her heart. And the longer she stayed, the more of Imager's love she absorbed.

An idea began to form. "Nathan, bring over that water from the dresser."

"No way!" he protested. "You can see how it's melting the stone already!"

"Bring it closer," she repeated.

"It could explode, or blow us up, or—"

"I doubt it." Denise looked up at him grinning. For some reason he no longer got on her nerves. Now she could see past his selfishness, his stubbornness, and everything else about him that drove her crazy. Now she saw the *real* Nathan O'Brien. And what she saw, well, strangely enough, what she saw she actually *liked*.

"Nathan, with all Imager has done for us, do you really think he'd destroy us with his own Bloodstone?"

"How should I know? He's not exactly easy to figure out."

"Bring the water here."

He threw a nervous glance at the boiling liquid letters and words in the dish.

"Nathan . . ."

"I'll burn my fingers," he whined.

"Use your shirt—wrap your shirt around it."

He turned back to the dish. Ever so slowly his expression began to change. Denise couldn't be certain, but it looked like he was watching the reflection of his brother—his suffering brother, his brother who could only be saved with their help. Or maybe he, too, was feeling the love from the Bloodstone. Whatever the reason, Nathan's own fear and selfishness seemed to be fading.

"All right . . . ," he finally sighed. He pulled out his shirttail and approached the dresser. "But if we die, you're going to live to regret it."

He wrapped the material around the dish and cautiously picked it up. Then he turned and started toward Denise and the Bloodstone. It was only a few steps, but by the time he arrived, the water was boiling so furiously hot that—"Augh!"—the dish fell from his hands, spilling the liquid onto the floor.

Well, not all of it spilled onto the floor. Much of it fell directly onto the Bloodstone. Immediately the liquid letters sizzled and spat. Soon the entire Bloodstone began hissing and bubbling . . . and melting. Within seconds it had dissolved into a boiling, blood-red pool of liquid!

Then the wind started . . .

It began as a faint wisp or two that rose over the pool. Then the wisps came together, swirling and intertwining until they formed a small cone . . . a miniature whirlwind.

Denise watched in amazement as the whirlwind began to grow until it was as tall as she was. As it grew it tugged at her hair, her clothes, papers on the desk, anything in the room that wasn't nailed down.

"What's going on?" Nathan shouted over the growing roar.

"I don't know!" Denise yelled.

And then, barely discernible over the wind, was another sound. The sound of three very familiar friends making a most welcomed entrance.

BEEP. . .

BOP . . .

BLeep. . .

BURP. . .

RE-BREATHED

"Listro Q!" Nathan shouted as the cool purple dude popped into the room.

"Aristophenix!" Denise shouted as his bearlike companion also appeared. She raced to him and buried her face into his thick fur. "Boy, am I glad to see you!"

Then of course there was Samson, darting over their heads, chattering at his high-pitched speed. Denise tried to jump up and give him a hug, too. But hugging a half dragonfly, half firefly is not the easiest thing to do—especially when you're standing next to a miniature tornado that happens to be roaring away in your best friend's bedroom!

Nathan shouted to them over the wind. "Bobok's taken Joshua!"

"And the Illusionist!" Listro Q shouted back. "In on this, too, is she!"

"You know what's happening?" Denise yelled.

Aristophenix nodded.

> "to the sea of justice,
> they have lured him away.
> now you must rescue him,
> to help brighten his day."

Denise winced. His poetry got no better with time. "*We're* not the ones to rescue Josh!" she shouted. "Only perfect people can enter the Sea of Justice." Suddenly her face lit up. "Wait a minute! That's you guys, isn't it? You're the perfect ones!"

Samson fired off a short reply.

"Perfect, not are we," Listro Q translated. "Perfection possible only for Upside Downers."

"There's nobody around here like that!" Denise shouted over the wind. "Bud said we'd find perfect people, but we haven't found a one!"

"Have you looked at yourselves?" Aristophenix yelled.

"*What?*" both children cried in unison.

Aristophenix tried to explain,

> "*you two, you're the ones,*
> *that's his plan, don't you see.*
> *but in order to be perfect,*
> *you must be re-breathed.*"

"What do you mean, *re-Breathed?*" Nathan shouted.

> "*the only thing perfect,*
> *is imager and his breath.*
> *you gotta let him fill you,*
> *and put your old breath to death.*"

"Whirlwind," Listro Q shouted as he pointed at the swirling cone of wind. "His Breath, that's what is this!"

Denise and Nathan stared, more confused than ever.

Nathan ventured a guess. "You mean this wind," he shouted, "this wind is Imager's Breath?"

All three creatures nodded.

"What do you mean, 'put our old breath to death'?" Denise shouted.

Listro Q explained, "All the wrong ever did you, or ever will do, destroyed, must be it!"

"But . . ." Denise searched for the words. "How?"

"The Bloodstone," Listro Q explained. "Absorb your wrong *all*, will it."

Both kids turned to the pool of red liquid that had once been the Bloodstone. It lay on the floor, barely affected by the raging Whirlwind above it.

"That?" Denise yelled over the roar. "That little puddle's going to take away all our wrong?"

> *"everything you have done,*
> *or ever will do.*
> *it's all gotta go,*
> *so his breath'll fill you."*

It was Nathan's turn for skepticism. "How can that little puddle do that?"

Listro Q answered, "The great price long ago paid by Imager."

"But you have to trust it," Aristophenix shouted.

"What do you mean trust?" Nathan yelled.

> *"you gotta trust in that pool,*
> *you gotta step in there, son.*
> *and breathe in his breath,*
> *so your wrong is undone."*

"You want us to step through that?" Nathan yelled, pointing at the swirling Whirlwind. "And into the pool?"

"Precisely," Listro Q nodded.

Samson chattered in agreement.

"You're crazy!" Nathan shouted.

"Perfect, only way become can you," Listro Q yelled. "So Sea of Justice, destroy you won't."

"You're *crazy!*" Nathan repeated. "No way! Absolutely not! If you think for one minute that . . ."

He continued to rant and rave but Denise barely noticed. Instead, she was once again raising her hands. But this time not to the Bloodstone. This time she was raising them toward the Whirlwind above the stone.

"Denny!" Nathan shouted. "What are you doing!"

"Feel it," she said, barely turning to him. "It's the same heat—just like the Bloodstone's. Nathan, I can feel Imager's love, I'm sure of it!"

Samson squealed a high-pitched reply.

"And why not?" Listro Q translated. "It's Imager part of. His Breath, is it."

Denise stepped closer to the Whirlwind.

"Denny, get away!" Nathan shouted. "Get back!"

But Denise wasn't listening. Ever so carefully she reached out her hand.

"Denny!"

Then, even more carefully, she stretched out her fingers.

"Denny, stop!"

Their tips touched the swirling wall of wind. She let out a little gasp. But it wasn't from pain or even surprise. It was from the sudden knowledge that finally, after all these months, she was actually touching Imager. True, it was only his Breath, but some of Imager was better than none of him. "Nathan," she whispered, "this is . . . *incredible.*"

Nathan yelled something back, but she paid no attention. She was too busy making up her mind, summoning up her courage. Finally, she was ready. Slowly, inch by cautious inch, she moved forward . . .

"Denny, no!"

. . . until, at last, she entered the raging, blowing Whirlwind.

At first all she felt was warmth—like before, but deeper, cozier—the type you feel snuggled up in a thick quilt around a fireplace on a snowy evening. But the warmth didn't stop at her skin. It soaked deeper—into her muscles, her bones, into the very center of who she was. It was like a warm hug whose love penetrated her very depths.

She heard Aristophenix shouting, "Step into the pool, Denny! You must step into the pool!"

She looked down and noticed her feet had not yet touched the red liquid. It lay at the base of the cone just ahead of her. Still cautious, she glanced back at Aristophenix and Listro Q. They nodded encouragingly. Then she heard Samson. She didn't have to understand a word of the little fellow's chattering to know what he said. The two of them were so much alike. Though they lived several dimensions apart and spoke different languages, she'd always sensed their closeness. She knew Samson wanted the best for her. And she knew that meant stepping into the pool.

Slowly she raised her foot and carefully, ever so carefully, stretched it out until, finally, she stepped into the pool that had once been the Bloodstone.

She was instantly struck by a feeling of lightness. It started in her head—as if a heavy darkness was being drained from it—as if all of the confusion and muddled thinking that had plagued her life was being drained away. She could actually feel the darkness leave, being drawn through her body, and out her feet into the pool. She didn't know the details, but she did know that the Bloodstone was pulling it out, taking it away.

When she glanced at the room she was astonished at how much clearer everything appeared. More real. It was as if she had been looking through dirty sunglasses her entire life and now, suddenly, they were taken away. Suddenly everything looked bright, sharp, and very, *very* real.

Next, she felt her neck and shoulders begin to relax. The darkness was being drained from them as well. And, as the darkness was removed, she noticed her fears also disappearing. Fears that she wasn't loved. Fears that she was never good enough. Fears that she was all alone. They were all being drained, sucked into the pool, disappearing forever.

Suddenly she broke out laughing. This joy, this knowing that she was loved no matter what she was, no matter what she did, it was more than she could handle. She tried to stop but couldn't. Not that she cared all that much. As a matter of fact, she didn't have any cares. They were all draining into the pool.

"What's happening to her?" she heard Nathan cry. "Her body's getting all clear—what's happening?"

Now the darkness was draining from her chest and stomach. It felt like many things, but mostly it felt like guilt. Guilt over all the wrong she had done, over all her failures. The heavy, oppressive weight of guilt was simply sliding away, disappearing into the pool. And for the first time in her life, Denise felt like she could breathe. *Really* breathe. And she wanted to with all of her might.

"Yes!" Aristophenix shouted as if reading her mind. "Breathe in. Breathe in as deep as you can.

> "HE'S REMOVIN' YOUR EVIL,
> SO YOU'RE CLEAR TO RECEIVE
> ALL OF HIS FULLNESS,
> BY BEING RE-BREATHED."

Denise nodded and exhaled, blowing out all of the old air from her lungs. Then she inhaled the wind, taking the deepest breath she had ever breathed—a breath she knew was entirely Imager's Breath.

"She's getting solid again!" Nathan cried. "What's going on?"

Denise looked down at her body. It was true. She seemed to be filling up with something else. Not the darkness, as before, but a sparkling *Presence* . . . a Presence more real than anything else in the room. She couldn't explain it, but she was being filled with a different Reality, a Reality more pure and real than anything she had ever seen or felt. A Reality that she knew was Imager Himself.

She looked at Nathan. His mouth hung open in astonishment. He was obviously amazed and perhaps a little jealous. He stepped closer. She could tell he wanted to join her. She could also tell that he was terrified.

"Come on." She smiled.

He looked through the wind into her eyes. She knew he saw her sincerity. And she knew he saw something else . . . something brand new, something she'd never experienced before. She knew he saw her love for him.

"It's incredible," she called. "Better than incredible."

He continued to stare, seeming to draw courage from her gaze.

She raised her hand, stretching it outside the wall of wind. "Come," was all she said.

Slowly, he raised his hand to hers until they were touching. He wrapped his fingers around hers. Neither took their eyes from the other.

Denise's smile grew. "Come," she whispered. She pulled ever so slightly and he responded by stepping forward. Soon the wind was blowing his hair and brushing against his face. Soon he also was smiling. "That's only the beginning," she said. "Come . . . step into this pool."

Nathan edged further into the wind. As it wrapped around and encompassed him, his smile grew. He looked down at the pool. It was just inches from his feet. He looked back up at Denise. She gave a gentle nod. Finally, he made the decision. He stepped forward and into the Bloodstone pool.

Denise watched in awe as the heavy darkness began draining from him—all of his confusion, all of his fear, all of his guilt. As it drained he, too, started to laugh. So did Denise. She couldn't help sharing in his joy.

Soon he was as clear as any crystal.

"Now breathe," she said. "Breathe in with all of your might."

Nathan nodded. And, as he breathed, he too was filled with Imager's sparkling Presence, a Presence more solid and pure than any reality.

Denise glanced over at the Fayrahnians. They stood watching in silent reverence.

And then it happened . . . a blinding flash of light.

Denise looked at Nathan and gasped. He was completely transformed. Suddenly he was like the reflection back in the stream at Fayrah—a powerful and majestic warrior clothed in glowing armor.

He looked at her with equal surprise. She glanced down and saw the reason. Now she wore a dazzling wedding gown made of shimmering pearls and light.

"You're . . . you're beautiful," Nathan whispered.

She looked up and saw he was awestruck. But she didn't blush or feel embarrassed because she knew he was simply telling the truth. She *was* beautiful.

"What's going on?" he whispered.

Denise could only guess. She remembered part of a conversation with Listro Q back at the stream. "This must be how Imager sees us," she said.

Nathan looked down at his new body and armor. He nodded. "And since this is how Imager sees us . . ."

Denise finished his sentence. ". . . this is how we are." She turned to the Fayrahnians for confirmation, but they were too busy dropping to their knees and bowing their heads.

Meanwhile, the Whirlwind was quickly shrinking and dying down. Soon it turned to nothing more than a breeze, then disappeared altogether. In a matter of seconds the room became absolutely silent.

Nathan turned to their friends. "That was incredible!"

But none of the Fayrahnians answered. Instead, they remained on their knees with their heads bowed.

"Guys?" Nathan called. "Guys, what's wrong?"

Finally Aristophenix spoke. He kept his head lowered and his eyes fixed at the ground. His voice was soft and full of respect.

> "now you are clean,
> now you are filled.
> now you are all
> that imager willed."

Denise and Nathan looked at each other, then back to the Fayrahnians who still remained on their knees with their heads bowed.

"Come on, guys," Nathan gave a nervous chuckle. "It's just us."

But the Fayrahnians did not budge.

"*Guys?* Look, this has been a lot of fun, but I got a brother to rescue, remember?"

"Please?" It was Denise's turn. "I don't understand everything that's happened, but we still need your help. Please?"

After another moment Listro Q slowly rose to his feet. He reached into his coat, pulled out the Cross-Dimensionalizer, and handed it to Nathan . . . all the time keeping his eyes lowered in respect. "Remember you still, how to use this?" he asked.

"Well, yeah . . . sure."

"And the water from the stream," Aristophenix said as he struggled to his feet—not an easy job for a bear almost as round as he was tall. He crossed to the canteen that had fallen from the dresser and brought it back to Nathan. But he still would not look him in the eyes. "You will also be needin' this."

"Nathan, look!" Denise pointed to the Bloodstone at their feet. It had solidified once again and had become a rock. She reached down and carefully picked it up. It was as cold and solid as ever.

"So, uh . . . what do we do now?" Nathan asked. "What's the next step?"

There was still no answer.

"Will somebody give us a clue here?"

After a moment Samson replied. But even at his high speed there was no mistaking his reverence.

"What did he say?" Denise asked.

Aristophenix's translation was simple and to the point: "Now you have Imager's Breath. Now you will know."

to the
sea

Back in the Sea of Justice, Joshua was on his knees sobbing. He had no choice. Wherever he looked, the mirrors reflected scenes of his past—every failure, every wrong, every mistake he had ever made. He'd forgotten most of them. But the mirrors hadn't. Not a one. And, as he continued to watch, the mirrors moved in closer and closer, their images filling more and more of his vision. Soon, he felt the cold hard surfaces of the mirrors touching his skin. They continued pushing in, pressing against his body harder and harder, squeezing him from every side tighter and tighter until he could barely breathe.

"Please," Joshua gasped, "no more, I can't . . . no more."

"But this is what you wanted," the Illusionist assured him. "This is Perfect Justice—the weight and pressure of its perfect presence."

The scenes continued to unfold—hundreds of them. Big wrongs, little wrongs, times he made Nathan cry, times he was selfish, times he lied, times he talked behind people's backs . . .

And with each scene, the mirrors pushed harder. The pain was unbearable. Something had to give. Unfortunately, it wasn't the mirrors. It was Josh's body. He could actually feel himself being crushed, hear bone and cartilage snapping. He wanted to scream but that meant having to breathe. And right now, with all the pressure, breathing was barely an option.

Then he heard it. He couldn't see where, but there was no mistaking the clear . . .

BEEP . . .

BOP . . .

BLEEP . . .

BURP. . .

. . . of someone cross-dimensionalizing.

When Denise and Nathan arrived it took a moment to get their bearings. (A billion mirrors pointed in a billion different directions can be a little confusing.) Still, they were beautiful mirrors—gleaming, dazzling, elegant. Mirrors that captured reflections within reflections within reflections—particularly of Denise in the splendor of her bridal gown and Nathan in his glowing suit of armor. But what of Joshua?

"Josh?" Denise called. "Joshua, where are you?"

There was no answer. Denise and Nathan exchanged puzzled looks. Aristophenix and Listro Q had promised he would be there. But where?

"Do him see you?" Listro Q's voice asked from the Cross-Dimensionalizer in Nathan's hand. "Do him see you?"

Nathan brought the Cross-Dimensionalizer to his mouth. "We don't see a thing, only mirrors."

"Are you sure you gave us the right coodinates?" Denise asked. "Remember, sometimes your aim isn't so—"

"Right coordiinates, have do you," Listro Q answered. "Somewhere there is he. You must look care—"

" . . . here . . . "

"What did you say?" Nathan asked.

"I didn't say anything," Denise answered.

"Neither, me," Listro Q replied.

" . . . here . . . "

There it was again—so thin and frail that Nathan wasn't entirely sure it was a voice.

"Here," it repeated, a little louder. "Over here."

Now Denise heard it, too. "Josh?" Then she spotted him. "Over there!"

Nathan followed her finger to two giant mirrors pressing together. Well, they were almost together. It seemed there was a thin something separating them. And that thin something with its feathers, six legs, and two heads looked very much like—

"Joshua!" Nathan cried. He raced around a dozen mirrors until he reached his brother. Denise was right behind him. Together, they tried to pry the giant mirrors apart.

"Help me," Josh groaned, "help me . . ."

"Hang on," Nathan gasped as he pushed, then shoved with all his might. "We'll get you out of there!"

They continued pushing, shoving, prying, and pulling. But no matter what they did, the mirrors would not budge.

"Going on, is what?" Listro Q called through the Cross-Dimensionalizer.

"The mirrors, they're crushing Josh!" Denise cried. "We can't . . ." She gave them a kick, but only managed to stub her toe. "We can't budge them!"

"That's because no substance has he," Listro Q answered.

"What?" Denise demanded.

"Imager's Breath inside Josh, is not," Listro Q explained.

"I don't understand!"

It was Aristophenix's turn.

> *"ONLY IMAGER'S BREATH*
> *HAS ENOUGH SUBSTANCE*
> *TO HOLD BACK THEM MIRRORS*
> *FROM THE CRUSH OF PURE JUSTICE."*

Listro Q continued. "Enough not flesh and blood. Imager's Breath only enough real to hold back mirrors."

Nathan thought he understood. The only thing stronger than the power of the mirrors was Imager's Breath. With Imager's Breath inside

Josh, the mirrors could not crush him. "But," Nathan called back, "how do we get his Breath inside him?"

The answer was clear and unmistakable. "Re-Breathed must too be he."

Nathan nodded. Somehow, they'd have to get Josh to be re-Breathed just as they had been. But how? He threw a look over at Denise. Unfortunately, she was nowhere to be found. "Denny? Denny!" He turned and shouted into the Cross-Dimensionalizer. "Denise has disappeared! I can't find her!"

"Find her, must you," Listro Q ordered. "Leave her alone, must not you."

"Denny!" Nathan shouted. "Denny, where are—" And then he heard it. Soft crying. Gentle weeping. It came from several mirrors away. "I'll be right back," he called to Joshua. "Don't go anywhere."

He raced around the mirrors searching until he finally spotted her. She was staring deeply into one of the mirrors. And she was crying . . .

"I'm sorry, Momma . . . I'm so sorry . . ."

"Denny?" Nathan shouted as he approached. "What's going on?"

But Denise didn't hear. She stared at the mirror, totally captivated by what she saw.

Nathan turned to see for himself and was dumbstruck. The reflection was of a much younger Denny. The little girl was yelling at her mother, saying awful things—things that made the poor woman break into tears.

And as the older Denise watched the reflected scene, she, too, was crying. "I didn't mean it," she shouted to the mirror. "Momma, I didn't mean it!"

"Going on, is what?" Listro Q called through the Cross-Dimensionalizer.

"It's Denny," Nathan answered. "She's looking at herself in one of these mirrors. Only it's her when she was a lot younger."

"The Illusionist!" Listro Q cried.

"What?"

"One of her favorite tricks is it. To destroy Denny, she'll try by showing all wrongs ever did she."

Once again Nathan had to rearrange the words. "You mean she's trying to hurt Denny by making her look at all the wrong she's done?"

"Yes and no," Listro Q answered. "Yes, they are wrongs Denny did, but no, exist no longer they."

"What do you mean?"

"Clean of all wrongs is Denny. Since her re-Breath, Imager completely has forgotten them."

Aristophenix continued. "Now it's a matter of who she wants to believe—Imager or the Illusionist."

"I'm not following you," Nathan said.

> *you two are now clean,*
> *imager sees you as perfection.*
> *but you must believe his truth,*
> *or you'll fall for her deception."*

"You mean the stuff in the mirrors happened, but they're not true because . . ."

Aristophenix finished. ". . . because Imager has completely cleaned you. He has forgotten all your wrongs so they no longer exist."

"So when the Illusionist says they're true . . . ," Nathan asked.

". . . lying, is she," Listro Q finished.

Denise cried out and Nathan spun to the mirror. The scene had changed. It was another argument, only this time between her parents. The two were yelling at each other as little four-year-old Denise stood in the middle crying, begging them to stop. But they wouldn't stop. Finally, her father turned angrily to the little girl and started yelling at *her.*

The older Denise watched the scene, breathless, through her streaming tears. "Daddy," she whispered, "please . . ."

"Stop that crying!" he shouted at the younger Denise. "Stop it right now!"

The little girl tried to stop, but couldn't.

"I said stop it!"

She cried even harder.

Finally, the man could stand no more. He turned and stormed toward the door.

"Daddy!" the older Denise shouted. "Daddy, don't leave!"

But the man obviously did not hear.

"Daddy, please! I'm sorry, I'm sorry!"

Grabbing his coat, he threw open the door, shouted a final oath, and slammed it shut behind him.

"Daddy!" Denise's knees buckled as she dropped to the ground in front of the mirror. She began to sob. "Daddy . . . I'm sorry . . . please, come back, come back . . ."

Suddenly the mother in the mirror looked out at the older Denise. Only she was no longer the mother. Nathan knew it instantly. She may have looked like the mother, but the voice was somebody else, somebody he recognized instantly . . . the Illusionist!

"You are the one!" the Illusionist shouted from the mirror. "You are the one who drove him away!"

"No!" Denise cried.

"He left us because of you!"

"Please!" Denise sobbed, covering her ears, trying to shut out the voice.

"It's all *your* fault! You are nothing but a mean-spirited worthless brat! *And he knew it!*"

"Momma . . . please, I didn't mean—"

"Your whole life has been worthless!"

"Daddy . . ."

"You have brought only pain and misery!"

"Momma," she cried. "Daddy . . ."

"WORTHLESS!"

"Daddy . . . Dad . . . D . . ." Denise could no longer speak. All she could do was sob.

But the attack still wasn't over.

"IT WOULD HAVE BEEN BETTER IF YOU HAD NEVER LIVED!"

Denise could give no answer.

"WOULDN'T IT?" the Illusionist demanded.

Denise continued to sob.

"WOULDN'T IT!"

Slowly, almost imperceptibly, Denise began to nod . . . as if she *was* worthless, as if she *was* a spoiled brat who brought only misery . . . as if it would have been better if she had never lived.

Nathan watched, astonished, unsure what to do. The Illusionist had her. It made no difference what the truth really was. It made no difference that Imager had absorbed all of her wrong and had made her perfect. Denise had chosen to believe the Illusionist. And by choosing to believe those lies, they became as real to Denise as if they were truth.

Suddenly, the Illusionist slammed her fist through her own reflection. It shattered into a dozen pieces of mirror that fell around the sobbing Denise. Now the Illusionist's reflection surrounded her on every side. "Do yourself a favor," she hissed from the broken shards. "Do us all a favor. Put an end to your wretched little existence."

Denise looked down at the reflections around her, each of them the Illusionist.

"Go ahead, you pathetic excuse for a person—pick me up—pick me up and do us all a favor."

Nathan watched in horror as Denise reached a trembling hand toward the biggest and sharpest piece of mirror.

"Do it," the Illusionist whispered. "Before you cause any more misery. Do us all a favor. Do it."

Denise hesitated.

"*Do it!*"

Finally, slowly she picked up the broken shard of mirror and took it into both of her hands.

"DO IT! . . . DO IT!"

She turned the pointed end toward her stomach, holding it like a sharp dagger.

"*DO IT! DO IT! DO IT!*"

She sucked in a final breath. She raised the dagger high over her head and—

"NOOOO!" Nathan leaped at her. He hit her so hard they both went rolling across the ocean's floor.

"Let me go!" Denise screamed as she tried to free her hands. "Let me do it!"

"It's a lie!" Nathan shouted. "It's not you anymore! It's a lie from the Illusionist!"

Denise was no match for the new, stronger Nathan. Soon he had both of her arms pinned to the ground.

"Let me go!" she screamed. "I know what I'm like!"

"It's not you anymore! Remember Imager! Remember what he did!"

"Let me go!"

"Forget what you were! Remember who he *is!* Remember what he made you!"

She continued to struggle.

In a flash of inspiration, Nathan grabbed her canteen of water. He unscrewed the lid and poured the liquid onto Denise's head and into her face. She coughed and sputtered until some finally splashed into her eyes. He took her head and forced it around to the nearest mirror.

"Look at yourself!" he shouted. "See who you *really* are!"

At first she fought and tried to look the other way. But soon her eyes landed upon the reflection . . . and then she saw herself as Imager saw her—the glorious, majestic bride in the shimmering gown of light.

She stopped struggling and continued to stare. She was beginning to understand. She was remembering who she was.

Slowly she started to nod. And then, at last, she turned to Nathan. "Thank you," she whispered hoarsely. "Thank you."

When he was sure she was all right, Nathan released her. But he knew it wasn't the end of the battle. For when he looked back at the broken pieces of mirror on the ground, there was no sign of the Illusionist. She had obviously returned to her first victim.

"Joshua!" Nathan spun around and started back to his brother. "JOSHUA!"

the
fiNaL
coNfLict

Denise and Nathan raced back to Josh. They didn't believe it could be possible, but the mirrors had actually crushed him flatter than before.

"I can't," he gasped, "I can't hang on."

"Joshua, listen to me," Nathan cried. "The only way to fight these mirrors is with Imager's Breath."

"I don't . . . I don't under—"

Denise interrupted. "Imager's Breath is more real than the power of these mirrors. With his Breath inside you, they can't crush you!"

"How . . . ," he gasped. "How do I . . ." He winced in pain as the mirrors closed in another fraction of an inch.

"The Bloodstone!" Nathan shouted to Denise. "You got it?"

"Right here." Denise pulled it from a fold in her bridal gown.

"Hold it out—let me pour the rest of the water on it."

"What?" she cried.

"Just hold it in your hand and—"

"You're crazy!"

"Denny . . ."

"You saw what happened the last time we poured water on it. No way am I holding it!"

"Ahhhh!" The mirrors moved in another fraction.

"Come on, Denny! He can't step into any pool the way he is. We have to pour the liquid Bloodstone *over* him."

Denise turned to Josh. She had never seen anyone in such pain. She looked back at the Bloodstone in her hand. It was already glowing and heating up. And for good reason. Nathan had already unscrewed the canteen's cap!

As the Bloodstone grew hotter, Denise tried not to panic. What would happen? Would it burn her? Melt her right along with it? Who knew? Who knew anything in this place?

But she did know one thing. She knew that Josh was her friend. And she knew that he could not stand any more pain.

Nathan reached out the canteen, waiting for Denise. She looked at him, then at Josh. Finally, she nodded and held out the Bloodstone.

Nathan poured the water. Its liquid letters and words splashed onto the Bloodstone, which immediately began to crackle and hiss. Denise winced at the growing heat, but she hung on. She watched in terror as the Bloodstone began melting in her hand. But she hung on.

Slowly, a small cone of wind sprouted from the red liquid.

"What's happening?" Josh cried as he strained for a better look.

"It's the Bloodstone," Nathan shouted. "It will make you perfect. And that Whirlwind, it's Imager's Breath. It will—"

"Liars," a voice calmly interrupted.

Suddenly Denise saw Bobok's reflection. He was inside the mirror that was crushing Joshua from the front.

Before she could respond, the Illusionist called to him from the other mirror, the one crushing him from the back. "There is only justice here, dear heart. Perfect justice. Here you receive exactly what you deserve."

"That's not true!" Denise shouted to Josh. "The Bloodstone will absorb your wrong—it will make you perfect so you can be filled with Imager's—"

"Most illogical," Bobok said to Josh. "In a rational universe one does not receive something for nothing. One must pay for what one has—"

"He's wrong!" Denise cried.

"It would go against all the laws of physics," Bobok quietly reasoned. "As a scientist, you know the need for absolute cause and effect. If there is but one exception to this logic, the universe would unravel. There would be no order. No justice."

Josh turned his eyes to Denise. The mirrors pressed tighter. "He's right," he moaned, clenching his eyes against the pain, trying his best to stay conscious.

"No!" she cried. "He's done nothing but lie to you from the start, why do you believe him now?"

"Because ... it's logic," he groaned. "Someone must pay for my—"

"That's just it!" Nathan shouted. "Imager has paid! The Bloodstone will absorb your wrong, it will take your punishment."

"Dear child." Bobok turned to Nathan in his kindest voice. "You have such great insight. If you would use it to its fullest potential, there's no telling what you could become. Why, with the proper training you could be one of the wisest, most sought after men in your kingdom."

Denise saw what was happening and immediately shouted, "Don't listen to him, Nathan! He's trying to seduce you like in Fayrah!"

But she was too late. Bobok had obviously remembered his weakness, and had gone for it. Nathan was already staring into the mirror, already being drawn into it by the creature's smooth, praising words.

"Do not let such a great mind as yours be wasted. Come, boy, come closer to the mirror. Take a deep look at yourself and see all that you could—"

"Don't listen to him!" Denise shouted. "It's a trick!"

But Nathan continued to listen ... and continued to look.

"That's it," Bobok purred, "look deep. Deeper still."

"Nathan!"

Scenes from Nathan's own life flickered upon Bobok's mirror.

Denise was beside herself. What could she do? She looked at the liquid Bloodstone still in her hand. Then, suddenly, without hesitation, she shoved it straight toward the mirrors, right at Bobok's reflection.

"Put that away!" Bobok screamed as he raced to the far end of his mirror and cowered.

The cry startled Nathan, seeming to break the spell. He blinked once, twice, then turned back to Denise. Good. He was back.

Quickly, she reached up and tried to dump the remaining liquid Bloodstone over Joshua's heads. But the liquid would not fall. It clung to her palm. She turned her hand completely upside down and shook it. Still nothing. It hung like glue. It was still liquid, but it would not fall.

The Illusionist broke into mocking laughter.

"What are you doing to it?" Denise demanded.

Bobok joined the Illusionist as their laughter reverberated back and forth in the mirrors. "Fool!" he taunted.

The communicator gave a crackle followed by Aristophenix's voice. "Denise—the decision must be Joshua's, not yours. He cannot be re-Breathed unless it's *his* decision!"

"Did you hear that?" Nathan shouted to his brother.

But Josh's pain was too great. He was losing consciousness.

"Joshua!" Nathan reached over and shook him.

Josh mumbled something but his eyes had closed.

"We have won!" the Illusionist shouted to Bobok. "Dear and trusted friend, the victory is ours!"

"Pity, to have only one destroyed." Bobok shrugged, as much as a blue orb can shrug. "But one is better than none."

"Josh, you got to listen to me!" Nathan shouted. "We can't do this for you. It's got to be your decision! Josh! *JOSHUA!*"

"Joshua O'Brien!" Suddenly, Denise was in his faces (both of them) and shouting at the top of her lungs. "You are the stubbornest person I've ever met!"

Josh stirred slightly, barely opening his eyes.

"This is killing you!" she yelled. "Don't you see that? You're being smashed to smithereens!"

"It's what I . . . deserve."

"The Bloodstone can change that! Imager paid the price!"

His eyes started to close.

"Don't do this! Don't you go and die on me, Joshua O'Brien!"

The boy struggled to open a single eye.

"All you have to do is trust it! I know it doesn't make sense. I know it's not logical. But maybe there's another type of logic here, a deeper logic. If you'd just . . ." Suddenly Denise's eyes welled with moisture. She hated it when that happened, but there was no way to stop it.

"Please don't leave us . . . Please, I need you." The tears spilled onto her cheeks. "Who is going to help me with my math? Who's going to stop me from beating up all those guys at school?"

"Stop that!" the Illusionist shouted. "Stop that crying this instant!"

"Josh, please . . ." Her throat tightened. The tears continued. "I know it doesn't make sense. But you got to trust the Bloodstone . . ."

"Stop her!"

"It's the only way . . ."

"Stop—"

And then the most curious thing happened. One of Denise's tears fell from her cheek. A single tear of her love. *Love* . . . something that the Sea of Justice had apparently never experienced. Because, as that tear fell onto a small mirror near her feet, the mirror suddenly gave a sharp and violent *CRACK!*

Everyone jumped in surprise.

Then it cracked again. Then again.

"Stop it!" the Illusionist screamed.

Then the entire mirror exploded. Dozens of pieces flew in every direction, some landing on other mirrors. Then *those* mirrors began to crack—and again, and again . . . until they, too, exploded!

"You're destroying justice!" Bobok cried.

Denise and Nathan watched in amazement as more mirrors cracked and exploded, sending hundreds of pieces onto hundreds of other mirrors, which also cracked and exploded. Somehow, without even knowing it, Denise had started a giant chain reaction.

"Joshua!" Nathan shouted. "Joshua, we got to get out of here! Joshua, can you hear me?"

Josh mumbled something.

"Do you want us to pour the Bloodstone on you?"

"Stop it!" the Illusionist screamed. *"Stop it!"*

"Joshua!" Denise cried. "Do you want to be re-Breathed? Joshua?"

Again Joshua mumbled. It might have been "yes," she couldn't tell. She turned to Nathan questioningly.

"Try it!" Nathan shouted over the exploding mirrors. "He might be saying yes. Try it!"

Denise raised her hand over Josh's heads to pour the liquid Bloodstone. And this time it worked! This time the liquid fell from her palm and onto one head, and then the other.

It wasn't much but it was enough. Slowly, it ran down his faces, dripping onto his shoulders. As it did, Joshua began to grow transparent. As the red liquid flowed down his body, all of the darkness, all of the wrong he had ever done was drawn to the surface and into that liquid.

And where the Bloodstone flowed, the Whirlwind followed. Instantly, the wind picked up all around him, completely engulfing him.

"BREATHE IN!" Denise shouted over the roar of the wind and the exploding mirrors. "YOU'VE GOT TO BREATHE IN!"

Josh's first breath was thin and shallow—but Denise saw some of Imager's presence enter him. And with that entrance, the mirrors pressing him were pushed back slightly. He tried again, taking a deeper breath. More of Imager entered and the mirrors were pushed back further.

"WE'RE UNDONE!" Bobok shouted over the kingdom as it continued shattering and exploding.

Josh breathed again, then again, deeper and deeper, filling himself more and more with Imager's. As he did, he continued to expand until the two mirrors pressing him began to crack.

"Help me!" the Illusionist shrieked from her cracked reflection behind him. "Help me!"

But there was no help for her or for her ice-blue friend. Joshua took another breath. More cracks.

"We're ruined!" Bobok screamed.

And then, with Josh's deepest breath, the two mirrors exploded in all directions. The dreaded Bobok and Illusionist shattered into billions of pieces of mirror. Billions of pieces of light.

"AGHHHHHhhhhhhhh . . ."

Denise looked on. Apparently evil does not die easily. It took a long moment for their anguished screams to finally fade. But when they had, they were gone. All that remained was a sparkling cloud of dust that sprinkled down upon the kingdom.

And from that downpour of glittering dust, a new and different Joshua stepped forward. No longer was he some pathetic two-headed feathered freak. Now he was a man, a mighty man. And in each of his strong arms he carried a clay pot filled to the brim with water—but not the water of earth. This was the water of liquid words and letters.

The mirrors continued shattering and exploding around them. The Sea of Justice was being destroyed—all from Denise's single tear. All from her love.

"Hurry!" Joshua shouted to Nathan. "Cross-dimensionalize us. This whole place is going to blow! Hurry!"

Nothing more had to be said. Nathan pulled out the little box and pressed the four buttons.

Beep . . .

BOP . . .

BLeep . . .

BURP . . .

the GREATEST aDVENTURES of aLL

The good news was that Nathan was a better shot with the Cross-Dimensionalizer than Listro Q.

The bad news was, he was still a beginner.

"Great," Joshua whispered in the dark. "Where'd we land this time?"

"Miye moph moow," Denise replied. It was supposed to be, *"I don't know,"* but it's hard talking when somebody's kneecap is in your mouth. Wherever they were they were definitely tumbled and crammed in tightly together.

"Here," Nathan said, "Just let me move my—"

"Ow!" Josh cried. "Your elbow's in my eye!"

"Oh, sorry."

Denise was the first to get an arm free. Unfortunately, she hit some sort of faucet and suddenly—*splishhhhhhhhhhh*—all three of them were soaked with water.

"Denny!" Nathan cried.

"It's our tub," Josh groaned. "We've landed in our tub."

"Oh, no . . ."

"Oh, great . . ."

"Oh, brother . . ."

The complaints soon gave way to giggles as the three finally untangled themselves and dragged their dripping bodies out of the tub . . . just as Aristophenix, Listro Q, and Samson entered the room. Apparently, they'd heard the commotion from Josh's bedroom and raced down the hall to join them. Although the kids were soaked, there were still plenty of hugs to go around.

Part of Denise was glad to be back in her regular clothes—her regular sloppy jeans, her regular sloppy sweatshirt, her regular sloppy everything. But a small part of her was already missing the bridal gown. "I still don't get why we were dressed up like that," she said. "Nathan like a knight, me like a bride, and Josh like a . . . a—"

"A water bearer?" Aristophenix said.

"Yeah," Denise nodded. "What does all that mean?"

> "IN time you will know,
> imager's plans will be clear.
> as you continue your journeys,
> and explore his frontiers."

"You mean there's more?" Nathan shot a dubious look at Josh and Denise.

"Choice is it of yours," Listro Q answered. "But many more adventures there are waiting for you."

"You don't mind if we get a little rest first, do you?" Nathan asked.

The group chuckled. It was true. It hadn't exactly been the easiest of journeys—two days and nights without sleep, running and searching for perfect people, struggling through various realms of perfection—not to mention blowing up a kingdom or two.

Denise turned to Aristophenix. "Now that we're re-Breathed, I thought the adventures would be over. I mean, from the beginning wasn't that what Imager wanted—for us to be re-Breathed?"

Aristophenix and Listro Q traded amused looks.

"No and yes," Listro Q said.

Aristophenix explained:

> "BEING RE-BREATHED
> IS BY NO MEANS THE END.
> IT'S ONLY NOW
> THE REAL ADVENTURE BEGINS."

"But Bobok and the Illusionist?" Nathan asked. "They're both gone."

"Right are you," Listro Q nodded. "Dust, became they."

Nathan let out a sigh of relief.

So did Josh.

Come to think of it, so did Denise.

"But same and different enemies, now have you."

"Same and different?" Nathan asked. "Like how?"

Listro Q grinned. "In time, friend my, in time."

> "DON'T WORRY 'BOUT THEM BAD GUYS,
> 'CAUSE WE'VE ALL SEEN YOUR TAPESTRIES.
> IF YOU STAY CLOSE TO IMAGER,
> THEY'LL MEET THE SAME, UH, CATASTROPHES."

The group groaned.

Samson commented and Listro Q quickly translated. "Perhaps leave we should now for home, before any worse get his rhymes."

Of course there were the usual "do you have to go's" and "can't you stay a few more minutes," but eventually reason won over. Everyone was just too exhausted. Besides, the sky outside was turning pink. Dawn was well on its way. And with dawn would come grown-ups. And with grown-ups would come thousands of questions. Questions they'd be happy to answer in time. But not just yet.

> "SAMMY BOY IS RIGHT,
> IT'S TIME THAT WE GO.
> LISTRO, PUNCH IN THEM COORDINATES,
> LET'S GET ON WITH THE SHOW."

Nathan tossed the Cross-Dimensionalizer over to Listro Q.

"Wait a minute!" Denise said. "The Bloodstone, where is the Bloodstone?"

"In the Sea of Justice," Listro Q answered. "Or where used to be the sea."

"It didn't get destroyed with the mirrors?"

"A symbol of Imager it is, impossible to destroy is it."

"But without the Bloodstone," Denise protested, "how will we signal you for another visit?"

Aristophenix grinned.

> *"we'll be here and around,*
> *we won't be long parted.*
> *'cause like we've already stated,*
> *your adventure's just started."*

Josh coughed slightly and cleared his voice. "Listen, guys, I just want to say . . . you know, *thanks.*" He glanced at the ground, a little embarrassed.

Each of the group nodded, seeming to understand.

"I tell you . . ." He took another breath. "I really learned my lesson. No way am I going to go around always trying to be Mr. Super-popular."

"Yeah, right," Denise smirked.

He gave her a look, then broke into a grin. "Well, at least not *all* of the time."

Everybody chuckled.

"We've all got stuff to work on," Nathan admitted.

Listro Q agreed and added, "But inside you now is Imager's Breath. Happen will changes."

It was Josh's turn to slowly nod. He seemed to understand.

Finally, Aristophenix signaled Listro Q to enter the coordinates. More hugs were given and goodbyes exchanged until the furry, bear-like creature cleared his throat and left them with one final poem:

> *"we best be a-movin',*
> *it's really time that we go.*
> *our beds, they're a-callin',*
> *so bye-bye, see ya later, tally——"*

BEEP . . .

BOP . . .

BLEEP . . .

BURP . . .

And, just like that, the Fayrahnians were gone.

Joshua, Nathan, and Denise stood looking at one another. It was hard to believe that it was over—that they could actually get some rest—and that things would finally return to normal.

Well, okay, so two out of three isn't bad. They were right about it being over and they were right about getting some rest. But as far as things returning to normal? Well, let's just say Aristophenix was right when he promised that now they were ready for the real adventures to begin . . .

the
taBLet

the SIGNAL

DENNNYYYYYY . . ."

Denise Wolff twisted and turned in the chair beside her mom's hospital bed. For the third time that night she dreamed of how her mother had fallen off the ladder. For the third time that night she saw her tumbling like a Barbie doll from their second-story window. And for the third time she heard the crack of shrubs and the sickening thud of her mother hitting the ground.

"Mom . . . *Mom!*"

No answer.

Denise raced toward the bushes, a coldness already knotting in her stomach. *"MOTHER!"*

She found her sprawled out on the ground, trying to catch her breath. "I'm all right, Denny," she gasped. "I'm all right, it's okay."

But it wasn't okay. Denise could see that in a second. It wasn't okay the way her mom kept trying to breathe but couldn't. And it wasn't okay the way one of her legs was twisted and pointed in the wrong direction.

Mom had been trying to change the storm windows, as she did every spring. Of course, if there was a husband around the house, she wouldn't have had to. Then again, if there was a husband around, they'd probably have enough money to buy windows that didn't need changing.

But Mom had no husband—at least not anymore. And Denise had no father—at least not one she could remember. He'd left when she was four.

Now it was just the two of them—mother and daughter. Of course, they had their fights—like over the torn and baggy clothes Denise always wore. But the two loved each other fiercely. And when the chips were down, they always knew the other would be there.

And that afternoon "being there" meant Denise calling 911, riding with Mom in the ambulance, pacing in the waiting room, and listening to the doctors say she had some bruised ribs and a shattered leg.

Everybody told Denise to go home and get some rest. "Your mother will be fine," they said. "She's under mild sedation—she'll barely know you're here."

But Denise wouldn't listen and she wouldn't leave. She'd already lost one parent; she wasn't about to lose another. Instead, she borrowed a blanket and pillow from an adjacent room and tried to get comfortable in the steel and vinyl chair next to Mom's bed.

Here she waited. And here her world-famous anger started to burn . . .

Why had Mom fallen?

Why did things always go wrong?

Why was life always so hard?

Of course, Denise knew Imager loved her. After all, she'd been to the Center. She'd even been re-Breathed. But sometimes that love seemed so far away. Sometimes it seemed as if Imager had forgotten, or that he didn't know, or, worse yet, that he simply didn't care.

"It would be a whole lot different if I were in charge," she mumbled as she drifted in and out of a fitful sleep. "A *whole* lot different."

The thought churned in her mind—of being in charge, of being the boss.

Unfortunately, she had no idea that the thought would trigger a little alarm—a little alarm for a creature who had sworn revenge upon her—a creature on the molten hot surface of Ecknolb . . .

T eeBolt! Come quickly!" cried the Merchant of Emotions. "It's happening, it's happening!"

The Merchant turned from his monitors and chuckled as he watched the huge, hairy TeeBolt gallop toward him. The animal's eight furry legs raced across the steaming rocks as fast as they could. He would have barked and yelped in pain, but he had nothing to bark and yelp with. In an outburst of anger the Merchant had destroyed TeeBolt's vocal chords many epochs ago.

"Look, my pet, it's the Denise—the creature who destroyed our Illusionist!" The Merchant of Emotions threw his claws up in joy. He fluttered his wings in delight. The Illusionist had been his sister— until Denise accidentally destroyed her in the Sea of Justice. Ever since then, the Merchant had vowed vengeance. Not only upon Denise, but upon all of her kind, upon all Upside Downers. The only problem was, he had been confined to the desolate planet of Ecknolb, forbidden ever to enter the Upside-Down Kingdom—at least on his own. At least without an invitation.

But all that was changing. For months he'd been monitoring Denise's thoughts, waiting for the opportunity. Now it was here . . . the beginning of distrust, the seed of rebellion. "The Denise is doubting!" the Merchant chortled with excitement. "What a fool. The Denise thinks it knows more than Imager!"

Of course, TeeBolt had no idea what his master was saying or why he was so excited. But it made little difference. The Merchant simply glanced down to the Emotion Generator strapped to his chest, scanned the dozens of silver switches, and flipped the one labeled "excitement." A misty cloud shot from the contraption's nozzle. It struck TeeBolt dead center and filled him with so much *excitement* that he couldn't contain himself. He was so thrilled that he began leaping on the Merchant and panting. The only trouble was that when he panted he drooled.

"Get down, you nincompoop! Stop that slobbering!"

Immediately TeeBolt hopped down and closed his mouth. For if he didn't hop down and close his mouth, he might not have any legs to hop down on or a mouth to close.

"Now if I can just get the Denise to dream about the Tablet—if I can just convince the Denise to begin writing on it." The Merchant spun back to the monitor before him and adjusted several dials. "Then the Denise will invite us into her world. Then I will get my claws on the Tablet. And then"—he began to grin—"then we will finally be able to destroy her wretched little world."

The Merchant broke into laughter. The joy of destroying Imager's precious Upside-Down Kingdom caused every crystal scale on his body to quiver with delight. TeeBolt was still too overwhelmed with *excitement* to understand the humor . . . until the Merchant reached down and snapped on the *laughter* switch.

Another cloud of mist shot out and struck TeeBolt. The animal began to laugh uncontrollably. He couldn't help himself. That was the power the Merchant of Emotions had over TeeBolt—over all creatures who gave him control. And it was this power that had been banned from the Upside-Down Kingdom.

But even from great distances he could sometimes direct dreams. Not a lot, mind you. But if the dreamer was angry enough, if there was enough rebellion in their hearts, then there might be room for the Merchant to nudge some of their dreams in his direction. He might even be able to influence a waking thought or two.

That's exactly what he hoped to accomplish with the Denise.

That's exactly how he hoped to enter and destroy her world.

Back in Grandpa O'Brien's Secondhand Shop, Joshua and Nathan were arguing again. Like Denise, they'd both visited Fayrah. They'd both been re-Breathed. And they'd both started to grow in Imager's ways. But when it came to good old-fashioned brotherly bickering . . . well, these guys were pros.

"You're the oldest," Nathan whined.

"So?"

"So, till Grandpa gets back from deliveries, let *me* visit Denny and *you* stay to look after the shop."

"No way," Josh argued as he stooped to adjust his hair in the reflection of a used toaster. "All you and Denny ever do is fight. She needs me at the hospital—somebody more mature and sensitive to look after her."

"Oh, please," Nathan groaned. He turned and limped toward the counter. His hip, the one that had bothered him since birth, was acting up again. But he wouldn't let his brother see the pain. No way. Not when he had an argument to win.

They'd been going around like this ever since Denise had phoned from the hospital, and they were no closer to an agreement than when they started. As far as Nathan knew, the only person more stubborn than himself was his brother. And according to Joshua, the only person more stubborn than himself was Nathan. So around and around they went . . . and around some more.

Fortunately, the standoff was about to end. Because suddenly they heard a very familiar voice.

> "*now come on, little buddies,*
> *don't get in a dither.*
> *put aside all yer fighting,*
> *and let us draw hither.*"

The brothers exchanged looks. Only one person in the universe had such awful poetry.

"Aristophenix!" they shouted.

Next came the familiar . . .

beep . . .

bop . . .

bleep . . .

burp . . .

. . . of three very good friends cross-dimensionalizing into their world.

And finally . . .

"Get us down—get us down from here!"

The brothers looked up to see Aristophenix, a roly-poly creature with checkered vest and walking stick, and Listro Q, a tall purple dude complete with a Mohawk and a tuxedo, spinning high above their heads. Apparently Listro Q's aim with the Cross-Dimensionalizer hadn't improved much. He and Aristophenix were caught on the ceiling fan, spinning round and round.

"Won't you—*whoa*—ever get—*whoo*—the hang of that thing?" Aristophenix cried.

"Cool, is it," Listro Q shouted. "Any day now, sure of it am I."

The third member of the party wasn't caught on the fan. He was darting about their heads chattering a mile a minute. Or was he laughing? It was hard to tell with Samson. The part ladybug, part dragonfly talked so fast it was hard to tell anything he said.

Nathan raced to the switch on the wall and turned off the fan.

Aristophenix didn't wait for it to stop.

> "tHaNk ya, DeaR NatHaN,
> tHeRe aiN't a secoNd to waste.
> tHe weaveR, He's a-caLLiN',
> so we'D betteR make Haste."

Joshua and Nathan traded glances. The Weaver—the kind old gentleman assigned by Imager to weave their life's tapestries—was calling *them* to Fayrah!

"But what about Denise?" Nathan asked. "Doesn't he want her to come, too?"

> "DeNNy's tHe ReasoN
> we're uNDeR sucH stRess.
> sHe's DReamiN' up sometHiN'
> tHat's causiN' a mess."

Again Joshua and Nathan exchanged looks.

"We can't leave just yet," Joshua said. "Not till Grandpa gets back from his deliveries."

"Worry don't about the store," Listro Q answered. "This part of world, freeze time will we."

From past adventures, Joshua could pretty much piece together his words. "You mean you're going to freeze time again and make it stand still?" he asked.

"But here only at the store. Rest of world will it be normal time."

Samson gave a quick chatter.

Aristophenix nodded. "Good thinkin', Sammy."

"What's he saying?" Nathan asked.

Listro Q translated. "Mr. Hornsberry, here is he?"

"My stuffed bulldog?" Nathan asked. "No, he's at home."

"Then swing by your home, better do we."

"Why?"

Aristophenix explained:

> "THIS ADVENTURE'S GONNA BE TRICKY,
> BUT HIS HELP WE CAN'T SKIP.
> WE'LL JUST HAVE TO ENDURE
> HIS SNOOTY AND SNOBBY LIP."

Nathan had to admit, his stuffed bulldog *was* snooty. And he *was* a snob. But from all the excitement, it sounded like they were going to need all the man and dog power they could get.

"Canteen of Imager's water," Listro Q asked, "still have you?"

"Not anymore," Josh replied. "We used it all up in that ocean of mirrors."

"Then loan you my own," Listro Q said as he removed a large water skin from around his neck.

Joshua took it and quickly slipped it around his shoulders.

"Ready to go are we, if are you." Listro Q said as he held the Cross-Dimensionalizer in his hand.

The brothers nodded. Without a word Listro Q punched in the four coordinates . . .

BEEP . . .

BOP . . .

BLEEP . . .

BURP . . .

. . . and they were off.

CHAPTER TWO

DReam ON

Denise woke with a start. For a minute she didn't know where she was—until she felt the jab of a steel armrest in her ribs, the sticky vinyl against her arms, and the cramp in her neck.

Ah, yes, the hospital chair.

She looked over at her sleeping mom. The sedative was still working. In fact, in the dim morning light her mother looked peaceful, almost happy. It was a look Denise hadn't seen for years. Not from Mom. And for some reason it made her throat ache with sadness.

"Life is hard, then you die." That's what Mom always said. Of course, it was supposed to be funny, but Denise knew better. All she had to do was look where they were this minute to see that it was no joke. Life *was* hard. *Too* hard.

Once again she felt the frustration stirring inside. Frustration at what had happened. Frustration at their life in general. If Imager was supposed to be so loving, then why were things always so hard? Why was there always so much pain? Why was there any suffering at all?

Stewing in her anger, she recalled the dream. Not the dream about the ladder, but the other one. She had no idea where it came from. It seemed so strange and yet so real.

In it she was upstairs all alone in her uncle's attic. A large black trunk sat in front of her. Slowly, she knelt down to it. This is where she'd found the Bloodstone. This is where she and Nathan had found Bud's cassette tape. And this is where the two of them had discovered the flat, thin stone at the very bottom.

Carefully, she had lifted the trunk's heavy lid. It groaned in protest. On the top were clothes. Lots and lots of clothes. She began digging through them until she reached the bottom, until she finally felt it— the cold, smooth stone. She hauled it to the surface and set it on the pile of clothes. It was exactly as she remembered—a big, flat rock— super thin and super smooth.

What she did not remember were the faint green lines running across the stone—like notebook paper—like it was some sort of writing tablet.

Suddenly, a felt marker appeared in her hand. And then . . . Well, then the dream was over—just like that. There was nothing more. It had ended and she woke up. And yet it remained in her mind, just as clear as ever.

"Weird," Denise sighed. She glanced over at her mom, then turned in her chair to go back to sleep.

But sleep wouldn't come. Not anymore. There was something about the dream, something so real about that stone. She lay in the chair wide awake, staring into the dark   wondering.

She didn't know how long she lay there—twenty minutes, an hour. But finally, she'd had enough. Throwing off the blanket, she looked at her watch.

6:50.

She hated to cross town and wake up her aunt this early. She knew the lady would think she was strange. Then again, everyone thought she was strange, so what was one more person added to the list?

Denise turned back to Mom. She was still sleeping. "I'll be back in a few minutes," she whispered. "I just gotta check something."

With that, Denise uncurled herself from the chair, grabbed her jacket, and headed for the door.

By now Joshua and Nathan were pretty used to traveling across dimensions. They were used to the blinding light and the sensation of falling. They were even used to seeing themselves as Imager saw them—Joshua as some sort of water bearer in a burlap robe and Nathan as a knight in a glowing suit of armor just a few sizes too big, carrying a heavy shield.

Master Nathan, Master Nathan . . .

He turned to see Mr. Hornsberry, his stuffed bulldog, traveling beside him. Moments earlier they had dropped by Nathan's bedroom to pick him up. Back there he was just as dead and lifeless as any other stuffed dog. But here he was alive and back to his usual snooty self.

How you doing, Mr. Hornsberry? Nathan thought (since speaking wasn't necessary when Cross-Dimensionalizing).

As well as might be expected, having been confined to your closet these many months.

Sorry about—

I trust you're aware of the distinct aroma those gym socks in the corner have been emitting.

Before Nathan could answer, Aristophenix interrupted.

> ꟑOOD to see ya, OL' Boy,
> But we're a comin' to the ceNteR.
> Best be thinkin' them ꟑood thouꟑhts,
> so more ꟑently you'LL enteR.

Nathan glanced down and saw they were approaching the brightly lit city. From past experiences, he knew what to do. Like the others, he closed his eyes and began thinking of Imager's greatness. Ever so faintly he could hear Aristophenix starting to sing. Someone else in the group was humming. Others quietly whispered. But no matter what they did, their purpose was the same—to dwell on Imager's greatness, to join with the rest of the universe in their love and adoration of him.

Soon they passed through a thin layer of fog and moments later they landed in the Center.

Nathan looked about in awe. Although he'd been to the Center before, his reaction was always the same: wonder and astonishment.

He was amazed at the beautiful lights, the incredible colors. But they were more than just lights and colors . . . they were living creatures. Living creatures that reflected Imager's greater light, his greater color. A greater light and color that blazed brilliantly just over the ridge.

Then there was the music. It came from everywhere—the trees, the grass, even their own bodies. Everything vibrated with marvelous chords and intricate melodies—all directed toward Imager.

But this time something was different. "Nathan!" Josh cried. "Look at us! We're not shadows anymore. We're real!"

Nathan looked at Josh, then down at himself. It was true. In their past visits to the Center they had only been misty shadows. It's not that they weren't real, it's just that everything around them had been so much *more* real. But now, all of that had changed.

"You're right," Nathan cried, tapping his armor. "You can't see through me! I'm totally here! We're both totally here!"

Samson buzzed their heads and chattered an explanation. Aristophenix translated,

> "it's 'cause you're re-breathed,
> now you've got imager's presence.
> you're no longer just shadows,
> since you're filled with his essence."

"'Cause his Breath is inside us?" Josh asked. "That's what makes us real?"

Listro Q nodded. "Ever since Whirlwind filled you, as real now you are as . . ." He turned toward the light glowing behind the ridge. "As Imager."

Nathan looked back toward the ridge and the blazing light behind it—a light so brilliant that it made all the others dim by comparison. But he knew it was more than just light. It had a quality . . . a *splendor*. A splendor so intense that it nearly destroyed Denise on an earlier trip.

"Aristophenix?" Joshua called. "Could we see him now? Now that we're solid and real and everything . . . would it be safe to see Imager?"

Nathan turned to him. "Are you crazy? You know what happened when Denny tried to see him!"

"But it's different now," Joshua insisted. "We're re-Breathed." He turned to Listro Q and Aristophenix. "Right?"

The Fayrahnians exchanged looks. It was obvious they were in a hurry, but it was also obvious they didn't want to deprive either of the brothers from experiencing more of Imager.

Samson chattered something, and with a heavy sigh Aristophenix agreed.

> *"weLL, if that's what you want,*
> *I ain't gonna spoil it.*
> *But we gotta hurry and save*
> *yer world from, uh . . . the toilet!"*

The group groaned as they started toward the ridge.

Denise heaved open the lid to the trunk. It gave a heavy groan—just like her dream. She peered inside and began digging through the clothes—just like the dream.

Her aunt, a frail lady, stood at the top of the attic stairs clutching her robe against the morning chill. She watched silently as Denise plowed through the old clothes and oddities.

"What's this?" Denise asked as she pulled out the camera she and Nathan had seen on their last visit to the trunk. As best she could tell it had no lens and it was impossible to tell the front from the back.

"You know your uncle," the woman sighed. "Just something he brought back from one of his trips. We'll have to ask him when he returns."

Denise looked at her. The woman smiled weakly. Her husband had been gone over two years. At first he'd returned from his documentary filmmaking ventures with strange and weird tales about strange and weird places. Then one day he disappeared and never returned at all. Everyone knew he wasn't coming back—everyone but his wife. Well, maybe she knew, too. Maybe she just wanted to keep hoping.

At last Denise reached the bottom of the trunk. There was a rusty jackknife and a beat-up pair of sunglasses. But it was the large, smooth stone that had her attention. It was about the size of a yellow legal pad and almost as thick.

Carefully she pulled it out. It was exactly as she remembered from the last time she was there, and almost the same as her dream.

"Almost" because there were no faint green lines on this rock. Nor was there any marker pen. She scowled slightly.

"What's wrong, honey?" her aunt asked.

"Something's not right."

Without a word she plowed through the trunk again.

But she found nothing new.

She plopped down on the floor, cross-legged. Pulling the tablet onto her lap, she began drumming her fingers on it, trying to think. The surface was smooth and hard, but not so hard that she couldn't make faint marks with her fingernails.

Her aunt turned and started down the steps. "Why don't I go and fix us some nice hot chocolate," she said.

Denise thanked her and continued to ponder. She knew it had only been a dream. But everything seemed so real, so true. So why weren't the lines there? And the marker? As she sat thinking, she absentmindedly began scratching her name onto the soft stone with her fingernail.

First a D . . . then an E . . . followed by an N . . .

It was no big deal, just faint markings she could easily wipe away.

But when she scratched in the final letter . . . it happened!

There was somebody else in the room.

She spun around, then sucked in her breath—not because she was frightened; the person in front of her wasn't frightening at all. It was not some strange creature from some strange dimension. In fact, she knew this person very well. Very well indeed. Because standing directly in front of Denise Wolff stood . . . Denise Wolff!

Somehow, by writing her name on the tablet, Denise had created another Denise . . . exactly like herself!

a LittLe stopoveR

Even with his clumsy suit of armor and heavy shield, Nathan was only a few steps behind Josh as they raced for the top of the hill. He wasn't crazy about the idea of seeing Imager, but he was even less crazy about being left behind.

Suddenly there was a blinding flash of light just on the other side. "What's that?" Josh cried.

Aristophenix was pulling up the rear by a dozen yards. His pudgy little body couldn't keep pace with the others, but between wheezes he managed to gasp,

> "*must be* GRADUATION (pant, puff)
> *for* UPSIDE DOWNERS, *take a peek.*
> GO *see what's* IN STORE (WHEEZE, GASP)
> WHEN *your* LIVES ARE COMPLETE."

Joshua and Nathan reached the top of the ridge just in time to be hit by another flash of light. It was so bright, so intense, that it knocked both of them to the ground. Being the scientific type, Josh found it difficult to believe that light could actually knock a person down. But when he found himself lying face first in the dirt it was a lot easier to accept. This light had *presence*—so pure, so intense, that it carried with it incredible power.

Since he was already on the ground, and since he was scared to death, he figured it wouldn't hurt to lie there just a bit longer. No real reason except that he enjoyed living and he wasn't sure that would continue if he got up. So there he stayed, cowering on the ground, covering his head right alongside his brother.

But not forever. Call it scientific curiosity or just plain stupidity, he wasn't sure. It didn't matter. The point was Josh *had* to see. He *had* to know what was going on. So, with eyes still clinched and head still covered, he leaned to Nathan and whispered, "We should really take a look."

"Are you nuts?" Nathan's voice echoed from under his shield.

"We just can't stay on our faces."

"Oh, I bet we can," Nathan said. "I got a few more things I want to do before I croak."

"Imager's not going to kill us."

"How do you know?"

"Listro Q says he's too cool, too loving. Come on, don't you want to take a little peek?"

"I'll take their word for it. Just lie here and keep quiet."

With eyes still shut, Joshua turned his head and called, "Aristophenix?"

"Josh, will you keep—"

"Aristophenix . . . Listro Q?"

There was no answer. Only another flash. A flash so bright that even with his eyes closed Josh could feel its power wash over him.

That was it. He could stand no more. Live or die (although living still had a lot more appeal) Josh had to see. Still clinching his eyes shut, he slowly turned toward the light.

So far so good. No heart attack. No vaporization. These were all encouraging signs.

Finally, he pried open one eye. Off to his left, Aristophenix, Listro Q, Samson, even Mr. Hornsberry, were all on their knees, faces bowed to the ground in the direction of the light. Carefully, he opened his other eye and slowly shifted his gaze toward the light. It grew brighter and brighter but he kept forcing himself. He knew the dangers of look-ing into the sun, but somehow this was different. The back of his eyes started to ache, but he pressed on. He had to. He shielded his eyes as he continued to look until finally, at last, Joshua O'Brien was gazing directly into the light.

And in it he saw . . .

Nothing.

Well, at first nothing. It was too bright to see anything. But as he squinted, he slowly made out a large, broad plain that stretched below them. It was so clear and smooth that it looked like water. But it couldn't be water. There were too many creatures standing on it. Mil-lions of glowing creatures.

And they were singing. They were all singing to an even brighter Figure standing in the center of the plain—a Figure carved out of the most intense, blazing light imaginable. Light brighter than the sun. Brighter than a thousand suns.

Josh squinted harder. You didn't have to be a genius to figure out who the Figure was. At first it stood directly in the middle of the plain. Then, suddenly, it was standing much closer. Then far off in the distance. Then somewhere to Josh's left. Then to his right. It was pretty confusing. As if it were everywhere at the same time.

Then there was its face.

Actually, it was too bright to see the face, but there was no miss-ing the profile—a profile that kept changing. One minute it was a giant bird, like an eagle; the next, some sort of bull; then an innocent lamb, followed by a lion. Back and forth it changed, again and again and again.

It was too much to comprehend. Josh's head began spinning. Everything was too strange, too weird. He grew dizzy, his brain over-loading. Then suddenly he heard a voice. It shook the ground like thunder, so loud that it made his ears ring. Yet it was softer than a whisper.

"HELLO, JOSHUA."

Josh spun around and gasped. The Figure was kneeling directly beside him! His head reeled. Instinctively, he bowed to the ground.

Still, he had to see. He had to look into the face. Slowly, and with great terror, he forced himself to raise his head. When their gaze finally met, he saw eyes as powerful as the voice . . . *and* as tender. They blazed with fire—a fire that burned deep into Joshua's mind.

He could not look away, even if he wanted.

The eyes held him. They searched his thoughts—seeing inside to his deepest, darkest secrets. Things no one knew. Things he did in secret, said in secret, thought in secret. Things that embarrassed him. Suddenly they were all exposed by the light. Every thought and action of Joshua O'Brien was in plain view of those eyes.

But he felt no fear. Because, as penetrating as those eyes were, as much as they saw his darkest secrets, they didn't condemn those secrets. If anything, they seemed to love and understand Josh more *because* of those secrets.

It took Joshua forever to find his voice. When he did it came out as a little squeak. "Who . . ." But that was as far as he got. He was too overcome to talk.

The Figure seemed to understand. He motioned toward the plain below them, toward all the different appearances of himself.

"I AM HE."

Josh wasn't sure if he was going to lose his mind or just die. But for some reason he did neither. It had something to do with the way those marvelous eyes held him.

He tried to ask another question. "How . . ." But he shook his head. He had no business asking anything. He had no business saying anything. At that moment he had no business *being* anything.

The eyes looked on kindly. The voice roared and whispered:

"ASK YOUR QUESTION, JOSHUA O'BRIEN."

Josh swallowed hard and tried again. "How . . . how can you be here . . . and down there at the same time? You're everywhere at once."

"YES, I AM."

"But . . . one minute you're a bird, then an animal, then—"

"YOUR MIND CANNOT GRASP MY FULLNESS, SO IT SEES ME IN SYMBOLS."

"But—"

"BEHOLD . . ."

The Figure pointed to a withered old woman on the plain below them. Unlike the others, she was shriveled and crippled. And, unlike the others, she was *not* glowing. He continued speaking, his voice lowered in quiet reverence:

"SHE'S AN UPSIDE DOWNER . . . LIKE YOU."

"You mean she's cross-dimensionalized just like—"

"NO. SHE HAS GRADUATED."

"Graduated?"

"BEHOLD."

Joshua looked back at the plain. The glowing Figure of Light was now standing beside the woman. Josh looked back at his side. The Figure of Light was also there. "Okay," he mumbled, trying to get a grip. "I can handle this. I hope . . ."

He turned back to the plain and watched as the old woman crumpled at the Figure's feet and began sobbing. But she wasn't the only one crying. So was the Figure.

A hush fell over the plain. All singing came to a stop. The millions of creatures watched in speechless anticipation as the Figure slowly stooped down to join the old woman. At last he spoke:

"I HAVE BEEN WAITING A LONG TIME FOR YOU."

The woman looked up. Tears streamed down her face. Tears streamed down both of their faces. Slowly, the Figure reached out his hands and helped her as they rose to their feet. Smiling, he wiped the tears from her cheeks. She looked up into his eyes, her face glowing in love and adoration. Then gently, tenderly, he pulled her into a deep embrace.

And with that embrace . . . came another flash of light!

Josh ducked his head as the wave of power roared over him. When it was finally safe, he looked back up and saw the woman was still in the Figure's arms. But she was different now . . . much different. Now, she glowed. Now, she shared a part of the Figure's brilliance—a part of his power. No longer was she bent and crippled. Now she was beautiful. Radiant. Now she was young, vibrant, and glowing with the Figure's own glory.

The two separated but continued gazing into each other's eyes like lovers who'd been apart for years. Finally the Figure took her hand into his. He said only four words.

"COME, SIT WITH ME."

The entire plain broke into applause . . . then shouts and cheers as the couple turned and headed through the throng.

Josh looked on, his own eyes burning with tears. The back of his throat hurt with emotion. He turned to the Figure of Light who was now beside him. He tried to speak, his voice hoarse and raspy. "Do you . . . do that . . . with everyone?"

There was no missing the moisture in the Figure's eyes as he smiled.

"I DO THAT WITH MY FRIENDS."

B ack in the attic Denise stared at the newly created Denise. But, never known for her shyness, the first Denise immediately demanded, "Who are you?"

"I'm you," the new Denise answered.

"You mean you're a picture of me—like a holograph."

"No, I'm you."

"But . . . how?"

"How should I know? You're the one who wrote me."

"Wrote . . . ?"

"Didn't you just write my name on the Tablet?"

Denise looked at the flat stone on her lap. "Well, no—how could I? I don't have anything to write—"

"With your fingernail," the new Denise sighed. "You just scratched my name on the Tablet with your fingernail."

"So?"

"So here I am."

"You mean . . . whatever I write on this thing—"

"—happens. Yeah."

"Let me get this straight. You're saying that whatever I write on this *Tablet* becomes real?"

The new Denise shook her head and muttered, "I didn't know I could be so ignorant. Yes! Yes! Whatever you write on that Tablet becomes—"

But she never finished . . . for immediately Denise reached over and rubbed off the name and immediately the second Denise disappeared.

She took a deep breath and blew it out. A little unsteady, she rose to her feet. Was this really happening? Could this thing . . . this *Tablet* . . . really create anything she wrote? Balancing the stone on one hand, she started to scratch in her name again until she noticed her fingernail was wearing thin. She changed her mind. Instead, she wrote: FELT PEN.

Instantly there was a black marker in her hand . . . just like the dream.

Denise blinked in surprise. She stared at the marker. Was this really true? And if it *was*, what did it mean? What were the limits? *Were* there limits? Possibilities filled her mind. She frowned and gripped the marker tighter. After a moment's thought, she started to scrawl out the letters C-A-R but stopped. She paused, and quickly wrote L-I-M-O-U-S-I-N-E, instead.

When she had finished, she looked down at the word, took another deep breath, and quickly walked to the window for a look. Sure enough—outside, parked in front of the house, was a black, shiny limo.

Denise leaned against the wall for support. This was too incredible. With the Tablet it looked like she could make anything she wanted—mansions, yachts, castles. But material things had never interested her much (well, except for a limo or two). One look at her wardrobe said that.

Then why, she wondered, was she the one given the . . . wait a minute. Of course. That was it, that's why she'd had the dream. That's why she'd been led to the Tablet. It wasn't so she could make her own selfish desires come true. No, of course not. It was so she could help make things better in the world!

The thought gave her a little shudder. She breathed harder, faster. What a privilege. She, Denise Wolff, had been chosen to change the world! Think of it. She would have the opportunity to make things better, to do away with suffering, to stop violence, to end starvation, disease, and poverty. She could actually help make things . . . *perfect!* This was no "genie in a lamp" time—no "make three wishes and get whatever you want." Forget the riches, forget the fame. Denise was chosen because she would do something greater. She would fix the world!

She felt the weight of the Tablet in her hands—its power, its possibilities. But where to begin? The world was in such a mess; where should she start?

How about something small? she thought. *Yeah, that's it. For starters, I should begin with something*—She had it! If she wanted to end all pain and suffering, how about starting off with her mother? Mom, who was filled with so much pain at the hospital.

She raised the Tablet and wrote the words: *NO PAIN.*

She finished and waited in anticipation. But nothing happened. Everything was exactly the same. She glanced back out the window. The limo was still there. Nothing else had changed. Or had it? There was only one way to find out.

She turned and headed for the stairs.

Joshua didn't know how long their conversation lasted. It could have been hours, it could have been seconds. But by the way Nathan, Aristophenix, and the gang were still on their knees, he voted for seconds.

The blazing Figure of Light continued speaking, his voice powerfully tender:

**"MY BELOVED UPSIDE-DOWN KINGDOM
IS IN DANGER."**

"Yes," Josh answered, "I know, but how—"

"DEAR DENISE."

Josh thought he heard a heavy sigh.

**"SHE NO LONGER TRUSTS ME.
SHE IS CREATING A DIFFERENT WORLD.
A WORLD SHE THINKS IS BETTER THAN MINE.
A WORLD WHERE SHE WILL INVITE
THE MERCHANT OF EMOTIONS."**

"Merchant of Emotions?"

**"HE WHO CONTROLS THROUGH EMOTIONS.
THAT IS WHY YOU AND YOUR BROTHER MUST HELP."**

Josh's mouth dropped open. "What . . . what can we do?"
The Figure smiled.

**"YOU WILL DEFEAT HIM.
AS MY WATER BEARER, YOU HAVE MY WORD.
AS MY ARMOR BEARER, NATHAN HAS MY FAITH.
TOGETHER YOU TWO WILL HELP
MY DENISE UNDERSTAND."**

"Yes, but why don't—"

"WHY DON'T I STOP HER?"

Joshua nodded.

"MY DENISE NO LONGER LISTENS TO ME."

"You could make her."
The briefest look of pain flickered across those magnificent eyes.

"SHE MUST TRUST ME BECAUSE SHE WANTS TO, NOT BECAUSE I MAKE HER."

Then, reaching out a hand, the Figure gently helped Joshua to his feet.

Of course, Josh wanted to say more . . .

. . . like, the only thing he and his brother had ever succeeded at doing together was fighting, so how could they save the world?

. . . like, shouldn't Imager chose someone else?

. . . like, did he really need *their* help?

But Josh didn't say a word. He knew Imager already knew. Now he felt his tender, powerful hand resting upon his shoulder.

"YOU ARE MY FEET, JOSHUA O'BRIEN. YOU ARE MY HANDS. YOU ARE MY VOICE."

Never in his life had Joshua felt so proud . . . or so helpless.

As if sensing his fear, the Figure drew him into an gentle embrace. There was no flash of light. No transfer of energy. No "graduation." Only the warmth and love of Imager holding his Beloved. It was fantastic. Joshua wanted to stay in that embrace forever. But he knew he couldn't, at least not now.

Finally they separated. Josh brushed the tears from his eyes and looked up just in time to catch the Figure doing the same.

"Will I . . . ever see you again?" Josh croaked.

The Figure broke into a gentle grin.

"YES, MY DEAR FRIEND, YOU WILL SEE ME. YOU WILL SEE ME WHEREVER YOU LOOK."

With that Joshua suddenly found himself standing in Fayrah. No cross-dimensionalizing, no traveling—one minute he was standing before Imager; the next, he and the entire group stood in one of Fayrah's Great Halls of Tapestry.

changes

The Halls of Tapestry were as dazzling as ever. In every room hung thousands of tapestries—beautiful, shimmering tapestries woven from glowing threads of light. Each was a masterpiece. Each represented a life Imager had created. Every living creature imagined had his or her own tapestry hanging in one of these magnificent halls.

Nathan was the first to spot the Weaver. The old man was pacing back and forth between tapestries at the far end of the room. Even from that distance Nathan could tell he was concerned.

As the group approached, the Weaver glanced up. "You're late" was all he said before he returned to his pacing.

Aristophenix tried to explain,

"they wanted to see imager,
a request we could not shrug.
and by the glow on josh's face,
it was somethin' he dug."

The Weaver shuddered. Apparently even he could not get used to the awful poetry.

348

"What's the problem?" Nathan asked as he approached, clinking and clanking in his armor. "And why are we still wearing these outfits? We usually lose them after we cross-dimensionalize."

"Those are your offices," the Weaver explained. "Yes, they are."

"But it's three sizes too big," Nathan whined as he tried to adjust the armor. "And this shield thing weighs a ton." Now Nathan didn't mean to whine. That was just his nature. As sure as Denise had her temper and Josh his ego, Nathan had his whine.

"You will grow into that armor," the Weaver patiently explained. "And the shield will come in most handy."

"Yes, but—"

"This is how he has imaged you, yes, it is. And this is how you will stop the Merchant."

"Merchant?" Nathan asked.

It was Josh's turn to explain. "The Merchant of Emotions. Imager said that—"

"Wait a minute," Nathan interrupted. "You talked to Imager? When?"

"I'll explain later. The point is—"

"I want to know now. When did you talk to—"

"Nathan, for once in your life try not to be the world's biggest brat."

"Who're you calling a—"

"Gentlemen, gentlemen," the Weaver sighed. "I know it's difficult to be civil to each other, but if you will look at these tapestries, you will see we have little time."

The brothers turned back to the tapestries in front of them. Something was wrong. Nathan could see it at once. The intricate beauty of their patterns was . . . disappearing.

Listro Q was the first to speak. "Tapestries, becoming unraveled is their weave."

It was true, each of the tapestries was slowly unraveling. Dozens of beautiful designs were coming undone. The glowing threads were being pulled out of their weave and hanging haphazardly in all directions.

"What's happening?" Josh asked in concern. "They're coming apart."

"An inappropriate observation," Mr. Hornsberry spoke up. "Upon closer examination you will note that many of the tapestries are actually reweaving themselves."

The group stepped closer for a better look. It was true. Some of the threads were actually coming together again, intertwining, forming their own patterns. But instead of the beautiful, glowing masterpieces, they were forming gross, clumsy designs.

Samson chattered off a quick question.

The Weaver shook his head and answered, "No, only the tapestries from the Upside-Down Kingdom are being rewoven."

"But . . . why?" Nathan stammered. "Who's responsible?"

The Weaver turned directly to him. He spoke only one word . . . "Denise."

The group stood, dumbfounded.

"But how?" Josh finally asked. "How could Denise, how could one person, do all this damage?"

The Weaver looked at him a long moment. Then he turned and stepped forward to one of the tapestries. When he arrived he pushed it aside to reveal a giant, round door. It looked like the door to a bank vault. "Come with me," he said.

The group glanced at one another.

"Where are we going?" Nathan asked.

The Weaver busied himself with dialing a combination in the center of the door, so Aristophenix answered:

> "if I ain't too mistaken,
> you'll enjoy this little stroll.
> it looks like we're enterin'
> someone's master control."

The combination was dialed in. The Weaver pulled on the handle, heaved open the heavy steel door, and stepped into darkness.

With more than a little trepidation, Nathan and the others followed.

Denise couldn't believe what she saw as her limo turned into the hospital parking lot. Outside there were hundreds of people. Most were wearing those silly hospital gowns—the type that never quite close in the back. But no one seemed to care. Not anymore. Everyone was too happy and excited.

The limo stopped and Denise threw open the door. Outside everything was chaos and confusion. Everywhere patients were running and leaping and laughing.

"What's going on?" she shouted as she stepped into the mob. "What's happening?"

No one seemed to hear.

"Would somebody please tell me what's going on?"

Finally an old man turned to her. He was very frail and weak. But he was grinning—from ear to ear his toothless gums glistened in the sunlight. "Haven't you heard?" he cackled. "We're healed! There ain't no pain no more!" With that he leaped into the air to click his heels. Of course, he failed miserably and fell to the ground in a crumpled heap. But he didn't care, not in the least—unless you call breaking into uncontrollable laughter "caring."

Denise looked around in disbelief. The place was like a school playground. Old-timers laughed and ran around like children. Pregnant mothers jumped rope. Accident victims played tag. Cancer patients slapped one another on the back, hooting and hollering with joy.

The only ones not smiling were the doctors. "Please, you are not well!" they kept shouting. "You must come back to your rooms."

But no one listened. Why should they? The doctors were obviously wrong. There was no pain. No suffering. Not anymore.

And Denise knew why. She couldn't help grinning down at the Tablet in her hands. The words *NO PAIN* were still written in permanent ink upon the stone. *She* had done this. *She, Denise Wolff*, had single-handedly rid the world of pain. With just two words she had erased all of the world's misery and suffering. Her chest swelled with pride and she shook her head in wonder over what she'd so easily accomplished.

She started through the crowd to look for her mom. After all, her mother was the inspiration for all this. "Mom . . . Mom, where are you?"

"Clear the way!" A couple wheelchair patients raced toward her. "Clear the way!" They nearly knocked Denise to the ground as they sped past. "Sorry!" they shouted as they disappeared into the crowd.

"Don't worry," Denise called back. "You couldn't hurt me if you tried!"

She wasn't bragging, just stating a fact. They *couldn't* hurt her. They couldn't hurt *anyone*. She had made the world too good for that. She wasn't sure why Imager had created the mess, but she was sure of one thing . . . with the Tablet, she was going to clean it up. She was going to make everything better, a *lot* better. She gripped the stone more firmly and searched the crowd. "Mom . . ."

"Denny! Denny, over here!"

Denise turned and spotted her mother hobbling through the crowd. Her face was glowing. All trace of suffering was gone. At the moment, she was doing her best to ignore a worried nurse who was pleading with her to sit down.

"Please, Mrs. Wolff, your leg's not ready—"

"Don't be silly. I'm fine."

Denise's grin widened as she pushed through the crowd toward her mother. She couldn't wait to tell her that she was the one responsible for—

Then Mom came into full view and Denise's joy turned to horror.

"Mom, your leg!"

The woman glanced down at her hospital gown. The lower portion was spattered with blood. But it wasn't the blood that concerned Denise. It was the way the leg had turned and twisted in the wrong direction.

"I told her it wasn't healed," the nurse cried as Denise joined them. "I told her it wouldn't hold her weight!"

"Nonsense," Mrs. Wolff laughed. "I feel fine. It doesn't bother me a—"

"But, Mom, it looks awful! And what's this white thing?" Denise bent down for a closer look. She wished she hadn't. The "white thing" was her mother's leg bone! It was still broken, still twisted, and now it jutted through the skin!

"Mom, sit down!"

"Sweetheart, I—"

"Sit down!"

Reluctantly her mother let Denise help her to the ground. Then, turning to the crowd, Denise shouted, "Is there a doctor? Please, I need a doctor! I need a doctor here, right away!"

the
chase
begins

W ow!" both brothers exclaimed as they entered the large round room. A single desktop circled the entire chamber like a giant ring. Sitting behind the desk, facing the center, were two dozen Fayrahnians. Each carefully studied a little 3-D picture that floated before them. Each carefully adjusted the complex knobs and controls on the desk below those pictures. But that was nothing compared to what floated in the middle of the room.

For there, directly in the center, nearly twenty feet high, was a giant 3-D projection of Denise! She was in a hospital room arguing with two doctors and a nurse over her mother's broken and bleeding leg.

The Weaver quickly explained to the brothers. "Behind each tapestry is a door leading to that person's Master Control."

"You mean each of us has a room like this?" Josh asked.

"Of course."

Josh and Nathan exchanged looks.

"My assistants here carefully monitor the decisions you make in your weave."

"Hold it," Nathan interrupted. "I thought you wove those tapestries the way Imager told you."

"I do."

"Then how—"

"You still have free will. If you refuse Imager's design, you may change it."

"But," Josh argued, "who would want to? I mean, his designs are so incredible."

The Weaver nodded and sighed wearily. "Yours is a most stubborn kingdom, Joshua O'Brien, yes, it is. Many insist on their own weave instead of Imager's." He motioned to the ring desk and continued. "Here we monitor your every decision, down to the tiniest details."

"The details?"

"They are often what change your life the most."

Josh looked at him skeptically.

"Not at first, but five, ten, twenty years into the future. It is the little choices that change your life. The little choices are often—" He was interrupted by a loud, buzzing alarm.

"Sir!" one of the Fayrahnians cried, "we have another Code 12!"

The Weaver quickly crossed to one of the desk stations to study the little 3-D picture floating above it. It was another image of Denise, but in a much different location. "Put it on the big screen!"

The assistant obeyed.

Immediately the big-screen image of Denise in the hospital was replaced by another one. In it she looked awful. She was haggard and very, very frightened. Instead of her usual uniform of baggy pants and T-shirt, she wore some sort of fancy riding outfit. And she carried a large flat stone.

She stood on a beach next to a burning bus. Heading toward her was a mob of people—some crawling, others staggering. But they all had one thing in common: their hatred for Denise. "Nightmare," they shouted. "You've created a nightmare!"

Tears filled Denise's eyes. "No, I . . . I created good!" she shouted. "This is supposed to be good!"

Other voices were heard. "Get the Tablet! Get the Tablet!"

She spun around to see another group—hundreds of them. They were awful to look at. Their bodies were broken and twisted beyond belief. Like the others, they staggered and crawled toward her. "Get the Tablet! Get the Tablet!"

"Monsters!" a third group shouted. "We're all monsters . . ."

Denise twirled to face them. They were equally as ravaged and twisted.

Filled with panic, she tried to run. But they came at her from every direction. Angry people, broken people, ruined people.

"Nightmare . . ."

They continued to close in.

"Monsters . . ."

They were nearly on top of her.

"Get the Tablet . . ."

"Mr. Hornsberry!" She turned to her companions. "Samson—do something! Help me!"

But there appeared nothing they could do.

Back in Master Control it must have been a shock for Hornsberry and Samson to see themselves up on the projection, but neither spoke a word as they continued watching.

Josh turned to the Weaver and shouted over the noise, "So this is what will happen in the future?"

The Weaver nodded. "*If* she makes the wrong decision in the hospital."

"What's that in her hand?" Nathan yelled. "It looks familiar!"

Aristophenix explained:

> "THE TABLET SHE HAS FOUND;
> IT CHANGES REALITY.
> IT'S THE THING THAT WILL BRING
> ALL OF THIS CALAMITY."

Joshua turned back to the Weaver for more information.

"This is the future," the Weaver explained. "Yes, it is. This is what will happen if Denise keeps changing Imager's reality."

"It's terrible!" Nathan shouted.

"It is nothing compared to what will follow." The Weaver turned to another assistant. "Punch in thirty seconds beyond what we're viewing."

The assistant obeyed.

The pleading Denise disappeared from the screen and was replaced by another creature. It was large with claws, crystal-clear scales, and huge black leathery wings. Wings that carried it silently through outer space toward a blue, cloud-covered planet that could only be—

"Earth!" Joshua cried. "He's heading for Earth!"

The Weaver nodded sadly.

"That's the Illusionist!" Nathan shouted. "I thought she was dead. I thought we destroyed her."

"Closely, look more," Listro Q called. "The Illusionist is not. Her brother is it."

"Her brother?"

The Weaver explained, "He is called the Merchant of Emotions. He is the creature you must battle, yes, he is. He is the one you must prevent from entering the Upside-Down Kingdom."

"But he's almost there," Joshua cried. "How can we stop—"

"Remember, this is the future you're seeing."

"Yeah, but—"

"Punch up 11–17 Quadrant E," the Weaver ordered.

Another assistant transferred another image to the center screen. It was a kingdom of towering buildings, crowded roadways, and deafening noise. Noise like a thousand stereos blasting at once.

"This is the present time. This is where he has currently landed. He has enslaved this kingdom as he waits to attack yours. You must stop him here."

"But, how?" Joshua demanded. "Imager said something about Nathan's suit of armor and I'm supposed to—"·

The Weaver nodded. "Nathan believes in Imager more strongly than you. That armor and shield are his belief, his protection from the Merchant's powers."

"What about me?"

"You are the water bearer. You have Imager's water in that water skin."

Josh instinctively adjusted the water skin around his shoulder that Listro Q had given him.

"Imager's liquid letters and words are your weapons."

"What good is—"

"Nathan told you how the water melted the Kingdom of Seerlo?"

"Well, yes, but—"

"You know how it helps you see as Imager sees?"

"Sure, but—"

"That is only the beginning of its power, yes, it is."

"Hold it," Nathan interrupted. "You're telling us that—"

Suddenly another alarm sounded.

The Weaver spun to the screen. "There's no time to explain!" he shouted. "You must stop the Merchant of Emotions before he reaches your kingdom—before Denise invites him into your world." Turning to Listro he called, "Have you entered their coordinates?"

"Yes, did I."

"Then give him one of the Cross-Dimensionalizers."

Listro Q reached over and handed Nathan the small control unit. "Still remember you, how to use it?"

"Well, yeah, but you guys are coming with."

The Weaver shook his head. "Only the re-Breathed can handle Imager's weapons; only you will be able to stop the Merchant."

"But—"

"Go!"

Again Josh protested, "I still don't see how we can—"

It was Aristophenix's turn for impatience.

> "DON'T BE A WORRYIN' 'BOUT IT,
> WE'RE HERE WATCHIN' THE SHOW.
> JUST USE THEM GIFTS WISELY,
> NOW HURRY AND GO."

"Yes, but—"

Another alarm sounded.

"Go!" the Weaver ordered. "Now!"

Joshua looked at his brother.

Nathan took a deep breath, pressed the four buttons on the Cross-Dimensionalizer . . .

BEEP . . .

    BOP . . .

        BLEEP . . .

            BURP. . .

. . . and they were gone.

The Weaver took a deep breath of his own and looked at the rest of the group. "This one's going to be close," he sighed, "yes, it is."

Back in the hospital, Denise clutched the Tablet and shook her head at her mother's doctors—an older gentleman and a younger, good-looking one.

"You don't understand," the older doctor tried to reason. "Pain is good."

"No way!" Denise argued. "Pain causes suffering, it causes misery. Everything's better now that I got rid of it!"

"Are you blind?" the younger doctor practically shouted. He pointed to her mom's twisted and bleeding leg. "You call that better? Without pain she doesn't know how badly she was injured. She'll just keep walking on it, making it worse and worse!"

Denise didn't like the young doctor. Not one bit. He was rude and arrogant. "You're telling me that we *need* pain?" she scorned.

"Yes," the older doctor insisted. "It's nature's way of saying something's wrong."

"You're crazy. I destroyed pain to make the world a better place!"

"You're wrong!" the younger doctor exploded.

"And you're jealous!" she shouted back. "Because me and this Tablet here, we just put you two out of business!"

"That's not it!" he insisted. "That's not it at all!" He raced to the window. "Look!" Before anyone could stop him, he leaned back and smashed his hand through the glass of the upper window.

"Doctor!" the older physician cried out.

But he paid no attention. Instead, he held out his bleeding hand to her. "Look! No pain!" He spun around and smashed it through the lower window.

"Doctor!"

Again he held it out. Only now it was in much worse shape. "Don't you see?" he pleaded. "I could do this all day and it wouldn't matter. I could get sick, burn myself, get hit by a truck—without pain I'd never know I needed help. Without pain I'd eventually kill myself!"

But Denise had made the world a better place. She wasn't about to let some doctor convince her to change it back. "No!" she insisted. "I made things better, and that's how they're going to stay!"

"We'll see about that," the younger doctor sneered. Suddenly he lunged for the Tablet.

Denise screamed and jumped back.

"Get the Tablet!" he shouted.

The older doctor and the nurse joined in. Soon they had Denise pinned against the wall as they tried to rip the Tablet from her.

"Stop it!" Denise's mom yelled as she hobbled into the fight. "Stop it!"

Denise continued screaming but it did no good. Hands came at her from all sides. She dropped to the floor and wrapped herself around the stone. She began kicking and biting—anything to keep them away.

Then she saw it. Between their legs. An opening. And past that, the door. She scampered between the legs and leaped up. In an instant she was out the door and in the hallway.

"Stop her! Stop her!"

She sprinted down the hall and knocked a couple patients off their feet. But it didn't matter. Since they didn't feel pain, they just sat there laughing.

She came to the end of the hall, looked in both directions, and darted to the right. She wasn't sure where she was going, but she could hear the younger doctor closing in from behind.

"Stop!" he ordered. "Stop!"

No way.

An open doorway came into view. She dashed into the room and tried to slam the door and lock it. But the younger doctor was too fast. Before she could get it closed, he was pushing against it. She pushed back as hard as she could, but he continued to shove it forward inch by inch.

"Denise . . . please . . . be reasonable."

She was losing ground. Any second he'd be inside. Suddenly she had an idea. If the Tablet could do anything, then maybe . . .

She pulled up the Tablet and fumbled for the marker.

"Denise . . ."

The door was nearly open. Already his arm and shoulder were squeezing in. Already he was reaching toward her.

Furiously, she scrawled the letters with the felt pen until she finally completed the words: *OBEY ME!*

But nothing happened! The doctor just kept coming! With a final push, he shoved through and grabbed her! She screamed, but it did no good. Why? What was wrong?

"Okay," he panted, "it's over. Give it to me." He held out his hand, waiting.

Denise's mind raced. *Why didn't the Tablet work?*

He grabbed the Tablet, but she still wouldn't let go. "All right, if that's the way you want it." He started prying her fingers loose—one at a time.

Suddenly she had it. Of course! He hadn't obeyed her because she hadn't given him an order!

The Tablet was nearly in his hands. Just two more fingers to go. "Be a good girl now and let—"

"Stop it!" Denise commanded.

Immediately the doctor stopped. A look of confusion crossed his face. Finally he spoke. "I'm . . . I'm sorry, Ms. Wolff . . . I don't know what came over me."

Denise watched him cautiously.

"I do hope you'll forgive me. May I walk you back to your mother's room?"

Denise hesitated, then slowly answered, "Sure." Just to be safe she pulled the Tablet in a bit closer.

The doctor held open the door for her and they entered the hallway.

Denise still wasn't a hundred percent sure. Was he just faking it or had the Tablet really worked? And if it worked, did that mean that no matter what she asked, he would have to obey her? She hated to do it, but there was really only one way to find out.

"Excuse me, Doctor?"

"Yes."

"Would you bark like a dog for me, please?"

The man instantly dropped to his knees and began to bark.

Everyone in the hall stared in amazement. Everyone but Denise. "Thank you, Doctor," she said with a contented smile, "thank you very much."

CHAPTER SIX

and now, for your entertainment

At first Joshua thought they'd cross-dimensionalized back home. This new kingdom looked exactly like any major city in any major country. Towering buildings, masses of people, and traffic backed up for blocks. But it didn't take long to see that things were just a little bit different . . .

First there was the noise. Deafening. Like a thousand stereos and TVs all blaring at the same time.

Then there were the windows. Actually the lack of them. In place of windows there were . . . movie screens. That's right. Whether they were the windows in cars, or the thousands of windows in a skyscraper, or the huge display windows of a department store, every pane of glass had been replaced by a motion picture screen. And every screen was playing a different movie! It was impossible to look anywhere without seeing at least twenty movies playing at the same time.

As a result, the people on the street barely moved. Why should they? What was happening on those screens, what filled their vision and blasted into their ears was a thousand times more interesting than real life. So they simply stood and stared.

"What is this place?" Nathan shouted.

But Joshua barely heard. The noise was too deafening. Not far away, he spotted a lone woman in rags. She seemed to be the only one moving as she pushed a rusty shopping cart down the street. He headed for her, with Nathan at his side.

"Excuse me, ma'am!" he shouted. "Ma'am, could you tell us where we are?"

"The Kingdom of Entertainment!" she shouted back.

"I'm sorry, I can barely hear you!"

"THE KINGDOM OF ENTERTAINMENT!"

Josh looked at his brother, still not entirely sure he understood.

The woman reached into her cart and brought out two sets of clear little balls, just slightly larger than marbles. She handed a pair to each boy and motioned for them to put them in their ears. Figuring he had nothing to lose, Josh popped them inside. So did his brother. And suddenly he heard . . .

Silence.

Beautiful, blessed silence.

"That will be 2,340 jairkens," the woman said, holding out her hand for payment.

Josh and Nathan traded looks. "I'm sorry," Nathan answered. "We don't have any of those . . . 'jairken' things."

"No jairkens!" she scorned. "Then give those back before I call the enforcers!"

"But," Josh protested, "without them it's so noisy we won't be able to hear ourselves think."

"That's the whole idea!" a voice boomed from behind.

The brothers spun around to see the same black-winged creature they'd viewed in Denise's Master Control. Its image was projected upon the glass panes of a revolving hotel door and it flickered as the panes spun around. Hiding behind it was the image of a large, eight-legged type of dog—frightened, but obviously trying to sneak a peek at them.

"It's the Merchant of Emotions," Nathan shouted to his brother.

"Very good." The Merchant grinned. "So tell me"—he gave a sweeping gesture with one of his claws—"what do you think of my world?"

"*Your* world?" Joshua asked.

"Well, it is now that they've made me their god."

"Why would they do that?" Nathan demanded.

The Merchant shrugged. "Appreciation, I suppose. All these people you see here wanted to be entertained. So I gave them exactly what they wanted."

"Which was . . . ?" Josh asked.

"Entertainment." He broke into a brief cackle. "Nonstop, never-ceasing entertainment. Now they'll never be able to hear themselves think. Most importantly, they'll never again be able to hear Imager's wretched voice. Their only relief is in buying silence—and that, my little friends, costs a pretty jairken."

"I should say so," the street vendor complained. "And they've just stolen four minutes' worth."

"Put it on my tab." The Merchant smiled.

"You have no tab," she argued. "And if I keep giving away silence I'll be as poor as a—"

Before she could finish, the Merchant reached for the machine strapped to his chest and flipped a single switch. A cloud of mist shot from a little nozzle and gently settled upon her stomach. Suddenly, she began to cry. Uncontrollably. Deep, gut-wrenching sobs that shook her entire body.

The brothers looked on in astonishment as she dropped to her knees and continued to weep.

"What did you do to her?" Joshua shouted.

"Oh, she's just feeling a little *sentimental.*"

"But . . . how?" Nathan stammered.

The creature grinned and gave the nozzle a small pat. "Just my little Emotion Generator."

"You mean you can control—"

"People's emotions?" the Merchant yawned. "Yes, that certainly appears to be the case, doesn't it? Would you care for a demonstration?"

"No!" Josh and Nathan shouted in unison.

"Yes, well, we'll see." The Merchant smiled as he carefully looked them over. "So, Imager has sent you two worthless creatures to try and stop my attack upon his Upside-Down Kingdom."

"We're not worthless," Josh said, taking half a step closer. "We've been re-Breathed and we have our weapons."

"Yes, a bag of water and a rather ill-fitting suit of armor."

Nathan shifted uncomfortably.

"You must remind me to give you the name of my tailor. He could do wonders."

Josh had had enough. If they were to stop this Merchant thing, then they would stop him. He started toward the revolving doors.

"Joshua!" Nathan shouted.

"Don't worry, he's just a reflection."

"Tell that to her," Nathan motioned to the old lady still crying on the sidewalk.

But Josh continued forward. He always had plenty of confidence in whatever he did. Why should this be any different?

"My, my, my, will you look at that, TeeBolt," the Merchant chuckled to the animal still hiding behind his legs. "The Josh is a brave one, isn't he?"

The animal whined and thumped its tail.

Joshua called back to Nathan. "Come on, we can take him." As he approached, he reached down and unscrewed the cap to his water skin. He wasn't exactly sure what he was going to do when he got there, but since the water was all he had and since it had proved its power in the past . . .

"The Josh has bravery," the Merchant said. "Shall we see if he has anything else?" He quickly reached to his Emotion Generator.

"Josh!" Nathan cried. "Look out!"

The Merchant flipped another switch. A thin mist shot out and struck Josh on the right side of the head.

Suddenly, Joshua began screaming in terror.

"Josh!" Nathan raced to him. "Josh, what is it?"

But Joshua couldn't speak. He was too terrified. All he could do was point down at the sidewalk and scream.

"Josh!"

Again he pointed—urgently, desperately—screaming for all he was worth.

"I don't understand! What is it?"

Joshua was beside himself. Why couldn't Nathan see it? It was right there on the sidewalk! Monstrous! Horrifying! An ant! And it was crawling straight toward him! Finally, in desperation, he raced to the nearby wall and cowered against it, whimpering and shaking like a leaf. Wouldn't somebody save him?

"Stop it!" Nathan yelled at the Merchant. "Whatever . . . doing . . . him . . . you better . . . now!"

Josh strained to hear the words but the kingdom's noise was returning. He turned toward the Merchant to see him laughing. When he spoke, Josh could only make out part of his sentence.

"You . . . no match.. . ha, ha, ha . . . will suffer . . . !"

Apparently, the marbles in Josh's ears were losing power. So he did the only thing he could do . . . he screamed louder and shook harder. Then he saw the Merchant reaching for another switch on his Emotion Generator and pointing the nozzle at Nathan . . .

After a few more barks and a long howl, the young doctor hopped back to his feet and continued down the hall with Denise. She could tell that he was embarrassed, but she had given him an order and, well, she *was* the boss. To have that much control felt good and, she had to admit, a little dizzying. Because she wasn't just the boss over the doctor. With the Tablet she was the boss over everybody. Now she had absolute power. Not that she ever planned to misuse it. But still, to have so much of it . . .

The elevator doors opened and two orderlies rushed out carrying an old man—the same one Denise had met when she stepped out of the limo—the same toothless gentleman who had jumped up and tried to click his heels. Only now he wasn't jumping. He wasn't even breathing.

Immediately the doctor was at his side. "What's wrong?"

"Heart attack!" one of the orderlies shouted.

"Set him down," the doctor ordered. "Get a crash cart, stat! We have a code blue!"

"The crash carts are all busy," the second orderly cried. "People are dropping like flies out there—everyone's overdoing it; they're all killing themselves!"

Without a word the doctor dropped to his knees and began pumping the old man's chest. Then he pinched the man's nose and began breathing into his mouth.

"What's happening?" Denise cried. "What's going on?"

"Without pain, no one knows their limits," the doctor explained as he turned from the man's mouth and began pumping his chest again. "Without pain, everyone will die."

The thought caught Denise off guard—but only for a second. If that was the only problem . . . and if she could control anything . . . Quickly she raised the Tablet and scrawled out two more words with her marker: *NO DEATH.*

Suddenly the old man came back to life—coughing, wheezing, and looking around very wide-eyed. But he was alive, there was no doubt about it.

The doctor stared up at Denise, his own eyes widening in astonishment.

"Well," Denise grinned, "that should take care of that."

Back in Master Control another alarm sounded.

Aristophenix, Listro Q, Samson, and Mr. Hornsberry had all been watching Denise on the main screen. And they all had cringed when she made the doctor bark like a dog. But now she was back to using the Tablet for good. Now things were getting better. Or so they thought.

"Alarm, what for?" Listro Q asked. "By eliminating death, didn't a good thing do she?"

The Weaver shook his head angrily. "Punch up the future!" he shouted to an assistant. "Punch up three hundred years into the future."

The big screen flickered. Now they stared at an incredibly old and outrageously fat queen. In fact, she was so huge that it took three thrones just to hold her. With all the wrinkles and rolls of fat, it was hard to recognize the face. But since this was Denise's Control Room, and since they were watching Denise, everyone had a pretty good idea who it was. She was so old and so fat that she couldn't move. And yet she was sighing in pleasure. Incredible, indescribable pleasure. The reason soon became apparent. The Merchant of Emotions was standing right beside her . . . covering her with thick mists of his emotions.

"Pull back!" the Weaver called.

The image pulled back to show more of the scene. Now they could see Denise's thrones were in the middle of a desert—an endless desert surrounded by thick, putrid air. Air so dark that it was impossible to tell whether it was day or night. Millions of people were crowded around her, coughing and choking, trying to breathe but finding it impossible.

Samson chattered a question.

The Weaver answered, "Without death, Upside Downers will overrun their kingdom and use up all its resources."

It was true. There were no trees or grass or even oceans—just people, billions and billions of swarming people. "Swarming" probably isn't the right word because to swarm you have to move. These people were so crowded together that they couldn't move. All they could do was cough and choke . . . and plead.

"Please," they begged the gigantic Denise. "Please let us die. Have mercy on us, please let us die, please . . ."

It appeared their bodies had simply worn out. Those who still had arms and legs could no longer use them. Yet, they could not die. They were forced to live century after century like this.

Still, they had no physical pain. How could they? That had been Denise's first order. But there appeared to be a different type of pain. A pain of the mind. A torture of having to live hundreds of years. A torture of having to survive in this harsh, impossibly crowded world. A torture of knowing things would only grow worse.

Aristophenix turned to the Weaver.

> *"you'LL Have to excuse me,*
> *i'm usuaLLy quite clever.*
> *But is this wHat Happens*
> *wHen upside downers Live forever?"*

The Weaver slowly nodded. "In the beginning, when Upside Downers turned from Imager, he commanded me to weave Death into their world."

"This, because of?" Listro Q asked, motioning toward the screen.

Again the Weaver nodded. "To live forever in any kingdom without Imager is impossibly cruel. Without Imager's rule, death is a gift, not a curse. Without Imager, death is mercy."

"But"—Mr. Hornsberry cleared his throat—"why is Denise so phenomenally overweight and insensitive?"

"She's done away with all of life's struggles, yes, she has," the Weaver answered. "Without struggles and hardships she has grown fat and lazy."

"Laziness of her body," Listro Q commented.

"And of her mind," Aristophenix added.

"And most dangerous of all," the Weaver continued, "there is a fatness to her soul, a laziness of her spirit."

The group stood looking on in silence.

"Still," Mr. Hornsberry asked, "this is not necessarily the future. If Master Nathan and Joshua are successful in their attempts to stop the Merchant, this will all change."

The Weaver nodded. "*If* they can stop him."

Silence again settled over the group. Only the choking and moaning from the screen filled the room.

Finally, the Weaver could stand no more. "Go back to the present," he ordered. Once again the projected image flickered and changed.

Samson began to chatter.

"Yes," the Weaver agreed, "in case Joshua and Nathan fail, a backup plan would be good."

Again Samson spoke.

Again the Weaver agreed. "Because of your closeness to her, she *might* listen. But the risk of a non-Upside Downer in this sort of situation is—"

Samson cut him off with another burst of chatter.

"I appreciate your devotion, but even if you did go, she still doesn't understand your language. She'd need a translator."

"Us have you," Listro Q offered.

The Weaver shook his head. "No, the risk of more than one non-Upside Downer there is too great."

The group stood a moment watching.

Again Listro Q spoke. "But, if somebody else from the Upside-Down Kingdom find could we—" His eyes turned to Mr. Hornsberry.

The dog shifted uncomfortably. "Did I miss something?"

"From the Upside-Down Kingdom, need we someone."

"Yes." The dog cleared his throat. "And your point is . . ."

Aristophenix turned toward Hornsberry, also seeing it. "Of course, someone of great courage . . ."

The Weaver nodded and joined in. "Someone of great intelligence . . ."

"And wisdom have must he," Listro Q added.

"Absolutely," Aristophenix agreed. Then, smiling at Mr. Hornsberry he asked, "Now, who do you suppose that special someone could be?"

Mr. Hornsberry swallowed nervously. As he was the only other citizen from the Upside-Down Kingdom, there was little doubt who they were referring to.

"I would be happy to volunteer," he coughed slightly, "most happy, indeed. However, if you recall, back home I am merely a stuffed animal. If you return me to the Upside-Down Kingdom, I'm afraid I shall once again become—"

"I could adjust your weave," the Weaver offered. "Temporarily, you understand."

"That would be most considerate, however . . ."

The group waited in hopeful anticipation.

"That is to say . . ."

They continued to wait.

Mr. Hornsberry gave another nervous cough.

They waited some more.

"Oh, very well," he sighed. "If anyone was created to save the day, I suppose it is myself."

"All right, Mr. Hornsberry!" The group cheered and slapped him on the back.

"What a guy!" Aristophenix said.

"A hero is he," Listro Q agreed.

"Yes, well," Mr. Hornsberry cleared his throat, "that goes without saying now, doesn't it."

"You'll need this." The Weaver suddenly and quite mysteriously produced another Cross-Dimensionalizer.

Mr. Hornsberry gave him a look. "You perceived that I would accompany Samson all along, didn't you?"

The Weaver gave the slightest shrug. "I am the Weaver, yes, I am." Then, without hesitating, he continued with further instruction. "Now, you must do your best to convince Denise to destroy the Tablet. And she must return everything to the original weave. Do you understand?"

Samson and Mr. Hornsberry nodded.

Without another word (and obviously fearful Hornsberry would change his mind,) the Weaver stooped down and hung the Cross-Dimensionalizer around the dog's neck. Then he quickly punched the four buttons . . .

BEEP . . .
BOP . . .
BLEEP . . .
BURP . . .

. . . and they were gone.

a CLOSE CALL

I say, this is rather odd!" Mr. Hornsberry exclaimed as he looked around the enormous room with its towering pillars, full-length windows, and sparkling chandeliers. "Do you have the slightest idea where we might be?"

Samson fired back a reply. It was long and loud. But no matter how long or loud, the answer was still your basic . . . "Nope."

Mr. Hornsberry started to trot around the room, carefully investigating. "Apparently it is some sort of mansion—a palace by all appearances. Yet, what would Denise be doing in such a residence? And what is that irritating ruckus outside?"

Beyond the windows they could hear an angry crowd shouting and yelling. Before they could look further, a large door at the far end of the room opened and a tall, stuffy butler appeared. He was stiff, and, if possible, even more snooty than Mr. Hornsberry. "May I help you?" he inquired.

Realizing the man's attempt at being a snob, Mr. Hornsberry rose to the occasion and tried to out do him. "That is your reason for employment, is it not? Now, be a good fellow and run along to fetch Miss Denise, Wolff. We'd like a word with her."

"I beg your pardon, but whom, or shall I say, *what* is calling?"

The butler was better than Mr. Hornsberry had thought. But that was okay, it would be nice to have a little competition for a change. Before he could return an appropriate insult, Samson started to buzz the man's head.

The butler appeared unfazed. Instead, he simply turned for the door.

"I don't believe you've been dismissed," Mr. Hornsberry called.

"Actually," the butler answered as he tried to swat Samson aside, "I was about to procure some bug spray."

Little Samson squealed in panic.

"No way!" Mr. Hornsberry cried. Then catching himself, he continued with a bit more sophistication. "That is to say, I see no purpose in implementing such barbaric actions."

"And while I'm at it, I think I shall call the dog pound. Talking animals can be such a nuisance."

"You'll do nothing of the kind." Denise appeared at the door behind the butler. Instead of her usual baggy pants and sweatshirt, she was decked out in a riding habit complete with riding whip and derby. She continued. "These folks are my friends and you will treat them with the respect they deserve."

"Miss Denise," Hornsberry shouted. He quickly trotted toward her, careful to turn up his nose while passing the butler.

Denise turned to the man. "That will be all, Chauncey."

"As you wish, ma'am." The butler turned to exit. As he did he fired off one last comment to Mr. Hornsberry. "Try not to shed on the furniture. Dog hair can be *so* loathsome."

For the briefest second Hornsberry wanted to sink his teeth deep into the man's calf. The fellow wanted loathsome, he'd show him loathsome. But somehow he was able to resist the temptation. After all, he did have a reputation to uphold.

Meanwhile, Samson, who was also excited to see Denise, began playfully dive-bombing her head.

"Hey, fella!" she giggled, trying to fight him off. "Cut it out. Come on now," she laughed, "stop it."

And, just that fast, Samson fell to the ground, unable to fly.

"Sammy!" Denise dropped to her knees. "Are you okay?"

"What happened?" Mr. Hornsberry cried.

"I don't know, I just . . . Oh, of course, I get it."

"Get what?"

"Well, I have this thing to write on." She held up the Tablet. "And whatever I write on it happens."

"Yes, we're well aware of that fact."

"Well, one of the things I wrote was that people have to obey me."

"I fail to see how—"

"I told Sammy to stop bothering me, and he had to stop."

Samson chattered a terse reply.

"Sorry, little guy," Denise said sympathetically, "but around here, I'm kinda like the boss. However . . ." she said, pretending to sound very official, "you hereby have my permission to fly again."

Samson took off and began giving Denise the lecture of her life, though this time he was careful to keep his distance.

Mr. Hornsberry didn't bother to translate. He figured Denise would catch the general drift. Instead, he had a few questions of his own. "Would you mind telling me why you are wearing such costly clothes?"

"Oh," Denise laughed, giving her riding whip a couple of slaps against her leg. "I saw this in a magazine and it was so expensive I figured I'd give it a try. You know, to see what the big deal was. When you can have anything you want, it's kinda hard not to go for the best."

"Yes, well, I'm afraid that's one of the reasons the Weaver has sent us."

"The Weaver sent you?" Denise asked. "Cool!"

"He knows all about the Tablet."

"So he's sent you guys to thank me for helping out?"

"Well, not exact—"

"I know these clothes and this palace are no big deal—anybody could wish for them. But it took some real thinking to figure how to make the world better for everybody."

Samson chattered off a sharp reply.

Mr. Hornsberry carefully translated, "Actually, in your admirable efforts to transform the world to a superior status, it appears you are actually destroying it."

Denise's mouth dropped. "I'm what?"

Mr. Hornsberry coughed slightly. "Destroying it."

"No way," she argued. "I'm making this place *better.* A lot better!"

Samson chattered his most stinging comment yet.

"Sure I am," Denise argued, not waiting for the translation. "'Course, not everyone understands it's for the best, but they will."

"Not everyone?" Mr. Hornsberry asked.

She nodded somewhat sadly, then motioned toward the balcony doors. "Don't you hear all that shouting and screaming outside?"

"That is directed toward you?"

"I'm afraid so." She crossed to the giant pair of doors. As she threw them open, the shouting and screaming grew louder.

"They want me to bring pain back into the world." She shook her head. "Can you believe it?"

Mr. Hornsberry and Samson moved to the balcony for a better look. Below them were hundreds of people—all shaking their fists and yelling. And for good reason. Their bodies were twisted and disfigured beyond belief. Many were doubled over with disease or sprawled out on the lawn unable to walk. Several looked as if they should have been dead. But, of course, in Denise's new world, that was no longer possible.

"A few even want me to bring death back." She sighed heavily. "They just don't get it."

"But my dear Denise. Pain and death . . . they're all part of Imager's plan. Can you not see how you are disrupting his Tapestries?"

"Disrupting?" Denise bristled. "I'm not disrupting anything. I'm only making things better."

Samson darted back and forth, speaking angrily.

Mr. Hornsberry translated. "Imager knows what's best. You've ignored his plans and changed the rules."

"No." She shook her head. "I've just added a few of my own to fix things up."

"And *your* rules," Mr. Hornsberry asked, referring to the shouting mob below, "you are certain they are 'fixing things up'?"

Denise stared down at the shouting crowd. "Hmm . . ." She tapped her foot, obviously thinking. "You know . . . you just might be on to something."

Mr. Hornsberry glanced at Samson in smug satisfaction. He'd been there less than five minutes and he was already solving the crisis.

"Yes," Denise said, beginning to nod. "That's my problem. You're right, there *are* too many rules."

"I beg your pardon?" Mr. Hornsberry asked.

She continued. "Not only do they have to follow all of Imager's rules, but they also have to follow mine. Of course. That's why they're so unhappy . . . there's way too many rules to follow."

"Miss Denise—" Hornsberry nervously cleared his throat.

"No one's really let them do what *they* want to do."

"Miss Denise—"

"If you really want people to be happy, you got to give them freedom." She broke into a grin. "Of course! Mr. Hornsberry, you're a genius!"

Hornsberry gave a shiver of delight in spite of himself. "How exactly has my intellect been of service?"

But Denise was no longer listening. Instead, she picked up the Tablet and pen and prepared to write.

"What are you doing?" Hornsberry asked.

Samson hovered over her shoulder for a closer look.

"Imager's got all these rules, right? *Do this, don't do that.* No wonder nobody's happy. What do we need all the rules for?"

Before Hornsberry could respond, she answered, "We don't. To really be happy we need to be free." She wrote on the Tablet as she continued speaking. "We should do only what *we* want to do. Live only the way *we* want to live."

She finished writing and flipped the board around for them to see. There were only two words: *NO RULES.*

Immediately, people below the balcony started screaming. "Get her! Get the Tablet! Get the Tablet!" Soon, the entire crowd joined in, "GET THE TABLET . . . GET THE TABLET!"

They began banging on the door below. "GET THE TABLET . . . GET THE TABLET . . ."

"Stop it!" Denise yelled down to them. "I command you to stop!"

But they continued pounding on the door. "GET THE TABLET . . . GET THE TABLET . . ."

"I thought they had to obey you!" Mr. Hornsberry yelled.

"They do!" She shouted. "I don't understand why—" Suddenly she broke into a sheepish grin.

"What?" Hornsberry shouted.

"GET THE TABLET . . . GET THE TABLET . . ."

"I just wrote that there are no rules, right?"

"That is correct."

"So now they don't have to obey me; now they don't have to obey anyone!"

"GET THE TABLET . . . GET THE TABLET . . ."

"If that's the case," Mr. Hornsberry shouted, "might I inquire if you have an alternate exit?"

"Sure," she yelled. "Why?"

"GET THE TABLET . . . GET THE TABLET . . ." Suddenly the crowd broke through the front doors, swarmed into the mansion, and started up the stairs.

Hornsberry shouted his answer. "So we may make a hasty retreat!"

In the Kingdom of Entertainment the Merchant's image still flickered in the revolving door, and Joshua still cowered against the building.

"Joshua!" Nathan shouted. "Joshua, can you hear me?"

But Joshua was too busy screaming to hear anything.

Nathan twirled back to the Merchant. "What was that? What did you hit him with?"

"Why, isn't it obvious?" the Merchant chuckled. "I just shared a little bit of *terror* with him."

Only then did Nathan see the Merchant had pointed the nozzle at him. Before he could move, the Merchant flipped another switch and another cloud of vapor shot from his Emotion Generator. Nathan tried to raise his shield and block the mist, but he was too late. It hit him dead center in the chest.

Yet nothing happened. Unlike Joshua, or the silence peddler who was still on her knees sobbing, there was no uncontrollable feeling. No all-consuming emotion.

Puzzled, Nathan looked down. Sure enough, there was the mist. It rested right there on his breastplate. So why had nothing happened? And then he realized the mist hadn't reached his body because of the armor. That clunky armor he hauled around had finally served a purpose. But not for long. For even as he watched, he could see the tiny droplets of moisture eating through the metal, turning it to a liquid goo, working its way closer and closer to his skin.

He spun back to his brother. "Joshua! Joshua, can you hear me?"

But Joshua was too busy screaming. At least he looked like he was screaming. Nathan could no longer hear. His marbles of silence were wearing off. The roar of the kingdom's speakers and movie screens filled his head.

The Merchant fired off another cloud of mist. This time Nathan was fast enough to block it with his shield. But when the mist hit, the shield itself started to dissolve. Nathan had no alternative but to turn and start running. But not away. No, he would not desert his brother. Instead, he ran to the silence peddler's cart and grabbed four more marbles. He quickly slipped two into his ears and rushed back to Josh with the other pair.

"What are you doing?" the Merchant cried. He reached down to his Generator and fired off two more clouds of mist. Nathan was so busy helping his brother that he didn't have time to raise his shield and defend himself. Both volleys hit him on the armor of his right leg.

But Nathan wasn't concerned about those hits. He was concerned about the first one. The one whose mist had finally eaten through his breastplate. Already he could feel its wetness touching his skin—and with that wetness came an uncontrollable emotion . . . *worry*. Worry about everything: Joshua, Denise, friends, school . . . he even began to worry about worrying. He knew it wasn't real. He knew it all came from the Merchant. But he also knew there was nothing he could do to stop it.

He dropped to his knees. "This is not happening!" he cried.

The Merchant of Emotions laughed. "You think that's something—wait until those other emotions eat their way through to you!"

Frantically Nathan looked at his right leg armor. The other emotions were quickly dissolving the metal just as the first one had.

"No!" he cried, fighting against the *worry*. "Nooo!"

The Merchant continued laughing.

"No! No! No!" Nathan screamed, but it did no good. The emotion was too strong to fight. In a final, desperate act, he cried, "Imager promised we would win! Imager promised!"

And with that cry, the strangest thing happened . . .

As Nathan shouted, as he declared Imager's promise, the mist of *worry* began to evaporate. Nathan could actually feel the dampness start to leave his chest. And, as it left, so did the *worry*.

Amazed, he shouted again. "Imager promised! We'll win! *We will win!*"

To his astonishment, not only did the moisture evaporate from his chest but the hole in his breastplate began to seal. The metal was actually sealing itself, becoming as smooth and shiny as if it had never been pierced. He looked down at his right leg armor. The same was happening there. He looked at his shield for the earlier hit. The same thing.

What had the Weaver said . . . *"The armor and shield are your belief—your protection."* Of course, that was it! They were his belief! They were his trust in Imager! Somehow as he held on to Imager's promise, he had activated their power.

Now the armor was as good as new. Slowly, with greater resolve, Nathan rose to his feet and turned to face the Merchant. He wasn't crazy about it, but by the looks of things, it was time for a little showdown.

Quickly, the Merchant fired off another round of emotion. And then another. But Nathan blocked each one with his shield. As they struck the metal, they spattered loudly and evaporated with a hiss.

"What has the Nathan done?" the Merchant shouted. "What has he done to my emotions?"

Nathan turned back to his brother, who was still screaming in *terror*. He'd already shoved the marbles of silence into his ears but it did nothing to stop the fear. "Josh!" he shouted. "Josh, you've got to listen to me!"

But Joshua was still overwhelmed.

What could he do? And then he spotted it. The mist the Merchant had fired at his brother. It was still on the side of his head, still glistening in the blue-green light of the surrounding TV screens.

Nathan reached out his armored glove to it. Ever so gently he touched the moisture. It spattered and hissed viciously.

Josh blinked.

Nathan touched some more. And every place he touched, the moisture evaporated . . . until it had completely disappeared.

Josh blinked again, then shook his head, trying to get his bearings. "What . . . what happened?" he asked.

Nathan leaned closer and looked into his eyes. As best he could tell the *terror* his brother had been experiencing was gone.

"What happened?" Josh repeated.

"It's the Merchant," Nathan said, pointing toward the revolving doors. "He was controlling you with—"

But when Nathan turned he saw the Merchant was no longer there. He had disappeared.

"Look!" Josh shouted, struggling to his feet. He pointed to the windows of the hotel, then to other buildings. "The TV and movie screens—they're gone. All of them! They're all glass again!"

"And the noise," Nathan said. He pulled the marbles from his ears to make sure. "It's also gone!"

It's true. Things were peaceful and quiet. Well, as peaceful and quiet as any big city can be . . . if you don't count the honking horns, squealing brakes, and screaming people.

"Do you see him?" Josh asked, looking around.

Nathan shook his head. "He's not here. He must have left."

"Good."

Nathan agreed. "At least for the people of this kingdom."

"So where do you think he'd go? I mean after he left this kingdom where would he . . ." Josh came to a stop. He turned to Nathan, his eyes widening in concern. "Quick, the Cross-Dimensionalizer!"

Immediately Nathan understood. He pulled the Cross-Dimensionalizer from his pocket and shouted into it. "Listro Q! Listro Q, you have to get us to Earth—*now!*"

The unit crackled to life. "At your home, he is not. One more kingdom, visiting first is he."

"Then send us there—we have to stop him!"

"Entering the coordinates now am I."

The brothers exchanged looks. In learning how to fight the Merchant, they'd nearly lost the first battle. Hopefully they'd be ready for the next.

"Ready!" Listro Q shouted.

Nathan nodded and reached down to press the buttons.

BEEP . . .
BOP . . .
BLEEP . . .
BURP . . .

the
OUT-OF-TIMERS

"Now where are we?" Josh asked.

Nathan shook his head. At first glance it looked like some kind of overgrown park. But a very weird overgrown park. There were lots of trees, yet they were all perfectly straight and had no branches. They were planted in single file and covered with ivy. Below them were wide, overgrown paths of concrete that stretched as far as the eye could see. And on those paths were . . . could it be? Yes. They were cars—broken-down, rusted-out cars. Hundreds of them. Which meant those concrete lanes weren't pathways at all, but overgrown streets. And the branchless trees in straight lines? What else but telephone poles!

Then there were the people . . .

Nathan saw them sitting inside the cars and on top of them chatting away. Like the cars and the rest of the kingdom, they were dirty and broken down—hair messed, faces unshaven, sporting the latest fashion in worn and tattered clothing.

Then there was the smell. *Their* smell. It was so strong that it made Nathan's nose tickle. It was a safe bet that soap and water weren't something this kingdom had discovered yet. Or if it had, then like the streets, cars, and telephone poles, its citizens simply didn't care enough to use them.

And, speaking of "not caring," no one seemed too surprised when the brothers suddenly cross-dimensionalized in front of them.

"Excuse me," Josh called to a nearby car. Its doors had rusted off and it was filled with a handful of elderly people. "Excuse me, could you tell us where we are?"

At first no one bothered to answer. They just continued their conversation.

"Excuse me!"

Finally a ragged, white-haired man from the front seat shouted, "We can't tell you where you *are*, but we can tell you where you *arrived*."

Nathan threw a look at Josh. "I'm sorry, what?"

"We were Out-of-Timers."

"*Out-of-Timers?*" Josh asked.

"That *was* correct. We *were* Out-of-Timers."

Again the brothers traded glances. "What do you mean, *were?*" Nathan asked. "What are you now?"

"We had no *now*. Nor will we have one in the future."

"What?" Josh exclaimed.

"What do you mean, you have no now?" Nathan asked.

The man turned to the group in the backseat. "I had forgotten how stupid youth was." The others chuckled and clucked their tongues in agreement. The white-haired man turned back to Joshua. "We neither had a *now* in the past nor will we have a *now* in the future. We will think only of our past or of our future. We have not lived nor will we ever live in the *now*."

Nathan turned to his brother. "You're the brain. What's he saying?"

"I'm not sure," Josh scowled. "But I think he's saying these people don't have a *present*."

"What?"

"It sounds like they can remember the past okay. And they can think about the future . . . but they don't have a *now*."

"They don't have a *now?*" Nathan repeated.

Josh nodded. "They can't enjoy the present."

"That's awful!"

"It *was* awful," the white-haired man agreed. "And it *will be* awful."

"Is that why everything is falling apart?" Nathan asked. "Because there is no *now* for you to fix things up?"

"We *have* fixed things and we *will* fix things, but we can't fix things now because—"

"—there is no *now*," Josh cut in impatiently, "yeah, I got it. But who is responsible for this?"

"There never was an *is* nor will there be an *is*."

"All right, all right, who *was* responsible for this?"

A beggar from the backseat spoke up. "The creature with the eight-legged pet—the creature with all the emotions had returned to us."

"The Merchant!" Nathan gasped.

"He'd been here before?" Josh asked.

"Yes, many times."

"And he's here now?"

"He *was* here. And he *will be* here, but—"

"I know, I know," Nathan sighed, "but there is no *now* so he's not here."

The beggar nodded with satisfaction. The group turned to one another and resumed speaking of the past, recalling how the Merchant had cast his spell—how he had stolen their *now*—how they could only have feelings and emotions for the past or the future.

Nathan tried to listen patiently, but it wasn't long before he broke in. "Don't you guys want to do something? Don't you want to fight to get those *now* feelings back?"

"Oh, we had tried in the past," the white-haired man explained. "And we'll try in the future—"

"But *now!*" Nathan exclaimed. "What about *now?*"

"There was and will be no *now.*"

"But . . . don't you see?" Nathan sputtered in frustration. "The future will always become the *now.* And then you won't be able to enjoy it or do anything about it because it's *now.*"

The group in the car looked at him blankly.

He tried again. "You will never do or enjoy anything, because when you try to, it will no longer be the future, but it will be the present."

The group shrugged and turned back to their conversation.

"Doesn't anyone care?"

There was no answer.

Josh tried another approach. "Okay, okay, why don't you just tell us where he's going . . . I mean, where he *was* going?"

"Into that swamp," an elderly woman with a fur hat said from the front seat. "When they heard you had arrived, the two of them raced into that swamp."

Joshua and Nathan turned in the direction she pointed. Not far away stretched a huge swamp, so large it could have been a small sea. It was covered with thick vegetation and shrouded in a dark, impenetrable fog.

"In there?" Nathan asked nervously.

"That's right!" the beggar nodded. "They ran in there and someday we will follow."

The other passengers nodded then resumed recalling their past and dreaming of their future.

"Come on," Josh motioned to Nathan, "let's get him."

"In there?" Nathan repeated.

"Of course!"

"By ourselves?"

"I don't see any other volunteers—come on!" Joshua turned and headed for the swamp.

Nathan hesitated a moment, then turned back to the car and tried one last time. "You sure nobody wants to help?"

"Yes, we will help," the white-haired man repeated. "Someday, we will."

Nathan let out a heavy sigh as he realized that "someday" would never arrive . . . and when it did, it would be gone. At last he turned to join his brother, his armor clunking with every step. Strange, the metal suit fit a lot better since their first encounter with the Merchant. Nathan wondered if he'd gained weight or grown a bit. And the shield, it didn't seem nearly as heavy.

But that did little to relieve his fears. The swamp loomed before him just as dark and foreboding as ever . . .

Back at Master Control one alarm sounded after another.

"What's she doing now!" the Weaver cried in frustration. "Project her image!"

An assistant transferred another image to the center screen. In it Denise, Mr. Hornsberry, and Samson were racing toward a beach.

Behind them was an angry mob, screaming: "GET THE TABLET . . . GET THE TABLET . . . GET THE TABLET . . ."

"Close in on Denise!" the Weaver ordered. "Let's hear what she's saying!"

The assistant obeyed as Aristophenix and Listro Q leaned forward for a better listen . . .

"Hurry!" Denise shouted as they arrived at the bright, sunny beach and started trudging through the sand. "The beach people will protect us. Look how happy they are!"

Unlike the wretched souls pursuing them, the crowd on the beach seemed to be having a great time.

"See," Denise cried to Mr. Hornsberry, "not everybody hates what I've done."

The group in Master Control also saw. Actually they saw too much . . . Hundreds of people were staggering about on the beach, screaming, shrieking, drinking, dancing, beating up each other, and . . . . well if you could name it, they were probably doing it . . . and worse! It was like a giant out-of-control party.

Mr. Hornsberry shouted over the din, "I fail to fully comprehend what has transpired."

Samson chattered in agreement.

"I added the one thing I'd forgotten!" Denise shouted. "Freedom!" She dodged a couple beer bottles flying in their direction. "If you really want people to be happy, then let them be free to do whatever they want!"

"I understand that you have removed the rules, Miss Denise, but—"

"But it shouldn't be like this!" Denise agreed. "Something's wrong. Something's not—Look out!" She pushed Hornsberry to the side just as a school bus roared past them. It missed the group by mere feet as it slid past, throwing sand over them. The driver of the bus obviously felt he didn't have to obey the road rules. But the screaming, hysterical children inside the bus obviously thought he should.

"What was that about?" Mr. Hornsberry shouted as he staggered to his feet, coughing and brushing himself off.

Before Denise could answer, she spotted a mom and dad pleading with their little five-year-old. Actually, she wasn't so little. In fact, she was as wide as she was tall, and for good reason. She was cramming her mouth with so many chocolate bars that she could barely breathe. The goop covered her face, her hands, her entire body. And still she continued to eat, practically choking as she shoved in one bar after another.

"What are you doing?" Denise demanded. She turned to the parents. "Make her stop! She's going to get sick, make her stop!"

"We're trying!" the father cried. "But since there are no rules, she won't listen to us! She won't stop!"

"GET THE TABLET . . . GET THE TABLET . . ."

Denise threw a look over her shoulder. The angry mob, the hundreds of broken and twisted people, were gaining on them. Before she could respond, another group approached her from the volleyball courts. They were young people. Very *angry* young people.

"We want to talk to you!" Their leader, a blonde-headed surfer, shouted. "We want to talk to you *now!*"

"What's wrong?" Denise asked.

"It's the radio stations," he complained. "They've gone off the air. Nobody wants to work in them anymore!"

"What?" Denise asked.

"And not just the radio stations," a freckle-faced girl in a scant bathing suit complained. "The malls are closed, too. And the theaters!"

"That's right," a boy with bow tie and glasses shouted. "And the hospitals, and the doctors' offices, and—"

"Wait a minute," Denise interrupted. "I don't understand."

"Without rules," the surfer shouted, " nobody wants to do anything, so nobody does anything!"

"But . . . ," Denise stammered. "They have to work . . . they have to eat."

"Not when they can steal," the girl yelled.

"Steal?"

"Of course! Everybody takes whatever they want from whoever they want!"

"But . . ." Frustration filled Denise and tightened her throat. "It's not supposed to be like this! Having no rules is supposed to—"

She was interrupted by the roar of the bus. It had spun around and was heading straight for them. The driver behind the wheel was laughing hysterically!

"LOOK OUT!" the young people screamed.

Denise dove to the ground as the bus roared by—missing her by inches. But the teens weren't so lucky. It slammed into the group, running over many of them.

"NO!" Denise shouted.

But thanks to the Tablet, they weren't dead and they felt no pain—though their bodies were smashed and destroyed beyond recognition.

The bus continued to slide until it plowed into a nearby refreshment stand, destroying it and wiping out another dozen people. As it skidded back onto the road it veered too sharply to the left. Tires screeched and smoked, before it finally toppled over, rolling once, twice—the children inside screaming—before it finally settled to a stop onto its back.

The air was filled with dust and the screams of children. They were trapped inside with no way out. Suddenly the engine exploded and caught fire, spewing thick black smoke into the bus. The children coughed and choked. Some tried to crawl out the windows but couldn't. Others pressed their faces to the glass, banging on it, begging for someone to come rescue them.

But no one did.

Denise stared in horror as the smoke filled the bus. She turned to the crowd and cried, "Isn't anybody going to help?"

A nearby lifeguard turned over on his blanket for a better look, but he did not move. A policeman quit his volleyball game and watched with interest. Others drew closer but only for a better view.

Denise was beside herself. "We've got to help them!"

"And ruin the show?" an elderly woman asked as she adjusted her beach chair to see better. "Why should we care?"

"Because they're going to die!"

"People don't die anymore, remember?" the woman said.

"What about their pain?" Denise cried.

"There is no pain," the policeman reminded her.

"You're just going to sit and let the bus burn up?" she screamed.

"Should be fun."

Denise spun back to the bus, hot tears burning her eyes as one child after another began sliding from the windows, overcome with smoke. This wasn't the kingdom she wanted! Nothing was turning out like she'd planned! Nothing at all!

She looked at the Tablet in her hand. If she could just remove some of the commands! But every one was written in the same permanent marking pen. Each and every command was impossible to erase.

the INVITATION

J osh . . . Josh, where are you?"

"Over here."

"Where?"

"Right over—ouch! That's my foot!"

"Sorry."

"Ow, that's my other one!"

It was dark in the swamp. So dark that the brothers couldn't see a thing, not even each other.

"This is impossible," Nathan complained as he waded through the thick, smelly ooze that clung and tugged at his every step. Then there was the dense undergrowth of branches that continually slapped him in the face. "How are we supposed to find the Merchant if we can't even see where we—"

"Shh . . . listen."

"I don't hear any—"

"Shhhh."

Nathan did his best to keep quiet. Not an easy trick when you're standing in muck and sinking to your waist, or when it's so dark you can't see, or when you happen to be a world-class whiner. But with great effort he somehow managed to hold off complaining, until he finally heard . . .

"What is that?" he whispered.

"It sounds like . . . panting," Josh whispered back. "Like a giant dog,"

In perfect unison, both boys whispered, "TeeBolt!"

"That means we're right next to them," Josh said.

"But where?"

In the darkness Nathan heard a faint click that sounded like a switch being flipped. Then he heard the gentle sound of falling mist. Suddenly his brother started to whimper:

"How come Imager gave *you* that suit of armor?"

"What . . ."

"It's not fair, you *always* get the good stuff."

"What are you talking about?" Nathan whispered.

"It's just like at home. Mom and Dad always treat you better—"

"Josh—"

"—just 'cause you're the baby."

"What's wrong with you?" Nathan asked. "Joshua?" He heard a faint chuckle just a few feet away and his blood went cold. There was no mistaking its owner.

"Sounds like the Joshua is feeling a little *jealous,*" the Merchant's voice taunted. This was followed by more sounds of panting and slurping—obviously from TeeBolt.

"You always get what you want," Joshua complained.

"Where are you?" Nathan whispered to him.

"Just 'cause of that stupid hip of yours—"

"It's the Merchant," Nathan explained, "he's controlling your emotions. Where did he spray you?"

"—everyone's always feeling sorry for you."

Reaching toward Josh's voice, Nathan tried to take hold of him. But he only caught part of his shirt and the water skin hanging around his neck.

"Get back!" his brother shouted as he yanked away.

The shirt slipped through Nathan's armored fingers. So did the water skin. But not before his sharp metal glove ripped a gash into the top of it.

"Now look what you've—"

But that was as far as Josh got before the glow stopped him. The glow of the water. In the utter blackness, the liquid spilling from the tear gave off a faint light.

"It's Imager's words!" the Merchant's voice cried.

Nathan spun around to see the creature just a few feet from them. He was covering his eyes and screaming, "Put it away! Put it away!" He turned and waded deeper into the swamp. "TeeBolt, come!" The giant animal splashed after him. "Not so close, you nincompoop! Not so close!"

Nathan turned back to Joshua. In the faint glow he could see the Merchant's moisture glistening on his brother's arm. "Here," he said reaching toward it, "let me touch that and—"

"Look how you ripped my water skin!" Josh whimpered. "It's no fair. Your stuff always lasts longer than—"

Nathan's glove finally touched the moisture. There was a loud hiss as the emotion boiled off of Joshua's skin. His brother blinked and shook his head as his senses returned.

"Are you okay?" Nathan asked.

"Yeah," he said, giving his head another shake. "Where's—"

There was a distant snapping of twigs. They both turned to see TeeBolt disappear into the darkness after his master.

"Let's get them!" Josh shouted.

"But—"

"We have to stop them before they leave for Earth!"

"But how?" Nathan argued. "We can't see a thing!"

"We've got this water!" Josh held up the water skin with the light glowing from its ripped top. "Come on!"

"But his emotions! They nearly had you again!"

"Just keep fighting them off with that armor of yours," Josh said. "You're doing great!"

"Yeah, but—"

"You defend us with your armor. I'll use this water to light our way. Come on!"

Before Nathan could argue, Josh started into the darkness. He held the water skin out in front of him, preventing any more from spilling out of its torn opening, while using its glow to guide each of their steps.

Their going was much faster now and soon they spotted the Merchant. As usual, he was berating TeeBolt as they stumbled and staggered through the darkness. "No!" the Merchant whispered harshly. "*You're* the pet. *I'm* the master. You go first!"

TeeBolt whined, panted, and slobbered in protest.

"Merchant!" Joshua shouted.

The Merchant spun around and for the first time since they met, Nathan saw fear on the creature's face. "Get away!" he shouted, shielding his eyes against the light of the water skin. "Keep that water away from me!"

"Oh, so this makes you a little nervous, does it?" Josh asked, holding the water out farther.

"Josh," Nathan warned, "be careful."

"That's right," the Merchant threatened as he reached to the Emotion Generator strapped to his chest. "Come any closer and I'll fire."

"We're not afraid of you," Joshua said as he continued to slosh forward in the swamp.

"Have it your way," the Merchant sneered as he flipped another switch.

"Look out!" Nathan cried. Without thinking he leaped in front of Josh to block the mist with his shield. It struck the metal with a violent hiss, then was gone.

"Thanks," Josh grinned. "You're getting pretty good at that."

Nathan grinned back, as amazed as he was nervous.

"Keep your distance," the Merchant warned. "Stay away with that water!" He reached for another switch.

Nathan raised his shield in preparation. Things were starting to make sense now. It was just as the Weaver had said. They each had their weapons. Nathan, his armor—Joshua, his water. And, if they worked together, maybe, just maybe, they could defeat the Merchant.

The creature fired another emotion.

Nathan easily deflected it with his shield.

"Let's get him," Joshua said.

Nathan nodded and they started forward.

"I'm warning you!" the Merchant cried, backing up. He began firing one emotion after another, in rapid succession. But with Josh's light Nathan could see each cloud of mist coming and was able to block it with his shield. As they hit the metal, each evaporated with a sinister hiss.

"TeeBolt!" the Merchant cried. "Attack!"

But TeeBolt was too busy running in the opposite direction to be doing much attacking.

"TeeBolt!"

As the brothers continued toward him Josh held out the water. "Sure you don't want a little drink?"

The Merchant began to tremble. "The Joshua must keep that away. The Joshua does not know its power!"

Nathan was not surprised at the Merchant's fear. He remembered all too well how the water had destroyed his evil sister's Kingdom of Seerlo.

Josh adjusted the rip at the top of the water skin so even more of the glow poured out—the glow that seemed to blind the Merchant, paralyzing him with fear. "Please"—he covered his eyes—"have mercy, have mercy!"

They were only two steps away now.

The creature dropped to his knees, cowering in fear. "Have mercy, have mercy!"

Josh came to a stop and raised the water skin over the creature's head.

"Please . . . I'll do anything the Joshua asks—please, please . . ."

"Anything?"

"Yes, yes . . ."

"You'll return to your own world? You'll leave the Upside-Down Kingdom alone?"

"Put it away, please—"

Josh repeated, *"You'll leave the Upside-Down Kingdom alone?"*

The children on the bus had all slipped from the windows. And still none of the beach people moved to help. In fact, they actually started to complain.

"That's it? No more explosions? No one is going to catch fire?"

Denise turned to them in astonishment. "Are you crazy? Do you *want* to see awful things?"

"Why not?" the old woman shrugged. "With no work, we need something to do."

"That's right," the lifeguard yelled. "We need some type of entertainment!"

"Yeah," the policeman agreed. "Entertain us. You've taken everything else away, the least you can do is entertain us."

Those around him started to agree. "Yes, entertain us." Others joined in. "Entertain us . . ." They began approaching her. "Entertain us . . . Entertain us . . ."

Denise started to back away.

They grew louder, more demanding, "Entertain us! Entertain us!"

Another set of voices came from behind her:

"GET THE TABLET . . . GET THE TABLET . . ."

Denise whirled around to see the first group from the mansion. They had finally arrived and were also closing in. "GET THE TABLET . . . GET THE TABLET . . ."

"ENTERTAIN US . . . ENTERTAIN US . . ."

Others approached from other directions . . . The father with his chocolate-covered daughter. Pain filled his eyes as he cried out to Denise. "You've made our lives a nightmare . . . a living nightmare!"

Then there were the mangled teens who had been hit by the bus. Some walked, others staggered, many could only drag themselves toward her. "Monsters . . . you've made us monsters . . ."

Tears filled Denise's eyes. "No, I . . . I created good! This is supposed to be good!"

"A NIGHTMARE . . . YOU'VE CREATED A NIGHTMARE . . ."

"ENTERTAIN US . . ."

"MONSTERS, WE'RE MONSTERS . . ."

"GET THE TABLET . . ."

Denise turned, trying to run, but they were coming at her from every side. Angry people, broken people, ruined people.

"ENTERTAIN US . . ."

"NIGHTMARE . . ."

"MONSTERS . . ."

"GET THE TABLET . . ."

"Mr. Hornsberry!" She turned to her friends "Samson—do something! Help me!"

But there was nothing they could do.

The mob closed in. "Don't you understand?" she cried. "I was trying to make things better!" Tears streamed down her face.

"NIGHTMARE . . ."

"MONSTERS . . ."

"YOU MUST BE STOPPED!"

They were nearly on top of her.

She pulled the Tablet closer. "NO! DON'T YOU SEE . . . I JUST, I JUST WANT EVERYBODY TO—" Suddenly, she had an idea. She reached for her marker and began to write.

"STOP HER!" the father screamed.

"GET THE TABLET!"

They lunged for her, but not before Denise had finished writing. She shouted, "I JUST WANT EVERYBODY TO . . ." she spun around the Tablet to reveal the words: *FEEL GOOD!*

The Merchant of Emotions let out a screeching laugh. "Too late!" he screamed into the boys' faces. "You're too late!"

Instantly, he vanished. Without a trace—except for the giant eight-legged pet who started whining at being left behind.

Back in Master Control, alarms and lights flashed everywhere.

"What's happening?" Aristophenix cried.

"Wrong, what's?" Listro Q yelled.

"Denise has given the invitation!" the Weaver shouted back.

"What?"

"She's invited the Merchant of Emotions to the Upside-Down Kingdom!"

CHAPTER TEN

ROUND
ONe

A shadow fell across the angry mob. They looked up from Denise and into the sky as a huge leather-winged creature blocked the sun, then dove directly toward them.

"It's heading for us!" someone cried.

Others in the crowd screamed as they started running, hobbling, and dragging themselves away.

Denise could only stand, staring. She watched as the creature swooped down in front of her and landed directly behind the people.

"Please," the creature called to them. "I mean the Upside Downers no harm. It is urgent that I speak to the Upside Downers. You must listen to me . . ."

The pleas sounded earnest and many in the crowd began to slow—

"It is so very important . . ."

Soon they came to a stop.

"Please . . ."

Some began to turn, listening cautiously to what the creature had to say.

It folded its wings and preened a few crystal scales. The braver and more curious took a step closer. Others followed. When it appeared to have everyone's attention it spoke again.

"I am here to help." The creature tried to look friendly and smile— not an easy job when you have a beak for a mouth.

The group murmured, uncertain, until finally the father of the chocolate-bar eater stepped forward. "Who are you?" he demanded. He was obviously trying to sound courageous. He might have pulled it off if his voice wasn't two octaves higher and shaking like a leaf.

Denise found her own voice. "Don't listen to her!" she shouted. "It's the Illusionist!"

Mr. Hornsberry cleared his throat. "Actually, it's the Merchant of Emo—"

Denise ignored him and stepped closer to the creature. "You're supposed to be dead! We destroyed you in the Sea of Justice!"

The creature turned from the crowd to face her. "The Denise did not destroy me. The Denise destroyed my awful sister—the Illusionist."

"She was your sister?" Denise asked suspiciously.

The creature bowed his head as if embarrassed. "Alas and alack, the Illusionist was the black sheep of the family. And, though her loss caused us great pain, we knew it was for the best." He took a deep breath, his beak trembling slightly. "And for that"—he swallowed— "for that we thank the Denise."

Samson chattered what sounded like a warning, but Denise didn't need anyone to tell her to be careful. "Why are you here?" she asked, taking another step forward. "What do you want?"

"I am the Denise's servant. The Denise summoned me here. What does the *Denise* want?"

"Me?"

"The great Denise summoned me with her wondrous Tablet."

Denise frowned, glancing down at the flat stone in her hand.

Once again the father of the chocolate-bar eater spoke. "Look, Mr., uh . . ."

"Merchant," the creature answered as he turned back to the crowd. "Just call me Merchant."

"Well, Mr. Merchant," the father took a step closer. Others followed behind him. "The point is, Denise here has made our lives unbearable and—"

"Unlivable!" another shouted.

"Impossible!" another cried.

The father continued. "And we've decided we must stop her."

"That's right!" other members of the group agreed. "She must be stopped." They moved closer. "She must be stopped at once!" As they approached, the Merchant reached down and adjusted something strapped to his chest.

"It's the Emotion Generator!" Mr. Hornsberry cried.

"What are you doing?" Denise shouted.

He turned to her and grinned. "Just setting my little machine here to maximum strength."

"Machine?" she asked.

"It's the Emotion Generator, the Emotion Generator!" Mr. Hornsberry cried as he hopped from side to side.

Pointing a nozzle at the angry crowd, the Merchant chortled, "I think it's time they loosen up a bit, don't you?" He flipped a switch and a mist shot out over half of the group. Suddenly they broke into laughter—uncontrollable, backslapping, hold-your-sides laughter. Many dropped to their knees, trying to catch their breath, but it did little good. They couldn't seem to stop.

"What did you do?" Denise demanded. "What was that?"

"Just a little *laughter,*" the Merchant chuckled. He redirected the nozzle toward the other half of the crowd. "And how about some *peace* for you folks." He flipped another switch and another cloud of mist shot out, raining down upon the rest of the group. Suddenly, they broke into dreamy smiles. Many closed their eyes, rocking back and forth as if they were in their own world . . . as if everything was perfect with no need to worry about anything.

"Stop him!" Mr. Hornsberry shouted. "He must be—"

The creature spun around and gave both Mr. Hornsberry and Samson a squirt as well.

"Sammy!" Denise shouted. "Mr. Hornsberry!"

But they no longer seemed to hear. If they did, they no longer cared. They simply closed their eyes and broke into mindless smiles.

"What have you done?" Denise shouted at the Merchant. "What have you done?"

"Your humble servant has done nothing," the Merchant replied. "The Denise is the one who invited me. The Denise is the one who commanded that all Upside Downers must feel good."

Denise looked down at the Tablet. It was true, the words FEEL GOOD were there just as bold as ever. She looked back to the crowd of laughers. By now they were rolling on the ground, gasping for air. While those hit by the *peace* mist were also sinking to the ground, apparently finding no need to stand.

"How . . . how long will this last?" she asked.

"The Denise wants Upside Downers to feel good, doesn't she?"

"Yes, but how—"

"If that's what the Denise wants, that's what she will get."

"But when will it wear off?"

"I'm afraid, like your Tablet, the effects of my emotions are permanent."

Permanent! The word hit Denise hard. "But . . . they can't get up. They can't go anywhere. They can't do anything!"

"That is correct, the Upside Downers will never go anywhere or do anything again."

"But . . . but they have to eat. They have to—"

The Merchant shook his head. "If the Upside Downers always feel good, why should they?"

"You mean they'll just—"

"Stay here forever." The Merchant nodded.

"But they'll starve to death."

"The Denise has destroyed death, remember?"

"So they'll just stay here until they . . . shrivel up for lack of food?"

"Or water," the Merchant agreed. "They'll stay here until they turn to dust and simply blow away."

"But . . . you just can't—"

"I have no choice," the Merchant sighed. "The Denise wrote it on the Tablet."

She turned and stepped toward the crowd. "You guys can't sit here like that!" she yelled. "You've got to get up and do something! Get up! Get up!"

Those who bothered to respond only laughed . . . or smiled dreamily.

"Mr. Hornsberry!" She turned to the dog, then to Samson. "Do something!"

But they sat on the sand, smiling away.

Fighting back her panic, Denise turned and walked into the sitting crowd. "What about you?" she shouted at the father who had tried to be the hero. "What about your daughter! Don't you want to save her?"

The man closed his eyes and smiled.

She waded further into the group, toward the laughers. She spotted the teen surfer. "You can't sit here forever!" she shouted. "Don't you want to do something—be something?"

The boy laughed all the harder.

The Merchant sighed. "I'm afraid the Denise has made quite a mess with that Tablet."

She looked around. He was right. What *had* she done? She was supposed to make things better. She was supposed to help their lives, not ruin them. But now . . . now the people were not only twisted and crippled, now they were smiling mindlessly or laughing insanely. By trying to make a dream world, she had, quite literally, created a nightmare.

Angrily she brushed at the tears springing to her eyes. "What am I supposed to do?" she demanded. "How can I make it better?"

"Perhaps . . ." The Merchant looked down to the ground and shrugged. "No, that would never work."

"What?"

"I don't think . . ."

"Tell me!"

"It's just . . . well, if the Tablet were turned over to someone more experienced . . ."

Denise looked at him.

"After all," he continued, "the Denise was right, she did improve upon Imager's work. Once she took charge, things did become better for a while, but . . ."

"But what?"

"The Denise simply did not have the experience."

"And you do?"

Again, he looked to the ground. "I cannot do it on my own, of course not." He gave another shrug. "But together—the Denise with her great understanding of Upside Downers and I with my vast experience—together we could make this the great world the Denise dreamed of."

"And"—Denise motioned to the crowd—"all this will stop?"

"Not only will it stop, but together, we will make this world *perfect.*"

Denise looked back at the Tablet in her hands. "But . . . how will I know?"

Again the Merchant tried to smile. "I guess the Denise will just have to trust me."

She frowned. How? How could she trust him? Look what he did to these people—turning them into mindless zombies, insane laughers. And yet, and yet . . . he was only following orders . . . *her* orders. It really wasn't *his* fault . . . it was *hers.*

The Merchant stepped closer. "The Denise would not give up power," he smiled. "She would simply share it. I will make no decision without the Denise. I give the Denise my word."

Denise felt herself weakening. It wasn't as if she was giving up control—she'd just have a partner. She turned to him and swallowed. "You promise?" she asked.

"Cross my hearts and hope to die." Again he smiled. "Please, just let me touch it. The Denise may hold it, only allow me to touch it."

"And things will be better?"

"Things will be . . . perfect." Gently, the Merchant reached out his claws. "Please . . . it will be for the good of the people—*your* people."

Denise looked back at the crowd of howling laughers and mindless smilers—a crowd that would remain that way forever unless . . . unless . . .

"For them . . . ," the Merchant whispered sincerely. "For them."

Finally, she began to nod. Then, slowly, she stretched the Tablet toward the Merchant. And just as his claws touched the stone . . .

BEEP . . .

BOP . . .

BLEEP . . .

BURP . . .

. . . Joshua and Nathan appeared. Oh, and one other traveler . . . an eight-legged dog.

As Denise turned toward them, the Merchant took advantage of the distraction and ripped the Tablet from her hands. But his possession was short-lived. For when the dog saw him, it broke into a grin and raced toward him full speed.

"No!" the Merchant cried. "TeeBolt! *Noo!*"

But love knows no bounds. Before the Merchant could stop him, TeeBolt leaped onto him with his front paws (all four of them) and sent them crashing to the ground—TeeBolt, the Merchant, and the Tablet. As they hit the sand, the stone was jarred from his hands.

"Get it!" Josh yelled. "Don't let him have the Tablet!"

The Merchant wiggled toward it—not an easy task with a three-hundred-pound pooch on your chest. "Get off me, you nincompoop! Get off me!" But the sound of the Merchant's voice gave TeeBolt even more joy, making him pant harder, drool gooeyer, and lick wetter. "No, boy!" The Merchant coughed and gagged. "Easy, fella, easy . . ."

Still, his claws were only inches from the Tablet. If he could just touch them. If he could just reach out and—

Denise spotted what he was doing and lunged for the stone . . . just as the Merchant did!

CHAPTER ELEVEN

GREED

Nathan watched as Denise and the Merchant rolled back and forth in the sand fighting for the Tablet.

"Let me—"

"It's mine!"

"The Denise doesn't know—"

The Merchant nearly had it in his claws before she yanked it away.

Pulling the marker from her pocket, she started writing the letters, M-I—

"The Denise must give it to me!" The Merchant wrapped his claws around it, ripping it from her hands—just as she finished the word . . . *MINE.*

Suddenly the Tablet flashed white hot and the Merchant dropped it to the sand screaming, "AUGH!"

Denise quickly scooped it up. But in her hands it appeared as cool as always. And Nathan knew the reason. It was the last word she'd written on it. Now, the Tablet would always be hers. Now, nobody would be able to touch it.

"Way to go, Denny!" he shouted.

"Nice work!" Josh agreed.

"We'll see about *nice,*" the Merchant sneered as he rose to his feet and smoothed his ruffled scales. "So the Denise doesn't want to share, does she? Fine. If the Denise wants to be greedy, let her be . . . *greedy.*" He reached to his Emotion Generator and flipped another switch.

Nathan shouted: "DENNY, LOOK OUT!"

But he was too late. Before Denise could respond, a mist of emotion shot from the Merchant's Generator and covered her entire body.

Suddenly her eyes grew wide with desire. She pointed to the first thing she saw—a nearby beach umbrella. "Mine!" she cried. As if caught in a mighty wind, the umbrella ripped from the sand and flew across the beach until it clattered onto the ground at Denise's feet.

Nathan looked at his brother in astonishment.

She pointed at the next thing she saw—the lifeguard station. "Mine!" she cried. Immediately it tore from its foundation and was at her side. A little tipsy from the sudden move, but there, nonetheless.

The Merchant started to laugh. "If the Denise wants to control the Tablet, let her. I'll simply control the Denise!"

"Mine!" Denise pointed at a pair of sandals on the feet of one of the laughers. Suddenly they were on her feet.

"You can't control her!" Nathan cried.

"Hasn't the Nathan learned yet?" the Merchant laughed. "Whoever controls the emotions controls the person."

"We'll see about that," Josh said, reaching for his water skin. "You may have her now, but not for long."

"Oh, yes, very long. And I'll soon have the Joshua and the Nathan as well."

"No way," Nathan declared, raising his shield and stepping beside his brother. The armor fit much better now. Nearly perfect. "With this shield and that water you can't touch us."

"The Nathan has a point. *I* can't." He turned to Denise and spoke. "Look at the Nathan's nice shiny armor. Wouldn't the Denise love to have that?"

Denise smiled and pointed. "Mine!"

Immediately the shield was ripped away and the armor torn off. Now Nathan stood only in his underwear.

"Denny!" he cried. But she didn't hear over the Merchant's laughter.

Suddenly the brothers were defenseless. They still had the water, but without the shield or armor, there was nothing to protect them from the Merchant.

"Let's see," he mused as he looked over the switches strapped to his chest. "What will it be? *Fear?* No, no, we tried that before. An interesting reaction, but not quite the effect we're looking for."

"Listen—" Joshua tried to reason.

But the Merchant wasn't listening. "Ah, here's an excellent choice. How about a little *hopelessness?*"

"A little what?" Nathan asked.

"*Hopelessness.* It's one of my favorites—and soon to be yours."

"Wait!" Josh shouted.

The Merchant flipped the switch.

"No!" Nathan cried, taking a step backwards.

But the mist shot from the Generator and gently rained down upon both of them.

Listro Q!" Aristophenix shouted over the alarms in Master Control.

The purple creature turned to his partner. No words were spoken. Each knew what had to be done. Listro Q reached into his pocket for his Cross-Dimensionalizer.

"No!" the Weaver interrupted. "It's too dangerous."

"Other choice, what have we?" Listro Q asked.

"There's no way of knowing the outcome," the Weaver warned. "The tapestries are unraveled, yes, they are."

"If don't go we," Listro Q said, "then destroyed will be our friends?"

Aristophenix agreed:

> "NOT ONLY OUR FRIENDS,
> BUT ALL UPSIDE DOWNERS AS WELL.
> WE GOTTA STOP THE MERCHANT
> FROM CASTING HIS SPELL."

"You don't understand," the Weaver insisted. "There is nothing I can do if you fall under his power."

Aristophenix nodded.

> "we know the risks,
> our chances are few.
> but they're imager's beloved,
> what more can we do?"

The Weaver took a deep breath. It was true. The Upside-Down Kingdom was Imager's favorite. No price was too great to save them. Imager had proven that by his own sacrifice for them, the one symbolized by the Blood Mountains. And if Imager was willing to pay such a price, how could he, the Weaver, prevent Listro Q and Aristophenix from doing any less?

The two quietly waited for his decision.

At last he nodded . . . slowly, sadly.

Listro Q entered the coordinates as Aristophenix fired off one last poem:

> "don't worry 'bout us,
> we're pros, don't ya know.
> them coordinates, they're a-entered,
> so let's get on with the—"

beep . . .

BOP . . .

BLeep. . .

BURP . . .

. . . and they were gone.

The Weaver stood alone. He could feel a lump growing in his throat, moisture burning in his eyes. Finally he turned back to the screen. "I'm going to miss those poems," he whispered hoarsely, "yes, I am."

a
test
of faith

By the time Aristophenix and Listro Q arrived in the Upside-Down Kingdom, the situation was hopeless . . . literally. The Merchant had fired the mist over the boys and now they felt completely *hopeless.*

"Oh, hello," Nathan greeted them flatly. "Sorry you had to come all this way just to get destroyed."

"Say what you?" Listro Q asked in surprise.

"He's got us," Joshua explained. "The Merchant's too powerful for us to win."

"Well, TeeBolt, what do we have here?" The Merchant chuckled to his panting pet. "More victims. Let me see . . ." He looked down at his switches. "What would be appropriate emotions for nosy, do-gooder Fayrahnians?"

Aristophenix turned to the boys. There wasn't much time to explain.

> "THOSE ARE ONLY EMOTIONS,
> OVER YOU THAT HE'S TOSSED.
> DON'T LET 'EM CONTROL YOU,
> YOU CAN STILL BE YOUR BOSS."

"It's no use," Joshua sighed.

"It's hopeless," Nathan agreed. "They've got my armor and shield. There's no way we can defend ourselves now."

The Merchant continued surveying his emotion switches. Apparently he was in no hurry. "Let's see, we have *anger, anxiety, apathy . . .*"

Aristophenix tried again:

> "DON'T ço BY yOUR feeLINçS,
> ço BY wHat you kNOw.
> tRUST IMaçeR'S pROMISE
> tHat you'LL oveRtHROw tHIS HeRe foe."

"I don't see how," Josh sighed.

"It's hopeless," Nathan repeated.

" . . . *bashful, bewildered, bitter . . .*"

Aristophenix turned to Listro Q, hoping he'd have a suggestion, but his partner was as clueless as he. If the brothers refused to believe, how could they force them?

Then there was the little matter of the Merchant and his Generator. " . . . *foolish, frantic, friendly . . .*"

Should they just grab Samson and hightail it back to Fayrah before they, too, got zapped? After all, they didn't create these problems, Denise did. As an Upside Downer it was *her* doing, *her* problem.

And yet, Imager had such love for these people. Come to think of it, so did Aristophenix and his partners. Throughout their journeys together a deep friendship had grown. A friendship so strong that they couldn't just leave the kids—even if it was their fault. No, Aristophenix and Listro Q had to stay. They had to stay and . . . and what?

Suddenly Listro Q's eyes lit up. He stepped toward Joshua. "Water still you have in the water skin?"

"Sure, but look how torn it is," Joshua whined. "Everything's ruined. Nothing's going right. The Merchant got Nathan's shield, he's controlling Denny, you're about to get hit with emotions yourself, everything's just hope—"

"The best defense, is offense," Listro Q interupted as he grabbed the water skin.

" . . . *optimistic, outrage* . . . That's it!" The Merchant grinned. "*Outrage* would be nice." He reached to the switch. "Yes, *outrage* would be very nice."

Aristophenix quickly whispered to Listro Q:

> "I DON'T KNOW WHAT YOU'RE PLANNING,
> BUT IT BETTER BE QUICK.
> 'CAUSE WE GOT 1.8 SECONDS
> 'FORE HE SWITCHES THAT SWITCH."

Listro Q unfolded the gash at the top of Joshua's water skin.

"Put that away!" the Merchant shouted. "Put that away this instant!"

"What are you doing?" Josh cried. "You're gonna make him madder—he'll make things worse!"

"Listen," Listro Q commanded, "carefully very listen."

"To what?"

But Listro Q didn't answer. Instead, he lifted the water skin over Joshua's head and poured the liquid letters and words over him.

"Stop it!" the Merchant shouted.

Next, he turned and poured some over Nathan's head.

"Stop it!" the Merchant cried. He quickly flipped the switch and fired the *outrage* mist . . . but not before Aristophenix shouted to the brothers:

> "TRUST IN IMAGER'S WORDS,
> WHAT YOU HEAR IS THE TRUTH.
> FEELINGS ARE FICKLE,
> BUT HIS WORDS ARE ABSOLU—"

That was as far as he got before the emotion hit him and Listro Q.

"What are you talking about?" Joshua whined. "What words?"

"Why do I have to explain everything for you!" Aristophenix snapped. "Use your brain for once!"

"Shout don't at them!" Listro Q yelled. He seemed equally as angry.

Aristophenix turned on his friend and shouted back, "Don't tell me what to do you, you . . . pretentious, purple . . . pinhead!"

Listro Q pulled up his sleeves. "Who are you calling purple?"

The Merchant roared with laughter. "So much for Fayrahnian love!" But he didn't laugh long.

"Listen!" Josh cried. "What is that?"

"I don't hear anything," Nathan whined.

"Shhh."

Nathan strained to listen. "It's nothing. Just the wind blowing in the—no, wait a minute. It sounds like . . . is that somebody whispering?"

The Merchant glanced nervously about. "It is nothing. You hear nothing!"

Josh turned to his brother. "Can you make it out?"

Nathan shook his head.

Both boys strained to hear. The words were very quiet. Very small. But they were very, very persistent.

"You will defeat him."
"You will defeat him."

"I still can't—"

"Shhh!"

"You will defeat him."
"You will defeat him."
"You will defeat him."

"Can you make it out now?"

"Almost. . ."

"You will defeat him."
"You will defeat him."

Nathan's eyes widened. He'd heard that voice once before. Once when Denise was trapped in the Experiment. "Is that . . . ?"

Josh nodded. "Imager. That's what he said when we were at the Center. Those were his *exact* words."

"I hear nothing!" the Merchant scorned.

The voice continued:

"You will defeat him."

"You will defeat him."

"You will defeat him."

412

"It's in the water," Nathan exclaimed. He ran his hand over the liquid letters and words still dripping from his face. "His voice is in this water."

"You will defeat him."
"You will defeat him."

"Of course it's in the water," Aristophenix angrily shouted. "It's his words!"

"But it's hopeless," Joshua insisted. "We can't defeat him."

"That's right," Nathan whined. "It's hopeless."

"Exactly," the Merchant sneered. "Trust your feelings. They are truth. Listen to your feelings, not these words."

Nathan turned to the Merchant. As he looked at him and listened, his feelings of *hopelessness* grew stronger. He glanced at Joshua. The expression on his brother's face said he felt the same thing. And as the *hopelessness* grew stronger, the voice of the water grew weaker . . .

"You will defeat him."
"You will defeat him."
"You will defeat him."

"Why is it fading?" Joshua cried.

It was Listro Q's turn to explode in anger. "Fading not is his voice! Fading is your hearing!"

"What?"

"If trust Imager's words, then will fade the power of feelings! But if trust your feelings, then power will fade of Imager's words!"

"That's right," Aristophenix snapped:

> *"tHe DecISIoN Is youRs*
> *wHo you'LL foLLow toDay.*
> *eItHeR ImaGeR's woRDs,*
> *oR youR feeLINGs oBey."*

"Imager's words," Joshua cried. "I want to follow Imager's words, but—"

Suddenly the voice grew louder:

"You will defeat him."
"You will defeat him."

"—but I *feel* so helpless."
Immediately the voice started to fade.

"No, Josh!" Nathan shouted. "We have to trust his words. His words are what's true."

"You will defeat him."
"You will defeat him."
"You will defeat him."

"But it's . . . it's so hard," Josh complained. "I can't."
Again the words started to fade.

"I know," Nathan cried, fighting against the feeling, "but remember . . . remember how they helped us in the Sea of Justice? How those words saved your life?"

Josh nodded. "Yes."

"And how his power saved me from Bobok's menagerie?"

Josh's voice grew a little stronger. "Yes . . ."

"Stop it!" the Merchant shouted as he fired another shot of *hopelessness* at him.

The mist covered Nathan even more thickly than before. Instantly, he felt himself sliding back into impossible hopelessness. He turned to his brother, pleading helplessly with his eyes for him to take over.

Joshua seemed to understand. He closed his eyes and took a deep breath. He set his jaw and then with great effort spoke. "Remember the way Imager saved Denny from the Experiment?"

"Yes," Nathan groaned, feeling the slightest stir of hope. Then, mustering all of his strength he added, "And how he saved me from the Illusionist."

"Yes," Joshua seemed to grow stronger.

"You will defeat him."
"You will defeat him."

"It's working, Nathan. Don't give up. Let's keep remembering what he's done!"

"Fools!" the Merchant shouted. "Your feelings are what is real! Trust your feelings, not some long forgotten—"

"How 'bout his power to reweave Denny?" Joshua exclaimed.

"Or how that water destroyed Keygarp," Nathan said, growing stronger.

"And Seerlo," Joshua added, his strength also increasing.

"You will defeat him."
"You will defeat him."
"You will defeat him."

"Stop it!" The Merchant cried. "Imager is nothing! His promises are noth—"

"No!" Josh shouted, spinning around to face him. "*You* are nothing! *You* will be defeated!"

"You are a fool!" the Merchant moved toward him menacingly. "Prove to me those past memories are real—"

"*Prove?*"

"You're the scientist! Can you touch those memories? Can you prove them?"

"Well . . . no," Josh started to falter. "They're just memories, there's no—"

"We will defeat you!" Nathan interrupted. "Joshua and I will defeat you! Right, Josh?"

Joshua tried to agree, obviously fighting to recover from the last blow.

"Right, Josh?"

His brother turned to him. It was no good. Nathan could see him starting to slip away. But, grabbing his shoulders, Nathan looked him straight in the face. "We can do this!" he shouted. "You and me together . . . Joshua, we can do this!"

He saw a glint of understanding return to his brother's eyes. He nodded to him encouragingly and saw even more strength returning. "Just like Imager told us," Nathan continued. "Together, you and I can do this. Together we can defeat him!"

Slowly Joshua began to nod.

"He's never failed us, has he?" Nathan said. "Not once. Not once!"

Confidence continued returning to Josh. He grew stronger by the second.

"Lies!" the Merchant shouted. "You are liars!"

At last Joshua's strength had returned. He spun back on the Merchant and shouted, "No, you're the liar! Imager's words have *never* failed!"

"You will defeat him."
"You will defeat him."
"You will defeat him."

"They destroyed the Illusionist!" Nathan yelled.

"That's right!"

"They destroyed Bobok!"

"Yes!"

"They destroyed Seerlo!"

Josh took a step toward the Merchant. "And they'll destroy you!"

The words were louder than ever:

"You will defeat him."
"You will defeat him."
"You will defeat him."

With full confidence, Joshua took the water skin from Listro Q and unfolded the gash at the top of it.

"What are you doing?" the Merchant demanded.

He began approaching the Merchant.

"Stay back! Stay away!" the Merchant ordered.

Nathan joined his brother's side and together they continued forward.

The Merchant backed away. "I'm warning you. Stay away with that!"

The brothers closed in.

In desperation the Merchant turned to his faithful companion. "TeeBolt—TeeBolt, attack!"

But TeeBolt was doing what he did best—running for his life in the opposite direction.

Now the Merchant was only a few feet away. Joshua held out the water skin. "I think it's time for you to leave our world."

"But I like it here," the Merchant hissed. Before Joshua could stop him, he fired off another volley of *hopelessness*. And another. And another.

Both brothers staggered under the impact.

"There's plenty more where this came from!" the Merchant shouted.

Imager's voice started to fade.

"Josh!" Nathan yelled. "Water . . . we need more water!"

Josh raised the water skin and poured it over his head.

The voice grew louder.

He tossed the skin to Nathan, who followed suit.

In a panic the Merchant twirled to Denise. "The Denise must do something! The Denise must write—"

But apparently Denise already had a plan. Still consumed with *greed*, she pointed to the water in Josh's water skin. "Want!"

Immediately the rest of the water was sucked from the skin and dumped onto her. From head to toe the liquid letters and words washed over her. She coughed and gasped, trying to catch her breath.

And for the first time, she also heard Imager's voice.

"You will defeat him."
"You will defeat him."
"You will defeat him."

"Listen to his words!" Nathan shouted to her. "Trust his words. Trust his words, not your feelings!"

"DON'T BELIEVE THEM!" the Merchant shrieked. "I CAN GIVE YOU ANYTHING YOU WANT."

Denise turned to him.

"JUST NAME IT. WE'RE PARTNERS, REMEMBER?"

She started to nod.

"NO, DENNY!" Josh cried. "NO!"

The Merchant grinned.

"DENNY! DON'T!" Nathan pleaded. "DON'T TRUST HIM! LISTEN TO THE IMAGER'S WORDS!"

Slowly Denise raised her hand and started to point. The Merchant's grin broadened. "Anything, my dear . . . just name it, anything at all!"

"DENNY—NO!" Nathan raced toward her, but Josh grabbed him, holding him back.

"Let me go, let me—"

"It won't do any good, *she* has to decide! Remember what Aristophenix said."

"But—"

"It has to be *her* decision."

Nathan looked at his brother, then reluctantly stopped struggling. Of course, he was right. It was up to Denise. He turned to watch as she opened her mouth. She spoke only three words. "That . . . ," she said, pointing at the Emotion Generator. "I want!"

Immediately the Generator was ripped from the Merchant's chest and resting in her arms.

"GIVE THAT BACK TO ME!" the Merchant cried.

"All right, Denny!" Nathan shouted. "Way to go!"

"GIVE THAT BACK TO ME, NOW!" The Merchant started toward her but hesitated as he saw that she was still dripping with Imager's water. "GIVE IT TO ME!"

"I won't give you this," she said looking down at the Generator and scanning the row of switches. "But I might have something else."

"What are you doing?" The Merchant started backing up. "Put that down! You don't know how to use it!"

Spotting a particular switch, Denise smiled. Then she pointed the Generator's nozzle toward the Merchant.

"The Denise doesn't know what she's doing! The Denise doesn't—"

Finally she fired a jet of mist.

"NOOO . . . !"

It fell gently over the Merchant.

"NO!" he screamed. "NO! NO! NO!" He began running in tight little circles. "NO, I DO NOT FEEL THIS! I DO NOT FEEL THIS!"

The brothers looked on in wonder as the Merchant continued to shriek in agony. Finally he unfurled his leathery wings.

"How 'bout one for the road?" Denise asked as she fired another volley onto him.

"NOOO!" he screamed. He flapped his wings and rose off the ground. "NO! NO! NO!" Then he turned, and with several powerful thrusts, headed off into the sky. "NO, NO, NO!" He grew smaller and smaller until he finally disappeared altogether. Only the faint echo of his cries remained. "No, no, nooooo . . ."

Nathan turned to Denise, and before he knew it, he was racing toward her and throwing his arms around her. "Denny!"

Soon his brother joined them in the hug.

"Come on, guys," she coughed, "knock it off. I can't breathe, I can't breathe."

But they had never bothered to let her have her way before, why should they start now?

"You okay?" Joshua asked as they finally separated. "You feeling okay now?"

"*Feelings?*" she said. "I don't know, I wouldn't put too much trust in *feelings,* would you?"

Josh broke out laughing. "No, I guess not."

Nathan joined in the laughter; so did Denise. It felt good. It had been a long time and it felt very good.

"But what did you zap him with?" Nathan asked. "What type of emotion could cause him so much pain?"

"Oh that's easy," Denise grinned. "I got him with the one he hated most."

"Yeah?" Josh asked. "Which is . . ."

Denise's grin broadened. "I nailed him with . . . *love.*"

another day, another saved planet

It didn't take long for Denise to get things back to normal. After all, she still had the Tablet—she still was the boss.

With a few strokes of her trusty pen, everyone in the group was back to their usual selves. Although they all seemed grateful, Mr. Hornsberry was particularly pleased, since it's tough to be a snob when you're sitting on the ground grinning like an idiot.

Denise sighed as she handed Aristophenix the Generator of Emotions. "Here," she said. "Do whatever you need to get rid of this thing, will you?"

> "I'll dispose of it quickly,
> on that you can depend.
> as of now the merchant's power
> is officially at an end."

"I tell you," Nathan said, "if I never feel another emotion, it will be too soon."

Listro Q shook his head in disagreement. "Good are emotions."

"He's right," Aristophenix said:

*"emotions are swell,
'cause they help us to deal
with life's ups and downs.
so it's good that we feel."*

Listro Q nodded. "Like instruments on dashboard. Emotions us tell inside what is happening to our minds."

Nathan frowned. "You lost me on that."

Joshua gave a shot at translating. "You're saying emotions are like gauges that tell us what's happening inside our minds?"

Listro Q agreed. "Gauges and thermometers of your mind are they."

Josh nodded then added, "We just have to make sure we're using them and they're not using us."

"Correct are you."

"Excuse me . . . excuse me, please?"

Denise turned to see the father of the chocolate-bar eater. Behind him stood the hundreds of people who had been on the ground laughing and smiling. Their uncontrollable emotions were now under control, but many of their bodies were still impossibly ruined.

"There's a lot more that has to be done," he said, motioning to the crowd. "We still need your help."

Denise nodded as she looked over the crowd. He was right, things were still a mess. A huge mess. She took a deep breath, sighed, and muttered half to herself, "Where to begin . . ."

"All things make, as used to be they," Listro Q said.

"You mean like Imager had it before I fixed up things?"

"Sounds like a pretty good deal to me," Josh said.

A murmur of approval swept through the crowd.

"But how?" Denise asked. "I mean, if I give them back pain, they'll all suffer. If I give them death, lots of them will immediately die. And what about all those rules I took away?" She sighed again and looked down at the Tablet. "I tell you, it would be better if I'd never even found this thing."

"Precisely," Listro Q agreed.

She looked at him. "What?"

"That very thing can happen make you."

"You're not serious?"

Aristophenix nodded:

> "none of this would be,
> if the tablet never was.
> so write, 'it never existed,'
> and see what it does."

"But . . . ," Denise protested, "then I won't have the power to make things happen."

"Correct are you," Listro Q said. "Then rely on Imager only must you."

"But . . ."

"Live by his plan, your only option."

"But—"

Aristophenix added:

> "either you trust him or don't,
> the decision is plain.
> either imager's the boss,
> or this insane life remains."

Denise turned back to the crowd. Things *were* insane, he was right about that. She'd only made a few changes, written a few little words, and look what had happened. She had tried to help these people, but had nearly destroyed them. Instead of perfect people, she had turned them into out-of-control monsters. Monsters who now stood silently waiting, hoping she'd make the right decision.

Denise hated the thought of losing control. But worse, she hated the thought of keeping it. It's true, there were thousands of things she didn't understand about Imager's ways. She probably never would. But she did know one thing—at least she did now. His ways were a *whole* lot better than hers.

Finally she brought the felt pen up to the board. "Well," she said with another sigh, "it's been real."

"Too real," Josh grinned back.

The others chuckled nervously as they waited.

"I guess I'll see you around," she said to the Tablet.

"Or not," Nathan corrected.

She nodded, "Or not." Then quickly and deliberately she wrote the words: *THE TABLET DOESN'T EXIST.*

Denise woke with a start. For a minute she didn't know where she was—until she felt the jab of a steel armrest in her ribs, the sticky vinyl against her arms, and the cramp in her neck.

Ah, yes, the hospital chair.

She looked over at her mother, who was still asleep—the sedative was still working. In fact, in the dim morning light she actually looked kind of peaceful.

But something had changed. Denise felt it immediately. Her anger about Mom was gone. She wasn't sure why. Maybe it had something to do with that strange dream she'd just had. Talk about weird.

She heard a gentle clearing of throats and looked up to see Joshua and Nathan standing in the doorway.

"Guys?" she said as she rose, struggling to stand.

"Sorry we couldn't come last night," Josh whispered as they stepped inside. "We had to watch Grandpa's store."

"How's she doing?" Nathan asked as he limped past Denise to look at her mother.

"Pretty good."

"You stay here all night?" Josh asked.

"Yeah," Denise said, rubbing her stiff neck. "It wasn't too bad. Except for the dream . . . talk about weird."

The boys exchanged glances.

"The *dream?*" Josh asked.

"Yeah . . . it was all about this flat stone, and me writing on it, and—"

"Was there a creature in it?" Josh asked. "Some guy with a machine strapped to his chest?"

"Well . . . yeah. How did—"

"And an eight-legged dog?" Nathan asked.

"How'd you guys know?"

Again the brothers traded looks.

Josh cleared his throat. "Nathan had the same dream."

"*What?*"

"So did I."

"You're kidding!" Denise exclaimed.

Her mother stirred slightly.

Nathan lowered his voice, "We both had it last night."

"You mean we all three dreamed the same dream?"

"About a Tablet," Josh said.

Denise nodded. "And some creep trying to take over the world."

"And you ruling it instead of Imager."

Denise leaned against the wall to steady herself. On the weirdness scale this was . . . well, it was off the scale. *Way* off. "How?" she finally asked. "Why?"

No one had an answer.

Then she asked another question, one she figured they were all thinking. "This has something to do with the Fayrahnians, doesn't it?"

"Probably," Josh answered.

Nathan agreed. "Next time we see them, we'll have to ask."

"Yeah." Denise nodded. "We'll have to." But even as she spoke and glanced back at her mother, she suspected that she knew. Somehow deep inside, she already knew.

Meanwhile, somewhere between the Upside-Down Kingdom and Fayrah, roly-poly Aristophenix, purple Listro Q, and the feisty Samson were cross-dimensionalizing home.

So bits and pieces, only they'll remember? Listro Q thought to Aristophenix.

Aristophenix nodded:

> *a foɢɢy DRea m*
> *is aLL tHey'LL RecaLL.*
> *But it'LL HeLp IN tHeIR ɢROWtH,*
> *of ɢIVINɢ ImaɢeR aLL.*

Aristophenix folded his arms in satisfaction. As the leader of the group, he was pleased with the way he'd pulled things off.

Actually, he was very pleased.

Only one question to ask have I, Listro Q thought.

Ask away, my good man, Aristophenix thought back. *Ask away.*

If normal, is back to everything . . .

Yes . . .

Then—Listro Q pointed past Aristophenix—*why a new companion have we?*

What new companion? Aristophenix thought as he turned. *We don't have a new*—

Suddenly he was hit by a galloping eight-legged dog. Before he could be stopped, the grateful animal hopped on Aristophenix's chest and began slurping, licking, and drooling.

Easy, fella! Aristophenix coughed. *Down, boy . . .*

Samson and Listro Q started to laugh.

Come on, fella . . . easy now . . . somebody call him off, call him off!

Although his buddies struggled to pull the animal away, there was something about their continual laughter that told Aristophenix they weren't trying all that hard. Yes, sir, by the looks of things, it appeared TeeBolt had found himself a brand-new master. And, by the looks of things, it appeared he would remain glued to Aristopohenix's side (drool and all)—traveling with him wherever he went . . . even on their future visits to three very special friends in the Upside-Down Kingdom.

Come on, fella . . . get down . . . easy now . . . easy . . .

Blood of Heaven
BILL MYERS

Mass Market: 0-310-25110-9
Softcover: 0-310-20119-5

Threshold
BILL MYERS

Mass Market: 0-310-25111-7
Softcover: 0-310-20120-9

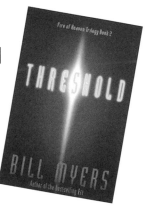

Fire of Heaven
BILL MYERS

Mass Market: 0-310-25113-3
Softcover: 0-310-21738-5
Abridged Audio Pages® Cassette: 0-310-23002-0

Eli
BILL MYERS

Mass Market: 0-310-25114-1
Softcover: 0-310-21803-9
Abridged Audio Pages® Cassette: 0-310-23622-3
Palm Reader: 0-310-24754-3

*When Everything Seems Lost, God's Love
Has a Way of Turning Life Around.*

When the Last Leaf Falls
A Novella

BILL MYERS

This retelling of O. Henry's classic short story,
The Last Leaf, begins with an adolescent girl,
Ally, who is deathly ill and angry at God. Her
grief stricken father, a pastor on the verge of
losing his faith, narrates the story as it unfolds.

Ally's grandpa lives with the family and has become Ally's best
friend. He is an artist who has attempted—but never been able—to
capture in a painting the essences of God's love. One day, in stubborn
despair, Ally declares that she will die when the last leaf falls from the
tree outside her bedroom window. Her doctor fears that her negative
attitude will hinder her recovery and her words will become a self-ful-
filling prophecy.

This stirring story of anger and love, of doubt and hope, speaks
about the pain of living in this world, and the reality of the Other
world that is not easily seen but can be deeply felt. Talented story-
teller Bill Myers enhances and updates a storyline from one of the
masters and brings to light the awesome power of love and sacrifice.

Hardcover: 0-310-23091-8

We want to hear from you. Please send your comments about this book to us in care of zreview@zondervan.com. Thank you.

ZONDERVAN™

GRAND RAPIDS, MICHIGAN 49530 USA

WWW.ZONDERVAN.COM